The

WAYFARER'S JOURNEY

Abi

A R Pearson

authorHOUSE®

AuthorHouse™ UK
1663 Liberty Drive
Bloomington, IN 47403 USA
www.authorhouse.co.uk
Phone: 0800.197.4150

Published by AuthorHouse 11/15/2018

ISBN: 978-1-7283-8061-2 (sc)
ISBN: 978-1-7283-8062-9 (hc)
ISBN: 978-1-7283-8060-5 (e)

Library of Congress Control Number: 2018913534

Print information available on the last page.

Contents

For Leoni, my beautiful daughter, who listened
to the story and loves it as much as I do.
Thanks for supporting me with your ideas and suggestions. I loved
it when you set up the awesome kitchen retelling of the book, using
various bottles and tins as the characters. It was a lot of fun!

For Shannon, Sebastian, and Merryn, my other wonderful kids.
Thanks for supporting your old Mug with her crazy dreams.

For Sarah, for always believing in her bestie, and for telling me the
one thing I always hoped I would hear after someone listened to a
chapter: "You can't leave it there—I need to hear the next one!"

For Richard, who gave me my first fantasy
fiction novel to read and lit the flame.

For all my friends, for promising to buy the book. I hope you enjoy it!

For my Twitter family, especially the Lennie's gang, meeting
all of you has been the highlight of this journey.

For my Goldfish, Butterfly couldn't have done this without you!

For Marisol at AuthorHouse UK, for convincing me to publish my
book and for supporting me every step of the way while I did so.

Prologue

———✾———

Orthrillium rushed inside his dome, where he dug out his hand-carved wooden quill and his largest dried leaves. He grabbed his pot of berry juice off the windowsill and sat down quickly to begin his letter. In his haste he accidentally spilled some of the purple juice onto his white gown, but he was too distracted to notice.

He needed Mother to see that he was sorry. If he wrote her a letter, she would be impressed by his new writing skills. It would show genuine effort; apologies should always be heartfelt.

He pondered whether he should write additional letters for his two fathers. The Dragon and the Unicorn had been most displeased that he hadn't given them back the powers from the Earth Stone. They'd said the damage couldn't be mended by him, or any human, because it was the two of them and Mother Fairy, as a trio, who had created the world.

Orthrillium decided not to write to them. He wished they understood he wanted to fix this mistake himself. He knew he could—he had a brilliant plan! He dipped his quill into the juice and started his letter.

"Dear Mother Fairy, I am so very sorry for what happened earlier. I know you are angry with me for breaking the Earth Stone. You told me not to try and touch the powers within it, but they were so fascinating I had to feel them for myself. I know it was wrong to disobey you. I hope you will forgive me when you read my letter."

Orthrillium reread the beginning of the letter. Pleased with how it sounded, he continued. "I don't know where you went, Mother, when the stone broke apart and the powers passed into me. I have never seen you *vanish* before. Father Unicorn and Father Dragon say you are gone forever, but that's just a trick, isn't it?

"I have a plan to fix my mistake, but I need to understand more about the powers. I am going to ask a group of my friends to help. If I share one of the eight elements with each of them, then they can study them and help me to learn the best way to fix the stone. I'll call the group the Theanic Order."

Orthrillium paused again. He already knew which of his friends he would ask to help him. To make sure he kept control of the powers, he would keep a portion of all of them, and he wouldn't gift anyone else the element of Light. He'd put Reanna in charge of the Theanic Order with him, because she was his best friend. He felt certain that everything was going to be fine.

"I will be dedicated to this project, Mother, just as I have been while cultivating the land and caring for the animals and plants. As soon as my friends and I have mended the stone, I will give it back to you, and we can carry on like before, can't we?"

Orthrillium signed his letter with his name and put down his quill. He'd leave the letter on the table while he went to find his friends. Mother would probably fly down and read it while he was away. He rushed out of his dome in search of his chosen friends.

Evelyn Maude saw Orthrillium running from his dome and down into the woods. She thought to him, but he didn't hear her. She entered his dome and, seeing the letter, picked it up and read it. She put it down again, feeling cross. Orthrillium had taken the power from the Earth Stone, and Mother Fairy was gone forever! Evelyn's nostrils flared. Mother had been teaching her for *ages* about the eight elements of creation, so why hadn't she been gifted the stone? That wasn't fair! She was the firstborn.

Orthrillium had rushed off to find Reanna, when he should be asking *her* to be the leader instead. She was so much cleverer then Reanna. She was so much cleverer than Orthrillium, too. If those powers were hers, she would know what to do with them.

Feeling determined Evelyn Maude left the dome in search of Orthrillium. She would make sure he gifted her with the element of Light, because that was the strongest. She would show her mother and her fathers, Orthrillium, and the other humans just what power in her hands could do. By the time she was finished, no one would ever overlook her again.

1

To Judelen, Boy

Jack pulled his horse to a halt and surveyed the bridge below him. It crossed the Judelen Pass. He admired the arches made of light-grey stone, which had been cut from the Great Mountains. They stretched down on thick columns into the River Nonnon. The bridge was high above the waterline, built securely into the valley and wide enough for two carriages to cross side by side.

If Bailey kept up a good pace, they'd reach Judelen City before dark. Jack hoped heading into such a big populated area was a wise thing to do.

A shiver ran down his spine, and he drew his cloak tighter. The morning air was bitter, and his cloak had seen better days; it did little to protect him from the chill.

Thinking he heard a distant screeching, he glanced nervously behind him, back into the savannah of Lanfar, but nothing stirred in the barren hills.

Pleased, Jack vaulted from his saddle and landed in the deep winter snow. Using small steps, he began to lead his horse down the steep slope towards the bridge. He studied the far side of the Pass as he walked. The opposite path wound steeply upward through a dense stand of silver-barked trees. The first peaks of the Great Mountains were visible beyond the forest, and although the city was not in view, Jack knew it was nestled amongst them, cut from their belly by magic.

The horse nudged his shoulder. "What?" said Jack, checking around in all directions. When he couldn't see or hear anything approaching, he relaxed his stance. "Are you after a fuss?" he said with a smile. He patted the golden coat of the animal; it felt rough beneath his fingers.

"You're looking the worse for wear, Bailey," Jack said seriously. "Not that I should talk, mind; I'm thin enough to be a skeleton. And I can't see a brush ever de-knotting this hair," he added, lifting a brown lock off his shoulder. "The first thing we're doing when we get to Judelen is finding an inn, with a good stable for you. Then I need a decent meal and a barber to chop this lot off." Bailey snorted; Jack took that as approval of his plan.

Of course, he needed money to fund a stay at an inn. "Perhaps I can do odd jobs here and there in exchange for food and shelter, until we get settled," he said to Bailey. "Maybe, if my identity isn't uncovered, we won't need to run ever again," he added hopefully.

Jack had been forced to wander as a wayfarer for long enough; it was no life for him or Bailey. They needed to settle down and become invisible, giving no one a reason to know their names. Bailey shuddered.

"You cold, boy? I think it will be warmer in the forest. We're exposed here on this side of the valley. Come on."

Bailey quickened the pace, snow crunching under his hooves. When they reached the steps onto the bridge, a sudden pull on the reins forced Jack to stop walking.

"What is it, boy?" he asked his horse. Bailey made a low, warning rumble in his throat. His ears were pricked forward, his eyes alert.

Jack could now hear the sound of galloping hooves somewhere out of sight in the forest ahead. He put his left hand down and unclipped the cover of his dagger.

Then a carriage appeared, pulled by a single black carthorse, the wheels spraying snow into the air. One man drove the carriage, he cried out harshly at the horse as it attempted to slow down before the bridge. With a crack of his whip, he forced it into maintaining the gallop.

Jack moved Bailey to the side of the road to avoid a collision; he wondered what was making the man drive so insanely. Jack had no desire to get involved. He'd let him pass and carry on his way.

With a sudden almighty crack, the carriage's back wheels exploded. The horse was pulled backwards; it screamed in pain and crashed in a heap on the ground. It was then pushed forward by the vehicle, which spun to the side and collided with the bridge wall, sending a section of the stone down into the river below.

Jack's breath caught in his throat. Pulling Bailey behind him, he ran up the steps and onto the bridge, slipping and sliding on the icy patches.

Jack reached the carriage and halted. There were deep snow banks around the wreckage. He looked down at the fallen horse, which was twitching in its harness, unable to rise. The animal had shattered its backbone and was beyond aid.

A moan full of pain gave away the driver's location. Jack approached the man cautiously; he was lying on the ground, trying feebly to pull his legs free from under the carriage. He heard Jack's approaching footsteps and looked round to find him. Half his face was badly grazed, blood was matted into his long black hair, and his clothing was ripped to shreds. Jack noted the outfit he wore was a soldier's uniform—just the type of people he was trying to avoid. But he couldn't help that now. Soldier or not, he wouldn't abandon anyone as badly injured as this stranger.

"Help," pleaded the driver. He choked and coughed up blood.

Jack knelt down beside him and weighed the damage to his legs, "Easy," said Jack gently. "Can you move your legs at all?" The man groaned in pain and shook his head.

Jack put a hand on the man's shoulder. "Just stay still then."

The man coughed again, bringing up more blood. He moved his lips in speech, but the salty liquid gargled in his throat, obliterating his words.

Jack surveyed the man's legs again. "I must get this carriage off of you," he concluded.

The man felt across the ground until he found Jack's hand. He squeezed it, getting Jack's attention. "Leave me," he croaked.

Jack shook his head. "No, I will find a way of freeing you; just hold on."

The man squeezed his hand again. "The carriage, there is someone…" His voice broke off into another coughing fit, and Jack waited for it to subside.

"There is someone inside," concluded the man.

The carriage gave a sudden jerk, bringing it closer to the edge of the bridge, where the stones had been dislodged in the impact.

"Lie still," said Jack urgently, jumping to his feet.

He moved to the back of the carriage. Part of it was now hanging over the edge, and the weight distribution suggested it could tip over. Jack used the front wheels to climb onto the side, and once up, he looked in through the window. A woman lay on the far side, unconscious, her hands and feet bound together with rope. She wore an embroidered red gown, and matching slippers. The carriage rocked, unbalanced by Jack's added weight. Carefully he lowered himself inside. He placed a foot on either side of the woman. Jack saw a welt on her forehead, but he couldn't see any other injuries. With difficulty, he pulled her upward and pushed her through the window until she was balanced enough for him to let her go. He then climbed out beside her and pulled her the rest of the way out. Slowly he climbed back down onto the bridge. He gently lifted her into his arms and carried her away from the wreckage.

Bailey had crossed over onto the forest path just beyond the bridge. Jack cleared away a patch of snow and placed the woman beside the horse. "Look after her while I go back to the man," he said, hurrying away.

When Jack laid a hand upon the man, he opened his eyes. "Is she—safe?"

"Yes," answered Jack. "Who is she?"

"She is the princess of Judelen," said the man.

Jack's eyes widened. "You're kidnapping the princess of Judelen!" he spat, feeling outraged.

The man shook his head vigorously. "Never! I was trying to save her."

"By binding her hands and feet? I think not, sir!" shouted Jack.

The man's bright-blue eyes were beginning to glaze over. "There is a plot—she doesn't know about it—her life is in danger!"

Jack looked down to see a pool of blood seeping from beneath the carriage; death was creeping closer. "It doesn't matter now," he said quickly. "You have begun to bleed from your wounds. I must free you—"

The man feebly shook his head. "No, leave me be! My legs are crushed—I am done for."

The wind picked up sharply; strong gusts blew across the bridge. "I can't just leave you," protested Jack.

Another section of the wall crumbled into the river. The carriage slid and halted halfway over the side, pulling the horse and man with it. He let out a scream of agony.

Jack seized both his hands. "It's going to go over the side," he panted. His arms were protesting from the strain. He was so much weaker than he had been since running away from Sanalow.

"There is nothing you can do," said the man. "Make sure she is safe. Don't trust anyone in the city; I don't know how deep the plot runs." The man's eyes began to close.

"Stay awake!" shouted Jack. "I don't understand about this plot. Who is plotting to kill the princess?"

The man didn't answer. "Come on, man!" roared Jack in an effort to keep him conscious. "How can I save her if I don't understand?"

The man's eyes flickered open. "Trust no one in the palace, not even the king. They are coming—the blackness—they are coming from the air! Can you see them?"

Jack looked over his shoulder into the sky; he saw nothing but pure-white clouds.

The wind was really howling now; it stung his eyes. The man was hallucinating from the pain, he concluded. He let go of the man, and with his dagger he began to hack at the horse's harness, to free the carriage from its weight.

"They have come to take me away," sang the man. "They don't want me to tell, but they are too late! I have told you their secrets, and you can save her now."

Jack continued to hack at the harness, the man continued to babble, and the pool of blood spread wider. The man looked straight at Jack. "You are too late," he shouted. "They are here!" Without warning, the carriage was caught by the wind, and it sailed over the side, taking the horse and man with it.

Jack leaped clear, landing on his front and grunting from the impact. He lay exhausted in the blood-soaked snow. He wiped a mixture of sweat and tears from his face. His hands were soaked with blood; he wiped them clean using snow and dried them on his trousers. Without looking over the edge, he stood and made his way back to where Bailey was guarding the princess.

The princess was still unconscious. Jack bent down and cut the bonds from her hands and feet before pulling her up into a standing position and then hoisting her over Bailey's saddle.

Wearily he climbed up behind her and turned her to rest in his arms. He brushed the loose strands of her long golden hair clear of her face. Her pale-pink skin was soft beneath his fingers. He felt an immediate overwhelming desire to protect her, but how was he going to do that?

He would have to return her to the palace. It was too dangerous to keep her outside of the city, but he knew he would not be content to hand her back over to the king knowing she was in danger from some secret plot. Until he could speak to her in private, he'd have to stay close by, even if it meant risking exposure. His honour would not allow him to do less.

Decision made, Jack adjusted his hold on the princess so he could steer Bailey, and he nudged him to begin walking. Bailey held his ground and looked back at Jack. He turned back the way they had come.

"No, boy, we need to take her home," said Jack.

The horse ignored his command and stepped onto the bridge.

Jack tugged sharply on the reins and turned him round. "To Judelen, boy," he said firmly. Bailey began to plod up the path towards the city.

The horse's unease was making Jack question his choice. What trouble was he getting himself into?

He looked down at the sleeping princess and smiled. Why did he feel so strongly that, whatever it was, she was worth it?

2

---❀---

QUESTIONS

Night had fallen by the time Jack rode Bailey to within sight of the city. The outer walls rose to a magnificent height; they loomed in the darkness.

The Great Mountains provided protection to the rear. The mountain chain was impenetrable. No man could cross it, and what lay beyond was a mystery.

A mighty river flowed down from the mountains, controlled via a dam. The water had been diverted to maintain a mile-wide moat, shaped like a crescent moon, around the rest of the city. There was only one access road across the moat, styled in the same fashion as the Judelen Pass and reinforced to cope with water corrosion and the constant footfall in and out of the city.

Judelen was the largest and most prosperous city in the kingdom. The smaller cities of Sanalow and Uxtellier held none of its grace or power. Once upon a time, Grimfar had been Judelen's twin city, but it had been destroyed during the War of Power.

Emiscial was rumoured to equal Judelen, but Jack had never been there to see for himself. There were rumours that the magus never allowed people to leave their city. It was known as the Heart of the Kingdom, protected by white magic, belonging to the Theanic Order. White magic's eight elements were the ingredients of creation itself. He knew it was the magic of the magus that had carved Judelen out of the mountains.

The evil black magus, Evelyn Maude, had destroyed Judelen during the War of Power. After the other magus had killed her, they'd rebuilt it—but then they'd abandoned it and their contact with the other cities after the final battle against Evelyn's son. To win the war and defeat the Dark Knight, they'd turned the world mortal. Jack couldn't blame them for running away. Who wouldn't go into hiding after invoking something as harsh as death upon innocent people!

Jack squeezed his eyes shut and refocused his mind to the present. He was nearly across the moat road. The city gates were still open and the drawbridge down. Aware that they could close at any time, Jack urged Bailey into a trot.

One of the powerful oaken gates made a protesting creek, and slowly it started to pull inwards, aided by massive chains on turn-wheels.

Jack increased Bailey's trot to a gallop. "Wait!" he shouted.

"Hold the gate," a guard ordered. "Rider approaching fast!"

Nine new guards appeared. They all drew their weapons. "Stop!" shouted the first guard; he held his hand in the air, palm extended towards Jack. Jack slowed Bailey and came to a halt before the gates.

The guard raised his sword. "State your business," he ordered Jack.

"I'm a wayfarer in need of entry to the city—"

"You come too late, traveller. Return in the morning. The city is closed to all tonight."

Jack drew himself up. "You will let me enter, guard," he said. "She is hurt and in need of attention."

The guard moved up next to Bailey and took hold of his reins. His eyes scanned Jack and his injured companion. He turned to the other guards. "Fetch a carriage from the palace. He carries the princess!"

There was a flurry of movement, as a guard ran back through the gate to follow the order while the others approached Jack.

"Dismount and lift her down, wayfarer," the original guard commanded.

Jack dismounted Bailey. Carefully he lifted the princess into his arms.

A tall man approached Jack. He had thick black hair, flecked with grey, tied back in a ponytail. "Give her to me," he snapped.

Jack passed the princess into his arms. The man walked her quickly through the gate and out of sight. Jack made as if to follow, but the gate guard blocked his path. "Don't move," he warned Jack.

"She is hurt! I must see that she is all right."

"Her bodyguard has taken her. She is not your concern now."

Jack stood waiting, tapping his foot. Another man came through the gate, also powerfully built, but with white-blond hair that fell across his eyes. His face was long, matching his nose and chin. Jack guessed he was in his mid thirties.

The man glanced at Jack before turning away. "Is this the man who brought her back?" he asked the guard, ignoring Jack completely.

"Yes, I am," answered Jack before the guard could open his mouth.

The blond man turned to study Jack. "Where did you find her?" he asked.

Jack frowned at his sharp tone. "On the Judelen Pass," he explained.

"Was she alone?"

"No, there was a man with her. Their carriage crashed on the bridge. I managed to free the princess, but I could not save the man before it went over the edge and fell into the river."

The blond man stared at Jack, his dark-blue eyes flashed. "Did you speak with this man?"

Jack hesitated, heeding the warning he had been given. "There was no time."

"How could you have known that you had saved the princess of Judelen if you did not speak with this man?"

Jack indicated to the guard standing next to him. "He just said who she was."

"It is true, I said she was the princess when I sent for a carriage," confirmed the guard.

The blond man had not taken his gaze from Jack. "What is your name and station?" he asked.

"Jack Orden, and I am a wayfarer."

Jack watched carefully, looking for a sign of recognition at his name, but the man showed no interest. Jack exhaled.

The blond man turned back to the guard. "Bring the horse inside and up to the palace stable. Master Orden shall accompany me."

The blond man studied Jack, a smirk appearing on his lips. "Do you have any other weapons apart from your belt knife?"

Jack nodded. "My sword is secured to my saddle."

The blond man raised an eyebrow. "How and why do you carry a sword, wayfarer?"

"It was given to me, and you can never be too careful," said Jack coolly.

The man smirked again. "A sword is only useful if you can wield it."

Leaning forward, Jack locked his eyes on the man's. "What makes you think I can't?"

Jack knew his question was stupid. It was obvious why the man doubted his ability. He was dressed in rags and looked too weak to even lift the thing, let alone wield it. The year of rough living had changed his appearance drastically. He might remember what he'd once looked like, but this man didn't know anything about him.

The blond man dismissed his comment. "Give your knife to the guard. It will be brought up to the palace with your other possessions."

Jack pulled his knife free from the holder and handed it over. He needed to be more careful. What if the man had pressed for more information? That would have landed him in it. He needed to rein in his temper.

The blond man turned on his heel. "Follow me," he said.

Jack did as he was told. Two of the other guards fell in behind him.

Jack glanced back. "Am I to be shadowed always?" he asked the blond man.

"You are a stranger to our city. Security is always tight around strangers."

"Even ones who return your princess?" enquired Jack. It annoyed him that he was being shadowed. He had expected that the city hero would get a warmer welcome than this.

"You did not know she was the princess until you reached our gates. How are we to know what your intentions were before you found out?"

"What are you implying?" shouted Jack angrily. He stopped walking; he would not take another step until that comment was explained.

Turning to face him, the man spoke to Jack in a slow voice, as if talking to a child. "You are a wayfarer from your own mouth; most are known as thieves and dishonest men."

Jack hated being patronised. "I brought her back to keep her safe," he said stonily.

The man smiled coldly. "Had you known she was the princess of Judelen when you saved her, I would find it easier to believe that you are honourable. However, you did not know, so forgive me if I choose not to trust you until I find you worthy of trust. That is not likely to come easy."

Jack's temper returned. "Who are you?" he shouted at the man.

"Who I am does not concern you, wayfarer,"

"Oh, really, well—"

Jack was prevented from giving his comeback by the arrival of a carriage. It swept up to the side of him. He saw two men driving; both were powerfully built. The blond man shoved him inside the carriage before he could take in anything more and then climbed in beside him.

"Is she secure?" he asked the two new men.

"Yes, Argon," answered one of the men. "She is being tended to by Mistress Stratton. Drake has sent us for the man."

Argon turned to Jack. "You are to travel with us to the palace of the king."

"Do I have a choice?" asked Jack sarcastically.

"No!" said Argon with a smile. He banged the side of the carriage twice with his fist, and with a jerk it began to move along the streets of the city.

Jack looked out of the window. No one was moving along the streets; he suspected it was past city curfew.

He turned away from the window and looked at Argon. "So, Argon, the princess is doing well?" he deliberately used his first name, just to see what reaction he would get.

Argon ignored him.

"I'm pleased to hear it," continued Jack; it was the honest truth, after all.

Argon looked at him sternly. "Do you always eavesdrop on conversations?" he snapped.

Jack felt amusement at the question. How could he not have heard the conversation? It had happened three feet in front of him!

Argon must have seen his smirk, because he looked livid. Jack knew he needed to stop goading him. He was carrying a rather large sword and no doubt had excellent weapons training. Jack turned back to the window in silence.

The carriage continued climbing the streets, passing through Low Town and Middle Town and up into Inner Town, where the palace of King Symon was situated.

As it climbed the vast labyrinth of streets, each rising level towards the palace showed details of class and riches. The poor lived in Low Town, in small clay houses in close proximity. Middle Town held the middle class, who lived in moderate stone houses. Throughout both towns there was no overcrowding and no overpowering smell of waste along the cobbled streets. As the carriage entered the gates of Inner Town, the dwellings of the rich began to appear; huge buildings of stone set on large plots of land. Taller still than any of these stood Judelen Palace. It sat upon the highest part of the city and was made from the mountains finest white rock. Like the city, it was fashioned to rise up in levels, the tallest containing the apartments of the royal family.

Jack was disappointed that it was dark. He wanted to know whether Inner Town was high enough to see past Lanfar and past the desert all the way to the sea. There the water was so wide you couldn't swim it without drowning and so salty it could not quench your thirst. He had always wanted to travel to the sea, but the desert was almost as impenetrable as the mountains. A handful of people had made the journey, but none had lived long after returning. Most people chose to stay in the centre of the kingdom, where it was safe.

The carriage stopped in a small courtyard. The men from the front climbed down and signalled for Jack to exit the carriage. Argon followed him out. "This way," he snapped.

The two men standing with Jack rolled their eyes in unison. Jack studied both men; he thought they must be brothers. They were identical in height, but one was slightly broader in his shoulders than the other. They shared the exact same shade of straw-coloured blond hair, but they each had a different style. The broad-shouldered man's was cut short, and the other's was down past his shoulders and secured in a ponytail. Both had light-blue eyes. Jack swallowed. He had forgotten that people born in each of the cities had specific eye colours. His were green, and that would identify his birthplace as Sanalow and likely lead to questions. Feeling concerned, he reluctantly followed Argon into the palace.

He passed through a maze of corridors and stairways. The deeper and higher he went, the more the décor changed around him. The lower floors were polished bare stone, while the higher floors were covered in smooth, rich-coloured carpets. More paintings framed in elaborate gold lined the walls as they rose higher, and each corridor seemed to have a different theme for the artwork. He hoped he would not need to make a hasty exit, because he had no idea how to get out.

The three men led him towards a door off the corridor. Argon opened it and went inside. Jack followed him through, and the two other men brought up the rear.

At a glance, he saw that the room was bare except for a simple wooden table and a stack of six chairs leaning against the wall in the far corner. There was another door leading out of the room on the opposite side. Jack was just studying it when it opened and another man entered. He recognised immediately the man to whom he had handed over the princess at the city gates. He was heavily built, but Jack knew it was muscle underneath his uniform, not fat. Jack noted that all the men were wearing the same dark-blue uniform, but a different style from the uniforms of the gate guards. It was cut from velvet, with no stitch lines showing, meaning it had been professionally made. He knew from his uncle that velvet was a tough material to sew.

Jack didn't have long to ponder the uniforms. The tall man sat down behind the table and laid before him parchment and an ink bottle, which he had brought in. Argon walked round the table to speak in his ear. Jack couldn't hear what was said, but the conversation soon came to an end.

Argon proceeded to the corner and took down one of the stacked chairs. He handed it to one of the men standing beside Jack and then handed another chair to the other man. Argon took a third chair, which he did not hand to Jack, but took over to the side of the table and sat upon himself, smiling at Jack as he did so. Jack tensed but made himself relax again; he would not give Argon the satisfaction of thinking he could get to him. Instead, he returned the smile and stood at ease before the table, waiting for the new man to speak.

The black-haired man cast a quick glance at Argon and then fixed his eyes on Jack. "You are Master Jack Orden?" The man had a deep, commanding voice, and Jack could tell he was a man with high authority.

Jack inclined his head to the man. "I am, sir," he answered simply.

The black-haired man looked past Jack at one of the men sitting behind him. "Ryan, fetch Master Orden a chair." The broad-shouldered man got up and gave Jack the chair he had been sitting on before fetching another for himself.

The black-haired man waited for Jack and Ryan to get seated before continuing. "Now that Master Orden is comfortable, we can begin. I don't know if you have been told, Master Orden, but the other men in this room and I are the personal bodyguards of Princess Lillian."

"The gate guard mentioned you were her bodyguard, sir," said Jack honestly.

The black-haired man cast Argon an unreadable look. He turned back to Jack. "You have been asked to come to the palace to give a statement about how you came to be in the company of Princess Lillian today. I will take your statement tonight to give to the king to review. Where are you staying in the city?"

"Nowhere as yet, sir. I was brought straight to the palace upon my arrival with the princess, so I have not had time to find lodgings."

The black-haired man nodded. "Of course; forgive me. In that case you are invited to spend the night here in the palace, as our guest. The king may call you to an audience tomorrow. In truth, I know he will, so it makes more sense for you to be here."

The black-haired man looked at Argon. "Please go and inform Mistress Stratton to prepare the guest suite." Argon nodded and left through the door behind the table.

The man turned back to Jack. "I'm sorry, Master Orden—where are my manners? I have not yet introduced myself. My name is Drake."

"Nice to meet you, Master Drake," answered Jack politely.

"Drake is my first name," corrected Drake. "The princess likes to have a somewhat informal household, so the bodyguards are always on first-name basis with everyone. Have the other men introduced themselves?"

The man who had handed Jack his chair stood up. "No, we have not," he said with a smile. "Argon is in one of his moods, so it was best to stay silent."

Jack was taken aback by such an open statement; he had thought these men would be very guarded in what they said. Drake simply nodded. Apparently Argon having moods was a normal occurrence.

"I am Ryan," said the man to Jack before sitting down again.

"I am William," said the other man, the one with the ponytail. "But please call me Will."

"You two are brothers?" asked Jack. If the bodyguards were happy to talk, then that was good, for he would learn a lot more.

Both men nodded.

"We are, and you are not the first to guess it!" answered Ryan.

"We take it you know the other man is Argon?" said Will.

"I do," said Jack. He smiled slightly. "He doesn't seem to like me much, though."

Drake cleared his throat. "Don't worry about Argon," he said. "We have all been going out of our minds today, with what happened. It has made his temper worse than usual. Take no offence."

Jack nodded, although he questioned the truth of the statement. "May I ask what did happen?" he voiced. He'd been surprised not to see search parties on his way to the city.

Drake sat up a little straighter on his chair, passing a quick look at Ryan and Will, who had both gone silent. Jack was convinced the air in the room had grown colder.

Drake looked back at Jack with a smile. It was forced and didn't meet his dark-blue eyes. "Well, we are hoping that your statement will get us to the bottom of today." The door behind Drake opened again, and Argon came back into the room.

"Let us begin," said Drake quickly. "Master Orden, can I call you Jack?"

Jack nodded.

"Before I begin the statement, may I ask you a few personal questions?"

Jack froze and his heartbeat quickened. *Just stay calm*, he told himself before nodding slowly.

Drake smiled and folded his arms. "Where are you from?"

"Sanalow, originally," replied Jack. He knew that was a test to check if he would be honest. These men would know as well as he did about the eye colours. He must have passed it, because Drake continued. "How old are you?"

Jack knew the answer he was about to give was going to lead to more questions, so he took a second to ready himself. "Twenty-six," he finally answered.

Argon raised an eyebrow and turned to look at Drake. Drake caught his look. Both men turned their attention back to Jack, who was ready for the interrogation he knew was coming.

Drake asked the next question. "You named yourself a wayfarer upon arrival here. Why are you not self-employed in a trade or in the army of Sanalow?"

Here we go, thought Jack. Drake had gone straight to the heart of the matter. He couldn't think of a way to avoid answering the question, so he opted to tell the truth and give as few details as possible. "I was in the army until a year ago," he replied.

Argon cut in. "Then what happened?" he asked, with his eyebrow still raised.

Jack cast him a dark look. "I resigned."

Argon opened his mouth to say more, but Jack cut him off. "Forgive me, sir, but I believe I am here to answer your questions about the princess and the man whom she was with. I think I have been perfectly co-operative with all of you so far, but I do not wish to continue explaining my past to you."

Jack heard both men behind him shift in their chairs. Argon was looking at him with a narrowed expression of clear distaste. Drake looked pensive; he locked eyes with Jack, and for a minute they stared at each other, until Drake finally broke the contact. He opened his ink bottle and dipped his quill into it. "Jack, would you please tell us where it was that you encountered the princess?" he began formally, ending the run of personal questions.

Jack blinked, surprised that he had got away with his outburst. He sighed inwardly and relaxed back in his chair to listen to what Drake was telling him.

"I will record what you say to present to the king. Once you have finished telling us your account, I hope you don't mind us asking you a few questions, just to make sure we have all the correct details. You may begin in your own time."

Jack took a deep breath and carefully began to tell his tale. He changed parts of the story, pretended the driver had been nearly dead, so he had abandoned hope of saving him, checked the carriage, found the princess, and rescued her before the man, horse, and carriage fell over the side.

For the whole telling, Argon sat with his eyes fixed on Jack, as if determined to read his mind. Jack kept his eyes on Drake and ignored Argon completely.

Ryan spoke out. "So you had no idea who you'd rescued?" he asked when Jack finished.

"No, not until the guard yelled that I had the princess. I was quite shocked," added Jack for dramatic effect.

Argon took over. "So it was chance you brought her to Judelen City?" he asked Jack.

"Well, I was heading for the city anyhow, in search of work, and the carriage came from the direction of the city, so I thought it was the safest place to try," said Jack.

Drake looked pensive. "The princess did not regain consciousness at all while you were with her?" he asked.

"No," said Jack, shaking his head.

"And the man with the carriage said nothing to you?" checked Drake again.

"I already told you, no," repeated Jack. He shifted in his chair but no one appeared to notice his mistake.

Will tapped Jack on the shoulder. "What made the carriage's crash?" he asked. "Did you see what it hit on the road to cause the wheels to come off?"

Jack frowned. "They didn't come off, they exploded!" he explained. "I've never seen anything like it—"

Drake sat bolt upright. "Well, it must have been pushing hard right from the city to try and get clear before the guards came after it," he interrupted, addressing the other guards. "That strain could easily have buckled the wheels."

"May I ask how the princess is?" said Jack quickly. He couldn't help himself; she was the centre of this story and the part he cared most about.

Drake gave him a searching look. "She is resting; her head wound is not serious."

Jack nodded, thankful to have been given an answer.

Drake put down his quill. "Well, I think you have told us all we need to know right now, Jack. I shall have you shown to the guest suite. I must ask you to remain in the suite for the rest of tonight. In the morning a guard will come and collect you. As a stranger to the palace, you might come to harm, if a guard who does not know who you are finds you in the corridors," he cautioned.

"Of course," said Jack. "My horse, is he stabled?" he checked.

"Yes, he is bedded down and quite safe."

Argon looked very interested in Jack's question. "He is a fine horse," he suddenly said.

Jack was taken aback. "Thank you," he said.

"The army let you have him, did they?'

Jack hesitated, thinking up an answer. "Yes, he was a gift for good service." Jack knew his lie was pathetic, and the look on Argon's face confirmed it.

"There is no earthly reason you could have for retiring at your age," said Argon sharply. "Which means you deserted the army, stole the horse, and now you are on the run, hiding as a wayfarer."

Jack knew he was finished. These men would take him prisoner and contact the steward of Sanalow, who would execute him forthwith. He felt so angry that he leapt up and moved forward to punch Argon, but the brothers restrained him.

Argon looked Jack up and down in open amusement. "The animal has a fault in his hind leg—did you know? He is only good enough for the meat carts now."

Jack shoulder-barged Will in an attempt to escape, but his grip didn't loosen. Drake was on his feet. "Enough!" he shouted. He rounded on Argon. "Whatever you, or the rest of us, think or feel, Jack is a guest here, and we are in his debt. I will not tolerate such abuse. If the princess hears of this she will skin you alive, Argon. Now apologise."

Argon looked ready to kill. He stood defiantly looking at Drake. Drake banged his fist on the table. "Now!" he shouted.

Argon gave him a sharp look before quickly turning to Jack. "I apologise," he said bitterly, before turning on his heel and leaving the chamber.

Drake watched him leave, looking angry. He turned to Jack. "Come, I will show you to the guest suite myself." Jack allowed the brothers to steer him from the room.

Drake turned back to speak to Ryan. "See that the paperwork is fit to present to the king. I will be back shortly." Ryan nodded and went back inside the room.

"You can go, Will," added Drake. Will let go of Jack's arm, and he left through a different door.

"This way, Jack," said Drake as he began to walk along the corridor. Jack followed silently.

"Tell me, Jack," said Drake after a while. "When you left Sanalow, did you leave behind family?"

"I have none," said Jack.

Drake gave him a sideways look. "None?" he repeated doubtfully.

Jack's hands balled up into fists. "They're all dead," he said, not wishing to discuss it.

Drake looked intrigued but he asked no more questions. They arrived outside the door of the guest suite. Drake opened it and steered Jack inside.

A plump woman with grey hair wound tightly in a bun was bent over the bed, patting it down. She straightened up at the sound of footsteps and bowed to Drake. "I am just finishing off," she said.

"Carry on," commanded Drake. He turned to Jack. "Jack, this is Mistress Stratton; she will see to you now. I must excuse myself. I have work to finish before supper."

Jack nodded and Drake left through the door, closing it behind him.

Mistress Stratton had finished the bed and now stood looking Jack up and down. "First things first, young man. I have drawn you a bath in the next chamber. Get behind the screen and strip out of those clothes, I will take them with me now and have them washed. Well, what are you waiting for?"

Jack jumped slightly and walked towards the screen. He had forgotten how to take orders, but this woman certainly seemed accustomed to giving them and being obeyed. Jack obediently walked behind the screen, but then he remembered he had no other clothing.

"Excuse me, mistress," he called out, "is there some spare clothing I could borrow?"

"Of course, of course. I shall bring some back into your room when I have taken these to the wash room. Mind you, stay in the bath chamber, though, unless you want me seeing parts of you I really don't need to see."

Jack coloured and was very glad he was hidden behind the screen. He wished there were spare clothes already in the room. Reluctantly he began to peel his clothes off, grimacing at how dirty and smelly they had become. He pushed them under the screen. He could hear Mistress Stratton collecting them on the other side; she was humming to herself.

"Is that everything, sir?" she asked cheerfully.

"Yes," answered Jack, "except my name is Jack Orden, and I am a wayfarer, mistress, so you shouldn't call me sir."

Jack could hear footsteps coming closer. Mistress Stratton spoke directly on the other side of the screen, making him jump. She spoke quietly, as if she didn't wish to be overheard. "Anyone who saves the princess's life and returns her home safely warrants being called sir. You are a good man, and I thank you greatly."

Jack was touched by the compliment; he sensed an opportunity. "May I ask you, mistress, is the princess well?"

"She is well, good sir. She awoke shortly after she was returned to the palace. The knock to her head has done nothing to stem her stubbornness, mind. She has been ordered to stay in bed until tomorrow by Sir Aidan, and she made a right fuss about it!" Mistress Stratton laughed gently. It was clear that she was a woman who knew the princess well and had a fondness for talking about her. "She will never be one to follow orders, that girl," she said affectionately.

"Who is Sir Aidan?" asked Jack, wanting to learn more about the princess and the palace.

It seemed Mistress Stratton was happy to answer. "He is to be her husband and future prince of Judelen."

Jack's shoulders slumped. Of course she was engaged; she was a princess. But he couldn't deny that he felt disappointed to learn the news.

Mistress Stratton continued, unaware of Jack's emotional conflict. "They will wed in the summer. He will be good for Lily; he is more than a match for her. I must admit that when I first met him I didn't like him at all; I don't much care for these foreign lords."

"Where does he come from?" asked Jack.

The mistress paused. "Well ... to tell you the truth, I couldn't say exactly; somewhere beyond the Great Mountains—I believe."

Not likely unless he can fly, thought Jack, but he said nothing and let her continue.

"Sir Aidan reached out to the king in friendship several years ago, and the king left the palace to visit his city. When he finally returned, he brought Sir Aidan with him and announced the engagement a week later."

"And the princess didn't object to being engaged to a stranger?" asked Jack, not believing anyone would agree to that.

Mistress Stratton chuckled. "Come now, good sir, the princess does what is best for king and country. I think she was taken aback in the beginning. Sir Aidan is older than she is and very different in looks, with his black irises and white skin. He is quite cold in his manner and, if I'm honest, very intimidating. He is always dressed from head to toe in black, which I find rather morbid. However, as the months have passed, she seems more content in herself about him. I think she maybe falling in love."

Jack frowned; he felt his disappointment growing deeper. He was being stupid, he knew. He could never win the affection of a royal, but as he stood there listening to the story, he felt desire burning in him. It was like nothing he had ever experienced.

Mistress Stratton remembered that she had work to do and scolded Jack for keeping her. "I'll be back shortly with your clothes. I must check on the princess, if Sir Aidan has managed to keep her in her rooms," she said.

"Thank you, mistress," said Jack. "Would you tell the princess, if you see her, that I am glad she is well?" he asked hopefully.

Mistress Stratton cleared her throat. "Mind you don't make too many enquiries of the princess if you like a quiet life, sir."

"But if you get the chance?" pushed Jack.

"I'll do my best," promised Mistress Stratton. She added in a hurried whisper. "In return, perhaps you would be kind enough not to mention anything I have told you about Sir Aidan to anyone?"

Jack smiled towards the screen. "I won't say a word about it," he promised. "How do you learn so much about the movements in the palace?" he asked out of curiosity.

"Servants are everywhere and always overlooked as unimportant. We hear a great amount of information, and so long as we are careful not to gossip openly, we can always be ahead of the scandals!"

Jack laughed. "A useful tool."

"Indeed!" agreed Mistress Stratton. "Now excuse me, sir, you best get to your bath before it cools."

Mistress Stratton left the room. Jack stuck his head round the screen to check the coast was clear before darting into the bath chamber and closing the door.

A large bathtub stood in the centre of the chamber, on a stone floor with a metal drain running through it. The floor was cold compared to the carpets in the main chamber, so Jack rushed over it and jumped straight into the bathtub. Far from the water being cool, it was decidedly hot. He stood up quickly, moving his feet up and down until they adjusted, and then he sank back down and began to wash. He ducked his head under the water, thoroughly scrubbing his hair; he tried in vain to pull some of the knots out with his fingers but gave up and lay soaking instead. His muscles began to unlock from the strain of long journeys and rough living. Jack stayed in the tub until the water began to cool and goose pimples started to appear on his skin. The main chamber door opened, and he turned to listen.

"I've put you some fresh clothing on your bed, sir," came Mistress Stratton's voice. "There is a tray of food and drink on the window table. Just put the tray outside the main door when you are done if you don't wish to be disturbed."

"Thank you," called Jack from the bathtub, his voice echoing in the chamber.

"Are you still in that bath?" asked the mistress in a disapproving voice. "You'll prune if you stay in it much longer."

The main chamber door closed again, and Jack got out of the bathtub. There was a piece of towelling on the floor beside him, which he used to dry himself. He then moved over to the door and made a quick check that the chamber was clear again before hurrying to the bed. He gasped when he saw the clothing Mistress Stratton had brought him: trousers made from fine black leather, a white shirt made from cotton, and a velvet jacket in deep red. There were also fresh undergarments and a shirt for bedtime. Jack put on the undergarments and the trousers; he was so thin he had to use the dinner fork to pierce a new hole into the belt to tighten it.

The smell of bread and meat stew enticed him back over to the window table to inspect the food. His stomach was reminding him that he had not eaten all day. Jack sat down and began eating the stew at a passionate speed. He sampled the drink and discovered that it was dark wine; it complemented the stew perfectly. In no time at all, the entire tray stood empty. Jack patted his stomach contentedly. He had forgotten how nice it was to have a proper meal and a full belly. He crossed the room and opened the door to the corridor to slip the tray outside. Movement beside him caught his eye, and Jack looked up into the face of a guard. He frowned as he silently put the tray onto the floor, stepped back into the room, and closed the door. He was not pleased about the presence of the guard, considering he was a guest and had already agreed not to leave the chamber. Still, it explained why Mistress Stratton had whispered so close to the screen.

Jack went back to the window. It was pitch-black outside; he estimated it must be very late into the night. The meal and the wine were making him drowsy, so he decided to retire. He blew out the candles around the room, and climbed into the four-poster bed. It was the most comfortable bed he had ever been in. Jack was too tired to change his clothes, so he blew out the last of the candles and lay back on the pillow. Sleep came quickly.

3

THE PRINCESS'S OFFER

Jack opened his eyes in the pitch-black chamber. He lay for a moment, trying to think what he had been dreaming of. Suddenly he realised that someone was entering his chamber through the main door. The person came inside quietly and then closed the door. Jack tensed and quickly tried to think of something to defend himself with should the person attack. His sword and dagger had not been returned to him, he remembered with a silent curse.

The person by the door stood still for a moment, studying the chamber, Jack guessed. He lay still, pretending to be sleep. The person moved slowly into the chamber, reached the end of the bed, and knelt down at the foot of it. Jack eyes had adjusted quickly in the dark, and he could make out the outline of a hand rising up towards his body. As quick as lightning, he sat up and grabbed the hand, expecting to find a dagger. A soft gasp escaped the mouth of the person kneeling on the floor. Jack let go as if stung—his would-be attacker was the princess!

"Forgive me, Your Majesty! I did not realise it was you," said Jack in an apologetic whisper.

"Master Orden?" said the princess in a gentle voice. "You startled me. I was just coming to wake you. Forgive me for coming into your chamber uninvited in the middle of the night, but I must speak with you," she whispered.

Jack nodded in her general direction. "Of course, Your Majesty."

The princess shuffled forward on her knees and came closer to the head of the bed. "I shall light just one candle so that we may see each other as we speak," she said softly. Then she cleared her throat. "Are you clothed at all?"

"I just need to put on my shirt, Your Majesty," answered Jack quickly.

"Good," said the princess, and she lit the candle. A soft glow sprang from it, illuminating just the head of the bed and the spot where the princess knelt.

Jack immediately reached down to the foot of the bed and retrieved his shirt. He slipped it on quickly and then glanced at the princess, who had her eyes on the floor. He couldn't tell if she had watched him at all. As her head came back up to look at him, Jack held in the sigh that his body longed to release. The princess was, if possible, even more beautiful now than she had been on the roadside. Her long golden hair hung loose, with natural curls running through it. It framed her oval face perfectly. She wore a dressing gown of pale-gold velvet, which covered her from the neck down.

Jack wished he didn't look so scruffy. He moved to climb out of the bed, so he could bow. The princess put a hand on his arm to stop him. "Please remain where you are." Her hand was warm on his skin. Jack was not cold, but a shiver ran up his body.

The princess fixed him with a hard stare. "There are questions I must have answers to," she said in a very formal tone. Jack waited for her to continue.

"I must ask you about what happened today."

"Your guards have taken a statement, Your Majesty," said Jack carefully.

The princess frowned slightly. "I know that. I have been informed that you pulled me from the carriage and brought me back home. I was told that Tomas is dead—is that true?"

Jack sat for a minute wondering who Tomas was. Then he realised it must be the driver of the carriage. "The man driving your carriage was killed, it is true," he said gently.

To his surprise, a tear fell from the princess's eye; she wiped it away in silence.

Jack felt awkward; he wanted to comfort her but was frightened of offending.

The princess dabbed her eyes. "Please, did he suffer at all?"

Jack winced. "I'm afraid he was in great pain, Your Majesty. His legs were trapped beneath the carriage and bleeding badly. When the carriage fell off the bridge, he was dragged with it."

More tears ran down the princess's face.

Jack swallowed. "I'm sorry, Your Majesty. I tried to save him, but I couldn't free him."

The princess sniffed and nodded, wiping her eyes. "Thank you for that, Master Orden."

"Jack, Your Majesty. My name is Jack," he blurted out. He needed her to trust him, and that wasn't going to happen if she didn't even use his name.

The princess regarded him for a moment; she managed a weak smile. "Jack it is," she said kindly. "I have another question to ask of you, Jack. My bodyguards tell me that you did not have time to speak with Tomas before his death. I don't like to ask a man this, but is that true?"

Jack sat quietly for a moment, looking at the bedspread. He opted to tell the truth. "No, Your Majesty, it is not true."

The princess's eyes widened, but not in anger, Jack thought she looked relieved.

"Please, Jack. I must know what he said to you, no matter how small it may seem," she said urgently.

Jack frowned at her. "Why is it so important to you?"

The princess frowned right back at him, and her lip thinned slightly. For a moment Jack saw a glimmer of mightiness rise within her, deep for her young years. He bit his lip to stop a smile.

"Tomas was one of my personal bodyguards," she said.

"Oh!" said Jack as clarity set in. "Well, that might explain a few things."

"What things?"

"He said that he was trying to save you."

The princess looked seriously at Jack. "Did he say what from?"

Jack sighed, and nodded his head. "Yes, he said that there was a plot in Judelen to kill you. He had found out about it and taken you to save you."

The princess stood up suddenly from the floor and began to pace by the bed.

"Your Majesty," said Jack carefully, "I don't know how much faith you can put in his words; he was hallucinating badly by the end."

"Did you believe him?" asked the princess.

"I didn't know what to believe," said Jack honestly. "I was overwhelmed by the whole situation. I had just rescued the princess of Judelen, who was bound hand and foot, in a carriage that was being driven so fast it crashed on a bridge, by a man who claimed he was conducting a rescue. It was a lot to take in."

The princess stopped pacing and came to stand by the head of the bed. "Why didn't you tell my bodyguards that you spoke with him?"

Jack sighed again. "Because he said that no one could be trusted, not even the king."

The princess raised her eyebrows. "So you *did* believe him?"

Jack shrugged. "I honestly didn't know what to believe. I thought it safer not to take any chances until I had spoken to you."

The princess covered her face for a moment. Jack thought she looked tired. He remembered her head wound, and forgetting about respecting her station, he stretched out and pulled her to sit on the bed.

"Do you think he was telling the truth?" he asked gently.

"Maybe," said the princess. "He was bound in my service and so could not lift a finger to harm me intentionally; none of my guards can harm me. Therefore, to get away with binding me, drugging me, and kidnapping me from the city, he truly must have believed he was trying to save me."

"What if he was mad, Your Majesty?"

The princess considered his question but appeared to dismiss it. "That doesn't make any sense. He was perfectly fine two days ago, although I didn't see him at all yesterday. The next thing I knew, he paid me a visit last night and brought me a drink. I passed out, and then when I woke up again in my chamber tonight, I was told I had been kidnapped. People don't just go mad overnight."

Jack knew that wasn't always the case. "Sometimes madness can come from nowhere, Your Majesty," he told her truthfully. "Maybe something triggered Tomas the day you didn't see him. I think that only you can decide whether you believe him or not. Maybe it would be safer for you to believe it, at least to become more alert about what goes on in the palace," he said reasonably.

The princess looked thoughtful. "You make an excellent point, Jack. I have known Tomas all my life. We played together as children, he and two of my other guards, and they all came into my service together. He was like a big brother. I could never believe him capable of hurting me; he lived to protect me." The princess bit her lip. "Of course, that leaves me with a terrifying thought—there really is a plot in Judelen. Someone is planning my death. What should I do, Jack?"

Jack leant forward. "For the moment I would do nothing, Your Majesty. No harm should come to you while you are within the palace, so long as you stay alert. Just keep your eyes peeled for any unusual activity."

"Should I tell my father what was said?"

Jack winced. "If you wouldn't mind, Your Majesty, I would prefer it if you didn't, as I have not told the guards and they took a written statement to show the king. It would not cast me in a very good light. I already have a bad reputation for being a wayfarer. Of course, if you think it is necessary, I will accept what comes after."

The princess smiled warmly at him and reached across the bed to squeeze his hand. "I shall say nothing," she promised.

A single quiet knock on the chamber door made her look round. "I have to go," she said quickly. "I have one more thing to ask of you."

"Your Majesty?" prompted Jack. He still had hold of her hand, but she slowly withdrew it. He felt disappointed but hoped she could not see it on his face.

"If I asked you to take service in my name, would you accept?"

Jack's mouth fell open. "Are you serious?" he asked.

"Please, Jack, I need to know," urged the princess.

Jack considered for a moment before answering. "When I rescued you, I vowed I would protect you, and if you want me in your service, then I shall accept."

The princess suddenly leant towards him and kissed his cheek. "Thank you, Jack," she said.

Jack blushed; he looked down to hide his ridiculous grin.

"Speak of tonight to no one. Tomorrow I will put my plans into action. You are to meet with my father at midday. I will see you then," said the princess.

Without another word she swept from the chamber. Jack took his shirt back off and lay back on his bed, feeling dazed and slightly delirious. He blew the candle out once more and lay in the dark, thinking about what tomorrow would bring, and the kiss, yes, mostly, he thought about the kiss.

4

THE BONDING

Winter sunlight flooded Jack's chamber. He lay on the bed, deep in thought. It was getting late into the morning. Mistress Stratton had been most displeased to find him still asleep when she had brought him breakfast. She had woken him and given him a few sharp words about his lazy behaviour. Jack had made things much worse by enquiring about the princess, calling her by her name instead of her title.

"Just because the princess drops you a visit in the dead of night, and asks you to keep her secrets, you think you can begin to call her Lily, instead of her title. You want to be careful, young sir! If the king or Sir Aidan caught you, your neck would break before nightfall!"

"How do you know she visited me?" Jack had asked in surprise.

"Who else do you think knocked on the door, and got her safely to and from her chambers, in the middle of the night, without anyone knowing!"

Jack should have been careful of angering the mistress further, but he had found himself asking more questions. It had ended with Mistress Stratton turning a dangerous purple colour and threatening to silence him herself if he didn't shut up. Jack had felt annoyed with her for not telling him more, but when she produced the scissors from her pocket and said she was going to cut his hair, he instantly forgave her. She completed the job and left him alone to clean up and eat his breakfast.

He now lay on his bed waiting, looking and feeling smart, dressed in his new trousers and shirt, with his jacket neatly folded on the end. Soon it would be time for him to go and meet the king. Jack didn't know what the princess was going to do, whether she has already arranged her plan or whether it would be dropped in at some point during the meeting. Jack thought it best just to act as normal as possible and remember he was only there to tell the king the events of the previous day.

A knock sounded on the door. Jack jumped off the bed. "Come in," he called. He quickly made sure his trousers were not creased and his shirt was tucked in properly.

Will entered the room, dressed in his uniform. He smiled pleasantly at Jack. "Morning! Did you sleep well?"

Jack was pleased that there was no awkwardness after his attempted escape the day before. He returned the smile. "Yes, I slept beautifully. This bed is so comfortable I had to be awakened by the mistress because I slept in!"

Will laughed out loud; he seemed much more relaxed today. Jack imagined the previous day must have been so hard for all the guards, dealing with the fear and loss they had suffered.

Will admired his new haircut. "I bet my brother a gold coin that Mistress Stratton would not let you see the king until she had tidied you up."

Jack grinned. "If I had a gold coin, I'd have paid it to her. She is a godsend!"

Will nodded. "She is wonderful, so long as you let her do things her way! So, are you ready to face the king?" he added lightly.

"I guess so," said Jack. "I must admit, Will, I am glad it is you who has come to collect me."

"Rather than Argon, you mean?" said Will, grinning.

"Oh yes, it would have been a tense trip to the king if Argon had come," confessed Jack.

Will laughed and picked Jack's jacket up off the bed. "Well you can rest easy, because you got me." He helped Jack put his jacket on to avoid creasing it.

"Thanks," said Jack, feeling a little self-conscious at being so fancily dressed. It didn't help that everything hung loosely on him.

Will smiled. "You look ready to me. Let's get going; you must not be late."

Jack and Will exited the room together and turned right down the corridor, then left, then right again. Then it was down a staircase and another right. Jack was soon as lost as he had been the previous day.

The entrance to the official greeting chamber came into view up ahead, and Jack saw Ryan and Argon standing outside. Ryan's face fell when he saw Jack's hair and he heard Will chuckle to himself.

Jack acknowledged both men with a small nod as he approached. Argon looked at him with a cold expression. To hide his annoyance Jack looked away at a painting on the wall. He stopped walking and stood transfixed. "The Trio," he whispered in delight as he surveyed the painting.

Will stepped up next to Jack. "It's a magnificent illustration of our creators, don't you think?"

Jack nodded his agreement. "It is just as I pictured them from the stories I was told as a child." He pointed towards the magnificent, pure-white horse with a single spiral horn growing from its head. "The Unicorn is my favourite."

Ryan came to join Jack and his brother. "Surely it should be the Dragon," he said lightly. He discreetly passed a gold coin to his brother for losing the bet. Jack stifled a laugh.

Will put the coin in his pocket. "Everyone always overlooks the Fairy," he said.

"Maybe because she broke the world!" argued Ryan, raising his eyebrows.

"You need to brush up on your history, little brother. Orthrillium broke the world when he broke the Earth Stone," corrected Will.

"I know! But it was the Fairy who gave it to him," insisted Ryan, "and look what happened because of her mistake. Evelyn Maude made black magic, and when Orthrillium found out she planned to overthrow him, he gave the Guardian the powers to protect the Light. Evelyn Maude killed Orthrillium, took what powers she could, and made her son, the Dark Knight. Together they started the War of Power against the good magus, but the dark forces lost, and the remaining magus now hide in Emiscial, doing who knows what." Ryan looked rather smug about his fact-telling.

Jack listened, fascinated. "You get to study the Creation in Judelen?" he asked.

Ryan nodded. "Oh yes. Every person in the city, whether they are poor or rich, has to receive a formal education on the Creation. Judelen has a library full of documents about the history of the world, the Black Order, the Theanic Order, and the War of Power," he said.

Jack frowned. "We don't get that in Sanalow, although I am not sure why I find it so compelling. I hate magic of any type."

Ryan and Will turned to study him. "Why?" they asked in unison.

Jack sighed. "Because magic has been the cause of every bad thing that has ever happened!"

"And of all the good things too! We all came from it, after all," said Will reasonably.

"Are you quite finished?" snapped Argon, walking down the corridor towards them. He looked crossly at the guards standing with Jack, who lowered their heads and moved away from the picture. "This isn't the time for a history lesson. You cannot keep the king waiting." Argon shook his head in disbelief, turned on his heel, and marched off.

Ryan whistled quietly under his breath and followed him in silence. Jack felt amusement rising up inside him, but he pushed it away. Now was not the time to provoke Argon. The men walked quickly to the door of the official greeting chamber.

Argon spun round and glared at Jack. "You are only just in time. It is not good practice to be sloppy when you are coming to see royalty."

Will looked crossly at Argon. "Enough, Argon," he said. "You had best give Jack the commands, or *you* will make him late."

Argon's eyes flashed towards Will, but he said nothing further on the matter. He turned back to Jack. "You are about to enter the official greeting chamber of Judelen Palace. The king has reviewed your statement from last night, and you are here today to answer any questions he may ask of you. When you enter the room, you will see that the king is sat directly ahead of these doors; he is positioned exactly one hundred paces away. The princess Lillian is sat to his right, and the princess's betrothed, Sir Aidan, is sat to his left. When the doors open, you will walk inside, looking directly ahead. Position your eyes to look just above the king's head. Count fifty paces into the room and stop. You will then salute the king with the salute of Judelen: place your left arm across your chest to join with your right shoulder and bow your head."

Jack nodded and kept listening.

"Next you will drop to the floor on your left knee, put your head down and your eyes on the floor. Do not lift your head or eyes at any point unless you are given permission to. Speak only when you are asked a question, and remain silent at all other times. Do you understand?"

"Yes," said Jack simply.

Argon sniffed. "Well, we shall find out. Get into position."

Will guided Jack to stand directly at the centre of the doors into the chamber. Then he took up his position on Jack's right, whilst Ryan stood on his left. Argon stood behind Jack, making the hairs on his neck stand up.

Ryan raised his fist and knocked three times on the door. A moment later the doors swung open, pulled by two servants.

Jack looked ahead, where he could see the king sitting upon his throne. He looked slightly overweight, but he radiated power in his posture. He wore a simple golden crown upon his short, curly blond hair, and his attention was focused on the group about to enter the chamber.

Will and Ryan began to move forward. Jack started walking and counting his steps. He kept his head up and his eyes above the king's head.

A small golden sparkle caught his eye, and he looked towards it without meaning to. It came from the crown the princess was wearing. She looked stunning, dressed in a red velvet gown with a light-blue underlay. Her golden hair was swept up off her face by gold wire, which wound down and around her hair. The same coloured wire wound up the sleeves of her gown. The princess caught him looking at her and smiled gently. Jack forgot what he was meant to be doing; for a moment he felt as if it were only the two of them in the room, and he smiled back. Lily dropped her gaze, and then Jack remembered he was supposed to look straight ahead. He had lost count of his steps. He felt sweat appear on his forehead. He quickly risked a look out of the corner of his eye at Will, who was looking directly ahead in concentration. Jack slowed his pace a little, hoping that if they all stopped he wouldn't take a full step ahead of them. Just as soon as he had thought it, the line came to a halt. Jack was in mid-step forward; he quickly tried to correct himself but ended up tripping. There was little chance that the king had not seen his mistake. There was nothing else Jack could do but quickly straighten up and salute with the others. He then dropped onto his left knee and gratefully put his head and eyes down. He felt as if every eye in the room was burrowing into him.

Will and Ryan, and Jack assumed Argon, had dropped to their knees also, but to Jack's horror they all stood up again, leaving him alone. He kept himself where he was and waited for someone to speak. It felt as if he waited for hours, but then, to his relief, Argon spoke.

"Your Majesties, I present before you Master Orden."

"Thank you," said a deep voice that Jack knew had to be the king's.

"Master Orden, you have been brought before me today to receive Judelen's blessing for the great service you performed yesterday when you rescued my daughter, the princess Lillian, from certain death."

There was a pause and Jack remained silent. When no one spoke, he began panicking, thinking it was his turn to speak. He licked his lips and opened his mouth, but then he heard the crunch of parchment being folded up, and he snapped his mouth shut again.

"I have read your statement of the events of yesterday, and I have heard the accounts of the bodyguards who questioned you. My daughter and I are in agreement that there is nothing further you can tell us of the incident—unless of course, anything has come to mind overnight. Is there anything else you would like to add?"

Jack cleared his throat. "No, Your Majesty. I can think of nothing new to tell you."

Again there was a pause. Jack hoped that the princess had stayed true to her word and not spoken to her father—or he had just signed his death sentence by lying directly to the king.

"Very well, Master Orden, there is nothing left to settle but your reward. For the great service you have performed for Judelen, I would like to offer you five thousand gold pieces."

Jack's eyes widened in shock. That amount of gold would set him and Bailey up for life! They could go anywhere they wanted.

"You will be free to leave the palace and Judelen, if you wish," the king continued. "There have been several new garments made for you to take, with our blessing, and enough supplies for yourself and your horse should you want to travel immediately.

"There is one condition with your reward. Out of respect for the royal family, you shall not mention the events of yesterday to anyone you meet upon leaving. The rumours in the city have been hushed. You can understand that I wish them to stay that way. Also, know that I will learn quickly if they should begin again. In that case, our grateful attitude toward you would end. You would be arrested and imprisoned. If you understand the conditions of the reward, then I believe that concludes our meeting. Master Orden, please rise."

Jack slowly stood up from the ground. The king and the princess both rose from their thrones. Jack risked glances at both of them and then at Sir Aidan, who had remained seated. He was unnaturally pale, and his hair was straighter than a razor edge, with hints of silver at the tips. He sat like a hawk surveying its prey. When Sir Aidan's eyes locked onto Jack, the black irises were so strange and unusual that they made him shiver, and he looked away.

The king bowed to Jack. "My thanks go to you, Master Orden; the thanks of my city carry with you always." Jack returned the bow.

The princess stepped forward and curtsied, spreading her gown widely. "It is good to look upon the face of my rescuer, Master Orden," she said gently. "You have shown yourself to be a man worthy of Judelen's love."

Jack held his breath. This was it; she was going through with her plan. Blood pumped in his ears. The king stiffened and watched his daughter from the corner of his eye. Noticing his reaction, the princess smiled, a winning smile, before turning back to look at Jack.

"My father has offered you a fine reward, Master Orden, and you may take it with our thanks. However, I would like to offer you an alternative way to accept my gratitude."

Straightening up, Sir Aidan looked round the king at the princess. The king stood looking at his daughter with open anger in his eyes. The bodyguards stiffened, and Jack tried to adopt a look of polite puzzlement, hoping it would mask his fear.

The king spoke in an angry voice. "There has been no discussion about an alternative reward, Lillian."

The princess bowed her head to him. "Forgive the suddenness of my actions, Father, for I have only just decided this myself."

"What is it you choose to offer Master Orden instead of gold?"

The princess took a deep breath. "I wish for Master Orden to take service as one of my personal bodyguards, in place of Tomas," she said quickly.

At these words the king exploded, all formality forgotten. "That is not acceptable! I will not allow it!"

The princess appeared unconcerned by her father's anger. "By the power vested in me, as Princess of Judelen, I may choose my personal bodyguard, and my choice cannot be overthrown by anyone, including you, Father," she said calmly.

The king stood staring at his daughter in shock. His mouth moved, but no words came out.

"If I may speak, Your Majesty?" said Sir Aidan quickly. The king glanced at him and nodded shortly.

Sir Aidan rose from his throne and walked to stand before the princess. He spoke quietly to her, but Jack caught every word. "This is an unwise choice, Lillian. You know nothing of this man or of his past. He has done you a great service by saving your life, and five thousand gold pieces is a very generous reward for doing that. Allow him to take his gold and leave."

The princess's mouth thinned slightly. "I know you speak words of wisdom, My Lord, but in this instance they hold no meaning. Should Master Orden accept my offer, the oath he will take will bind him to my service in complete loyalty."

The king interrupted, looking furious. "Oaths may be broken, Lillian! Does yesterday not prove that?"

"Should that be the case, Father, then I can trust none of my bodyguards. My safety can no longer be assured," said the princess. "We agreed last night that Tomas had, sadly, lost his mind. He believed he was saving my life when he fled Judelen with me; therefore his oath was not broken."

The king and Sir Aidan opened their mouths to argue further, but the princess turned from both of them and walked towards Jack. "The question that needs to be answered before more arguments break out is whether Master Orden would choose to accept my offer. Will you accept?" she finished.

Jack knew it needed to appear as if he was in careful consideration of the offer. So he stood silently, waiting for a suitable length of time to pass. The king was watching him with an expression like stone; Sir Aidan was also watching him, his expression blank. Jack wondered what he was thinking. He looked back at the princess; she raised an eyebrow at him.

Sir Aidan broke the tense silence. "You have overwhelmed Master Orden," he said. "May I suggest that this matter be settled later, Lillian, so he has time to consider properly."

"Master Orden can have all the time he wishes," the princess said, not taking her eyes off Jack. "Do you need more time to consider my offer?" she squeaked in nervousness.

Jack decided he had wasted enough time; he shook his head. "I don't need further time, Your Majesty. I choose to accept your offer and take service."

Jack heard Will whisper, "By the fires of the Dragon!"

Argon broke from his position and stepped towards Jack. The princess noticed him and raised a hand. "Remain at your position, guard," she said firmly. Argon stepped back, barely hiding his anger.

The princess bowed her head to Jack before turning back to her father. "The decision is made, Father; let's not waste time arguing over it. Master Orden has chosen to accept. Let us bind him into service without delay."

The king's chest heaved up and down, but he said. "Very well, daughter; the decision was yours. The oath requires two of the guards to witness the swearing. Do two of you volunteer?" he snapped.

Will and Ryan stepped forward, and Ryan spoke. "We shall witness the swearing, Your Majesty." Jack felt a rush of gratitude towards him.

The king drew himself upright. "Very well, as it is the power of the princess, she will head the ceremony with Master Orden and the guards. Everyone else may leave the chamber."

Argon turned around and stalked from the chamber.

The king turned to Sir Aidan. "Will you accompany me back to my private chambers? My daughter has chosen and won her right to a new bodyguard; however, by *my* rights, I shall not bear witness to his joining."

The princess flushed slightly and moved to speak with her father, but he raised a hand to silence her and swept from the room. Sir Aidan cast the princess a cold look before following the king.

The princess looked frustrated as she watched the king go. No one remaining in the room spoke. Jack moved his weight from one foot to the other. The princess sighed deeply. "Let us begin," she said quietly.

She reached inside a pocket in her gown and produced from it a symbol in the shape of a five-point star. It was made of gold, and it covered the palm of her hand. Four points on the star lit up red under her touch, but the fifth one glowed black.

The princess looked from the star to Jack. "This is a *serfdom*. It is a magical device, which I am able to use to connect my bodyguards together. It creates a connection between minds, allowing all those bonded to feel each other's emotions. It does nothing more than that. It cannot read minds or demand obedience, as it only has the power of whispering infused within it. Because of the personal nature of the connection, it has been proven, loyalty increases, as those who are bound have chosen to join freely."

"*Whispering?*" asked Jack. He wasn't familiar with that element.

"Yes, the power of the lost communication—telepathy—from a time before the War of Power. The feeling of emotions is one part of it."

Jack felt himself relaxing. That didn't sound too bad, and he liked the thought of having an emotional connection to the princess, a way to always know that she was safe.

"There is one important thing to note about the magic," continued the princess. "It cannot be broken easily. Death will sever it, and I have the power to sever it, but I would not do that lightly, for the loss of the bond will cause pain to all those bound to it, including myself.

"If you accept, you will be agreeing to spend the rest of your natural life serving and protecting me and the men already bonded—"

Jack suddenly frowned as he remembered. "But wait a minute. Humans can't use magic! After Evelyn Maude was killed and her son was left behind, trapped in human form and weak in power, the Theanic Order made the world mortal to destroy him and his magical human army and finally end the war."

The princess smiled kindly at him. "Your facts are correct, but since then, the royal family and the magus have had a strong relationship. Over the centuries they have gifted Judelen with many protections. The serfdom is a fairly new one, made first for my mother, a year before her death. Then I inherited it."

The princess paused and swallowed. "Forgive me, it is sometimes painful to talk about my mother." She cleared her throat. "The serfdom cannot be used as a weapon and so is not affected by the curse of mortality. Drake and Argon served my mother as faithful bodyguards, and they asked me to accept them into my service. Sadly, her other three guards died when their bonds were severed upon my mother's death, so I replaced them with Will, Ryan, and Tomas," she said in conclusion.

"I'm sorry about your mother," said Jack. He silenced the questions burning inside his brain. He didn't want to be rude by asking them after she had shared something so deeply personal. Jack longed to hug her and tell her he understood what it felt like to lose a parent. He sighed deeply; they had a lot in common.

The princess smiled, a sad smile, and then signalled for Ryan and Will to move closer to her. "We shall give you a minute to think over what you have been told. You may still change your mind, but if you agree to continue with the next step, then you will not be able to turn back." The princess moved back to her throne, Will and Ryan following her.

Jack stood alone, thinking over what he had been told. He had already made the promise to protect the princess, and he was ready to accept, but there was one thing he felt afraid of. He massaged his temples.

The princess sat upon her throne watching him, her face impassive. Jack knew he would have to make a decision soon.

Gently the princess rose from her throne and stepped towards him; she signalled to her bodyguards not to follow. Jack watched her approach, but she said nothing to him until she was stood directly in front of him.

She kept her eyes on his as she spoke: "It is unfair of me to ask you to commit to my service on such short notice. The others knew what was expected of them a long time before they made the choice. You have not been given that time, and for that I apologise. It is frightening to think of the bonding when you are not already bound; however, it doesn't have to be so. Is there something you fear you would lose if you became bound?"

Jack looked down. He had so many secrets. How could he explain his feelings to her without exposing them?

The princess placed her hands on his shoulders. "What do you fear, Jack?"

Jack looked up; he could answer this very simply. "I fear failure," he said.

The princess smiled kindly. "Of all the things in this world, that is what I fear the least from you."

Jack looked up in puzzlement.

"You've been protecting me since we met," she whispered. "I knew yesterday when I came to you that even without my offer of service you would not have left Judelen. You would have stayed in the city, trying to find some way to protect me, to carry out the duty you promised yourself you would do. That tells me you don't accept defeat easily."

Jack was impressed with her observations. "I would have done as you say. I would have stayed in Judelen until I knew you were safe." he said.

The princess looked smug. "Then stop worrying about failing me. Let us agree that it won't happen, unless you find you have no other choice," she finished firmly.

Jack frowned. "Are you sure you want a wayfarer as a bodyguard?"

The princess's eyes sparkled. "I am sure I want you."

Jack blinked in surprise at her seductive comment. He smiled, and leaning forward, he whispered in her ear. "If you truly want me, then I shall continue."

The princess blushed; she drew away and bowed her head to Jack. She turned and looked at Ryan and Will, who came forward to stand on either side of her.

"Why do you need two guards for the ceremony?" asked Jack.

"It can be done with all of the guards or with just one and myself. However, it has proven to be easier for the person who is to swear if there are at least two guards present," answered the princess.

"Why?"

The princess cleared her throat. "It is better I don't tell you, Jack. You will know soon enough."

Jack looked at her in alarm, but she said nothing further on the matter. "We shall begin," she said gently.

She held the serfdom out on the palm of her hand and moved it towards Jack. Her eyes swept over the brothers on either side of her. "Will, Ryan, please show your presence."

Will and Ryan each put out a finger and each touched one of the points on the serfdom. The points beneath their fingers turned from red to blue.

The princess looked at Jack. "There are no spoken words needed for this ceremony, Jack. All you need to do is place your finger on the black point, and then the serfdom will bond you to me."

41

Jack raised his hand and brought it to hover just above the black point. The princess nodded at him in encouragement. Swallowing a lump in his throat, he slowly lowered his finger until it touched the black point. The black glow turned a pure white. Jack felt a sensation like ice-cold water running through his finger and along his arm. It travelled through his body until it found his heart, and it seemed to engulf it. Jack felt his heart grow tight and contract against the pressure. Suddenly pain racked his body. Panicking, he tried to break contact with the serfdom, but his finger was stuck. Jack felt arms grabbing him under his armpits. His vision was growing blurry, but he could just about make out Will and Ryan holding him steady. Jack could hear someone screaming, and he realised it was himself. He looked wildly around, trying to find the princess. She was still standing directly before him, with the serfdom on her outstretched hand. Her eyes watched Jack, focused and alert. Jack tried to speak to her, but he couldn't.

She raised a finger to his lips to silence his attempt. "Don't struggle. It will be over soon," she said gently.

All of a sudden the pain ended. Jack stopped screaming and stood gasping. His body was covered in sweat, and he shook involuntarily. The only thing holding him up was the grip Will and Ryan had on him. Jack shook his head to clear his vision. His finger came away from the serfdom; where it had been there was now a red point, which matched the other four.

The princess put the serfdom back into her pocket and moved closer to Jack. "Are you all right?" she asked in genuine concern.

"Tell me," asked Jack, panting, "is that why you have two or more guards with you during the ceremony?"

The princess smiled sheepishly. "Yes, I am sorry I could not warn you, but it is a part of the bonding. I don't know why it happens, but I think it is the serfdom cleansing the body of past pain, readying to begin anew, in service."

The brothers nodded their agreement to her explanation.

"I have never felt pain like that!" Jack was still panting.

Ryan squeezed his arm. "I assure you that you have, Jack. It might not have been physical, but at some point in your life you have experienced something which has caused you that amount of pain," he said. "My brother and I both had the same experience, and we had suffered a loss before joining service. The serfdom helped make it feel less consuming. We didn't forget anything, but we felt as though we had made peace with it."

Jack nodded to indicate he understood Ryan. Still breathless, he slowly straightened and signalled that they could release him.

The princess took another step closer. "It is done, and you need not speak of your bonding or past pain to anyone. All who are with you now will never discuss it."

Jack stood holding his chest, his heart pounding underneath his fingers. "I feel a strange tightness," he said.

Will looked kindly at him. "It is normal," he reassured him. "It is a residue left by the binding. It will always be with you, but you'll learn not to notice it."

Jack closed his eyes. "I can sense you and Ryan inside me. I can also feel one of the others, I can't tell who right now, but either Argon or Drake are feeling incredibly angry."

The princess looked at Jack in interest. "You are gaining your senses quickly, but don't push yourself too hard too fast. It is best that you go and rest now. You need to recover from the bonding and be helped back into proper health—although I see Mistress Stratton has already begun to sort you out," she added, touching one of his short curls. Then she seemed to remember the other guards were present and withdrew her hand. "Ryan and Will can show you to your chambers," she finished quietly.

Jack bowed to the princess. "Thank you, Your Majesty."

The princess bowed her head in return. She looked at the brothers one at a time, saying. "Ryan, Will, make sure Jack gets settled."

She turned from the men and walked to her throne. "When you see Drake and Argon in the corridor, tell them I am waiting here for them."

Nodding, the brothers left the chamber, taking Jack with them. Once the three men were out of earshot, Will and Ryan looked at each other seriously. Ryan spoke quietly to Will. "So, what do you think?"

"I think Judelen Palace has been turned on its head! What was going on in there?" said Will seriously.

Jack looked from one man to the other. "Are you talking about my bonding?" he snapped.

Will looked at Jack. "Sorry, Jack, we should not have spoken over you like that. We don't mean your bonding. We are talking about the meeting with the king that has just taken place."

"What about it?" asked Jack.

Will looked at Jack. "Even you must have noticed that meeting was not carried out like any other official meeting would have been," he said in disbelief.

Jack was confused; he had never attended a meeting with a king. "What should it have been like?" he asked.

It was Ryan who answered his question. "Well, for one thing, Sir Aidan would not have been allowed to speak at all, let alone over the king," he said. "And the king should never have allowed such raw emotion to be displayed in front of guards and guests at an official meeting. Did you hear the way he spoke to the princess?"

Will nodded. "What about the way he left the chamber, stopping her from speaking? It's just not how the king should behave."

Jack didn't see what the big deal was. "Well, I guess it came as a shock to him when she offered me service," he said reasonably.

Ryan shook his head. "It makes no difference, Jack. The king was taught from babyhood that a man of his position should remain calm and in control at all times."

"At least he didn't say 'by the fires of the Dragon' under his breath," said Jack in amusement. Will nearly tripped over, and Ryan burst out laughing, punching his brother lightly on the arm. "And that was because I accepted!" finished Jack. The look on Will's face was priceless, and he couldn't help grinning.

Will steadied himself. "Well, you were not meant to hear that, Jack. I admit I was totally shocked when you said yes. You'd had no time to think about it, and it is a huge thing to do. Frankly, I never thought you'd be up to the task," he said apologetically.

Jack smiled. "Don't worry, Will. I understand why you feel that way."

The three men turned the first corner in the corridor, and there they met Drake and Argon. Drake spotted the three guards and quickened his pace toward them. He ignored Jack altogether, instead focusing on Will. "I take it the ceremony went well?"

Will nodded. "Yes, we are just taking Jack to his new chambers."

Drake looked disconcerted; he seemed to be trying to work out what to do next. Slowly he turned to face Jack. "Welcome to the bodyguard, Jack," he said, but he sounded distant and unimpressed.

"Thank you, Drake," replied Jack, keeping his observations to himself. Argon offered him no congratulations.

Drake swallowed hard and looked at Argon. "As everything is under control here, we should return to our work." He turned to leave. "We shall see you at supper. Be sure to show Jack where everything is before then."

Ryan stopped Drake by touching his shoulder, and Drake turned back to regard him.

"The princess is waiting for both of you in the official greeting chamber," Ryan told him.

Drake looked very put out. "Now?" he asked.

Will smiled wickedly. "Oh yes, she is in quite a temper now. Then again, you already know that!"

Drake drew himself up and signalled to Argon to follow him. Once they were out of earshot, Will let out a snort of laughter. Ryan joined him. Jack grinned again, and then he closed his eyes, wondering if he could feel Lily's bond yet. He concentrated on her, and the connection came rushing into his head. He gasped—her line was stronger than the others', and there was no mistaking the anger she was feeling.

"She is in a temper!" he said and laughed. The others joined in, and they all set off again down the corridor.

"I take it you two don't get on so well with Drake and Argon," said Jack after a time. He felt there was no time like the present to learn about his new brothers.

Ryan turned his head to regard him. "Well, that is a half-truth, really. Every one of us has a different personality, and some personalities clash; that's all it is, really."

Will snorted. "It is more than that, and you know it," he said shortly. He turned to Jack. "Firstly, they are older, Argon by ten years and Drake by fifteen. Secondly, they have much more experience, because of their service to the queen, rest her soul. So, when Tomas, my brother, and I joined the bodyguard, we always felt as though they considered us beneath them, although we are all supposed to be equal. It's a hierarchy thing really, then—"

Jack raised a hand to interrupt, curiosity taking over. "Forgive me, but I know nothing about the queen of Judelen, other than what the princess told me before my bonding. What happened to her?"

Will suddenly looked uncomfortable and sad; he sighed heavily. "It has been nearly five years since her suicide."

"Suicide!" said Jack in alarm.

"You are one of us now, Jack, so you might as well know the facts," said Will. "The queen was found in her chambers. She had doped her evening wine with a fast-acting poison."

"Why?"

Ryan stared darkly at Jack. "It was never discovered why she did it," he said.

"That is a tragic way to leave the world," said Jack.

Will touched Jack on the shoulder. "That is not the worst of it. The queen was with child when she killed herself."

Jack stopped dead in shock. The brothers both nodded sadly.

"The baby was a boy; he would have been the king of Judelen when his father died," said Will. "King Symon was maddened with grief and anger at his loss. After spending a year in mourning, he should have married again, but he refused, stating that Elizabeth, the late queen, was his true love and no one else could take her place. He told Lily that the throne was hers after his death and that her children would be the future kings or queens of Judelen."

Will paused, letting Jack absorb the information before he continued telling his story. "He already had a groom picked out for her, a lord from a land beyond the Great Mountains whom he had been communicating with—Sir Aidan. He was drawing up a marriage contract and making deals to expand the empire, but he would not sign the agreement until he had seen Shangol for himself."

"I've never heard of Shangol," said Jack truthfully, "and as far as I know, no one can cross the mountain range."

"We all thought exactly the same here in Judelen," continued Will. "I think even the king was sceptical. He went to see for himself, leaving the city in the hands of advisors, because the princess was only 15 at the time; she couldn't rule until she turned 18."

"How long was he gone for?" queried Jack.

"Nearly three years. I think Lily started to believe he was not going to return. Then, finally, the winter before this one, he did return, and he brought with him Sir Aidan. He put Lily and Sir Aidan into the arranged marriage contract. They are to wed this summer, now that Lily is old enough. Shangol and Judelen will be joined when the marriage is complete, and the empire will expand."

The thought of arranged marriage still annoyed Jack; he shook his head. "In Sanalow, people select for themselves whom they marry. I could never agree to marry a girl someone else picked out for me."

Ryan laughed, but his tone was kind. "It is different when you are royal, Jack," he said. "No royal can marry for the luxury of love. It is all about the empire's interest, not the individual's."

Ryan suddenly looked alarmed. "You do know that you can never get married or raise a family now you are bonded, don't you?"

Jack grinned and nodded. "I wasn't told so, but I assumed that a lifelong service would mean having no other life to distract me."

"Well, it is not all bad," said Ryan. "The inner city has some of the best inns in Judelen, and there are certain things you are permitted to do in your free time, if you get my meaning."

Will sighed loudly. "Yes, and don't we all know when you are doing it!" he said to his brother, tapping the side of his head as he spoke.

Jack assumed he was indicating the bond. "We know when each other are …" Jack searched for the right words. "Being intimate?" he finished awkwardly. Ryan grinned, but Jack felt horrified.

Will regarded his expression and patted him on the back. "Relax, Jack. No, we don't know that. I merely meant you would know when my idiot younger brother is, because you will feel such a surge of pride from him. He does it on purpose, I think."

"Just because you're a prude doesn't mean I have to be one," said Ryan, still grinning.

"Sometimes I swear you are still twelve, not twenty-two, Ryan," said Will, rolling his eyes.

The three men walked up a staircase. "How old are you?" Jack asked Will, steering the subject onto less embarrassing ground.

"Twenty-four," said Will. "Not much older than Ryan physically, but mentally—well, I'm in my fifties, compared to him. He likes to think he's some sort of stud, but I chose to adopt a celibate life and focus on my work, like the others—"

Ryan cut him off. "Excellent!" he said. "Let's leave Drake and Argon to carry on being boring, and Jack can help me to convert you back into a normal person. I'm sure he has many skills, gained from all his years of experience."

Will whispered to Jack. "If you do, please teach Ryan what love is actually all about," he said with a wink.

Jack stayed silent. He wasn't about to confide to these two that his first encounter with love was with the women they all protected or that her secret kiss on his cheek had been the only one he had ever received. Jack felt his face flush with heat; he looked at the floor.

Will looked at him quizzically. "I see you're going to be a tough one to work out, Jack," he said softly.

Jack smiled to himself; it was definitely time for another topic. He looked up. "You both must be really annoyed that today a complete stranger was selected for service by the princess," he said.

The brothers exchanged glances, Ryan indicating for Will to answer. "It was a shock that the princess selected you for her new bodyguard, that is true," he said. "And it is a struggle to take in what Tomas did and the fact that he is dead. We are grieving for our loss, and it will take time for each of us to adjust and get to know you." He rubbed his temple. "I don't know why, but it feels right having you in my head, Jack, as if you were always meant to join us."

Ryan nodded. "Yes, I feel that way too," he added. "The princess knew everything about you that we knew, and she made her choice to call you into service. I trust her judgement."

Jack nodded. "Thank you both for the compliment."

Will pointed to a door they were approaching. "Jack, this corridor holds the chambers for the personal bodyguards. The royal apartments are above us. Your room is this one." Will moved ahead and opened the chamber door, and the three men filed in.

Jack studied his room. It was moderate in size and simply furnished. There was a single bed against one wall and a table and chair against the other. The window was a good size, and despite it being winter, it allowed plenty of sunlight into the room. Jack noticed another door exiting the chamber and proceeded to explore. It was the washroom; Jack was thrilled to have his own bath! He stepped back out into the main chamber. Someone must have been there earlier, for there were clean clothes laid out neatly on the bed. He rubbed his fingers over his new uniform and smiled. Mistress Stratton was a wonder—he owed her a thank-you.

Will steered his brother towards the door. "We will let you get settled in now," said Will. "Don't wander off; we'll come back to get you in an hour or so to show you round the rest of the palace. You need to try and rest and let your body adjust to the bond."

"Thank you," said Jack to both the men. They smiled, bowed their heads, and left Jack in peace.

Jack walked to the window and looked out at the view, sighing loudly. He wasn't high enough to see the sea, but he could see deep into the desert. He had a view of the inner town's main square, where he could see a dais. It must be the place important announcements from the palace were made.

Jack needed to go and visit Bailey before dark, to check he was settled into his new home. He was happy knowing he had done right by his trusted friend.

Jack's head was constantly filling with different emotions from the others; it made him feel slightly dizzy. Jack was feeling such a strong surge of anger from Drake's link; it made him shuffle his feet nervously.

The princess was no longer in a temper; from her link Jack got a feeling of satisfaction.

Jack felt for Argon, and the connection appeared, just as Lily's had in the corridor. Argon was feeling worse than angry—he was livid! Whatever the princess had said and done in the greeting chamber had left him raging. Jack now feared his revenge.

5

DARK FORCES

King Symon stormed through the door into his personal chambers. He waited for Sir Aidan to follow him inside before slamming the door shut so hard that the crash vibrated down the corridor. Then the king stormed to his writing table. His mood none the better for slamming the door. He turned over the table, sending countless documents flying into the air to land scattered all over the floor. The table hit the ground on its side with such force that it cracked along the middle. The king let out an almighty cry of frustration and kicked the table, which broke in two along the crack. He stood panting and not focusing on anything.

Sir Aidan remained to the side of the chamber door; he had watched the king's actions with a blank expression on his face. He did not move from his position or speak.

After a few moments, the king regained a sense of where he was and turned to regard the mess that lay before him. He shuffled some of the documents away with his foot. He knew Sir Aidan was standing behind him, but he did not turn to face him.

Sir Aidan appeared to realise that the king was not going to speak first, so he slowly walked towards him. "Have you quite finished?" he asked in a cold, calm voice. The king shifted his stance and shrugged his shoulders but didn't answer.

Sir Aidan's eyes flashed dangerously. "I asked you a question, Salzar. Do not refuse me an answer unless you wish to feel the full extent of my wrath."

The king straightened up and turned to face Sir Aidan. He met his eyes for a brief moment before dropping his head in fear. "Forgive me, Overlord. I lost control."

Sir Aidan sniffed. "That is obvious."

The king kept his head down.

Sir Aidan moved closer to him and raised a hand to grab his face. Slowly he lifted his chin. The king tried to look every way except at Sir Aidan.

Aidan smiled as sweat began dripping from the kingly forehead. "It is good that you fear me, Salzar," he hissed. "You have disappointed me today, with your sloppy actions. You might have endangered all my plans through them. For that I might well have to kill you and give the king's body to another of my creatures."

Salzar whimpered and began to shake. *"Be quiet!"* snapped Sir Aidan. Salzar stopped whimpering instantly, but the sweating and shaking continued.

"I chose you for this mission because you were reliable, Salzar. If you cannot control your host, then I will have to replace you."

"Forgive me," whispered Salzar.

Sir Aidan suddenly pulled his arm high into the air, lifting the king's body off the ground. Salzar hung helplessly, gasping for breath. Sir Aidan held him there for a moment before throwing him back to the ground, where he lay sprawled in a heap, coughing as the air returned to his lungs.

Sir Aidan stood watching him with no concern for his distress. "I do not forgive, Salzar."

Pulling himself onto his knees before Sir Aidan, Salzar swallowed painfully. "Let me serve, Overlord. I shall do better," he croaked.

"It may be too late for that," spat Aidan. "Everyone who was in that chamber today knows the king does not behave like that. You have caused a lot of damage, forcing me speak out to resolve the situation over you. You should never have lost control."

"But Overlord, the introduction of a new bodyguard would damage our plans significantly. I was just trying to—"

"Be quiet, you fool!" snapped Aidan. It had been clear that nothing could be done from the moment the princess had asked the boy to join her service. It had been obvious from his lack of reaction that he'd already known she was going to ask him. That meant she must have spoken with him the day before and arranged it. *"How* is what I want to know! How did she get to speak with the boy, when I had confined her to her chambers and set guards?"

"Maybe someone asked him for her?" suggested Salzar.

Aidan shook his head. "No, he would never have accepted the word of another; it must have come from her. She knew that if he accepted you would be powerless to stop her from bonding him. Lillian would never have risked asking him in the chamber before us unless she knew his answer. I'm surprised he didn't change his mind and leave when you made him your offer of gold. He is a wayfarer—why didn't he snatch it from you and run? Instead, he took service for a girl he knows nothing about. He is unpredictable and could cause big problems with the next stage of my plan."

"That is why I tried to stop her bonding him, Overlord. I knew he could be a danger," said Salzar, keen to please.

"Yes, but through your actions you have caused bigger problems than the boy," snapped Salzar.

"How, Overlord?"

"The boy's death can be arranged; that is not a problem. How we repair the damage of your unofficial outbursts is more difficult. By now the servants will have spread the tale throughout the palace. King Symon would never have reacted so angrily. You have control of his body and mind; what if you become exposed? You would destroy both of us and my years of careful planning."

Salzar frowned. "The king was fighting me so strongly in the greeting chamber, Overlord. It is hard to focus when he really struggles to take control again. He is stronger than I expected."

"And yet you assured me before we left Shangol that you had him under control. Stand up," snapped Aidan.

Salzar quickly got to his feet. Sir Aidan took hold of his head with both hands and closed his eyes. Salzar shuddered, as if a great cold were sweeping through him.

Sir Aidan opened his eyes and released his head. "The king will not regain control of his body, Salzar; he is nearly dead. If I let you keep this host, then you better not disappoint me again."

"Never," answered Salzar, his voice shaky.

Sir Aidan smiled a cruel smile. "Never stop fearing me, Salzar. The day you do, I will end your life and I can promise you it will be painful and long, just like the dear king's death."

Salzar wept in relief. "Never, Overlord." He knelt before Sir Aidan and kissed his feet. "Th-thank you," he stuttered.

Sir Aidan kicked him away. "Enough! We have work to do."

Salzar staggered back to his feet. "When shall I have the boy killed?"

Aidan shook his head. "Leave the boy alone for now. If we kill him too soon it will look suspicious. I think it safe to assume that we cannot possess him; Tomas proved that to us."

Sir Aidan gave Salzar a very sharp look. "That is something else you messed up. Tomas managed to kidnap the princess from under our noses. She should never have been able to leave the city without my knowledge. It is lucky she did not learn of our plans from him. You had better figure out how he managed to do it. It was also fortunate that the spirit creatures sent out to find Lillian were successful, although nearly putting her into the river was a careless error. I destroyed them for that stupidity!"

"Forgive —" began Salzar, but he stopped himself saying more under Sir Aidan's stare.

"You are learning," said Aidan in an amused voice. "We shall continue with the next stage of the plan. If you can link Tomas's kidnap into the framing, then do it. I must prepare my spells for use on the princess and keep her close, so she doesn't suspect anything."

Salzar nodded enthusiastically. "Yes, Overlord."

Aidan walked towards the chamber door. "The bodyguards will be on their way to you shortly; you shall have this mess sorted out before they arrive."

Salzar looked at Aidan in confusion. "What shall I tell them about the table?" he asked.

Sir Aidan smiled. "Tell them you were with your mistress and the combined weight buckled the table."

Salzar looked shocked. "But that will make me look like a fool! A king keeps his personal affairs well hidden from the palace staff."

"Consider it punishment for today," said Aidan as he left the chamber.

Salzar's legs gave way as the door closed behind Aidan. He wept again, feeling relieved that the Dark Knight had let him live.

6

THE PUNISHMENT

Jack sat in the hay of Bailey's stable, with his back to the wall and his eyes closed. He was glad it wasn't cold; hiding in the stable all day would be miserable if it were.

He sat pondering his new life. Yesterday Will had told him he had been in Judelen for two months; he'd been shocked to find the time had gone by so quickly. The winter had melted into spring without him even noticing. They had been feeding him so much that his figure was fuller than ever before, and his face had filled out. He guessed that he must have become better looking, for he was getting very suggestive smiles from the serving girls when he walked down the corridors.

He'd been thrown into his new life the morning after his bonding. He had begun training and the duties that ran alongside it. Both his training and his duties were enough to fill his days, but he'd had the extra work of learning his way around the palace and the city itself. At least he only needed to know Inner Town well, he thought gratefully. Since the death of the queen, the royal family rarely travelled beyond it.

The bodyguards' training was to the highest standard, especially when it came to weapons handling. Jack didn't like thinking back on his old service, but he reluctantly admitted he was grateful for the training he had received in the army. Now that he was stronger, he could wield a sword as well as any of the other guards, but he had no knowledge of other weapons; he was starting from scratch with them.

All of the guards had a speciality, so Jack's training was divided up between them. Will was a superb teacher for archery, and he quickly had Jack hitting the set targets from a standstill. Now Jack was busy learning to fire from the back of a horse whilst moving. He'd had several rather painful falls, but he felt he was getting the hang of it.

Ryan and Drake were both experienced with a variety of hand weapons, including the axe and the ball and chain. Jack smiled to himself at the memory of dagger-throwing with Ryan. It had been a lot of fun, especially while galloping on Bailey—except for the bird Jack had accidentally hit instead of the fence post, but Ryan had sworn not to tell anyone about that.

Jack had spent hours worrying about learning with Drake, in case he still held a grudge against him; however, his worry had been in vain, as Drake had been nothing but professional. He was a fair teacher, and Jack was progressing well under his tutelage.

Jack had begun training with Argon, guessing he would be horrible, and he had been right. Argon was spending every minute available making sure Jack knew he had not forgotten the grudge. He was teaching him long-handled weapons, mainly the spear, but they were using lances to practice balance and striking. These were excellent at causing damage without risking death. Argon had used all of the lessons so far to bully Jack and inflict on him as much pain as he possibly could. He delighted in discussing his poor performance with the other guards, trying to rally Jack into an argument. Jack had admirably managed not to rise to the provocation, but his patience was wearing down.

The day before, Argon made him do a mock joust on Bailey. No doubt he had been hoping Jack would refuse, but he had not given him the satisfaction. He'd paid for his defiance by being knocked to the ground, but he was so determined not to let Argon win that, like an idiot, he had gotten back up and continued the joust.

Jack might have won the battle morally, but he paid for it physically the next day. The pain in his chest kept him awake for most of the night, and in the morning, when he examined himself, he saw he was a mess. There was bruising all over his chest and stomach, and every breath he took was painfully done. He'd had to skip breakfast, knowing he couldn't hide the injuries from the others. Instead he had spent the early shift sneaking through the palace until he got to Bailey. Jack knew the others would be feeling him in the bond, but he was so angry, he hoped they would be picking that up over his pain.

Bailey stood eating oats from his manger, happily leaving Jack to his resting. A warning snort from him made Jack open his eyes and look towards the stable door.

The princess had appeared in the doorway. She looked around the stable and spotted Jack sitting on the floor in the hay.

She raised her eyebrow at him, but a smile crossed her face. "So this is what you do on your rest day!"

"It is, Your Majesty," replied Jack, looking up at her from the floor.

The princess's smile grew wider. "Could you spare a minute from your exhausting rest to come with me, Jack?"

Jack groaned under his breath. He couldn't move, but he didn't want to refuse her.

"Are you down here alone, Your Majesty?" he asking, buying himself time.

The princess indicated over her shoulder. "Will is with me."

"Just Will?"

The princess frowned. "I only need one guard to escort me to the stable from the palace, Jack."

Jack nodded idly.

The princess tilted her head slightly. "Are you going to come with me?" she asked with a bite of impatience.

"Yes, Your Majesty." Jack sighed. He was out time and couldn't think up any more questions.

Wearily, he began to stand up. He held onto the wall to pull himself upright. The pain in his chest throbbed, and he hissed sharply.

The princess watched his struggle and became alarmed. She quickly turned to Will and motioned him over. She opened the stable door herself and went in. Bailey gave her a cautious look before returning to his oats.

The princess stepped past the horse and took hold of Jack's arm. "What has happened?" she asked seriously. Will appeared from behind the princess, and he also looked down on Jack in concern.

Jack felt as if he would pass out. "Just training, Your Majesty," he said vaguely.

The princess looked horrified. "Training? Where have you been training—in a war!"

Jack tried to pull himself up a bit straighter, but he couldn't. Will stepped past the princess to grab his other arm.

"I'm all right," insisted Jack. "It's just a bit of bruising; it goes away by supper."

Will tried to lift Jack's shirt. "Let me see it," he insisted.

Jack pushed his hand away. "I'm fine. There is no need to worry."

The princess adopted her serious voice. "Jack, show me the bruising," she demanded.

Jack dared not disobey a direct order. Feeling defeated, he lifted his top. Both Will and the princess gasped. Jack looked down at his chest. It was definitely worse than it had been that morning.

Will carefully ran a hand over Jack's bruising, to assess the full extent of the damage. "You've broken a rib," he said seriously. "You are damn lucky it has not caused you to bleed beneath your skin. That could have killed you."

The princess looked from Jack's chest to Will and then met Jack's eyes. "How long have you been receiving injuries like this?" she asked.

"Just this once," he lied.

The princess gave him an annoyed look. "If it was just this once, how then do you know that the bruising will go away before supper?"

Kicking himself, he gave up lying and told her the truth. "I have been getting these injuries for about eight weeks now," he said sulkily.

The princess didn't look at all happy. "How?" she snapped.

Will adopted a softer tone. "You said something about training?" he prompted.

"It was training," said Jack. "I get them during my lance and spear training with Argon."

At these words the princess screwed her face up in anger. "I should have known! He has been holding a silly grudge since I bonded you into service. I never knew he would be so stupid as to go this far!"

"I have been able to work through it, Your Majesty," said Jack, trying to pacify her.

The princess fixed Jack with a furious stare. "I thought you had more sense. You should have come to me eight weeks ago, when this first happened. Now you have a broken rib, and you are going to have to be taken off duties for weeks, until it heals."

The princess turned to Will. "I'll go and call a servant to fetch Ryan, to help you get Jack back inside."

"I'll go," said Will quickly. "The king will have harsh things to say if I let you wander alone, even if it is just to the palace."

The princess looked ready to argue, but Will cut her off, turning back to Jack. "Can you stand for a moment, while I go?"

"Yes," said Jack. To prove it he held onto the wall firmly.

Will turned to the princess. Her lip had grown dangerously thin, the way it did when she was very angry. "I'm sorry, Your Majesty, but I have to follow orders. At least here you will not be alone," he said.

The princess sniffed, and Will left quickly, before she could say anything else.

"I can't be left alone, for my own protection, so I get left with a man who has a broken rib!" she muttered under her breath.

Jack tried to lighten the mood. "Do you remember saying that I would only let you down if I had no other choice? Well, can we include *now* in that, please, Your Majesty?"

The princess tried to look displeased, but she gave up and smiled. "What am I going to do with you?" she said playfully.

"I beg you, Your Majesty, nothing physical!" Jack said jokingly.

The princess laughed. Jack laughed too, but his vision went blurry. Shaking his head, he reached out his other hand, trying to grab anything to help support him.

The princess noticed his struggle and took a firmer hold of him. "Put some of your weight onto me," she said.

Sighing, Jack transferred his weight over slightly. The princess slipped her arm round him, and he gratefully took hold of her waist, so he was evenly balancing between her and the wall.

"Thank you," he said sincerely.

The princess looked at him and smiled again. Flustered, Jack tried concentrating on the stable door. It was becoming very clear to him that he had fallen in love with her. He didn't know what Lily felt towards him, but he knew their relationship was different to the others'. She was always seeking him out to spend extra time with him. She enjoyed learning about his hobbies and interests; she had even taken it upon herself to begin teaching him about the history of creation. He loved spending all the extra time in her company—but not acting upon his feelings was getting harder every day.

He hoped he wasn't flooding the bond with despair. He tried talking to ease his worrying. "What was it you wanted to show me?" he asked.

"Oh," said Lily, "I wanted to show you my new horse. Sir Aidan had her brought from his homeland for me. She is a Shangol breed, most unlike our horses. I knew you liked horses, and I wanted you to tell me what you thought of her."

"I'll look at her tomorrow, when I've rested a little, if you don't mind," said Jack.

"I do mind, Jack. You will not be leaving your chambers until that swelling has gone down. The horse can wait."

Jack rolled his eyes, but luckily the princess didn't see him. She seemed surprised by his silence. "Are you *not* going to argue?" she asked.

"Would there be any point?" said Jack.

"Actually, no. But it is most unlike you not to try, Jack!"

Jack smiled. "I only argue when I think I can win!"

The princess licked her lips. "If that is true, why do you argue with me at all?"

She had given him an opening, and it was too perfect to pass over. "It is fun to watch your lip thin the way it does when you are preparing for an argument," he said, grinning.

The princess looked shocked, but then she grinned back. "Is that so, Jack Orden?"

Jack laughed, relieved she had taken his comment the way he'd intended. "It is so, Princess Lillian," he said, liking her reaction to his teasing.

The princess went quiet. "Lily," she said suddenly.

"Pardon?" blurted Jack, not believing what he was hearing.

"You can call me Lily, Jack."

Jack felt incredible.

"At least when we are in private," warned the princess.

"As you wish," said Jack, "Lily." How he loved calling her by her name! The way she looked at him told him that she loved it too.

"Thank you, Jack," she said gently.

Jack smiled, studying every curve on her face. She sighed and put her head onto his shoulder. Jack heard footsteps; he shifted slightly, and Lily moved away.

Will and Ryan arrived at the stable door, looking slightly out of breath. "Sorry we were so long, Your Majesty," said Will. "We had to go the long way around to avoid Argon. We guessed you would not want him alerted before you got to him."

"Very true," said Lily. "I'll deal with Argon as soon as Jack is back in his chambers."

Will and Ryan moved inside and took Jack from the princess. Together they helped carry him from the stable. The princess followed and closed the door after them. The four of them proceeded into the palace.

They got several looks from servants who were going about their duties. The last one they spotted didn't even wait to be out of sight before she darted off down the corridor.

The princess sighed. "Well, I'm afraid that the whole palace will know by nightfall, Jack," she said hopelessly.

Ryan smiled. "Hopefully Argon won't find out, though!"

Will and Ryan steered Jack around the corner into the bodyguards' corridor. They were nearing his chamber when Argon appeared, just leaving his own room. The princess spotted him, and moved to go ahead of Will and Ryan. They stopped walking and let her past. Jack stood watching in silence as she approached Argon. Argon's eyes passed over the princess and down onto the three men, narrowing when he focused on Jack. Feeling murderous, Jack glared back at him.

"I'm glad I have found you, Argon," said the princess. "I want you to go to the greeting chamber immediately and wait for me there."

"Your Majesty," said Argon, snapping his eyes from Jack back to her. "What is this about?"

"I will tell you when I arrive, Argon. I suggest you go and wait for me there."

Argon cast another look at the three men. "Your Majesty, what has happened here?" Jack shook his head. If that had been an attempt at sounding concerned, it was a bad one!

"Go to the chamber now, Argon!" shouted the princess.

Argon looked shocked. The princess glared at him. Upon realising she was not going to say any more, he bowed and walked away. Jack gripped Will slightly harder as he passed. Noticing, Will stepped slightly in front of Jack, shielding him from Argon.

Once he was out of sight, the princess put a hand to her head and sighed. "I should not have shouted," she said in regret.

Will looked at her. "I think you had every right to shout, Your Majesty," he said gently.

"After the telling-off I gave my father for doing the same in front of guards, I really don't have the right, Will—but thank you."

Will smiled at her, and he and Ryan began moving Jack again. The princess opened the door and held it, letting the men bring Jack inside.

Mistress Stratton was waiting inside the room. At the sound of the door, she turned around, and her eyes widened in shock when she saw Jack being carried inside. "What have you been doing?" she shouted. Jack groaned. She hurtled towards him, looking deeply concerned and began touching him. She poked him in his chest so much that Jack debated killing her but only cried out loudly.

The princess came to his aid. "Let him be, Maggie. He is in a lot of pain," she said, pulling the mistress away.

"What are you doing here?" demanded the mistress. "If you have witnessed whatever trouble he has been in, I will be most displeased with you, young lady."

"Jack's not been fighting, Maggie. He has been injured during training. He has suffered a broken rib, and there is a lot of swelling to his chest and stomach."

The mistress's eyes narrowed. "How do you know that? You didn't look for yourself, did you?"

Lily coloured slightly. "Of course not! Will examined him and reported to me."

The mistress made a noise in her throat. Jack sensed she didn't believe Lily, but she said nothing more. "Put him on the bed, and let me see how much damage he has done."

Will and Ryan guided Jack to the bed, and the mistress turned to Lily. "You leave him to me now, Your Majesty. Out you go, before I examine him."

The princess clucked her tongue. "Really, Maggie, I don't know what the fuss is about. It is only his stomach you need to look at; that will hardly do me any damage."

"That is for me to decide," said the mistress firmly. "Out!'

The princess rolled her eyes and turned away from the bed. "I'll speak to you later, Jack," she called over her shoulder.

Will looked at his brother. "Ryan, go with the princess," he ordered. "I'll stay with Jack."

Ryan nodded to Will and then to Jack. "See you later, Jack. Take care," he said.

The mistress looked angry. "What harm is he going to come to with me watching him?" she asked.

Ryan starting grinning, but he said nothing as he followed the princess from the chamber.

Jack sighed as he watched the door close. He regretted that Lily could not have stayed with him a little longer.

Will was watching Jack. "Don't worry. The princess will handle Argon without any problems."

Jack was glad Will had misunderstood what he had been thinking about.

Mistress Stratton had gone to the wardrobe for a night-shirt from Jack's supply. She returned to the bed with it clutched in her hand. "Let's get you undressed, so you will be more comfortable while I examine you."

Jack's held out his hand for the shirt, but the mistress kept hold of it. "There is no way you are going to be able to undress yourself. Just sit up and I'll do it."

Jack felt his face burning. "I can manage," he said.

The mistress put her hands on her hips. "Two people had to carry you through the palace because you couldn't support yourself, and you really believe you can undress yourself?"

"I can!" shouted Jack defiantly, and reaching forward he snatched the shirt from her. Pain shot through his ribs, and feeling sick, he lay back down.

The mistress threw her hands in the air. "I knew it! You have caused yourself even more pain, and look how pale you have gone from doing it! No more arguments, I will undress you."

Feeling defeated, Jack didn't bother arguing further. With the help of Will, the mistress removed his jacket and his day-shirt without causing him any more pain. She then proceeded to unbutton his trousers. Jack took hold of her hand to stop her, glancing at Will, hoping he would understand his silent plea for help. Will chuckled quietly and stepping forward, clearing his throat. "I'll help Jack out of his trousers," he said, his voice sounding slightly higher than normal.

"I can manage," said the mistress.

"Of course you can," said Will quickly, "but I think Jack would be more comfortable if I helped him."

The mistress gave Jack one of her looks. Trying to win her round, he gave her a dashing smile, but it just made her lip thin. Jack turned back to Will, in need of rescuing. Will started coughing, but it sounded more like laughing to Jack. The mistress gave him the look too, sniffed loudly, and turned her back.

"Let's get you comfortable," said Will after he'd regained control of himself. He pulled the covers higher and gave them to Jack to hold while he removed his trousers. After a minute he brought them out from under the covers and told the mistress he was done.

"Thank you," said Jack.

Will didn't speak, but his lips kept rising at the corners, making Jack debate killing him too.

"Can I examine you now?" asked the mistress firmly.

Nodding, Jack lowered the bedcovers, bringing them down to just below his waistline, letting the mistress see his bruising. She began feeling over his ribs with her fingers. Trying to stay still, Jack focused on the ceiling. It felt like hours before she had finished examining him.

She turned to Will. "I will need some bandage to strap up these ribs. Can you fetch me the longest roll you can find from the store, please?"

Nodding, Will left the chamber.

The mistress looked at Jack. "Well, you have broken one rib and badly bruised the others. I am going to have to strap your ribs up, and you will have to keep them strapped for the next month at least. You must stay in bed for the next three days, until the swelling goes down. I will mix you up a medicine that you are to take three times each day; it will aid in the repair of the rib. I will also collect some wasps' root for you to eat, to relieve the pain."

Questions burst out of Jack mouth in a verbal explosion: "Mistress, when will I be able to return to my duties?"

"When you have fully healed," she answered firmly.

"Does that mean I can't train until then as well?"

"Of course it does! I'm not patching you up so you can go and damage yourself all over again, am I!" she shouted at him.

"I can't be off work for a month. I could understand three days, but a month!" shouted Jack back. "I need to see Lil—the princess. She will need to know that I won't be able to protect her for much longer then I imagined."

"She already knows that, Jack," said Mistress Stratton in a gentler tone.

"I can't believe I've failed her," said Jack sadly. He felt as if he'd been punched in the stomach.

The mistress sighed deeply. "If these injuries were not your fault, then you have not failed her." The mistress paused for a moment, apparently in thought. "A month *is* a long time to be away from your duties. I'll speak to the princess and see if some light duties can be arranged until you are healed."

"At least I would be able to do something," said Jack, feeling more positive.

"Don't go getting yourself all excited," warned the mistress. "You will not be leaving this chamber until I am happy that you can't cause any more damage."

"I understand," said Jack. "Thank you."

The mistress smiled and patted Jack's shoulder in a motherly fashion. Then she fluffed up his pillows and sat him up straighter.

Will returned with the bandage, and Jack let her begin strapping him up. The bandage was tight, pinching his skin, but it was definitely supporting him. The mistress carefully pulled on his night-shirt. Jack grimaced when he tasted the medicine; it was vile, and he swallowed it as quickly as possible. He was feeling more exhausted with every second that passed.

Ryan returned to tell Jack and Will that the princess had seen Argon. "I can't tell you what she said, because I was not in the chamber," he recounted, "but whatever it was, it was serious. The rumour is that Argon's bond might be severed and he will become an ordinary bodyguard to the king."

Will looked amazed by the statement. "She would cast him out of service?" he said.

"It would seem so," said Ryan. "She has confined him to his chamber until she decides what she's going to do. Argon is certainly not happy; you can feel his rage pulsing through the bond. And I have never felt Lily so angry."

"The princess," corrected the mistress, who stood listening in interest. Ryan gave her an apologetic look and fell silent.

Jack felt apprehensive at this news. What damage might this do in the future? Yawning, he closed his eyes. He heard Mistress Stratton whispering for everyone to leave, but he didn't say anything. He was too tired, and sleeping was more important.

Jack sat up in the bed, screaming. He was covered in cold sweat, and everything hurt. A drum was beating a tattoo inside his skull. He heard a loud snapping noise—what could that be? Looking round the dark chamber, he felt terror. He hid his head in his hands, willing all the sensations to go away. Then he felt it, the severed connection. Argon's emotions were gone from inside his head. Lily must have gone through with destroying the bond. Jack felt his eyes rolling and his head hitting the pillow as unconsciousness took him.

7

THE MAGUS

Jack was bored. He had been lying in his bed for three days, being nursed by the mistress. It was so frustrating not being allowed to get up! He wanted out of his chamber so he could get on with his duties. Will and Ryan's daily updates were only making him feel more useless.

Drake's visit to Jack had been a surprise. He had come the day after Argon's bond had been destroyed. He'd not been angry or resentful; instead, he had talked Jack through a new training program, as he was going to continue the spear training.

Jack thought he was healing nicely, but he had no say in the matter. He had to wait for Mistress Stratton to clear him. The only thing he was allowed to get out of bed for was to use the chamber pot, and he'd had to fight to be allowed to do that unaided. He was longing to go and see Lily; she had not been to visit him once. He knew from Ryan that she was suffering after severing the bond, and knowing it had killed people in the past, he wanted to make sure she really was all right. Mistress Stratton said she was resting and doing well, but he wouldn't believe it until he saw for himself. Feeling daring, he decided he would risk paying her a visit.

Just then there was a knock on the door. "Come in," he called, but he was irritated that someone had turned up just as he had decided to sneak out. He was expecting to see Will or Ryan but looked up to see Lily instead.

Jack checked she was alone before speaking. "Lily! It is good to see you! I have been so worried about you."

Lily moved into the room and sat down on the end of Jack's bed. She looked paler than normal; however, she smiled warmly at him. "Maggie told me you were getting restless and that you were asking after me. She said I had better come and visit you, before you do something silly in your haste to check up on me!"

"You are just in time!' said Jack honestly. "I was just about to come and visit you."

Lily looked amused. "Well it is a good job I came, then. Maggie warned me she would hold me responsible if you injured yourself."

Jack smiled. "I would not have wanted to get you into trouble, Lily. I just wanted to know you are well."

Lily nodded. Jack realised how tired she was looking; there were purple rings under her eyes.

"Are you all right, Lily?" he asked in concern.

Lily reached across the bed; he thought she was going to hold his hand, but she seemed to think better of it and withdrew again.

"I'm fine, Jack," she said with a sigh. "I am just a little tired. The severing of the bond caused me a lot of discomfort. I have had to rest in my chamber for the past three days, just like you. Sir Aidan and Maggie have been looking after me, Sir Aidan would have had me lying in bed for another three days, but luckily Maggie made him agree to let me out of bed, to see how I got on."

Jack folded his arms. "How are you getting on?"

"Better now. It was hard moving about for a while, but I am starting to feel more like myself again. I think everyone, including me, forgot that it is not that long since I lost Tomas. I am still feeling the effects of his death."

She went quiet, so Jack sat in silence watching her. She was studying the bedspread, running her hand over the material. Jack felt the strange awkwardness between them; he didn't like it at all.

"The mistress says that I can get out of bed tomorrow, so I wanted to ask you if I can return to duties, so long as they are light, for the next month. The mistress said it would be fine for me to do that," he said keenly.

Lily looked up sharply. "Certainly not! You need to heal, and you can't do that if you are doing duties."

Jack felt as if she had slapped him. "But—"

"Jack, I understand your need to be back working. It can't be easy having to leave your duty, but you are no use to me if you are not fully healed," said Lily.

Jack's arms flopped to his side. "What can I do then, if I can't do my duties?" he asked grumpily.

Lily regarded him for a moment before dropping her eyes back down onto the bedcover. "It is best that you rest for now. We can discuss your returning to duty in a few weeks."

Promising to visit him the following morning, she said goodbye and left him alone. Jack wondered what he had done to make her grow cold towards him. No doubt it was this stupid injury. Would he ever learn to stop letting Argon get to him! In annoyance he snatched a pillow from behind his back and threw it at the chamber door.

Lily entered her chambers and quietly closed the door.

Sir Aidan stood looking out of the chamber window. "You have been gone a while," he said in a cool voice. "Have you been with the boy all this time?"

Lily crossed the room towards him. "Yes, My Lord. Jack wishes to return to duties, and he didn't take it well when I told him he couldn't."

Sir Aidan moved away from the window towards Lily. "It is for the best. You created quite a stir amongst the guards when you broke Argon's bond. It is safer you keep the boy out of the way until the dust settles."

Lily raised her head defiantly. "I am keeping Jack off duty so he can heal quicker. I am not hiding him away from Argon or anyone else!"

Sir Aidan smiled. "Of course not, Lillian. You only have the boy's best interests at heart."

Lily watched Sir Aidan for a moment; he also watched her, his face blank.

"I must change for supper," she said flatly.

Sir Aidan bowed. "I must be leaving in any case."

Lily frowned. "I thought we were having supper together."

Sir Aidan nodded. "Your father has asked us to dine with him this evening; there is business about the wedding which must be taken care of. I need to speak with him on another matter before supper, so I'll meet you there."

Lily looked down at the ground.

"Is something wrong?" Sir Aidan asked her.

"You have been here for over a year, and we have spent very little time alone together since you arrived. How am I supposed to get to know you if we are never together?" said Lily angrily.

Sir Aidan approached her and put a hand under her chin, raising her head. "A lady should not speak in such high volume," he said firmly.

Lily looked into his eyes for a moment before looking away. "Forgive me, My Lord."

Sir Aidan released her head, and he sighed. "You are a riddle, Lillian. Sometimes I look at you and see the powerful ruler you will be, but other times I look at you and see little more than a child, crying because she can't have everything her own way."

Lily stared open-mouthed at Sir Aidan. "I am not a child!"

"Then why do you behave like one?"

"I don't—"

"If that is true, then, why are you sulking?"

When Lily didn't answer, Aidan smiled cruelly. "I have affairs to take care of. I have great demands upon my time. I am the ruler of Shangol, and I am to become the joint ruler of Judelen. I am devoting my time to making Judelen and Shangol the most powerful empire in the kingdom. I am striving to become the greatest ruler there is. You are going to be a queen, Lillian. You should be devoting your time in the same way."

Lily listened to Sir Aidan in silence.

"You have nothing to say?" he asked in disbelief.

Lily raised her head to look Aidan in the eye. She kept her voice steady and cool. "Judelen is my city, and I am doing all I can to better it. How dare you say I'm not!"

Sir Aidan looked pleased. "Finally, I see that you are able to control yourself, just as a queen should."

"I shall be the greatest queen Judelen has ever known."

Sir Aidan laughed at Lily's words.

"You don't agree?" she asked calmly.

Sir Aidan tilted his head and regarded her. "With my help, maybe, one day you will be a great queen. But for now you are still very young."

"I am not much younger than my mother was when she became queen."

"You are eighteen and so inexperienced," said Aidan coldly. "It will require patience and hard work on my part to make you a ruler."

"I already am a ruler here, My Lord. Don't forget who is the outsider."

Aidan's eyes flashed. "Well, your father does not agree with you there," he said bitterly. "That is why he came to me with his offer of marriage, not because he needed it to secure the empire. He wanted someone experienced sitting beside you on the thrones of Judelen, fearing that if he left you as lone ruler his life's work could be ruined."

Lily's face went white. "That is not true."

Aidan smirked. "When your father first came to me with the offer I nearly turned him down. I could not imagine marrying someone as young as you. The thought that you, at your age, were going to rule Judelen was laughable. I was almost twice your age before I was given my rule, and I had to earn it. Here it is different; the rule is passed down to the next of kin, no matter what. All that leads to is people like you getting to play kings and queens, thinking they hold the power of a city when all they really hold is the power of a blood link. That does not make a great queen, Lillian."

"Leave!" commanded Lily.

Sir Aidan folded his arms and didn't move.

"I do not want you in my chambers anymore! Leave!"

Aidan stood, completely unfazed by her demands. "You have no power over me, Lillian, and it is about time you learnt that. You may not like what you hear from me today, but every word of it is true."

"I may not have power over you, My Lord, but I have power over my life choices. I choose to end our marriage contract. You are free to return to Shangol as soon as you are ready."

Sir Aidan eye's glinted mischievously as he pushed Lily back into the wall. He moved his body up next to hers and ran a finger across her cheek. "Such innocence," he said fiercely.

Lily flinched from his touch. "I said leave," she whispered.

"I'm not going anywhere, Lillian," Sir Aidan promised her. "Our marriage contract is between the king and me; you have no say in it. You should remember that if you want a happy marriage, for I will not tolerate your behaviour once we are wed."

He grabbed her face and turned it upward. He leant in and kissed her mouth while gripping her cheeks between his fingers. Lily stood frozen, trying to clarify her feelings about her first ever kiss; she felt both disgust and delight. Aidan broke off and released her. She touched her mouth, feeling stunned.

"Still so much to learn," he said in a disappointed voice.

Without another word, he pushed away from her and left the chamber. Lily waited for him to leave before allowing herself to cry. She felt trapped and humiliated. All she wanted was for him to love and respect her, so that they might make their union together pleasant. Since meeting Jack, she knew exactly what that felt like, and it broke her heart that she could not be with him instead. She had thought once that she loved Aidan, but now she knew better.

Lily wiped the tears away from her eyes and walked into her bedchamber to change for supper. Her mind felt numb, and she undid her buttons without thought.

The door to her main chamber opened and shut. Lily raised her head at the sound, for no one had knocked. She put her head round the bedchamber door and saw a young female servant standing inside the chamber.

Lily's mood, already less than friendly, lost its last thread of patience. She stormed from her bedchamber to confront the servant. "How dare you enter without knocking! Get out of my chambers this instant, before I call the mistress and have her whip you all the way down the corridor!"

Lily turned her back on the servant and walked back to her bedchamber, where she continued undoing her buttons. The bang of the bedchamber door shutting made her heart jump. Lily spun round to see the servant standing by the closed door. She stared at her angrily. "How dare you come in here when I have ordered you from these chambers? Get out now, before I dismiss you from my service!"

"I am not in your service," said the servant.

Lily puffed herself up in anger. "How dare you speak when you have not been ordered to? Leave now and go to the mistress. Tell her to whip you until you bleed as punishment for your arrogance!"

"Enough!" said the servant firmly. She raised her hand towards Lily. "Be silent and listen."

Lily moved forcefully towards the servant but stopped in her tracks. Her eyes widened in fear. The servant had suddenly changed in appearance. She was now wearing a green silk dress, with an emerald cloak. She was still young-looking, but her hips and bosom placed her as a woman. Her hair had changed; it was now long and black, fixed in two partings and wrapped around her waist. She had lightly tanned skin and a narrow face. Her yellow eyes were fixed upon Lily. "Are you ready to listen now?" said the woman, calmly.

Lily found her voice. "Who are you?" she asked.

The woman proudly raised her head. "I am a magus."

Lily stared openly at the magus; she had only seen one of them once before, when the serfdom had been delivered to her mother. Lily couldn't remember whether it was the same one, though.

"What do you want with me?" asked Lily.

The magus raised an eyebrow at Lily's tone. "I have very little time. I will not waste it arguing with you! I have come here to deliver you a warning."

Lily frowned. "What warning?"

"What I am going to tell you will be shocking to learn," said the magus quickly. "I don't have time to explain everything, so you need to trust me." She took a deep breath. "The Theanic Order have been keeping a big secret from the kingdom. The War of Power is not over, Evelyn Maude is not dead, and neither is her son, the Dark Knight!"

Lily opened her mouth, but the magus waved a hand at her. "Listen, please! Judelen is in trouble. Your palace has become infested with black magic, and I believe the Dark Knight is here."

Lily put her hands to her throat. The Dark Knight was the stuff of nightmares, a heartless creature created from black magic and bound by Evelyn Maude—with the blood and skin of Orthrillium, after she betrayed and murdered him. She called him her son, and he had no conscience or compassion; he was a liar and manipulator, a ruthless embodiment of evil."

"He can't be here," pleaded Lily.

The magus grew impatient. "I was delivered a warning, through my gift of whispering, from a horse within the city—there is black magic in

Judelen. Horses were made by the Unicorn's power; they are very intelligent and they know all about magic. If there is black magic in Judelen, it must be the Dark Knight creating it, because Evelyn Maude is trapped in a prison."

Lily looked at the magus in shock. "Why tell the kingdom she was destroyed if she wasn't?" she demanded.

The magus sighed. "After Evelyn destroyed Grimfar and our army a thousand years ago, she used a spell to destroy King Rain, the Guardian of the Light, but it backfired and hit her, too. The magus thought they both died.

"The Dark Knight, who was already weaker, being trapped in his human shell, was left to fight us alone. After the mortality spell destroyed his army, he fled, and we thought him too powerless to cause any further harm.

"Five hundred years passed, the kingdom continued, and the people in it adapted to their mortality. The magus stayed out of the way, watching in case the Dark Knight tried to rise again, but he had disappeared."

Lily lowered her hands from her throat. "So, how do you know Evelyn Maude isn't dead?" she asked.

"It was the warriors of Grimfar who found the Guardian five hundred years ago, trapped in a magic prison, deep below the ground. They knew who he was, and they protected him until they could tunnel through to the surface, close to Emiscial. They only succeeded a few years ago, and a messenger was sent to tell us he had been found. That was when we found out there were survivors from Evelyn Maude's destruction of Grimfar and before Grimfar and Sanalow's war began. Using magic, the magus dug a secure tunnel from Emiscial to the Guardian's prison, and we spent a year trying to free him. Eventually we succeeded. It was then that he told us of the mirror prison that Evelyn Maude is trapped in, but we didn't know its location.

"The Guardian also warned us that the prisons hold a link between them, so if he is freed, she will be freed too. Until we knew more, he insisted we seal him back inside. Once every year, on different dates, we open the prison to formulate plans, hoping the Dark Knight doesn't have time to do the same with his mother."

Lily stepped forward. "Clearly he was able to, though."

The magus frowned. "Yes, we believe the reason he disappeared was that he found his mother's prison and stayed near to it, in case it opened. The theory was confirmed a few years ago when we opened the prison to tell King Rain of a plan we thought would save the world. We proceeded to put it into action, but the Dark Knight appeared and thwarted it. We felt the twisted magic growing stronger very near to Judelen, so the magus now believe her prison is somewhere near to your city."

Lily straightened up. "What plan did the magus have to save the world?"

The magus raised her eyebrow at Lily. "That doesn't matter. All you need to know is that it failed and we sealed the prison again."

"Is that why you made the serfdom for my mother?" asked Lily. "Because you know the prison is near to Judelen, and you wanted to protect us?"

The magus hesitated and then said, "Of course. Why else would we gift it? It was designed to provide protection from the dark forces. It appears to be working, because I conducted a soul search over the palace. Most of your people have been taken over by black magic creatures, but you have not been caged, and neither have your bodyguards. That is why I can trust you to help me uncover the plot."

Lily felt terrified. "Do you really think one princess and four loyal bodyguards can save Judelen?"

The magus blinked. "There are only three pure souls joined to the serfdom with you."

Lily felt bile rising in her throat. "No, I have Drake, Will, Ryan, and Jack. How could one be taken? You just said they were protected."

The magus rubbed her head. "This is bad; I was certain those bound to you must be safe. I don't know how the Dark Knight has combated the mortality spell to cage people, and I don't know how he has defeated the serfdom! It shouldn't be possible." She looked up sharply. "Something is keeping you safe, but until we know what, you can't trust anyone."

Lily covered her face in her hands in horror. "What do you think he wants?"

The magus looked sadly at Lily. "Control of your city to make a new army, I am guessing." She looked back at the door. "I must leave. I have never seen the Dark Knight in person, and I can't risk detection. I need to return to the safety of my hiding place in the city and contact the head of the Theanic Order for further instructions."

Lily looked up sharply. "Can't you sense him and know where he is?"

"He is shielded. He could stand in front of me and I wouldn't know it was him until he touched me. Then he would sense my power, and I would sense his," said the magus, moving towards the bedchamber door. "If he finds out I am aiding you, he will kill me. Now I have told you all I can. It is up to you to investigate, and try to identify him." The magus opened the bedchamber door and left through it, Lily following her out.

"You must not tell anyone that I was here or what I have told you," warned the magus.

"If I learn something important, how am I to let you know?" asked Lily.

The magus turned to look at Lily. "I will be watching the palace every day. If you need to contact me, pick some red flowers from the garden and hang them outside your chamber window. I will contact you as soon as I can after seeing your signal."

Lily moved closer to the magus. The magus raised her hand to stop her advancing. "I know you are frightened and confused, and I'm sorry. But please understand that I must leave." Before Lily's eyes she turned into the servant girl once more. "Remember to be discreet, and don't trust anyone. I fear dark times are ahead for Judelen."

The magus shut the door behind her and was gone. Lily stood frozen, and then the shock began to take over. She was alone and fighting in a war beyond her powers of comprehension. How could she possibly identify and defeat the greatest evil ever known?

A loud knock on the chamber door made Lily jump. For a moment, blind panic took her. Her eyes darted around the chamber, trying to find a way out. The knock sounded again. Lily looked towards the door, trying to think who it could be. Then, remembering that no one could be trusted, she ran towards her bedchamber. The latch on her door clicked open. Lily was halfway to the bedchamber, and she kept running, not looking back.

"Your Majesty?" said Will's voice. He sounded urgent.

Lily stopped running and glanced over her shoulder. Will had entered the chamber and closed the door behind him. He was watching Lily, looking confused.

"What do you want, Will?" she snapped.

Will appeared shocked by her tone of voice. "Are you all right?"

"Yes," said Lily in a high-pitched voice. "Did you want something?"

"I'm here to escort you to supper with the king and Sir Aidan," explained Will.

"I don't need an escort."

Will was looking really worried now; he moved further into the chamber. "You always have an escort, and Sir Aidan commanded me to do it." His eyes suddenly raked Lily's back. It was then that Lily remembered that her dress was unbuttoned.

She quickly turned round to face Will and hide her back from him. "I am not ready," she said with as much dignity as she could muster.

Will cleared his throat and dropped his eyes. "I'll wait here until you are."

"Very well." Lily moved backwards toward the bedchamber so as not to expose her back again.

Will looked up with a frown on his face. "Your Majesty, are you sure you are all right? It is just that I can feel you through the bond, and you feel frightened."

Lily paused in her backward walking. "I'm fine, Will, honestly. I am just a little late getting ready for supper."

Will studied her, looking pensive. Lily smiled at him and moved through the door, closing it behind her. For a moment she leant against it, breathing hard, trying to make herself relax. How could this be happening to her? The palace was her home; it had always been the safest place to be. Now that was gone.

Lily moved away from the door and slipped out of her dress. She slowly put on her other outfit. As she did up the buttons, she wondered what she could do about the situation. She had to defeat this evil and win Judelen back, there was no question about it. But how could she alone defeat the dark forces, with no clue as to where to start?

"I've got to do this," she said quietly to the empty bedchamber. "I am the only one who can."

Lily took a deep breath and left the bedchamber. Will stood waiting by the door, and he smiled warmly at her. Lily forced herself to smile naturally back at him.

As they walked along the corridor, she kept telling herself that she must be strong and must act normally. She began to run over all the names of the people closest to her and think about how she could lessen their involvement in her life. The bodyguards were the biggest problem, for she couldn't go anywhere without them. It then occurred to Lily that she could remove one of them by following Sir Aidan's advice.

"Will, can you do a job for me?" she asked.

"Of course, Your Majesty."

"I think it is best if Jack remains in his chambers while he heals. I am thinking he would do better to stay away from palace life as much as possible for now. I haven't got the time to visit him again today, so would you tell him for me?"

Will frowned. "Is this because of Argon?" he asked. "It is not fair that Jack should get punished for Argon's mistake."

"It is nothing to do with Argon, Will; I think it is for the best. Now, will you tell him?" Her short tone seemed to do the trick. Will agreed to pass the message on.

Lily and Will walked towards her father's chambers in silence. Lily kept running over the conversation she had had with the magus. Every possible idea she came up with seemed impossible to do. As a result she spent the supper with her father and Aidan playing with her food and not engaging in their conversation.

Her father kept glancing at her and then at Aidan, as if looking for the answer to her silence. Aidan merely shook his head. He knew she was still sulking about the argument in her chambers, which he had taken great delight in causing.

Finally Lily excused herself and said she wanted to get some sleep. After waiting for Ryan to come and escort her, she left for her chambers, and again she walked in silence.

In bed, Lily tossed and turned, her mind groaning under the strain that had now been placed upon it. It was sheer exhaustion that put her to sleep in the early hours of the morning.

8

---※---

THE GRIMFAR PLOT

noise in the corridor outside her room made Lily stir in her sleep. The banging of her chamber door being thrown open woke her fully. She sat bolt upright in her bed. "Who's there?" she shouted.

Sir Aidan rushed into her bedchamber. "It is me," he said gently. "Are you all right, Lillian?"

"I was before you charged into my chamber!" said Lily angrily.

Candles suddenly lit the room. Lily was shocked to see Drake, Argon, Will, and Ryan, all with swords drawn. Her eyes grew wider when she saw her father, too.

"What is going on?" she asked, pulling her bedcovers higher in fright.

Sir Aidan moved over to the bed and sat down. He took hold of Lily's hand. "Thank goodness you're safe."

Lily shivered; she felt cold all over, and her head began to ache. "Why wouldn't I be safe?" she asked.

"The city guards intercepted a group of men tonight, inside our city walls. They had plans of the palace and a mapped route to your chambers, my dear," said the king.

Lily's eyes widened. "Who were they?"

"They were Grimfar warriors, Lillian, deadly people from a land shadowed by the Black Mountains," said Aidan.

"I know of them, but why would they wish to attack me?"

"We have no answers yet," said Aidan, "but the plans of our city must have been given to them by someone inside the palace. We feared they were coming to kidnap you or harm you in some way. We came to you as fast as we could, to make sure you were safe." Aidan squeezed her hand more tightly.

"I have heard no one moving around outside in the corridors," said Lily truthfully.

"That is good, but for your own safety, tonight at least, I think it is best if you come and stay in my chambers," said Aidan.

Lily nodded her agreement.

The king also nodded. "Drake and Will, you escort Sir Aidan and Princess Lillian to his chambers. Argon and Ryan, you will come with me."

The king turned to Aidan. "The guards will remain with you for the rest of the night."

"Good," said Aidan. "They can sleep in the outer rooms of my chambers; we cannot be too careful."

With another nod and a signal to the guards, the king left Lily's chamber.

"Come on, my love, let's get you to my chambers," said Aidan gently. Lily obediently slid from the bed and Aidan wrapped her up in the bedcovers. "There is no time to get dressed," he said, leading her towards the door.

Lily allowed herself to be steered along the corridors. She was still so cold, and she shook in Aidan's arms. He wrapped her tighter in the bedcovers. Once she was inside his chambers, the guards began to take up their positions.

"I hope you will forgive that tonight I must share this bed with you," said Aidan, once they were alone in his bedchamber. "I don't wish to leave you alone, even for a moment."

Lily shook her head. "I want you to stay with me."

Aidan climbed under the covers, fully clothed. Lily felt instantly relaxed by his weight beside her, and her heartbeat calmed in her chest. Despite the events of the night and the argument they'd had the previous evening, this time sleep found her easily.

When she woke, Aidan had gone. Lily lay for a while thinking about how wonderful it had been to feel him lying beside her. He had held her hand all night, and she felt that her spirit could never be lowered again. She had been wrong about him; he did love her. Last night had proved it. She felt a strange pulling feeling inside her mind, as if there was something she'd forgotten, but she dismissed it. Everything was so good in her life—except for the unfortunate business of the Grimfar plot—that she couldn't think what the pulling was. Lily decided to stop pondering things and finally got out of bed. She looked into the outer chamber and found Mistress Stratton busily tidying up the sleeping rolls of the guards.

She looked round to see Lily standing in the doorway. "Finally you're awake!" she said firmly. "I have brought you a dress to change into. Sir Aidan insists you remain here for a while."

"Where is he, Maggie?"

"With the king, I would guess. He wouldn't tell me why you spent the night here. I only hope there was a very good reason!"

Lily laughed at Maggie's disapproval. "You're so old-fashioned!"

"And rightly so! A princess has a duty to behave to the highest standards, even with the man she is to marry. Honestly, Lily, you are not some inn girl who sells her rights to feed herself!"

Lily walked over to her kind mistress. She often forgot that Maggie had been around for such a long time. She had been her mother's mistress first, and even though, to Lily, she always looked wonderful, her age was starting to show. Only her amazing energy seemed unaffected by her advancing years.

"Don't go getting yourself all worked up, Maggie. Nothing dishonourable happened between Aidan and me last night."

Mistress Stratton's still didn't look convinced. "So, why are you here?"

Lily looked down at the woman in front of her. She had known Maggie all her life. She had never kept a secret from her in all those eighteen years, and she knew she couldn't start now. "There is a plot against me. Men were caught last night with plans of the palace and a route mapped to my chambers!"

Maggie gasped and covered her mouth. "Oh, child, that is terrifying." Tears appeared in her bright-blue eyes.

"Rest easy, Maggie. They didn't get me last night, and now that Aidan and the guards are alerted, they will have no chance of finding me," Lily reassured her.

"Who are these men?" asked Maggie quietly.

Lily frowned. "My father said they were from the land of Grimfar."

Mistress Stratton bit her lip. "The land near Sanalow, with the underground city that's only just been discovered beneath the dead lands."

Lily nodded. "Yes, it is between the western desert and the Black Mountains. It is said Grimfar warriors are monsters!"

"Does the king know much about the people?"

"I don't think anyone in Judelen knows much about them, Maggie. We have never had dealings with the people from Grimfar."

Mistress Stratton looked excitedly at Lily. "Young Jack will know! He was in the army of Sanalow, and they are at war with Grimfar!"

Lily looked surprised. "I didn't know he was in the army. I guessed he was from Sanalow because he has green eyes, but neither he or my guards have ever mentioned that he was a soldier."

Mistress Stratton looked uncomfortable. "I think they may have agreed to hide the fact from you, to protect your reputation after you chose to bond him. I mean no offence to you or Jack by that, but from an outsider's point of view, it doesn't look very good that you bonded a deserter."

Lily blinked in surprise. "No!" she said feeling slightly disgusted. "Jack, a deserter? I can't believe it!"

"He is young, Lily. It must have been awful to see war and to take part in it. I don't think it is fair to judge him, though, until you know his reasons."

"I must speak with him about Grimfar," said Lily firmly. "Are there guards on the door?"

"Of course! When aren't there?"

Lily smiled and lowered her voice. "In that case, I need you to sneak me out!"

Maggie sighed. "As you wish, Your Majesty."

A knock sounded on Jack's chamber door, but he ignored it; he really wasn't in the mood for visitors. Then Lily suddenly came bursting through the door, shutting it quickly behind her.

Normally Lily bouncing into his chambers would be a dream come true, but Jack wasn't feeling at all pleased to see her. "Your Majesty, what a nice surprise." He hoped she heard the bitterness in his tone. He was still very angry that she'd made Will tell him he was confined to his chambers without having the decency to explain why. To further show his annoyance, he didn't bother getting off his bed to bow. While Lily hovered by the door, he crossed his arms and waited for her to speak.

"I'm sorry, Jack," she said gently.

"Sorry for what?" he asked coldly.

"For bursting in on you, of course," she said more firmly.

Jack laughed bitterly. Did she really think she'd get away with that answer?

Lily softened her voice again. "I'm also sorry for making you stay in your chambers," she added quietly.

Happy with the apology, Jack smiled and uncrossed his arms. "Does that mean you'll let me leave them now?"

Lily didn't answer, and Jack had a horrid feeling she was about to cry. "What's wrong?" he asked. He knew something had terrified her the previous evening. but the bond didn't give away any feeling of fear now. He frowned. "Lily, what's troubling you?" he said quietly.

Lily burst into tears. "I'm frightened, Jack," she sobbed. "I was trying to hide it, but I can't do it anymore!"

Jack sat himself up carefully. "Come and sit down, Lily, and tell me what's happened," he said gently.

Lily took a moment to dry her eyes. Then she pulled Jack's small chair out from his desk and sat on it near the foot of his bed. He wondered why she hadn't just sat on the bed; perhaps she hadn't wanted to rock him, he concluded.

She looked at Jack, and her worries poured out like a waterfall. "Last night the city patrol came across a group of men who were acting suspiciously. These men attacked the patrol, but the patrol fought them and managed to defeat them all.

"The patrol checked the bodies and discovered detailed plans of our city. The plans held the seal of Grimfar. The men have been identified as natives of Grimfar. They managed to get into the city after the gates were shut for the night.

"My father examined the plans they had with them. They held a detailed plan of the palace, and my chambers were highlighted. Father is sure that I was their target. What do you think?"

Jack raised a hand to silence her. "That's a lot of information, Lily. Give me a minute to think about it." He massaged his temples as he thought. "If everything you have said is correct, then it does look that way. However, it doesn't make sense. Grimfar and Judelen are not enemies. Why would they plot to kidnap or kill you?"

Lily shrugged. "I don't know. Father doesn't know either, but at the moment he is more concerned with the other problem."

Jack must have missed that part. "What's the other problem?" he asked.

Lily looked at Jack seriously. "How the natives of Grimfar managed to get detailed plans of our city and palace."

Comprehension dawned. "What you mean is, who they got them from. For them to have been so comprehensive, someone inside the palace must have drawn them. There is a person, or persons, here, at the centre of this plot."

Lily dragged her chair closer to Jack. "Do you remember what Tomas said, what we discussed the night you were brought here?"

"Of course. If this has happened, then Tomas was right, you are in danger. And it could be anyone in the palace who is working against you."

Lily bit her lip. "What should I do?"

Jack considered the options and began listing them. "Keep a low profile, stay near to those whom you know you can trust—your bodyguards, the king, and Sir Aidan are the least likely to be the people who would harm you. Don't trust anyone too much, though. Until we know more about these plans, no one can be ruled out."

Lily nodded, still biting her lip.

"Where are the bodies of the Grimfar men?" asked Jack. He wanted to go and see them for himself.

"They are here in the palace, waiting to be burned. Father wants no one in the city to learn of the plot. Only he, Sir Aidan, our bodyguards, and I know anything about it. The patrol that found the group are being kept within the palace on strict orders not to discuss their findings."

"Good. The fewer people who know the plot was discovered, the more chance we have of catching the people involved." Jack felt the bandage over his ribs. "If only this hadn't happened, I could be of more use! Well, I can still protect you in other ways—"

"No," said Lily firmly. "You have to heal. You could cause more harm than good if you attempt to help while you are in this state."

Jack felt his anger returning. "But you are in danger! I cannot sit back and not help you! It is my duty," he spat, outraged.

Lily sighed. "If you want to argue about it, then you can do it with the king. He is holding a meeting tomorrow morning. Only the people who know of the plot will be there. As far as anyone else is concerned, it is a hearing about Argon's punishment. That is the only thing that would allow all the people in our group to meet and not look suspicious."

"Then I should be there anyway. After all, I was the one he injured," said Jack stonily.

"You have not seen him since the bond was severed. Be careful you do not do anything silly when you do see him," warned Lily.

Jack raised his eyebrows. "I would not give him the satisfaction. I'm not a child, Lily!"

She ignored his comment. "It is settled, then. Come to the greeting chamber at dawn, and we shall find out what's going to happen next."

Lily paused and looked at Jack, a frown creasing her forehead. She was looking at him in the oddest way, as if desperate to ask him something.

"Is there something else, Lily?" he asked.

"Jack …" But then Lily shook her head, leaving her sentence unsaid. "No, there is nothing else." She got up and headed for the door.

"Where are you going now?" snapped Jack, but she didn't pull him up on it.

She didn't look back at him when she spoke. "Aidan's chambers. I shall remain in them until tomorrow morning. Goodbye, Jack," she said shortly.

Jack frowned as the door closed behind Lily. What did she mean about going to Aidan's chambers? Whatever was going on, it was disturbing. Something didn't feel right. Why would Grimfar suddenly plot against Judelen? How had they gotten into the city, and how had the patrol managed to bring down the whole group without sustaining injury themselves?

Jack remembered the battlefield of Sanalow, the horror he had felt seeing Grimfar warriors for the first time. Their deformities were terrifying to look at, but despite their physical handicaps, they could fight better than any of the soldiers in Sanalow. The casualties had been numerous before the end of the first day. The nickname "monsters" had come from the front line, and Jack had thought it fitting at the time—until he had discovered the chilling truth.

The door of Jack's chamber burst open again. Jack jumped and then hissed in pain. It was Will who had entered.

"What is the matter?" said Jack, angrily rubbing his ribs.

"Have you heard?" asked Will.

Jack put a finger over his lips. "Shut the door, Will," he said quietly. He waited for the latch to click. "If you mean about the group of men who were killed last night in the city, then, yes, I have heard."

Will moved away from the door and came towards Jack's bed. "There is something unnatural about this attack, Jack; I can feel it."

"I was just contemplating that myself. Come and sit," he offered, signalling to the chair.

"I saw the princess leaving your chambers. I knew she would have told you about the attack," said Will as he sat down quickly.

"Why shouldn't she tell me? I'm one of her guards too," said Jack defensively.

"After you were injured, Sir Aidan told her not to tell you anything. He thought that because you were out of action you shouldn't be involved."

Jack ground his teeth.

"That is why I'm here, really. If she hadn't have told you, then I would have," added Will quickly.

Jack breathed out deeply. "I thank you for that, Will. Well, Sir Aidan is going to be disappointed tomorrow when I turn up for the meeting at dawn!" he said, feeling smug.

Will smiled. "I think it will do some good to remind these outsiders that they can't go taking over."

"I'm as much an outsider as he is," said Jack carefully.

"There are outsiders and there are outsiders, Jack. Sanalow is much closer to home than his country is." Will looked round the chamber and lowered his voice. "Did the princess tell you what was found on the Grimfar bodies?"

Jack whispered his response. "She said they had detailed maps of inside the palace. I told her that it must have been someone inside the palace who had drawn them."

"I had concluded the same," said Will in agreement. "My mind has been turning over all the information, and I am starting to think that maybe it is Sir Aidan who is our traitor."

Jack sucked in a breath. "Be careful what you speak out loud, Will. Accusations like that could get you killed!" His ribs pulled; he hissed again and shifted into a more comfortable position, trying to ignore the pain.

"I have only spoken to you, Jack, and I will not speak to anyone else, not even my brother," said Will quickly.

"Why trust me? For all you know of me, I could be your traitor!"

Will studied Jack. "I trust you for two reasons. One, our bond protects me."

Jack sighed. "It protects the others too, Will. Why else?"

"Why else? That will be answered with my next question," said Will mysteriously. "The men who took the Grimfar bodies into the palace are being held, so they cannot talk to anyone about what happened. The bodies themselves are going to be burned; Sir Aidan has arranged it.

"No one from Judelen has ever seen a person from Grimfar, but we have heard rumours from Sanalow about them, that they are supposed to be monsters. Is it true?"

"Yes, the army of Sanalow nicknamed them monsters," confirmed Jack.

"Is it because of how they fight?"

Jack shrugged. "That was one of the reasons, but mainly they were named so because of their terribly deformed faces and bodies."

The colour slowly began to drain from Will's face.

"What is the matter?" asked Jack, fearing he might collapse. He reached forward to grab his arm, and the movement made his chest throb.

"I saw the bodies! I managed to see them before they were locked away," said Will in a daze.

"And?" Jack questioned through gritted teeth. Will looked composed, so Jack let him go and leant back, exhaling sharply as he did so.

"They were just ordinary men, Jack. Not monsters—no deformities at all," said Will. Looking up at Jack, he saw the pain in his face. "Are you all right?" he asked with concern.

Jack raked a hand through his hair. "Broken rib!" he said sarcastically. He thought hard about the bodies. "Will, there is something really wrong here! Those bodies can't be men of Grimfar if they are not deformed. Do you know the history of the land?" he asked.

Will looked thoughtful. "I know from studying the creation history that the city was originally the base for the magus's army, and Evelyn Maude destroyed it during the War of Power. She used molten lava rivers to decimate the land," he said. "We all learned about the hidden underground city and the survivors from the Sanalow reports a few years ago."

Jack nodded. "It was the foul gases left behind from the attack that caused their deformities. It affected the unborn, the children, the men, and the women; no one was untainted by it."

Will leant towards Jack. "If you were the traitor, Jack, you would not have revealed the truth about Grimfar to me, because it exposes the lie."

Jack had a sudden thought. "If I am the only one to know about the deformities, it's possible that the people of Judelen have just assumed this was the work of Grimfar."

Will shook his head. "What about the seal upon the plans? It is the seal of Grimfar. The records show that, and if the men are not natives from Grimfar, somebody wants us to believe they are."

Jack frowned. "Why, though? To hide another country's involvement?"

"That would make sense," said Will. "But what country wants to stay hidden from us?"

"What about the princess?" queried Jack suddenly. "She said the king believes the attack is aimed at her. If Grimfar is not behind it, who else might want to harm her?"

Will stood up. "I really don't know, Jack. There is still an awful lot we must uncover. I have to go back to my duties. Will you think about this and talk to me later?"

Jack nodded. "Don't speak to anyone else, Will," he warned.

"I don't intend to, Jack. The same goes for you. That way, if anything happens and we are discovered, we know it can only be the other of us who has spoken."

Jack watched Will leave. He didn't know what was really going on, but he was going to find out.

9

DETERMINATION

Jack got up in plenty of time for the meeting; he knew he'd need extra time to get dressed because of his injuries. He was annoyed that Mistress Stratton had refused to help him in any way. She was very angry that he was going to be moving around before her say-so, but she couldn't overrule the princess's order.

Jack was walking along, thinking about Argon and trying to imagine different scenarios for when they came face to face. He was just picturing an epic sword fight in the greeting chamber, which ended in him cutting off Argon's head, when he turned the corner and ran straight into him. Groaning, he stepped away and massaged his ribs. They locked eyes and stared, unblinking, in a silent challenge. Jack could feel the very air around them prickle. The tension was broken by the arrival of Ryan.

Ryan cast a quick look over Jack and Argon and swiftly moved to intercede. "It is good to see you up and about, Jack," he said, placing a hand on Jack's shoulder to steer him down the corridor. "Morning, Argon," he said quietly as they moved past him. Argon merely nodded, and followed Ryan and Jack, keeping a little way behind them.

As the three men reached the greeting chamber, they were met by Drake and Will. Drake looked slightly surprised to see Jack, but he said nothing. Will met Jack's eyes for a moment; they both nodded gently, so the others wouldn't notice.

The doors to the chamber opened, and the bodyguards filed in. The king, Lily, and Sir Aidan were all sitting upon their thrones, and chairs were lined up in a neat row before them for the guards to sit on. Jack took particular care to watch Sir Aidan from the minute he entered the chamber; his expression turned out to be similar to Drake's, his body stiffening and his face going rigid when he saw Jack. His eyes flashed dangerously towards Lily. Jack was beginning to think more than ever that Will had the right measure of Aidan. He took his seat in silence and cast a quick look at Lily, who gave him a small smile.

King Symon spoke to the gathering from the seat of his throne. "This meeting has been called to discuss the attack upon Judelen by warriors of Grimfar," he said formally. "All who are in attendance today are reminded that this matter is to be discussed with no one outside of this meeting."

The king looked very sombre, indeed. In fact, Jack thought he was looking upon the bodyguards with mistrust in his eyes. Puzzled, he sat in silence to listen to what was said next.

"I have already begun an investigation into how these warriors breached the city's defences in the dead of night. Although that is a matter of importance, I feel there is enough focus upon it. Instead, I wish to focus upon the more serious problem, which is known only to those in this room and the guards who were attacked. That matter is, of course, the safety of Princess Lillian."

Jack glanced at Lily again. She sat in her throne straight-backed and cool, as if determined not to look frightened.

The king didn't look over at Lily; he merely cleared his throat before continuing. "You are all aware of what the warriors had in their possession. There are a vast number of people who could have drawn, or described such plans, as many people have free access into and out of the palace, so we must look from the servants to the highest-ranking palace guards. There are a lot of people to choose from. Of course, there are ways to narrow down our field of search, this part of the palace, the royal chambers, and the bodyguards' chambers have strictly limited access. The servants here are not permitted to work in other areas of the palace, which means we could narrow our search by up to half the original numbers. Although servants have an unfortunate habit of gossiping, I feel it is unlikely that this plot could have been directed from them."

Will abruptly stood up from his seat, and every eye in the room turned to regard him.

"You have something to say?" asked the king, with a bite of impatience in his voice.

Will nodded slowly. "I wish to ask if the bodyguards in this room are under suspicion along with the others in the palace?"

Jack turned from Will to look at the king. The king waved a hand impatiently. "Sit down," he commanded. Will remained standing.

The king's face turned an ugly shade of red, but before he could speak, Lily rose from her throne. "The bodyguards here are not under suspicion, Will," she said firmly. "You are all known to be completely loyal. I would never suspect any of you."

Will sat down slowly.

Lily turned to regard the other guards. "I do believe that the person or persons behind this plot are people who have clear access to me on a daily basis. I do not know why anyone would wish to plot against me, and I do not know why Grimfar warriors are involved. I do know, however, that I trust each and every one of my bodyguards with my life. Together we shall uncover who is behind these dealings." Lily sat back down gracefully and turned her attention back to her father.

"There is much work to be done," said the king quietly; he indicated Lily and Sir Aidan. "We shall personally be giving instructions to each of you, and we shall see you individually, to make certain that no information can be overheard. You are all ordered to keep your instructions secret; they are not to be discussed between yourselves under any circumstances.

"Regular meetings, like this one, shall be held to give updates and discuss new developments. Should you uncover anything you believe is significant, bring the information directly to the princess or myself. These are dark times for Judelen, and we must now work together to bring our city clear of them."

The king, Sir Aidan, and Lily all stood up. The bodyguards followed suit. "You may return to your duties," the king ordered. Each of the guards saluted, and they began to make their way across the chamber to the doors.

"Master Orden, would you remain?"

Jack stopped walking in the direction of the doors and turned back to regard the king. Will cast him a curious look, but Jack moved back towards the thrones before he could speak. He thought it would be unwise for Will to speak out of turn twice in one meeting.

The king, Sir Aidan, and Lily had all returned to their thrones, and Jack remained standing before them. The distant thud of the doors closing signalled that the room was now clear of the other guards. Jack saluted the king and waited.

It was Lily who spoke to him. "Jack, we have kept you back so that you can be given your instructions." Lily cast a quick look at the king before continuing. "Today is your first day out since your accident. How are you feeling?"

Jack frowned before he could stop himself. "I'm sorry, Your Majesty. *How am I feeling?*"

The king looked crossly at him. "It is a simple enough question, Master Orden," he cut in. "If we are to evaluate your usefulness to us at this difficult time, we must know how you are coping with your injuries."

"Of course—I'm sorry, Your Majesty. I am managing my injuries well, and it is good to be out of my chambers. I am still suffering with stiffness, but I am confident that should have eased in another couple of days," said Jack politely.

The king looked at Lily with a firm expression on his face.

Jack felt nervous. "What is the problem, Your Majesty?" he called.

"I thought that would be obvious, Master Orden," said the king mockingly. "Originally you were to be excluded from this meeting today, because due to your injuries, you are not fit enough to aid the princess. Now Lillian, I presume, went against my better judgement and allowed you to attend. I fear it will make things much more difficult."

"Your Majesty, I can still be of use to you in the investigations, even with my injuries—"

"All you can do is sit in on the group meetings and offer advice on what you hear. I cannot post you on guard duty, I cannot post you to question suspects, and should the worst happen and warriors gain access to the palace, you cannot attempt to fight in your condition. Am I right in believing you would anyway?"

Jack scowled, and the king looked triumphant. "In your current state, you are more likely to be killed and put the other guards in danger, and I cannot allow that." The king paused for a moment, his face hardening. "I'm afraid I must ask you to return to your chambers and remain there until you are fully healed."

Jack's legs felt weak. "Your Majesty, you cannot ask me to do that—please! There must be something I can do. If not aiding the investigations, at least allow me to leave my chambers."

"I fear you will not be able to resist interfering with the investigations if I allow you to wander freely. You must already be feeling frustrated by not being fully active. No, I'm afraid I stand by my order that you remain in your chambers."

Jack knew he must look furious, but he didn't care. He stood silently, breathing quick, anger-fuelled breaths.

Lily had a pitying look on her face, but that only made him feel worse. He looked away from her as she caught his eye.

"Perhaps it could be arranged for Jack to have some time outside his chambers?" she said gently.

The king looked at Lily. "I don't see any way of arranging that."

"He could walk with me once a day. I swear that I shall tell him nothing of the investigations."

Jack felt a rush of gratitude towards Lily. He looked back over at her.

"I'm afraid that is out of the question, Lillian. You are the target here, and I shall not allow you to roam around with Master Orden and make it easy for the plotters to attack you."

"Very well, Father. Instead of me, let someone else escort him—Mistress Stratton, perhaps?"

Jack's mouth thinned, and Lily cast him a stern look. The king, however, was looking thoughtful. "Yes, I suppose that might be an idea. The mistress is so strict she will not be bullied into speaking; she is also outside of the investigation." He turned to regard Jack. "I must insist upon two rules, Master Orden. Firstly, you are not to ask or answer any questions from the mistress, or anyone else. Should you be asked anything suspicious, you are to report it to me or the princess."

"Of course, Your Majesty."

"Secondly, I must isolate you from the other bodyguards, until you are returned to full health. You are not to speak to any of them or ask questions; they, in turn, will be told not to approach you. Should I find you are not obeying these commands, then I shall once again order you to remain permanently within your chambers."

Jack nodded that he understood.

"You may go now," said the king, swiftly dismissing him. "Stay in your chambers until I send the mistress to you, and speak to no one."

Jack saluted the king and stalked from the chamber. He felt so angry that he could no longer feel the pain in his ribs. His head was throbbing with the injustice of the situation, but he had a clear thought in his mind of how he would quickly release himself from it. He would train hard during his time outside, and he would pull himself back to full health as fast as he could. How could they ask him to step aside and do nothing while the woman he'd sworn to protect sat in danger? His bond pulled at him to do his duty, and he had to fight against it. Also the king had put a stop to him speaking more with Will about his thoughts on Sir Aidan.

Jack had no idea how he reached his chambers; his journey had been clouded by his determination to fight. The moment he entered the chambers, he tore his shirt off and began to undo his bandaging. It restricted his movement, and he needed to be able to stretch his muscles. He focused his mind and began to work out his new routines; the bandages lay forgotten on the floor.

10

REVELATION AND REVENGE

Jack stood in the training area with his eyes shut, preparing to begin his exercise program. He called upon the "deep calm", a meditation method that helped him block out everything going on around him and focus his mind completely on the session in front of him. His leader in Sanalow had taught him and the other soldiers how to call upon the deep calm to focus their minds before battle, and now Jack was using it to aid his return to full health.

Two weeks had passed since the king had called the meeting. True to his word, Jack had been allowed time outside his chamber with the mistress. He had begun his training program on his first walk, and despite the hard start, he was now almost totally healed. The mistress had been furious to learn of his plans, but Jack had stuck with them. Now Mistress Stratton sat silently under the rose arches, watching him prepare to do his exercises. She'd found very little to argue about once she had examined him and learnt for herself that he really had cut his healing time in half. Although she would never admit it, Jack knew she was very impressed; she had certainly increased his time outside after the first few days.

A cool wind blew gently across his face, bringing with it the scent of the roses. Jack breathed deeply. While he was in the state of deep calm, his senses were more advanced, sharper, and deadlier.

Jack snapped his eyes open and moved into his first pattern. Without a weapon, he appeared to be dancing. Weapon play was all patterns, weaving, and delicate footwork. He moved quickly and carefully. Although the movements seemed delicate, the air whipped around his body from the force of his blows.

Jack kept working his patterns for nearly fifteen minutes, unaware of anything but his movement. He moved into the final formation and drew to a halt. He allowed his deep calm to ebb away and became more aware of the sweat on his body and the quickened pace of his heartbeat.

Mistress Stratton rose from her seat and came towards him. "How do you feel?" she asked firmly. That was always her first question to him after a training session.

Jack wiped sweat from his brow. "I feel no pain whatsoever. I wish to begin again, with a weapon this time."

The mistress frowned slightly but then nodded. "If you wish to begin with weapons, then I shall agree, but you are not to start now. I want you to eat two good meals first, and then you can begin this evening, when the air cools."

Jack nodded without argument. It was still morning, and the air was thick with heat. By midday it would be hard for people to walk round, let alone work patterns.

"Well, I have work to do, Jack," said the mistress firmly. "I'll see you back to your chambers now."

"Mistress Stratton, I must go to the stables," said Jack quickly. "Bailey's surgeon wants a word about his leg."

The mistress suddenly looked concerned. "How is the animal's leg? I heard he was likely to be unable to walk if the fault spreads further."

Jack swallowed hard. It was true that Bailey's leg had begun to seize. He had developed the defect when a sword had caught him in the top of his back leg during the war. The muscle had never really healed, and living rough for a year hadn't helped it at all. Much to Jack's shame, the injury had become even worse following Argon's mock jousting session. He would never forgive himself if anything happened to Bailey.

"He'll get better," answered Jack in a strangled voice.

He felt a hand on his shoulder and looked down upon Mistress Stratton. "I'm sure he will be fine, Jack. The palace has the best workmen for many miles. The horse surgeon will make him right." The surgeon was a very skilled man, and he had been raised with horses. Jack had every confidence in him, but even confidence gave way to worry at times.

"Let's go and check up on him, and then maybe, depending on your training session tonight, I could visit the princess and tell her that I believe you are now ready to return to full duties."

Jack grinned. "You'll tell her that I'm ready?"

"If you can do a full session of patterns with a sword, I will! Now, let's get to the stable. I have lots of work to do!"

Impulsively, Jack hugged Mistress Stratton. Upon realising he was sweaty, he let her go, issuing a hurried apology. He led the way to the stable feeling better than he had done since the meeting.

The following morning, Jack rose and dressed in his uniform. He had completed a full training session with his sword, and Mistress Stratton had been true to her word; she had informed Lily that Jack was fit to return to duties.

He set off down to the hall for breakfast, feeling bright. His visit to the stables the previous morning had brought good news. The horse surgeon thought Bailey would recover, with the proper exercise and medicine. Until he was satisfied Bailey was stronger, Jack had been loaned another horse.

Jack quickened his pace as he approached the hall. As far as he knew, none of the others would know yet that he was returning to duties. He couldn't wait to surprise Will and Ryan. He also wanted to see Argon's face when he strolled in two weeks earlier than expected!

As soon as he stepped through the doorway, all eyes turned to regard him. Drake got to his feet and crossed the room, looking angry. "Jack, you are not supposed to come here."

"I am returning to duties today, Drake. You can confirm with the princess if you wish. I, however, am hungry and do not want to miss breakfast, so if you'll excuse me …" He ducked round the side of him and kept walking.

Drake didn't attempt to stop Jack coming further into the room. He didn't hurry off to find Lily either. Jack guessed he was using the bond to sense his emotions. He turned around and followed Jack.

Will and Ryan got to their feet as Jack stopped at their table. They both looked slightly concerned. Ryan spoke first. "You're not here against orders are you, Jack?" he mumbled.

Will stepped forward. "The king will come down hard on you if he catches you," he added.

Jack felt slightly put out by their reactions. "Of course I'm not," he said shortly. "I am back to full health, and I am beginning duties again this morning."

The brothers split into identical grins, and they both patted him on the back, laughing. Jack grinned—that was the reaction he had been hoping for.

Will clapped Jack on the shoulder. "You heal fast! I thought you would be out of it for a month, at least! It is good to have you back."

Ryan nodded his agreement, and all three men sat down.

A serving woman approached the table, and Jack placed his order. He glanced round the room. "Has Argon already left?" he asked, hoping he hadn't missed him.

Ryan bit off a mouthful of bread. "He hasn't come for breakfast yet," he said, chewing his food and then swallowing it down. "I can't wait to see his face when he sees you here!"

Drake frowned at Ryan as he came to the table. "I would have thought you'd have settled this silly feud by now."

Ryan pointed his bread at Drake. "He broke Jack's rib, Drake. He abused his teaching sessions against a fellow bodyguard. You may be able to forgive and forget, but personally, I think Jack has every right to stay angry."

Drake shook his head. "Whatever Argon has done, he has paid for it. That is an end to it."

Ryan did not respond but continued eating his bread. The serving woman returned with a bowl of porridge and a loaf of bread for Jack. He had just begun eating when Argon walked into the chamber.

Ryan saw him first and smirked; he nudged Will. Drake said nothing, but his eyes fixed onto Jack.

Argon glanced round the room and spotted the men at their table. He began to walk towards them. Upon noticing Jack, he stopped abruptly. For a moment he looked shocked, but he quickly hid it, and his face became set like stone. He started walking again and came to rest at the table.

He turned to Drake. "Is he supposed to be here?"

Before Drake could answer, Jack got to his feet. The room went quiet. "Of course I'm supposed to be here, Argon. Do you think the other guards would be sat with me, eating breakfast, if I wasn't?"

Argon had tensed as Jack stood up. Now he eyed him up and down, searching for some sign of his injuries.

"Are you healed already?" he said, trying to sound bored and uninterested.

"Fully," goaded Jack.

Argon looked mildly impressed, despite his efforts not to show it.

Drake cleared his throat. "Shall we continue breakfast?" he asked, a note of pleading in his voice.

Argon sniffed and slid into a chair next to Drake. Jack waited for him to sit before sitting himself. Ryan looked deeply disappointed by the lack of action. Everyone began eating again. Jack kept glancing across the table at Argon, who would catch his eye and glower. For a while no one spoke, until Ryan decided to talk to Jack.

"I was wondering how your horse is doing, Jack."

The other men looked up to listen. Drake looked relieved that some conversation was beginning again.

Jack swallowed his last spoonful of porridge and began to tell Ryan about Bailey. "So the surgeon met me yesterday, and he is confident he will be fine," he concluded, after filling Ryan in on how the injury had come about.

"Have they lent you another horse?"

"Yes. I have not ridden him yet, but he has a good look to him. Still, I'll be very glad to have Bailey back in action. I've had him from the beginning of my training, and he has become a part of me now."

"Like an old friend," said Ryan, smiling. "I feel the same about Dancer. They are amazing creatures really, horses. They are loyal, intelligent—" Ryan broke off as the door opened again.

To everyone's amazement, it was Lily who walked in. Jack was surprised to see her alone, but then he noticed Mistress Stratton standing in the shadows by the door.

All the guards got to their feet. Argon made a show of finishing his bread first, making certain he was the last one up.

Lily smiled round at each of them. Her smile faltered a little when it rested on Argon. She motioned for them all to sit.

"I've come for Jack. If you have finished eating?" she added to him.

Jack moved his chair back and issued a quick goodbye to the others before following Lily out of the hall.

"The king wishes to see you later," she told him as they walked. "Now you are fit for duty, you will need to be filled in on your roles in the investigation."

Jack's heart did a flip; finally he got to be involved!

"As you wish. What time does the king want me?"

"This afternoon," said Lily. Jack thought she looked distracted.

Lily turned to Mistress Stratton. "Jack can guard me from here, Maggie. You may go about your business."

Mistress Stratton curtsied and turned back down the corridor. Lily watched her out of sight before turning back to Jack. "Before I assign your new duties, I would like to talk with you. Will you accompany me on a walk?"

"Of course," said Jack. He had been missing their time together so badly.

They made their way outside of the palace. The air was warm even though it was early, promising another hot day.

For a while they simply walked, making polite conversation and jokes. They were walking through the guard's stables when Lily turned to Jack. "You have not seen my horse yet," she said brightly.

"The one you wished to show me before I was injured," remembered Jack. "Where is it stabled?"

"The royal stables are this way," she said, leading him away from the guard stables.

The royal stables were kept in the best of condition. There was no smell of dirty straw, and roses hung all round the stables, sending their strong, sweet scent into the air. The guard's stables were kept clean and tidy, but against these they seemed poor. There were ten stables in the royal area. Only three were occupied.

Lily led Jack over to the one tucked furthest away. Inside it was a pure-white mare. She was large for a mare, but her body and legs were bony. Her face was tight for a horse, as if the skin was simply stretched over the bone. She held her neck in an arch, and her eyes held a deep fierceness. She watched them as Lily led Jack over to her door. Her eyes didn't blink often.

"This is Afillia, Jack. Do you like her?"

Jack regarded the horse for a moment. He had never seen an uglier animal anywhere, and he disliked her build. "She is certainly different from our horses," he said softly. "What is she like to ride?"

"She is a good ride—although I sometimes feel she has more control then I do," said Lily with a frown.

"Sir Aidan brought her for you?"

"Yes, and he brought a stallion for my father as well as his own horse. I'll show you." Lily motioned Jack to the other stables.

Jack looked into the stable containing the king's new horse. This one was also white, but it had a black mane and tail.

"This one is called Neo. Sir Aidan told me that all of the Shangol horses are white. The females are pure white, and the males have black manes and tails. They kill any that are born outside of these colours, because they consider them bad omens."

Jack frowned. "Sounds like a waste of good horses to me."

The stallion tossed his bony head. Jack moved on to the next stable to regard Aidan's horse. By far this one was the biggest and ugliest. Jack didn't like him at all. Lily gave a small shudder next to him.

"What is the matter?" asked Jack in concern.

Lily regarded the horse for a moment before moving away. Jack followed her. "I don't like Rittard, he gives me the creeps," she admitted. "I don't like speaking in front of him, because I feel like he is listening to every word I say." Lily laughed nervously. "It is silly, really. I mean, he is just a horse, but I am not looking forward to riding to Shangol with him next to me all the way."

"When are you going to Shangol?" asked Jack in surprise.

Lily gave him a disbelieving look. "Don't you pay attention, Jack? I go to Shangol as soon as I am married. I am to spend my first years in marriage learning their customs so that Judelen and Shangol can become one empire."

Jack frowned. "I thought Sir Aidan would stay here with you. I never thought that we would be leaving Judelen."

Lily sighed. "I must talk with you about that. Let's go to my garden."

Lily led the way to her private garden, situated beyond the stables, towards the back of the palace. It was a stone-walled garden with only one entrance. The walls were high, sheltering anyone inside from view. It had borders of beautifully coloured flowers and a weeping willow with a stone bench beneath. Once they were inside, she told Jack to sit down, and then she sat beside him.

"Why do you need to talk to me about going to Shangol?" asked Jack straight away.

"I thought it fair to ask you if you would be happy to go there."

Jack felt bemused; he couldn't believe she didn't know the answer to that. "I'm bound to you for life, Lily. I'll follow you anywhere you go."

Lily smiled. "Then there is nothing to discuss. I shall have three of my bodyguards with me."

"Three, but ... who isn't going?"

"My father wishes Drake to remain in the palace. Will and Ryan will remain with me, so they shall travel to Shangol with us."

Jack regarded her. "So you'll be two bodyguards down by the time we leave," he said. That thought was making him nervous.

"I am to select two new bodyguards from Shangol. My father believes that will help show confidence in the union between our lands. That is why no one has been selected to replace Argon."

Jack sat chewing his finger. Lily fell silent, and for a time they both seemed content to sit with their thoughts. Finally Jack spoke the question that had been rising within him.

"Lily, what is the real reason you asked me whether I was happy to follow you to Shangol?"

Lily looked surprised for a moment, but she quickly made her face smooth once more. "I told you, I thought it fair to ask."

"Did you ask Will and Ryan, or did you just know they would come with you?"

Spots of colour appeared in her cheeks, matching her pretty pink gown. "Well, I didn't ask them directly ... I mean to say ... I have known them for a long time; I knew how they would react better than you."

"The bond between us should have been enough to tell you what my choice was too," said Jack, his temper flaring. "Why don't you just tell me the real reason?"

Lily's mouth thinned. "I may allow my guards to possess a personal relationship with me, Jack, but I limit what I shall allow to be acceptable, and your tone is certainly beyond that limit!"

Jack jumped off the seat and glared down at her. "I have a right to know why you place my loyalty to you below the others'," he shouted.

Lily stood up so fast Jack took a step back. "I'll not be spoken to this way! Now sit down and calm down, or I shall discuss nothing with you!"

Jack stood his ground, but he felt as if he had swallowed a sword. He closed his eyes tightly. "Did you ask me because of my past? Was it because you believe me to be a deserter?" He snapped his eyes open. Lily dropped her head, looking embarrassed.

Jack snorted in disgust. "You have much to learn about me yet!"

Lily looked up sharply, her eyes shining. "How dare you vent your anger on me, when it was you who told the others you were a deserter!"

"I didn't tell anyone that," spat Jack. "That was Argon's assumption, and at that time I was unwilling to discuss the truth with men I did not know—or trust!" He laughed a low bitter laugh. "You were going to ask me in my chamber when you came to tell me about the Grimfar plot, weren't you, but you changed your mind. Why, Lily? Did the thought disgust you? Were you sorry you'd bonded me?"

"For a moment, Jack, that is how I felt," confirmed Lily.

Jack stepped away from her. He knew she didn't understand, but he was deeply hurt by her reaction. He turned around so he couldn't see her.

"How am I to know better if you don't tell me the truth! Have you told anybody?" she shouted at his back.

Jack knew that was a fair point. "No," he answered quietly. Turning back round, he went and sat back down on the bench. He couldn't bring himself to look at her.

Lily's eyes lost their anger. She relaxed her stance and stood regarding him. "What has happened to you that was so bad you would rather people think you are a deserter?" She sat down beside him and placed her hand on his. "You don't have to tell me, but I can see this secret of yours has you trapped in a web of pain, and I would like to help you, if you will let me."

Jack sighed and met her gaze. "Have you known all along that I had not revealed the truth?"

Lily smiled. "I knew you had secrets; that wasn't hard to see. Your eyes hold a hardness of someone blotting out past pain and memories that are better forgotten. I have seen soldiers all my life, and even the ones who have faced war and death do not hold the hardness you do. You have faced something more painful than the war you fought in."

Jack stared hard at the floor. "I have seen things no decent man should ever see." He squeezed her fingers gently. "If I tell you, will you keep it to yourself? I don't wish for the others to know."

"On my life. I swear I will tell no one," said Lily very firmly.

"Then get comfortable, Lily, because this is a long story," warned Jack. He began telling her his painful tale. "It is common knowledge that Sanalow and Grimfar are at war because Grimfar began to invade Sanalow's lands. But only the steward of Sanalow and the army know the real story. Grimfar's people were already in our lands, long before the war began."

Lily looked puzzled.

Jack sighed. "Let me explain. The steward of Sanalow, Orbressen Fanlar, was the greatest, most loved steward Sanalow had ever had. He believed in helping anyone in need, so when the first survivors from the land of Grimfar appeared in Sanalow's hills, he rode out and asked if they needed aid. On first sight of the people, I believe even he was scared. How could people with such deformities be anything but evil or cursed? Grimfar people have grey eyes, which people find disturbing, because they are a mixture of black and white. They think it makes them untrustworthy.

"Fanlar didn't condemn them on first sight, though. He listened to their stories, and he understood that what they told him was the truth. Far from being monsters, these people were no different from you and I. They had, however, suffered greatly at the hands of the climate they had been forced to live in for hundreds of years." Jack paused for a moment to catch his breath.

Lily leant towards him. "I know about the destruction of Grimfar, but I don't know about its history after that point."

"I didn't either, to be honest," said Jack. "It was King Niar of Grimfar who educated me about his people. Evelyn Maude attacked Grimfar and decimated the magus army in the High City, but she had no idea that there was a secret underground city below it. Hundreds of people became trapped after the attack. For many years the people fought to tunnel out, and eventually they broke through to the surface. But far from their problems ending, they were forced to face new ones. The land was ruined, and the air had become poisonous; too much exposure to it killed. Learning this quickly, they were able to seal themselves in the underground city once more. They began a new mission to tunnel free of their lands completely. Although being in the tunnels again was successful in stopping more people from dying, it was too late to stop the fumes that had invaded their bodies. The children that were born after the breakthrough to the surface were born deformed—missing eyes, ears, fingers, toes, and mouths. There was nothing that could be done to stop it."

Jack shifted on the bench. "Although the deformities were terrible, the children born also possessed strength higher than any of the men in the tunnels, and they grew quickly. The people found that they were able to tunnel faster with the children aiding them, so they continued to have babies."

Lily had her hand over her mouth. "What an awful amount of suffering those people went through," she said, shaking her head sadly.

Jack touched Lily's face gently. "King Niar has quite a unique deformity; he has a deep diagonal scar that runs from below his right eye all the way to his chin." He traced a line with his finger across her face. "His wife, Maria, has missing toes and a missing eye. Niar must be forty or so now, so it shows just how potent that air is, as the generations before him were trapped nearly one thousand years ago."

Jack withdrew his hand. "As I said, Fanlar heard this story and aided them all he could. He gave them land so that they could start a colony outside of Grimfar, in hopes of stopping the deformities and giving the people of Grimfar a chance at a new life, away from their dark city.

"The colony was successful; the deformities began to lessen. King Niar was thrilled when he was blessed with his son, Revir, the first child of Grimfar to be born without deformity. For four years there was peace, but naturally that all changed when Fanlar died."

Lily gasped, "How did he die?"

Jack's face grew dark, "He was found in his chambers; he had been bludgeoned to death. It was deeply disturbing, and the Grimfar colony was immediately blamed."

"Did you think they did it?" Lily asked uncertainly.

Jack nodded. "Yes," he sighed, feeling ashamed. "After Fanlar's death, Jarrad Morridread was raised to steward of Sanalow, and he raised me to under-steward. It was my duty to help drive the people of Grimfar back to their dead land." Jack raked a hand through his hair and glanced at Lily, waiting for her reaction.

Lily was staring at him in amazement. "You are the under-steward of Sanalow!" she said in shock.

Of course that was the bit she was most interested in, thought Jack. "I *was* the under-steward of Sanalow," he corrected. "I lost my title when I betrayed Morridread."

Lily leant forward and grabbed his hands. "How—what happened? Under-steward of Sanalow—Jack!" she finished breathlessly.

Jack groaned and continued the story. "Sanalow and Grimfar fought for five years in an ugly battle. The people of Grimfar were terrified of returning underground. I begged Jarrad to reconsider, but he wouldn't listen to my council, so I secretly began negotiations with King Niar. I pleaded with him to flee to Emiscial and ask the magus for aid. Jarrad's army was no match for the warriors, so he changed his attack plan and sent me to kill all the women and children in the colony."

"Please tell me you didn't attack the women and children!" said Lily, looking disgusted.

Jack pulled his hands away from hers. "Of course I didn't, I'm not an animal. I went straight to Niar to warn him. But what I didn't know was that Jarrad had found out my duplicity, and he had sent men to the colony to begin killing everyone."

"What did you do?"

Jack looked up at the sky. He remembered the hopelessness he had felt; it was a painful memory. "I didn't know what to do. The scene in front of me was sickening. The soldiers were killing and torturing everybody. I spotted a boy cowering under a broken cart; I recognised him as Revir. I couldn't see his mother anywhere. Bailey and I galloped to save him from a soldier. I got there just in time before the soldier had the chance to kill him. Making a stand for what was right, I murdered the soldier and took Revir to safety. Niar found me making my way towards the mountains with a group of survivors. He understood that I had forfeited my life, and honouring me beyond words, he offered me a place with his people."

Jack stood up, feeling irritated; he began to pace, making patterns in the dust with his feet. "Then Jarrad found us. Niar and I fought him, letting the others flee. We were defeated, but I think they made it to Emiscial."

Lily was perched on the edge on the stone bench; she looked horrified. Jack came and sat on the floor in front of her. She put a hand on the top of his head, and he leant forward onto her lap. He began to cry, and she let him lie there until he stopped.

Jack looked up at her with bloodshot eyes and swallowed, knowing he had reached the crux of his story. "Niar and I were returned to Sanalow for execution, but I had two loyal men inside the hall, Sam and Leon, and they set me and Niar free. I disguised the escape to protect them, leaving them unconscious in the hall, and ran to collect my family, so we could flee."

"I didn't realise you had any family—" Lily broke off when she saw the fresh tears in his eyes. She moved off the bench and onto the floor next to him, putting her arm around his shoulders. "Oh, Jack ... I'm so sorry."

Jack wiped his face. "My parents died in an accident when I was five, and my Uncle Jon and his wife, Shannon, raised me. They had a son themselves a couple of years after I joined the army; he was called Tommy." Lily squeezed his shoulder in comfort.

Jack's voice grew hollow. "I was too late in reaching their house. Jarrad had already taken them all. Niar told me I had to flee, for there was nothing I could do to save them. But I had to try, so I made my way back into the central city, and Niar came with me. As we approached the circle, the alarm bell began to sound—my escape was known. Niar pushed me into the shadows, so we were hidden before the soldiers began to search the city; however, the soldiers never came. I could see straight before me the wide stone courtyard of the circle, and beyond that lay the steward's hall. In the middle of the circle rose the scaffold and the hanging ropes meant for Niar and me. I saw in the moonlight that the scaffold held three ropes. Then it all happened so fast. Guards led Uncle Jon, Shannon, and little Tommy out into the courtyard. I began running, but I didn't stand a chance of reaching them before the ropes went on, and there they were, swinging in the moonlight." More tears poured down Jack's cheeks. "I stood screaming—I was in full view—but no one moved to take me. Niar hurried me away."

Lily was now also crying silently. She kissed the top of Jack's head. "There was nothing you could do, Jack. Getting yourself killed would not have avenged your family," she said. "So that is how you came to leave the city?"

Jack wiped his face on his sleeve. "Yes. Niar and I fled in the direction of Emiscial. We spent several days in the mountains, and eventually we found some of his people. They told us that they had returned to Grimfar, the place they felt safest, but this group had left to search for their king. I refused to return with Niar. I planned to take revenge on Jarrad for the murder of my family. I vowed I would not rest until he was dead. Knowing my mind was made up, Niar let me go. He returned to his family, and I became a wayfarer." Jack rubbed his throbbing head. "The soldiers were sent out to search for me, but I remained hidden from them. Everywhere I went I heard stories from Sanalow. One morning I was hiding in a hayloft behind an inn when I heard a tale that chilled my blood. Jarrad Morridread was dead; he had taken a fall and broken his neck. The news shook me. I had stayed to carry out my revenge, but now Jarrad was dead. I had failed to avenge my family. It was too late for me to think of a life in Grimfar, because I didn't know the way into the city. I thought about Judelen, and I began travelling. I took the very long road through the savannah of Lanfar." Jack shrugged. "For some reason, I felt like Judelen would be where I could settle down into a new life. I longed to find something to live for again, and as luck would have it, I found you." He leant across and touched Lily's cheek. "You have given me a reason to survive, Lily, and for that I will always be grateful. You will never need to question my loyalty again—I am yours."

Lily lifted his hand off her cheek and kissed his palm. Jack felt his heartbeat increase. He gently took hold of her face, and leant towards her, wanting to feel her lips upon his.

The sound of footsteps running snapped them apart. Lily leapt up, straightening her gown. Jack rose too, feeling flustered. He turned to see who was approaching. It was Will. He flew into the garden and skidded to a halt before them.

He took a few gulps of air before he spoke. "Jack, I have come to find you—something awful has happened."

Lily stepped forward in concern. "What has happened, Will?" she asked.

"Your Majesty, it is Jack's horse."

Jack felt his heart leap to his throat. "Is his leg worse?"

Will shook his head. "He has been taken away to the slaughterhouse."

"What?" Lily and Jack shouted in unison.

"No one knew anything of it, until the stable hand told Ryan a short while ago, when he went to take Dancer out for his ride. He will already be dead by now. They kill their animals upon arrival!"

"How could this happen?" yelled Jack. "People can't just take the guards' horses!"

Will looked fearfully at Jack. "Argon did it. He must have ordered it straight after breakfast."

Jack felt rage rising inside him. He cursed loudly and pushed past Will and Lily; they both missed grabbing him. Lily ordered him to stop, but Jack ignored her and started running.

He raced towards the training area. It was Argon's rest day, and he would normally be found working the patterns. Sure enough, as Jack approached, he saw Argon alone in the ring. Jack pulled his sword free. Argon heard him approaching and turned.

He took one look at Jack's face and laughed. "You look upset about something, Jack!" he mocked, flicking his hair out of his eyes.

"I'll make you pay for what you did to my horse, Argon."

Argon raised his sword. "Didn't I tell you when you arrived, Jack, it was fit for nothing but the meat carts? I was doing it a favour."

"This was a cruel attack upon me, Argon—do not deny it," screamed Jack.

Argon smiled. "It was well worth doing just to knock you down a peg or two, Jack. I take a dim view of people who tell tales outside of my lessons. I can't kill you, but I had no problems killing that dumb animal of yours instead!"

With a cry of pain, Jack threw himself into the ring. His sword met Argon's and the bitter grating of steel upon steel rang around the walls. Jack's rage made him strike harder and faster than ever before. Argon fended off his blows, but soon sweat appeared on his face from the effort of stopping Jack's blade. On and on Jack fought, working through the patterns, willing his sword to find Argon's flesh. Argon pulled back and pushed for an attack. Jack took the opening he had given and brought his sword down onto his arm. With a cry, Argon dropped his sword, his hand moving to cover the wound on his arm from Jack's blade. Jack swung his leg round and toppled Argon onto his back, where he lay panting and cradling his wound. Jack raised his sword into the air and was preparing to push it down into Argon's heart when someone slammed into his side and knocked him to the floor. All the wind left his body, and his sword clattered to the ground.

"Get off me!" yelled Jack, pushing free of his attacker. It was Drake. Jack saw above him the faces of Lily, Will, and Sir Aidan. Ryan was pulling Argon to his feet. Drake got up and dragged Jack up with him.

"Don't move!" he warned as he lifted Jack's sword from the floor and went to remove Argon's.

Sir Aidan moved further into the ring, pointing a finger at Jack. "Place him under arrest," he told Will and Ryan.

"No!" shouted Lily stepping forward. "He shall not be tried for this! This was provoked!"

"He would have killed Argon if Drake had not have thrown him clear," said Aidan firmly. He turned his eyes onto Jack. "Do you deny that, boy?"

"No," said Jack defiantly, his chest heaving from the exertion of the fight. "I meant to kill him, and I will still kill him for what he has done!"

"This is over a horse, I believe. A horse is not worth doing murder for!" Aidan looked again to Will and Ryan. "Take him to his chambers and confine him there, until the king makes his decision."

Will and Ryan reluctantly moved to stand beside Jack. Will cast a look at Lily, waiting for her instructions. "Take Jack to his chambers," she said quietly.

Jack stared at her sharply. Lily moved closer to him and touched his chest. "Go, and wait, Jack. I must see my father. He could order you executed. If you want to stay alive, don't resist. Just go, and put your faith in me now."

Jack nodded and allowed Will and Ryan to lead him from the training area. Neither of them spoke to him as they led him through the palace to his chamber. They both cast him consoling looks before shutting him inside.

Jack leant against the door, breathing deeply. The rage had left him now, but the pain of losing Bailey began to throb in his heart. He let the tears flow freely down his dust-stained cheeks. He had failed his family and now his horse. He was facing a hangman's rope once more, so now he could add Lily and the other guards to his list. Jack slid to the floor and smashed his head backward against the doorframe, feeling like a failure and wanting to be put out of his misery.

11

THE SECOND STAGE

Salzar sat behind the king's desk in his personal chamber, casting nervous looks at Aidan. "Are you sure the second stage of our plan is ready to be carried out?" asked Aidan for the third time.

"Yes, Overlord, I have already hidden the seal in the chamber. There is more than enough evidence to convict them. No one will be suspicious, not even her, Overlord."

"Good," said Aidan crisply. "Have you informed Lillian of your decision for the boy, yet?"

"Yes, Overlord," said Salzar, wiping his forehead. "I have told her he is to be put to death for his attempt on Argon. She tried to make me change my mind, but even she knew he was doomed. I told her I would allow Jack to remain in his chambers until the actual date. I am delaying the execution for a few days, just to allow her to think I care for her feelings."

Aidan smiled. "Argon shall be rewarded for getting the boy worked up into committing that fool-brained attack. Salzar, tomorrow you shall execute our second plan. In a few days the boy shall be killed too. My manipulations over Lillian appear to be working. By the time he is dragged out to the ropes, she will be far from upset to see him die. We will be free of our problems for a while, once he's dealt with."

"Yes, Overlord."

Aidan moved towards the door. "See there are no hitches tomorrow. I must go now. I have left Lillian in my chambers, waiting for me. I must keep on making her believe that I love her, especially in her hours of need.

It is the key to taking control of her! I shall arrange for her to be there again tomorrow morning, so she is well out of the way while the plan is being carried out. Make sure the boy doesn't leave his chambers when he feels what is happening."

Salzar nodded again. Aidan cast one look towards him before leaving the chamber.

Lily sat behind the large harp in Sir Aidan's chambers, plucking the strings idly. The sun was rising slowly, filling the chamber with light. Sir Aidan had woken her early this morning so she could come and share breakfast with him.

Lily sighed deeply. She had been to visit Jack the previous day, after his attack on Argon. Her father had left it to her to tell him he was to be executed. Jack had accepted the news with no fuss. Lily believed he thought it was deserved. Jack had been grateful to her for allowing him to stay within his chambers and not the cells until his death day. He had sworn not to attempt escape. He had asked if she would consent to visit him each day while he waited, and she had been happy to say yes. She hid her pain from everyone except her guards. Through the bond they could feel her despair; even Jack could feel it, and she could feel his in return. The brothers spent a lot of time with her, and with Jack, trying to ease the pain they were all feeling. Her father would not change his mind about the sentence, and Sir Aidan had refused to try and make him do it; he believed justice must be done.

Lily pulled on a string of the harp again; it hummed as she released it.

Aidan came from his bedchamber, dressed in his usual black outfit, and moved behind her. "Come now, my love, you can play that so well! Play me a happy tune."

Lily smiled, although it was not a warm smile. "I am afraid there is little happiness in me today."

Aidan bent down and kissed her cheek. "You feel blue because of Jack?"

Lily nodded.

"Well, don't," said Aidan, his voice going hard. "He was ready to kill Argon, and a man who cannot control his temper is a danger to himself as well as you. He has accepted the fact he is to be executed. Why do you think that is?"

Lily shrugged her shoulders.

"It is because he knows he has done wrong and he wishes to keep his honour—what he has left of it, anyway—intact while he dies. If you grieve for him, you are insulting his honour, and he does not want that!"

"I see," said Lily firmly. "Well, I shall speak with him and ask him myself what I am allowed to do."

Aidan straightened up. "You are a fool, Lillian. You have much to learn about men and life. Still, go and ask him later if it makes you happy. Go and insult his honour."

Lily rose from the harp. "If you'll excuse me, My Lord," she said, not looking at him.

Aidan placed a hand on her shoulder. "You shall remain here now and see him later. Jack isn't going anywhere, and you must learn that you cannot run away and sulk just because someone puts you in your place!"

Lily sat back down. "As you wish," she snapped.

Aidan removed his hand and moved to the door. "You shall learn the lessons, Lillian, whether you wish to or not!" He stepped from the chamber and closed the door behind him.

Lily put a hand to her head. She was trapped, and she had no way out. All that lay before her was a miserable and controlled life.

Her head began to throb again; it had hurt so many times over the past two weeks, ever since the plot had been uncovered. Lily shook her head, willing the pain to go away. A noise behind her made her turn her head. She let out a gasp. A woman wearing a green silk dress and an emerald travelling cloak stood in the chamber with her.

Lily stood up angrily. "Who are you? How dare you enter here without permission!"

"You've spoken to me like this before, Lily," said the woman, moving closer to her. She raised her hand. "The Dark Knight has been tinkering in your head, and you have forgotten me. Remember?"

The woman touched Lily's forehead. Lily felt a cold sensation, and her memories came flooding back. She remembered the magus and the dark forces in Judelen.

The magus stood and regarded her. "Do you know who I am?"

"I remember now," said Lily, touching her head where the magus had touched her. "You visited me and told me of the dark forces. How did I forget it all?"

"The Dark Knight has been trying to manipulate you," said the magus.

Lily gasped. "He can cast spells on me? Could I have told him about you and not known what I was doing?"

"I believe if he had discovered about me I'd have been hunted down by now," said the magus carefully. "I think whatever he has been trying to do to you is to help progress his plan, and it appears you are a big part of it. He is hiding inside your inner circle, Lily. You must be vigilant."

The magus moved away. "I will be certain to contact you in person every day in case anything else happens. In the meantime, do you remember how to contact me?"

"Yes, but—"

"Then we'll speak soon. Be careful," said the magus abruptly, and a moment later she was gone.

Lily sat back down at the harp. Now that she could think clearly again, it could not be denied that there were differences appearing in the palace. They had started with Tomas kidnapping her. He had told Jack of a plot. Was he speaking of the dark forces invading or the Grimfar plot? Either way, how had he found out about it?

Another change had been Argon abusing his position and leaving her service for it. Now Jack was to hang for attempting to kill Argon! Her future husband had eyes for the glory of Judelen and Shangol, yet recently he had become kinder and gentler in his manner. Did he love her after all?

Her father was more distant these days; in fact, ever since his visit to Shangol he had been different. There was his erratic behaviour and lack of secrecy regarding his personal affairs, much to Lily's disgust. He never spent quality time with her anymore; instead, he gave all his free time to Aidan. Lily couldn't understand why he'd changed so drastically. A shudder rippled through her. Maybe the black magic had taken her father! He was the king, after all, and the best target was the head of the city.

Lily gasped out loud; it was no good! If her father was being forced to act by black magic, then she could do nothing to stop him. He had the final power over everything, except her personal bodyguard—but how could she use her bodyguard to her advantage? Maybe there was no way.

Her serfdom had not been successful in keeping one of her guards loyal, yet the Dark Knight had not been able to take her fully, so perhaps the magic was at least delaying him. Who was it, she wondered? If her loyal bodyguards were providing protection, then perhaps she had aided the Knight without realising it by removing Argon. Soon Jack was to be killed, and she had no power to save him.

Lily sighed and rubbed her head. She looked up sharply when she heard hurried footsteps approaching; she watched the door apprehensively. It burst open without anyone knocking. Lily expected to see Sir Aidan, but she was shocked to see Maggie instead, out of breath, with a look of horror on her face.

Lily stood up and rushed across the room; she took hold of Maggie's shoulders. "Maggie, whatever is the matter?"

Mistress Stratton stood before her, pale as snow and shaking. "I've come to tell you, Lily, about Ryan and Will."

"What about them?" asked Lily.

"They've been taken away by the guards; they're on the way to the gallows now!"

"What—no—that is not possible! Maggie, wherever did you hear that?"

Mistress Stratton stood wringing her hands. "I saw it, Lily. I saw Argon and Drake leading them down the corridor. I was ordered not to tell you; they said the king didn't want you distressed. They've found the traitors you told me they were looking for. Will and Ryan are the traitors!"

Lily wanted to be sick. Will and Ryan where her oldest and dearest friends; they would not betray her. This couldn't be true.

Lily felt faint. "No, Maggie, I don't believe this. I must question them myself," she resolved.

Lily felt for the bond between her and the two men, but it was dull and hazy. "I can't sense them, Maggie," she said in surprise.

"Lily, if you want to see them, you must hurry. They will be gone in a few minutes."

"The king cannot hang two people immediately, without trial," said Lily, shaking her head. "They must be on the way to the cells. I shall go and learn what has happened."

Lily began to leave the chamber, but Mistress Stratton ran to block her path, parts of her grey hair hanging loose from her bun.

"Please, Lily, you must listen to me! There is to be no trial. They are to be hanged today in the main square. I learnt from one of the servants on my way here that Sir Aidan found a seal in Will's chambers; it is the seal of Grimfar. Somehow they have forsaken their oaths to you and joined them. They have been under suspicion since Tomas kidnapped you. They think he was working with them too, and now that proof has been found, the king wants immediate execution!"

"Will and Ryan are the reason Grimfar warriors could find me in my palace?" said Lily in shock. "My father knew and said nothing? There is something not right here!"

"The land of Grimfar can't come again and attempt another attack, Lily! People will panic."

"Then why is my father hanging them in the main square, where the city will see? He will be telling the people about the attack if he does that!"

Lily felt the blood run from her face. If her father was taken, what could this mean? She gripped Maggie's shoulders again. "Tell me how to reach them before they get out of the palace," she ordered her.

Maggie pulled her off down the corridor and into an old storage room about halfway along the passage. Lily looked at her in surprise. Maggie pressed her hand against one of the cold stones in the wall. The wall slid away, revealing a spiral staircase, which wound downwards and out of sight.

"What is this?" asked Lily.

"The palace is full of these. They are escape routes and passageways that only us servants know of; we've used them for years. Now you must go down as far as you can go. When you reach the dead end at the bottom, touch the darkest stone to move the wall. You should arrive in a storeroom by the side entrance to the palace. That is the way the guards will be taking Will and Ryan."

Lily stopped admiring the hidden stairway. She nodded to Maggie and quickly took to the stairs, moving as fast as she could without falling. Her head began to throb, and it throbbed harder with each step. This wasn't real—how could this be happening?

Lily grunted as she turned the last spiral and fell into the stone wall. She quickly began searching for the darkest stone, which was hard in the dim light. Upon finding it, she pressed it quickly, and the wall slid away. She ran quickly from the staircase and into the small storage room, and she heard the wall sliding shut behind her. As she burst from the storeroom, the sudden increase in light made her shield her eyes. Her head thumped worse than ever.

The sound of footsteps came from along the corridor. Will and Ryan appeared from round the corner; both were bound and gagged. Argon and Drake were leading them with the aid of two other palace guards.

Lily rushed forward. "I demand to know what is happening here!" She glanced quickly at Will and Ryan. Both men looked extremely relieved to see her. Drake and Argon looked slightly stunned by her sudden appearance, but when Drake spoke he sounded as cold as ice. "It has been revealed that Will and Ryan are the palace traitors. They have been sentenced to immediate execution, on the king's orders," he barked at her.

Lily shook her head. "I shall not allow you to take them until I myself have questioned them. You shall remove their gags."

"I am afraid I have been ordered not to allow these men to speak to anyone. They must be hanged quickly, so as to destroy the plot against you and stop Grimfar from being able to plot any longer."

"Surely they must be questioned, Drake. Surely the king needs to know how powerful the Grimfar army has become, and I need to know if they really have been behind this plot on my life. I trusted them; I must be certain they betrayed me."

Lily looked at Will. Tears blocked his eyes, and he shook his head. Ryan tried to speak against his gag; worry lines creased his brow.

Lily touched each man on the cheek. "I don't believe you betrayed me." She looked away from both of them, tears in her own eyes. "I demand their release, Drake."

Drake stared hard at Lily. Lily gasped and stepped backward, covering her mouth in fear. Drake's irises had gone black. Lily glanced at Argon and saw that his were the same. She looked at Will and Ryan and felt her tears fall, they had the same light-blue eyes they had always had.

"The king has made his orders clear. The traitors are to go for immediate execution," said Drake coldly. Both men appeared not to have noticed Lily's shock.

"Escort the princess back to her chambers," Drake told the guards. The two of them grabbed Lily.

She began to struggle. "I won't let you do this!"

"It is done," said Drake sharply.

Lily looked at Will and Ryan, both were watching her with fear and pleading etched on their faces.

"I'm sorry," she whispered to them. "Forgive me."

Before anything else could happen, Drake shoved them away down the corridor, while the other two guards pushed her away. She looked back over her shoulder, screaming, until one of the guards covered her mouth.

She shook herself free of the guards as they reached the corridor for her chambers. "Leave me," she ordered. "I cannot try to save them now!"

The two guards made quick bows and moved away. Lily noted that both had black eyes. Once they were out of sight, she began to run towards her father's chamber. She reached his door and knocked once before entering.

Her father sat in one of his high-backed chairs, and Sir Aidan sat opposite him. Both had glasses of wine, and neither seemed concerned about the traitors waiting to be hanged.

Lily made a quick bow to her father. Before she could speak he stood up and walked towards her. "I take it you know the news of your bodyguards," he said calmly. "Your face tells me that much, and I shall stop you now before you can begin to argue with me. They are to hang today—shortly in fact. I am on my way now, with Sir Aidan to witness it."

Lily nodded. "I understand, Father."

The king frowned slightly. "I thought you'd be more upset than this, my dear. If I had known you would take it so calmly, I would not have ordered my suspicions and their arrest kept from you."

Lily smiled a weak smile. "At first I was shocked, Father. Wouldn't anyone have been? I could not understand such betrayal, but then I heard the evidence, and it made me sick to my stomach. I shall show no sorrow for traitors who work with monsters to kidnap me!"

Aidan stood up. "For your safety, I am taking you to Shangol as soon as possible. You and I shall wed as soon as Master Orden has been dealt with. I suspect he was in on the plot; Will and he spent much time having long detailed talks. I fear your most loyal bodyguards have always been Drake and Argon."

"And Tomas?" asked Lily.

The king patted her arm awkwardly. "He tried to kidnap you, my dear. Surely, knowing how close he was with the brothers, you cannot believe his actions were for your benefit. It is even possible he spoke to Jack on the road when he found you," he said reasonably.

Lily stared at her father and listened to the lies calmly, showing no outward sign of the horror she felt. His irises were black too! Aidan's had always been black, so if he was a part of the plot, how could she tell? Then it hit her—Aidan was the Dark Knight! It took all her will power not to scream in terror. Now it made sense! Tomas had discovered Aidan's identity and tried to save her life. Argon and Drake were both taken, so the Grimfar plot, the seal, and the city plans had all been set up to murder her other loyal guards. She knew what she needed to do.

"I am glad that this business is at an end, Father," said Lily with a bow of her head. "If you will excuse me, I shall retire to my chambers to prepare myself for the severing of the bonds."

Lily turned to Sir Aidan and curtsied. "My Lord, you were right to believe me young and a fool. I have much to learn. May you still wish to teach me to grow into a great queen."

Aidan smiled smugly. "You are already learning. May I suggest you hurry to your rooms now? The execution shall be happening very shortly."

Once outside her father's chamber, Lily rushed away up the corridor. She needed to see the magus again. She ran to her own chambers, pulled the fresh-cut red roses from their vase, and hung them from the window, hoping the magus would come quickly. Lily turned her thoughts to Jack. He must be loyal to her, for surely they wouldn't kill one of their own people. Lily checked that the corridor was clear before heading off towards the bodyguards' chambers.

Jack's hands were tangled in his hair. He was pulling it so hard it hurt, but the pain was nothing compared to the sensation of fear that was pulsating inside him. He knew something awful was happening; his brothers were in terrible trouble. He turned quickly at the sound of the door opening and watched Lily fly into his room.

He felt an immediate rush of relief and ran to her, grabbing her shoulders. "Lily, thank goodness you're here! Something is happening with Will and Ryan—you must help them!"

Lily stepped away from him suddenly. She grabbed his hair and pulled his head backwards; the light from the window hurt his eyes. She sighed, sounding relieved, and let him go. Then she threw herself at him and hugged him tightly. Jack felt confused, but there was no time to ponder. The brothers needed him.

He pulled away. "Lily, please listen to me. Will and Ryan are in trouble! I felt both of them briefly, and their fear was so strong! Then I felt Drake, and it was shocking—he felt pleased, and he didn't seem concerned at all. I know Will and Ryan are still alive, because the bond is here, but it's like they're sleeping. Can the bond be masked?"

Lily looked at Jack and sighed. "Yes. Something terrible is happening. There is evil at work here, and you and I must leave the palace now."

Jack frowned. "Evil?" He took hold of Lily's arm. "Never mind that; there is something you need to know. Will and I have been talking since the night the Grimfar warriors were killed in the city—only they weren't really Grimfar warriors, Lily. Will saw them before they were burnt, and they were just ordinary men, like you or I. Will suspected Aidan as the traitor; we were searching for proof."

Lily made a vexed noise. "You are right, Jack. Aidan is the traitor. He has ordered Will and Ryan executed. We must leave and find the magus; she came to me to tell me that Judelen has been taken over by the Dark Knight."

Jack stood, feeling confused. "The Dark Knight is dead."

Lily grabbed his hand. "No, he's Aidan, and I can't stop him alone. My father has been taken, and so have the guards: Argon, Drake, and many others. They want you dead! You were set up so they could get rid of you, just like the brothers. They haven't been able to take you three, so you have to be destroyed. Jack, I need you to remember something. When you were with Tomas, what colour were his eyes?"

Jack thought back to the Pass. "I remember now, they were blue. I saw death creep upon him through his eyes."

Jack felt as if his brain was connecting up a jigsaw, and he gasped. "On the bridge, when the wheels of your carriage collapsed, there was no real reason for them to do that. Tomas said he could see the blackness coming for him, and the moment he said it had arrived, the carriage went over the bridge. That could have been black magic."

Lily looked scared. "I can't fight magic. My only chance of saving my father and my city is with the help of this magus. Please, Jack, we must leave and find her."

Jack nodded. "All right. I'll get you to her, and then I'll come back for Will and Ryan. I can't leave them, Lily."

Lily pointed to the window. "Didn't you see the crowd around the main square? It has gathered for their executions. We cannot reach them in time; they are already lost. We must save ourselves."

Jack's eyes grew wider with each of Lily's words. He rushed to the window and stared down at the crowds around the main square. His breath caught in his throat when he spotted his brothers, bound and gagged, on the dais.

Lily ran up to him and tugged on his hand. "We must go now! As soon as they are dead, my father and Sir Aidan will come back here. We must be gone, or it will be too late."

Jack understood her urgency, and his face set in determination, "How can we escape the city without being seen leaving one of the exits?" he asked.

"I have a way," said Lily, running for the door. "At least, I hope I do." Jack prayed it was more than a hope.

Lily moved out into the corridor, checking it was clear. Jack stayed right behind her. "What way?" he asked quietly.

Lily didn't answer but kept moving until she reached the maids' storage room and pulled Jack inside. He wondered what an earth she was doing. As he turned to close the door, "Leave the door slightly open. I must have light," she told him.

Jack frowned but didn't argue. He scanned the storeroom, looking for weapons. He spotted a small scabbard on the wall; it contained a dagger. He took it and quickly slipped it onto his belt. A sudden grating noise made him look up. Lily was rising from where she'd been crouched by the wall, and the wall was disappearing from view. Jack could see the spiral stairs winding downwards. He glanced at her for an explanation.

"I'll tell you later, Jack. Right now we must go! Close that door now, and hurry through here."

Lily stepped onto the staircase, he pulled the door shut, and he ran back to follow her. He held her arm to stop her from slipping on the climb down.

"Where does this lead to?" he said in a whisper.

Lily stopped for a moment. "I don't know, exactly. There are hidden stairways all through the palace. I just hope that this one leads outside."

"What do you mean you don't know!" hissed Jack.

"We had to get away quickly, Jack, and these stairways are not known to any but the servants. I thought it might just give us time to get away." Lily began moving again. Jack followed, saying nothing.

Suddenly he heard a noise, and he tugged on Lily's arm. "Did you hear that?"

Lily stopped walking and listened. Jack was certain he could hear distant footsteps echoing up the stairs towards them.

"Do you think it is a servant?" he whispered. He dreaded to think what they would do if they discovered them.

"Just be ready to act," Lily replied firmly. Understanding the instruction, Jack carefully moved past her, ready to silence the person if need be.

A light appeared below them. It grew bigger as the footsteps grew louder. Jack flattened himself against the wall. The stranger climbed the final steps, Jack felt Lily tense next to him, torchlight flooded the area, and the stranger glanced up from under a hood. Jack pounced and grabbed one arm, pulling the torch away. He reached up and tore the hood down, preparing to use it as a weapon.

Lily suddenly tugged on his sleeve. "Release her, Jack. It's the magus."

12

THE CHILD OF LIGHT

As Jack stared at the magus standing before him, he felt a mixture of fear and hatred. He'd read about their yellow eyes and flawless features, protected by immortality, and the descriptions in the history books were incredibly accurate. Of course, with his hatred of magic, he'd never desired to meet one in real life. She stood regarding him in shock. She heard Lily's voice and glanced at her; then she looked back at Jack and tilted her head, looking cross. When Jack let go of her arm, she motioned for the torch, and he handed it over.

Lily made a quick curtsy. "Forgive us. We did not know it was you."

The magus straightened her travelling cloak before fixing Lily with her stare. "I was not expecting to find you here either!" she said firmly. "I was coming to answer your summons. I take it there have been some developments."

Lily nodded and opened her mouth. The magus quickly raised her hand. "This is not the place to discuss it. Why have you fled to these secret stairways?"

Lily glanced at Jack, but he shrugged at her. He hardly knew what was going on. It was better for her to explain it.

"We have left because Jack is in danger from the Dark Knight. He has not been taken, so his death has been arranged. My other two loyal bodyguards are also about to be executed in the main square."

"How do you know he is not caged?" asked the magus, eyeing Jack suspiciously. He narrowed his eyes at her in annoyance.

"I found a way to identify the Dark Knight and those under his power. You can see it in their eyes—the irises become black. I learnt that my other guard, Drake, is taken, and so is my father. I have seen guards and servants alike with the same signs." Jack listened in horror.

"The only three men who I found unchanged are Will, Ryan, and Jack. My mistress Maggie is also all right—oh no, I've left her behind!" Lily turned to run back up the stairs towards the palace. Jack grabbed her at the same time as the magus.

The magus spoke quickly. "You cannot go back. She should come to no harm for the moment," she reassured Lily.

She studied Jack again before turning back to Lily. "We shall return to my home in the city and make preparations to leave Judelen. If the king has been taken, then you cannot remain here, for he can order you, and you must obey him."

The magus held out her hand. A ball of red magic appeared in it, then rose into the air, and shot away up the staircase.

"Was that magic?" asked Jack.

"Yes, I have sealed the doorway above so none can enter this stairway." The magus began walking down the stairs. "We must begin moving. We need to be back at my home before your escape is detected."

Jack glanced at Lily, who signalled that he should follow her. The stairs wound down for a short while before coming to a dead end. The magus did not locate the darkest brick but instead produced another ball of red magic, which she sent into the wall to make it open.

"I sealed this passageway against the palace servants, so I could use it without being detected," she said before Jack could ask.

The wall slid open to reveal a long tunnel. The magus moved inside, and Jack led Lily in behind her. He moved to walk beside the magus and lowered his voice. "What, exactly, is going on?"

The magus kept looking ahead, but she answered him. "You already know the Dark Knight lives. He has come into Judelen City to carry out a plan for his mother. She is also still alive, but she is trapped in a prison. I don't know what the plan is, though," she stated calmly.

Jack rolled his eyes. "Let me get this straight. The Theanic Order have known all along that the witch and her son still lived." Why was he not surprised by that fact? "Why an earth should we trust you then?" he snapped.

The magus did look at him this time, and she didn't look pleased. "I came to aid you. Without me the princess would not have known of the danger growing in her city." She glowered at him and turned away.

Jack moved back to walk with Lily, and he slipped his hand around hers. "The magus are liars, Lily. Are you sure we should go with this one?" he whispered.

Lily sighed. "I don't know what else to do, Jack. I know Judelen is in danger. I have seen that much for myself, and I don't know anyone but her who can help me."

Jack sighed. It seemed he had no choice but to accept the circumstances. "Does she have a name?" he asked Lily.

The magus turned round to face them. She looked Jack squarely in the eye. "My name is Mia, and despite your lack of trust, Jack, I am here to help you, for I am a protector of this world. It is my job to help destroy the Black Order."

Jack frowned. "Can you actually do it, or is that just another lie?"

He could tell Mia wasn't at all impressed by his smart comments. Her tone of voice grew sharp. "The Theanic Order made a mistake thinking Evelyn Maude was dead and the Dark Knight was powerless. We work tirelessly to find a way to destroy their magic, and we will win the war, make no mistake about that!"

Jack screwed his hands into fists in irritation. "You're like children playing with fire!" he said angrily.

Mia pursed her lips. "You know nothing, Jack, about magic or its formation. You are the child here. Keep quiet and leave the Order to their work," she said acidly.

With a gasp, Lily fell down in a faint. Jack felt the snapping of the bonds at the same instant. He could hear the snapping of two necks pounding inside his ears. Will and Ryan were dead.

Mia moved forward. "What is wrong?" she asked dropping to her knees next to Lily. Jack also fell to the floor, fighting for breath. His eyes stung and his body shook. He felt a sensation like hot needles sticking into his skin and gritted his teeth against the pain. Mia took hold of his head in her hands. "Are the two loyal guards dead?"

Jack nodded weakly. His vision was blurring in and out of focus, and he felt sick.

"You must not let the sensation clog your senses, Jack. What you feel is less than half of what the princess is feeling right now. You must stay strong and help me get her to my home. I cannot give you any treatment for the pain here. If you don't help her, Jack, she could die," said Mia urgently.

Jack heard her words. He blinked and blinked again, to clear his vision. He suddenly thought to seek the deep calm he used for training. He felt his vision begin to clear, and he pushed away the pain. He glanced round to find Lily; she was unconscious, her breathing ragged and uneven. Jack forced himself to get up. He knelt next to Lily and placed her head onto his arm. Then he scooped her up, staggering backward. Mia reached out and steadied him.

"I'm all right," he said simply. "Lead the way, Mia." She wasted no time in rushing ahead up the passageway. Jack felt the sobs rise in his chest. He didn't fight them; he knew it was vital to mourn his brothers and let healing begin. Mia kept glancing back at him but kept her pace fast. Jack's arms began to burn from carrying Lily's limp weight. It felt like hours passed before, finally, a wall appeared ahead, blocking the tunnel. Mia sent more magic into it, but the wall did not slide away.

Mia turned to Jack. "Beyond this wall lie the ruins of the original city. My house is close now, but we must pass through the streets. Wait here while I check that we have a clear path."

Jack knew that if they had reached the old ruins, the tunnel had transported them as far as the edge of Middle Town. Mia stepped through the wall and vanished. Blinking in surprise, Jack placed Lily on the floor and sat down next to her. He hoped Mia wouldn't be long. He leant out and touched the wall she had walked through—it was solid. *Magic*, he thought bitterly.

Mia eventually reappeared as suddenly as she had vanished, making Jack jump. He climbed to his feet and picked Lily up again, Mia touched his arm and gently guided him to step through the wall. Passing through the magic barrier sent shivers down his spine. She led him round several corners and past many deserted buildings, until finally she moved directly towards an old house, which looked ready to collapse. The walls were cracked and the windows void of shutters. Many of the roof tiles lay scattered on the street below. Jack could see holes through the roof. He glanced at Mia in confusion.

She motioned him to the doorway. "Step inside, Jack."

Jack moved past her and stopped before the doorway. He could see nothing inside but blackness. He stepped through the doorway and then stared in amazement. Light filled the hallway he now stood in. It ran down straight ahead of him into a kitchen. Jack could see the scrubbed oak table through the far doorway. The walls, floor, and ceiling were clean and made completely of grey stone. A deep-red rug ran down the hallway, covering the stone floor. There was a doorway off either side of the hall; each had a wooden door hung from its frame.

"Please step through the door to the right," said Mia from behind Jack. He turned round and saw behind her a wooden front door, closed to block out the street.

"How can this be?" he asked in wonderment.

Mia moved past him to the door on the right, she opened it and stood aside to let him through with Lily. "Welcome to my house, Jack," she said as he walked past her into her sitting room. "Lay the princess down on the double chair," said Mia as she crossed to a small table in the corner.

Jack placed Lily carefully down and looked around. "What magic made this house?"

"It is called an illusion, Jack. It is a spell I can perform with my gift of whispering. I needed a house in the city where no one would find me. The old city proved perfect. I cast the spell that makes people see what I want them to see, from the outside, but I rebuilt the inside to suit my needs." Mia smiled and regarded the room with pride.

A thought occurred to Jack. "How is it that your magic is not detected by the Dark Knight?" he asked.

"This part of the city is naturally filled with white magic, so he would not sense anything unusual," she answered shortly.

Mia came over to him with two glasses in her hand. "Sit down, Jack. You must rest whilst your body works through the stress of losing those bonds." She handed him a glass. "This medicine will ease your physical pain. I have also added an herb that will affect how much you feel through your bond. There is still one attached to you whom we don't wish to feel your emotions."

A part of Jack still couldn't believe Drake was a part of the dark forces. He had no problem accepting that Argon was, but Drake had often shown kindness. It hurt Jack to think of him as an enemy. "Will I still sense him?" he asked Mia.

"No, this medicine cannot only act for one person."

Jack looked sceptically into the glass of dark liquid; he drank it down in one gulp, grimacing from the bitter taste. Mia moved from him to kneel by Lily. She held her head up enough to open her mouth and pour the same mixture down. Lily's eyes flickered slightly, but she did not wake.

"She will be all right, won't she?" asked Jack, staring at Lily's limp form.

"She should come around shortly," said Mia, standing once more. "There is little time to waste now. I must consult my orb to see if I can access the palace."

Jack watched as Mia placed a large glass sphere onto the floor close to the fireplace. "I shall need your help, Jack. My magic can only do so much. I need you to enhance my abilities."

Jack stiffened. "But I have no magic!"

Mia smiled. "I am aware of that. I need you to sit opposite me and place your hands on the sphere."

Jack hesitated but decided this was not the time to wage war on magic. He sat down as instructed and placed his hands onto the sphere before him. It felt warm to the touch. Mia placed her hands onto it, and it lit up like a ball of white flame, burning Jack's eyes.

"Close your eyes, Jack," commanded Mia. "I need you to think of the palace and see it clearly in your mind."

As Jack thought of the palace, it appeared within the white light of the sphere. The image showed the palace from the main gates.

"Jack, you must move into the palace, through your mind, and follow the paths to the royal apartments." The images in the sphere shifted as Jack sought out that part of the palace.

"Remember what time of day it is, and focus on where you think the king will be now."

Jack moved to the official greeting chamber. It was empty.

"Where else could he be?"

Jack moved to the king's chambers, but they were also empty. He frowned.

"Who might he be with, Jack—the other guards?" urged Mia.

Jack thought of Aidan, and the image moved to his chambers. The king appeared in the sphere alongside Sir Aidan.

"Keep focusing on the king and this man, Jack, I can now use my magic to hear them speak."

For a moment there was silence. Jack held the images firmly in his head. Suddenly their voices filled the sitting room. Jack opened his eyes to look into the sphere.

"She cannot have gone far," said the king in an urgent voice. "The palace guards will find her shortly. She could not have made it out of the palace in so little time."

"What of the boy, Salzar?" said Aidan in a deadly whisper.

"He cannot have gone far either, Overlord,' said the king, wiping sweat from his brow.

Mia gasped. "The Dark Knight is revealed!" she said quietly.

"Why was she not being guarded?" spat Aidan across the room to another person standing in on the conversation.

"I ordered guards to escort her back to her chamber, Overlord. I don't know why they left her," said Drake's voice.

"Find the guards you assigned and learn why they left her. After they tell you, kill them for failing me," said Aidan crossly.

The sound of a door opening filled Mia's house.

"Drake, if she is not returned, then I shall punish you for failing. Do I make myself clear?"

Drake's voice trembled. "Yes, Overlord. I shall find her," he said. The chamber door closed.

"Wherever she has gone into hiding, she has taken the boy with her, Salzar. He is a threat to my plans more now than ever before. I should have killed all three guards together when I had the chance. If he is not killed, he could destroy my chances of securing the vessel."

Mia gasped again, but she said nothing.

"How can that be, Overlord?" asked Salzar.

"He is in love with her, you fool, and she loves him, even if she dares not admit it."

Mia's eyes flashed to Jack briefly before returning to the sphere.

Aidan covered his face with both hands. "This human form makes me weak and foolish. Of course love provided her with a protection against me. I should have been quicker in preparing Lillian to become the vessel, but I've been distracted cleaning up all your mess! Tell me now why I let you live!"

Salzar stood visibly trembling before Aidan. Aidan moved closer to him. "What type of death did I promise you? A slow one, I believe, full of pain. Well, I shall not kill you yet, Salzar, but I think pain would help you remember that I do not accept failure."

Black magic shot from Aidan's hands and surrounded Salzar. Jack could see the agony he was in without needing to hear the screams. His body stood rigid, and his skin turned bright red. Blood began to seep through and fall to the floor around him, until all his skin was open and bleeding.

Salzar fell to the floor like a sack; he lay twitching and gasping for air. A knock sounded at the door.

"Enter," said Aidan casually. "Argon, you have news for me?"

Argon entered the chamber; he glanced at Salzar, twitching on the floor, and grimaced.

"Your report, Argon," said Aidan, more firmly.

"Overlord, I searched the area in the main corridor where the princess stood waiting for us with the prisoners. There was only an old storeroom close by. Upon closer examination, I found that it contained a secret staircase, leading to the upper levels of the palace. It must have been how she beat us to the ground floor."

Aidan looked surprised. "Did the king know of these stairways, Salzar?"

"No, Overlord, he had no knowledge," whimpered Salzar.

"If the king didn't know, then the princess didn't know, either. Someone told her of it. Who else could have known of hidden stairways in the palace?"

"I may know the answer, Overlord," said Argon carefully. "Drake and I encountered Mistress Stratton when we were leading Will and Ryan from their chambers. We told her nothing of what was happening, but there were servants about who must have filled her in on the story. I believe she would have gone straight to the princess to tell her the news. She must have used a stairway to reach your chambers, inform the princess, and instruct her to beat us to the main corridor."

"Of course!" said Aidan. "If anyone knows this palace like the back of a hand, it will be her and the other servants. Find her and bring her here immediately."

Argon nodded and left.

Aidan looked down at Salzar. "Have you learnt your lesson?" he asked menacingly.

"Yes, Overlord."

"Good. Then I shall seal your skin, but the pools of blood on the floor I shall leave for you to wipe up with your own hands, as a further reminder."

As they watched, Salzar's skin healed over.

"Clean up your mess now," ordered Aidan.

Salzar shuddered; he began to mop up the blood on the floor.

Another knock sounded on the chamber door. Drake and Argon entered, with Mistress Stratton between them. She glanced round nervously. When her eyes came to rest on Salzar, mopping up the blood, she screamed in horror.

Aidan moved forward and seized her round the throat. "Silence!"

Mistress Stratton stopped screaming and stood panting in panic.

"Tell me, Maggie, how many secret stairways are there in the palace?"

Mistress Stratton's eyes darted around. "I don't know what you are talking about," she whispered.

"Do not waste my time with lies, Maggie. Tell me what I ask, or I'll put you on the floor to mop up blood with the king."

Mistress Stratton whimpered and began to cry. "There are many stairways on all the palace levels. I don't know how many exactly," she blurted out.

"Do they all start in a storeroom?"

"Yes."

"Do any of them lead outside the palace?"

"Some do lead into the inner city. There may be others that go further. Most just run through the palace levels."

Aidan turned to Argon. "Go to the boy's chambers and begin a search of all the storerooms closest to his room. They will have wanted to leave quickly without being seen."

Argon left the chamber immediately.

"Drake, begin a full search of the city. She must be found and brought back to me. You can kill the boy on sight."

Aidan turned back to regard Mistress Stratton, who he still held firmly in his grasp. "You have been very helpful, Maggie. For that I shall not make you mop up blood from the floor."

Mistress Stratton gasped in relief.

Aidan's lips curled. "I cannot let you run off and tell anyone about our little meeting, either."

Mistress Stratton's eyes widened in terror again. Aidan twisted her head round until she faced the door behind her; her neck snapped under the pressure. Aidan let her body drop to the floor. "When you have finished on the blood, Salzar, take care of the good mistress for me."

A scream sounded in the room, but it was not from the palace. Lily sat on the double chair, staring at the image in the sphere, her hands clawing at her cheeks and tears running down her face.

13

DECISIONS

Jack jumped up from the ground and rushed towards Lily. Mia made a vexed sound as the image in the sphere faded away, but then she, too, turned towards Lily.

Lily stared hopelessly at the now-black sphere.

"Is it true?" she asked, her voice shaking.

"Your mistress is dead," said Mia calmly. "Everything you saw and heard in the sphere is happening now."

"You said she would be safe!" Lily screamed in anger.

Jack glanced at Mia and then back to Lily. "How much did you see and hear?" he asked quietly.

Lily rubbed her forehead. "All of it," she said, just as quietly. "But there is so much I do not understand. Mia, what did Aidan call me?"

Mia stood up from the floor and moved to sit in one of the other chairs. "He called you 'the vessel'," she said. "It appears the Dark Knight has stolen an idea originally thought up by the Theanic Order and twisted it to suit his needs. He has chosen you to harvest a child that he believes he can use to destroy the world of everything light."

Jack frowned. "Did you know before today that Lily was to be turned into 'the vessel'?" he asked.

"Certainly not, or I would have removed her from Judelen immediately."

"That still doesn't explain much," said Lily. "You said this idea of a vessel was yours originally, so what was it supposed to do?"

Mia leant forward on her elbows and regarded Lily. "We created a vessel and planned to use it to make the Child of Light, a child born from love, an innocent soul, infused with the element of light, something the dark forces couldn't touch. The combination would have been strong enough to undo the black magic and cleanse the world."

"Then why didn't the Child of Light come to be?" asked Jack, sitting by Lily. He rubbed her back to help keep her calm.

"Because Evelyn Maude thwarted our plan by destroying our vessel," spat Mia bitterly. "But now the tables have turned again. We have a second chance to make the Child of Light, through Lily."

Lily looked terrified. Jack hugged her tightly and glared at Mia. "You are not doing anything to Lily! I will not let you!"

Mia frowned. "You don't understand, Jack. This is a good thing! Lily can have the Child of Light and save the world. We need to get to Emiscial immediately. The Dark Knight must not know his secret has been discovered before we turn his plan on its head and secure his vessel." Mia laughed loudly. "Finally the Theanic Order have the upper hand in this war again!"

Jack's blood boiled. He stood up and moved until he stood looming over Mia. "I said no, Mia!" he hissed in a deadly whisper. "You are not involving us in your magic war. Lily is not a pawn for you to use."

Mia stood up, looking flabbergasted. "Jack, you have no choice here. This has to happen. The war must be won for the Light."

"You vile witches and your magic!" screamed Jack.

Mia recoiled then, her face growing red in anger. "Don't you dare speak to me like that! I am a magus of Emiscial, boy! You will show me some respect."

"Call me boy again, and I'll—"

Lily leapt to her feet and grabbed his arm. "Calm down, Jack, please. We don't know everything yet. We need to hear Mia out. Let her explain about this plan in more detail. Then we can decide what to do—together."

Jack and Mia stood locked in their battle of wills, both breathing heavily and neither prepared to give up the fight. Lily moved forward to stand a little in front of Jack, but she held on to his arm.

She faced Mia. "You need to explain this plan in more detail, Mia. Tell me exactly how this child is supposed to win the war," she said firmly.

Mia's eyes flickered to Lily, and she sighed deeply. She cast another nasty look at Jack before retreating to the chair and sitting down. "What do you want to know?"

"Just start from the beginning," snapped Jack.

Mia clenched her fists; she ignored Jack and focused on Lily. "I can't tell you everything right now, Lily; we simply don't have the time. The Dark Knight is searching for you. I need to get you to the safety of my city and to my sisters. Once there, you will be safe, and I can explain everything to you in as much detail as you like."

Lily nodded. "All right, Mia. We'll agree to leave Judelen with you now, so long as you promise to explain all this later and promise to let me make up my own mind about it."

Mia stood up. "Fine," she said quickly. "We need to make preparations to leave right now. You must help me."

Jack didn't move. "Surely this problem can be dealt with here and now," he said quietly.

"I just told you we don't have the time!" spat Mia.

Jack shook his head. "I mean, surely we can create the Child of Light right now."

Mia looked confused. Jack pressed his advantage. "You said that the Child of Light would be born of love, an innocent child, infused with the power of Light. Well, I love Lily, and she loves me. We could marry right now and create the Child of Light together. I assume you need to use some kind of white magic on the child, but as long as you swear it will be fine, I don't see why we couldn't end this war today."

Jack turned Lily round to face him. "That is, of course, if you would do me the honour of consenting to be my wife."

Lily stared at Jack with wide eyes. A smile suddenly spread on her face, and she nodded wildly. Jack's face split into a grin, and he bent down to kiss her.

Mia let out cry and leapt in between them. "Stop it, you foolish children. You have no idea what you talking about!" She glared at Jack. "You cannot marry Lily. The Child of Light will not be your child. King Rain, the Guardian, must create it. If you two start taking to each other's beds, you will destroy the power of the vessel, so do not touch each other again!"

It was Jack's turn to recoil. "But you just said—"

"I know what I said, but it is not as simple as you think!" cut in Mia. "We need to leave for Emiscial," she said, moving away towards the door.

"Get back here!" shouted Jack. "What are you saying—that Lily and I cannot be together, even though we are in love?"

Mia turned back to regard him. "That is exactly what I am saying. Now, I will not discuss this further! Remember your place, bodyguard. Lily is a princess, and her future lies with a king. She will marry King Rain and secure the Child of Light." Mia stalked from the room and slammed the door shut behind her.

Jack turned to Lily. "No way are they doing this! This is wrong; we love each other. They can't stop that. They are making a mistake!"

Lily regarded Jack calmly; then she sighed and stepped away from him. Jack watched her move away. Confused by her action, he reached out to take her hand.

"Don't, Jack," said Lily quietly.

"Lily, I don't understand," said Jack, lowering his hand.

Lily raised her chin and looked Jack in the eye. "Whatever is going on right now, it is bigger than the two of us. We cannot afford to be selfish, if the world is at stake by our actions. We need to be just bodyguard and princess until we escape the city and get to Emiscial."

Jack stiffened; he felt hurt beyond words. "Fine," he said quietly.

Lily nodded and left the room in search of Mia. Jack gave himself a moment to process his thoughts before going after the two women.

They began preparing to clear the house. Mia barked out instructions for Jack and Lily to follow, whilst she herself moved around collecting things she would not leave for them to pack. Most of her belongings were to be abandoned, for the three of them needed to travel as lightly as possible.

As Jack placed the last pack down in the kitchen, he raised the question he had been thinking about. "How are we getting to Emiscial, anyway?"

"We are riding, of course," said Mia simply, her tone still cold towards him.

Lily frowned. "We don't have horses," she said.

Mia laughed. "Did you think I would not be ready to leave the city quickly if the time came? I have brought two extra horses. I admit, I did not know Jack would be joining us, but he can ride the one I was going to use for a packhorse. He is big enough to take his weight."

Mia led the way out through the kitchen to the stables beyond. A bay mare hung her head from the first stable. She had a star and snip on her face. Her delicate figure and thin, silky coat named her a native of Emiscial. "This is my soulmate, Leena," Mia told them.

"Why do you say soulmate?" asked Lily. "She is a horse!"

Leena snorted loudly. Mia shook her head and raised her hand to calm the mare. "You do not understand my people and our ways. I do not own Leena. She chose me to raise her; she is my friend."

Leena pawed the ground inside her stable. Mia made a soothing noise. "She does not understand our ways, Leena. Do not be angry."

Lily looked at Jack. "Do you understand?"

Jack nodded slowly. "I understand that a horse can be your closest friend and that it can show you a form of love more devoted than any other." Jack turned to Mia. "I admit I do not know your ways, but I know from experience how deeply attached you can grow to these fine animals."

"You speak like one who has lost," said Mia gently.

Jack pictured Bailey in his mind, and his voice died in his throat. "Jack's old horse was the only thing he kept from his past," explained Lily. "One of my old bodyguards, Argon, had him killed for revenge."

Mia nodded sadly. "People can be so cruel." She moved away to the middle stable. "Lily, this mare is to be your mount." Lily looked inside the stable. Her mare was short and a good deal plumper then Leena. She was a dappled grey colour and built for hard labour. Jack took her for a Judelen farm horse.

"Have you named her already?" asked Lily, patting the mare on the nose.

"I did not choose her name; that was for her mother to do!" said Mia impatiently. "She is called Apple. She was born in an orchard outside the city, four summers ago. I brought her from the meat yard. Her owner had come to be in great debt, so he had sold her to help pay it. I arrived just in time, for she was to be killed that day." Mia took a steadying breath. "I despise these cities and how they run their industries. They would kill a perfect and intelligent animal for meat. It is sick enough that people think they have the right to buy and sell them at will!" Mia took another steadying breath. "Forgive me, I cannot control my emotions when I think of how this world has turned out." Mia patted Apple's nose. "She is a steady-footed lady, and although she is not as fast as Leena, she will carry you safely to Emiscial."

Mia moved towards the last stable. "You must take good care of this horse, Jack, for he is hurting from both physical and mental pains. I managed to save him from the meat yard when I picked up Apple. I think a part of him wished I had left him there to die."

Jack shook his head in pity. "What is his name?"

"He will not talk to me, so I do not know his name. He was most reluctant to leave Inner Town."

Jack moved past Mia to peer inside the stable. For a moment he thought the horse had gone, then he saw him lying in the straw. He certainly did look very unhappy.

Mia carried on explaining. "He is a native of Emiscial; I can tell from his colouring. No other city in the kingdom can breed the golden coat of Emiscial horses. I don't know how he ended up in Judelen," said Mia. She looked at Jack and gasped in alarm, for tears were running freely down his face.

"What is wrong?" she asked.

Jack wiped his eyes and laughed aloud. "I can tell you how he came to be in Judelen, and where he was before that. I can even tell you his name. It is Bailey, and he has been my friend for a very long time!"

Lily, who had remained talking softly to Apple, looked up when she heard Jack. "Is it really him?" she screamed in excitement. "Oh, Jack—it *is* Bailey!"

Bailey had heard Jack's voice and risen from the ground. Jack opened the stable door, and Bailey shot through it into the courtyard. He began to run in circles, kicking his legs in celebration. Jack and Lily laughed as they watched him cavort. Mia had a hand over her mouth in disbelief.

After a minute or two, Bailey stopped dancing and trotted over to Jack. He placed his head down and allowed Jack to wrap his arms around his neck in greeting. "I've missed you, boy," said Jack, patting his neck. "I'm so sorry I was not there when Argon took you. I should have been. Forgive me."

Jack buried his head into his friend's mane and cried. Lily wiped tears from her eyes as she watched them reunite.

"Well, it is safe to say I did not expect this!" said Mia smiling. "I am sorry to have to break up your reunion, but we must get moving. The guards in the city will be looking for us by now."

Jack broke away from Bailey, who raised his head and snorted contentedly. "Will he be fit to travel? He has an injured leg."

Mia nodded. "I have given him some medicine; his leg should be fine now." She patted Bailey on the neck. "For appearance' sake we shall tack the horses. I have removed the bits from the bridles to make them more comfortable. Each of us must carry a pack."

"How long will it take to reach Emiscial?" asked Jack.

"If we ride hard and fast, we could do it in three days and three nights. We must leave Judelen and travel into Lanfar. Once we are clear of the savannah, we can follow the River Nonnon along the border of Sanalow. We must avoid most of the major towns and sleep out in the countryside. However, if our journey is trouble-free, I will allow us to stop off in the village of Lowfar, Sanalow, to stock up on supplies. We have very little to take with us now, and hunger will set in by the second night."

Lily looked over at Jack. "Is it wise to stop in Sanalow?"

"Lowfar is the safest stop we can make; there should be no problems for us in Sanalow," answered Mia.

Lily continued to look at Jack; Mia looked at them both. "Is there a problem?"

"No," said Jack quickly.

"But what about—" Lily cut off at the look on Jack's face.

Mia frowned. "You two keep too many secrets between you. If there is a problem, then you must share it with me now!"

Jack looked at Mia. "There is no problem," he said.

"Very well, then. You had better go and prepare yourselves and your horses for the journey; we shall leave shortly."

Mia left Lily and Jack alone. Jack stood silently staring at the ground until finally Lily turned and walked away without a word. Jack turned his attention back to Bailey. His faithful friend butted him gently with his head, and Jack knew he understood his problems.

Twenty minutes later, Jack was seated on Bailey's saddle. He had a pack secured to his back, and he was feeling nervous about the journey he was about to undertake.

Lily sat upon Apple; she appeared to be looking at nothing, but Jack caught her glancing his way every now and then.

Mia had made a final sweep of her house and was just climbing up onto Leena. She turned to speak to both of them. "The guards are out looking for us, but I do not intend to make it easy for them. I am going to perform a spell that will make us look different to anyone who views us. It is illusion similar to what I used on the house. It will not harm you in any way."

Lily nodded that she understood. Jack swallowed his distrust and followed suit.

Mia closed her eyes. Jack felt cold; a moment later it was gone. Jack didn't feel any different. He glanced over at Lily and cursed. Lily looked nothing like Lily now! She was older, and her long golden hair was now dark and short, with grey streaks running through it. Lily was regarding Jack with similar shock. "What do I look like?" he asked.

"Different!" said Lily with a laugh. "You have short, reddish hair, and your face is much wider and older. You look just like a trader!"

"That is the idea," said Mia gently. She now appeared no older then fifteen. "A trader, his wife, and helper will draw no looks from the guards. We should hopefully move out of Judelen without any problems," she explained.

Mia moved a now-white Leena behind Jack and Lily. "I must ride behind you. A helper follows her employees. I can also observe better from this position. If for any reason we are stopped, you, Jack, must do all the talking. Tell them we are travelling to Sanalow in time to buy the summer dyes; they should not question you on it. If they ask you for a name, tell them you are Master Turner, your wife is Juliet, and your helper is Mimi. If the guards check, they will find you have residence in Middle Town."

"So where are this trader and his wife now?" questioned Jack.

"They are in Emiscial. As far as anyone here knows, they are travelling round the lands collecting new products to sell. We are covered with this story."

Jack nodded that he understood his instructions. He began to ride a now-black Bailey out of the stable yard.

14

LEAVING JUDELEN

Mia had been right about the presence of guards searching for Lily; the streets were crawling with them.

Jack led them out of Middle Town into Low Town, being stopped several times by different guards. Jack had tensed at the sight of Drake coordinating the guard's search at the main gate, but luckily they passed by without having to explain themselves to him personally.

The journey through Low Town was quieter. No one walked the streets except the guards, who were searching each and every property. The poorer folk had hidden away from the disturbance, which both annoyed and pleased Mia. The sounds of distant shouting and screaming sometimes rang through the air, as the guards found another household to search.

The reason Mia was displeased was fairly easy to understand; very few travellers walked the streets, so they stood out. They were stopped frequently, and Jack repeated over and over who he was and where he was going.

On the other hand, the fact that the people of Low Town were hiding away in their clay houses meant that the guards' search was taking far longer than intended. This bought them time to get out of the city before the patrols moved further afield.

Two city guards moved past Jack's party, both looking tired and angry. One of them was speaking crossly to the other. "It is crazy not to close the city gates! How can we be certain that they won't slip out somehow?"

The other guard sighed. "They have stopped any wagons and carriages from leaving. The only way you can leave is on horse or foot, so you can be clearly seen. The guard on the main gate is one of the king's own bodyguards; he knows what he is doing. They have to let these prisoners think they can escape, to draw them out. It is not our job to argue." The guards moved away, taking their conversation with them.

"Argon must be on the gate," Jack whispered to Mia. "Are you certain he will detect nothing in us?"

"Completely," answered Mia. "It is the Dark Knight we would need to fear."

Jack fell silent. Although he trusted Mia, he was certain things wouldn't be as simple as they sounded. He led the way to the city gate with an uneasy mind.

The two guards they'd overheard had been right about Argon manning the gate. He stepped out to meet them as Jack approached.

"Hold," he bellowed, raising his hand out. Jack reined Bailey up short, Lily drew up a step or two behind him, and Mia brought up the rear.

"Dismount!" commanded Argon. Jack swung himself off Bailey.

"All of your party," he ordered.

Jack moved round to help Lily from the saddle, leaving Mia to fend for herself, as a master would.

"No one is allowed to leave this city without my permission, master."

"Why is that?" asked Jack politely.

Argon smiled smugly. "The reasons of the palace are none of your concern, master."

"They are if they delay me from getting along on my travels, sir. I am a trader. I need to keep ahead of my schedule if I am to arrive at my destination in time to purchase my goods."

"And where is it you are going to?" asked Argon.

"Sanalow, sir. It is the time of year that myself, my wife, and helper go to buy up the summer dyes."

Argon's eyes fell across Lily and Mia, who kept her head down.

"I shall need your names and your house before you may leave the city."

Jack smiled politely and moved away from Lily and Mia to give the details.

After he had finished, "You may leave," Argon told him. Jack moved quickly to Lily and helped her back onto Apple. Mia scrambled back onto Leena again without help. Jack climbed back onto Bailey and began to move him forward. Argon stood by the gate, ready to watch them leave, his arms folded lazily. Jack moved to pass him, but as they drew level, Bailey lunged forward and bit Argon firmly on the arm.

With a yell Argon stood up straight and looked down upon his bleeding arm. The bite was close to where Jack had cut him with his sword. He looked up at Jack in anger.

"My apologies, sir! The horse is new to me—he must have been spooked," said Jack quickly, hoping he could smooth over the situation.

"Get out of my sight!" yelled Argon, covering his bleeding arm.

Jack heeled Bailey out of the city gates. As soon as they were over the moat and into the forest, he increased the pace to a gallop. They kept up the speed for several hours, until they reached the Judelen Pass and crossed over the bridge. Jack saw the wall had been repaired where Tomas's carriage had hit it.

Mia drew Leena alongside Bailey. "That was close!" she snapped.

"I guess he wanted revenge on Argon for selling him," said Jack, patting Bailey's neck.

"You should know better! You could have made it impossible to leave!" shouted Mia.

"I didn't tell him to bite Argon!" said Jack defensively.

"I'm not talking to you, Jack," said Mia shaking her head. "It's a good job I put the illusion over the horses too." Bailey let out a snort.

Lily glanced behind them nervously. "How long do you think it will take the guards to search the city?"

Mia answered, "With a little luck, a few days. Those guards were right, though. The Dark Knight would have done better to seal the city."

"Let's just be thankful he didn't," said Jack.

15

DISCOVERY

Aidan paced around his chambers, feeling murderous. A servant had reported finding a sealed doorway inside one of the secret stairways. Aidan had examined it himself and been repulsed to feel the trace of white magic upon the seal. A magus had been in the palace and had aided Lillian's escape.

Aidan rubbed his head. He could still recover her, but he needed to act quickly. The magus would take Lillian to Emiscial that was certain. It would take them at least three days to get there, and if they'd left immediately at the time of the executions, they only had a one-day head start from Judelen.

Aidan ran to the chamber door and flung it open; he found Argon standing outside.

"I have a job for you to do," he said harshly, as he beckoned Argon inside the chamber. "The princess is no longer in Judelen. I fear a magus has been aiding her and is now taking her to Emiscial."

Argon nodded that he understood but said nothing.

"Tell the guards to stop searching the city. I hold most of Judelen's people in my power. I shall invoke the spells, which will give my spirit creatures full control over their hosts."

"Overlord, that will reveal us," said Argon quickly.

"The witches of Emiscial already know of our presence here; that is why one is aiding Lillian. We must take control of the city now! We need to turn its people into our army."

"Do you suspect they know she is the vessel?" asked Argon.

Aidan grimaced. "I hope not, or I have just lost our advantage. Argon, I need you to take the three Shangol beasts from the stables and go after the magus, Lillian, and the boy.'

Argon's face lit up. "With pleasure, Overlord! What are your orders for when I find them?"

"Bring Lillian back, alive and unhurt. Do what you like to the boy and the witch."

Argon's lips curled in pleasure.

Aidan waved him away. "You're wasting time."

Argon moved towards the door.

"Argon, one more thing," said Aidan, stopping him in his tracks. "If you don't succeed in returning Lillian, I suggest you don't return at all. All that awaits you here, if you fail, is death. Do I make myself clear?"

"Yes, Overlord," said Argon. "I won't fail you." He crossed the rest of the chamber and left through the door, pulling it shut behind him. Once out of Aidan's sight, he wiped the beads of cold sweat off his forehead. He would not fail—he could not afford to fail.

16

❁

THE JOURNEY TO EMISCIAL

Jack, Mia, and Lily rode along the open road through Lanfar. Soon they would reach the border of Sanalow and be able to follow the river.

The first night had been hard on Lily. She was not used to sleeping rough and she had not settled at all. Now she sat on Apple's back, hardly able to keep her eyes open. Jack rode close to her to make sure she stayed in the saddle. Mia continued to push the pace. She was determined to reach Emiscial as soon as possible; she accepted no excuses for delaying.

The path went up and down over small hills, where nothing much grew but spiky, dry grass. Jack remembered travelling through here to Judelen. He remembered how depressing this place was and how he had longed never to come here again. It seemed even more depressing the second time round.

Lily let out a long moan from her saddle and slumped forward. Jack reached across to steady her.

"I can't carry on, Jack," she said wearily.

"You have to, Lily. It is only just midday. We can't stop now, you know that."

Jack glanced at Mia, who regarded him coldly. "We are not stopping, Jack, not until night falls."

Jack rolled his eyes. He gave Bailey a pat and asked, "Are you up to carrying a little extra weight, boy?"

Bailey moved closer to Apple to signal his approval. Jack took hold of Lily and dragged her over onto Bailey.

"What are you doing?" snapped Mia.

"She is nearly asleep," said Jack in annoyance. "If we can't stop, then I shall carry her for a while. Why can't you strengthen her with medicine, anyway?"

Mia looked furious. "I cannot magic away her fatigue." She took hold of Apple's reins and turned back to face the road. Lily adjusted herself in Jack's arms; her eyes were already closed.

Jack kept his eyes on the road ahead, not because he needed to but because his temptation to look upon Lily was too strong. However much it hurt him, he did know that she was right about them. He had a duty to protect her, and she had her duty to protect Judelen, even if that meant they could never be together.

The journey through Lanfar continued in silence. Lily slept peacefully in Jack's arms. It was a relief to reach the river and see trees and grass again. Darkness fell over the party, and Mia finally ordered them to stop for the night. They settled on the riverbank, behind some large bushes, to help conceal them from the road.

Lily woke when Jack lifted her from Bailey, but she was more than happy to go straight back to sleep once the bedrolls were laid down. Mia didn't seem to be in the mood to talk, so Jack settled himself down close to Lily. He kept handy the sword Mia had given him, and although he would sleep, he would be alert to the slightest noise around them.

The night passed by uneventfully. As dawn came, Mia woke first and roused Jack and Lily from their blankets. They sat together eating breakfast, which consisted of the last of their supplies.

"We should reach the town tonight, before dark falls again, and be able to buy supplies," said Mia as she brushed away the last crumbs from her dress.

Lily was rubbing her stomach. It would be a long day without any further food or water. Mia had told Jack that the river wasn't a safe water supply, and although she had forewarned them that the food would run out by the second night, that wasn't going to help Lily.

Jack approached her as she was saddling Apple. "I have saved the last of my supplies, Lily, so if you feel hungry, please tell me, and you can have them."

Lily smiled warmly at him. "That was very kind of you, but won't you be hungry?"

"Not as long as you're all right!" said Jack, with a smile. "I spent a year travelling around the outskirts of Sanalow and many months of that was in this savannah, hiding from soldiers, until I finally reached Judelen. I am used to having limited food. You, however, are not."

"You make me sound greedy, Jack," said Lily angrily.

"I'm not saying that at all. I am merely pointing out a fact. Princesses rarely go without a proper meal."

Lily shrugged away his explanation and went back to saddling Apple. Jack felt rejected. He moved away and began to saddle Bailey.

Mia approached him. "You are right to tell her the facts, Jack. She is not in Judelen now."

Jack shook his head. "Out of the three of us, Lily has it the hardest. She can say whatever she likes to me; I understand where she is coming from."

Mia barely hid her impatience. "Jack, may I ask you a question?"

"I suppose," said Jack, still working on Bailey's bridle.

"Who were you before you joined Lily's service?"

Jack looked at Mia in puzzlement. "Who I am has not changed, Mia. *What* I was, though, was a wayfarer."

Mia's eyebrows rose. "How did a wayfarer come to be joined in service to the princess of Judelen?"

"I saved her life whilst on my way to the city," said Jack honestly. "Lily asked me to join her service, as an alternative reward to the gold her father wanted to offer me."

Mia's eyes narrowed. "You are hiding something," she said.

"So what if I am?" said Jack shortly. "I choose not to tell you every detail of my life, until I know for certain I can trust you."

Mia laughed. "You are wise for your years, Jack. Let me ask you this: were you from Sanalow originally?"

Jack nodded. "I was from Sanalow, and before you ask, I was in the army, but I left."

"Why?"

Jack glared at Mia. "It is none of your business! I had my reasons, and that is all you need to know."

Mia looked far from angry at his outburst; instead she smiled warmly at him and moved away to saddle Leena.

"What was that about?" asked Lily after Mia had gone.

"She asks too many questions," said Jack, feeling flustered.

"Did she ask you about Sanalow and why you left the army?'

"Yes, but I don't want to discuss that with her. It is between you and me, and that is the way it will stay."

Lily nodded agreement. "You know I will say nothing, Jack, but don't you think you should tell her to miss off the Sanalow village stop?"

"Do you want to go today and another night without food, Lily?" snapped Jack.

"Of course not—"

"Then say nothing to her."

Lily's mouth thinned. "Very well," she said shortly before moving off to see to Apple again.

Mia came rushing back over. Jack was not in the mood for more questions. "Before you ask, it is nothing to do with you what Lily and I talk about," he said before she could speak.

"Idiot boy!" hissed Mia, her face pale. "There are more important things! There is something on the road behind us, and they're full of black power. The horses can sense it and hear them whispering."

Jack looked up in alarm. "Is it Aidan?"

"More likely one of his men and some sort of creature the Dark Knight has twisted with magic," said Mia. "We must go now—it is closing on us as we speak!"

"But we are protected—they will not know it is truly us because of the illusion!"

Mia shook her head. "I doubt any spell will save us now."

The party quickly mounted and sped away at a full gallop. Mia kept glancing behind them every now and again. Jack shouted across to her, "Whoever it is, they can't be that close yet."

"Bailey can hear them getting closer," Mia shouted back. He could only just make out what she was saying over the rush of the wind and the drumming of the horse's hooves. A scream from Lily turned both their heads. Three horses and one rider had just come over the hill behind them.

"We can't outrun them!" shouted Mia. "We must fight!"

A group of trees growing by the river came into view up ahead. "Use those trees as cover for you and Lily," ordered Jack. "I'll fight off Aidan's man."

The three riders pulled their horses up at the trees, and Jack turned Bailey, ready to meet their attacker.

"Jack, get off Bailey," said Mia quickly.

"I can't defend myself as well if I'm on the ground," Jack told her.

"Bailey is of more use to you if you get off him and let him fight with you! Quickly, get his bridle and saddle off!" Jack dismounted and did as instructed. Lily and Mia did the same.

"Keep Apple and Leena near to you. I cannot protect you as well as fight!" said Jack, drawing his sword. "Can your magic help?"

"My gift is to whisper. I can do little good in a fight!" shouted Mia.

Swirls of dust rose on the path as the three Shangol beasts and their one rider came upon the party, drawing to a stop in front of Jack.

Jack gasped. The Shangol horses looked nothing as they had in the royal stables. Now they had sharp, pointed teeth that stuck out from their mouths and ugly black horns, curled around their ears. Jack looked upon the man who rode one of them and found he was staring into the face of Argon.

"Is that you, Jack?" said Argon, trying to see past the illusion. "Why did you stop running, boy? I was looking forward to chasing you down. Now you have made my job all too easy."

Jack regarded Argon with a feeling of complete hatred; he carefully pushed his anger out of his body and sought the deep calm.

"Killing me won't be as easy as you hope, Argon," he said coldly.

Argon smiled. "You think so? You're outnumbered, Jack, four to one."

Bailey charged forward and sunk his teeth into the neck of Argon's mount, Rittard. The beast reared up and toppled Argon from his saddle.

Jack stepped forward. "I think you'll find you got the odds wrong, Argon."

Argon let out a growl as he jumped to his feet. "Afillia, Neo, take out the witch and the other animals," he shouted. He sprang towards Jack with his sword drawn.

Jack met Argon's blow and sent his own towards him. The crash of steel and the screaming of Rittard fighting off Bailey rippled through the air. The other two Shangol beasts moved towards Mia and Lily. Jack saw that they had armed themselves with thick tree branches. Leena and Apple stood before them, ready to defend.

He made to intercept the beasts, but Argon struck at him again and again, making it impossible for him to move towards Lily.

Jack roared in anger. With all his might, he increased the strength of his blows, forcing Argon to abandon striking at him and defend himself. Jack kept pushing him backwards, trying to make his stumble so he could make a good strike.

A powerful blow caught him in the side, throwing him into the air. He landed painfully and tasted blood. Dazed, he looked round. The Shangol beast Neo had struck him with its horns and was now advancing upon him.

Jack scrambled through the dirt, trying to reach his sword, which he had dropped in the attack. He reached it and rolled onto his back, as the beast reared over him. He saw the underside of his black hooves, aiming for his head. He thrust the blade of his sword up into his underbelly, pushing it deeper with all his might. Warm droplets of blood splattered all over him, and with a scream, Neo fell. Jack rolled out of the way before he crushed him. A flash of steel whistled down beside him, and he quickly rolled again, this time to avoid Argon's blade. Bringing his sword up, he managed to defend the next strike.

"I'm going to enjoy killing you!" spat Argon.

"I'm not dead yet!" answered Jack, kicking Argon in the stomach. With a grunt, Argon fell backward. As Jack staggered to his feet, he glanced at the trees and saw Afillia advancing on Mia and Lily. They were using their branches to keep her back. Apple lunged at her, but the beast kicked her in the ribs, sending her over. They were no match for her strength.

He was too distracted to notice Argon creeping up on him. His sword caught Jack on his upper arm, ripping his skin. It burned sharply; he cried out and backed away, blood seeping from his wound. Steadying himself, he attacked again. Argon's blows were stronger, pushing Jack backwards. Jack kept trying to attack, but his arm wound was interfering. He growled in frustration.

"I'm beating you, Jack," said Argon and laughed. "You could never beat me!"

"Funny," said Jack, defending. "I thought I did beat you, back at the palace, when my sword was aimed at your heart!"

Argon grew red. "All for a stupid horse!" he snarled. "But where is he now?"

Hooves connected with the side of Argon's head, sending him crashing to the ground. Bailey drew up beside Jack, covered in the blood of Aidan's own stallion, Rittard.

"Right here, actually!" said Jack to Argon. He allowed himself a minute to catch his breath. Then, patting Bailey once on the neck, he advanced upon Argon, feeling victorious.

Argon lay on the ground, panting, his sword lost. "That horse is not yours," he spat.

"He is mine!" said Jack, swiftly kicking Argon in the ribs. "That was for training!" he hissed. He kicked him again, even harder. "And that was for trying to kill Bailey!"

Argon cried out in pain and covered his body. He stared at Bailey, and his eyebrows contracted. He touched the place on his arm where Bailey had bitten him.

"You couldn't beat me alone," he hissed through bleeding lips. "You may kill this host now, but you'll always know that, Jack."

Jack laughed coldly. "That doesn't matter to me, Argon. The point is—you're dead!" He raised his sword and drove it down into Argon's heart, killing him instantly. Jack stared at Argon's lifeless body. *Good riddance*, he thought.

A scream from Lily whipped his head round. Afillia had forced Mia into the open. Jack yanked his sword out of Argon and raced towards Mia. He could hear Bailey cantering behind him.

Afillia hit Mia with her horns, sending her crashing to the ground; she reared up ready to crush her.

"No!" screamed Jack. Bailey overtook him and crashed into the side of the beast, bringing her feet clear of Mia. Jack ran to her and pulled her to her feet.

"Get back into the trees, and mount the horses!" he told her before turning to face Afillia, who was locked in battle with Bailey.

Moving around Bailey, Jack aimed a strike at the beast, but her hooves hit him in his leg, causing him to fall painfully. She pushed Bailey away from her and managed to rear up, striking him with her front feet. Bailey fell to the ground.

Jack staggered up and moved in front of Bailey to defend him. The mare let out a whinny as she charged at him.

Heart in his mouth, Jack raised his sword and swung it with all his might. It cut deeply into Afillia's neck, sending her crashing down onto her side, screaming in agony. Rushing towards her, Jack swung his sword again as hard as he could. It connected with her already-open neck, the final blow bringing her head clean off. The path around them began filling with blood.

Jack stood panting. His body ached all over, and his wounds stung sharply. He looked around him at the dead bodies of the Shangol beasts and Argon. It was over, for now at least!

Lily rushed to his side. "Jack, you're hurt!" she said, studying his body from head to toe.

"I'll live," he said gently, taking her face in his hands. "What happened to you?" he asked, looking at the bruise on Lily's head and the blood on her riding dress.

"Afillia knocked me into a tree. She managed to bite my arm, but I don't think it is serious," said Lily, showing Jack the wound.

Jack kissed the top of her head. "I let you get hurt," he said, hugging her to him.

Lily returned the hug. "You saved my life, Jack, and Mia's. Please don't start thinking you've failed me because I have a few cuts," she said.

Jack stroked her hair softly. "Are you sure you're all right?"

"Yes, but you had better check on Mia and the horses; they're wounded too."

Reluctantly he let go of Lily. He made a quick check on Bailey, who had got back to his feet and appeared to have no serious injuries. He went over to Mia, who was standing with Leena. "Are you hurt?" he asked her.

Mia touched his arm. "My head hurts from the fall, but I have no other injury." she said, squeezing him. "Thank you, Jack. You saved our lives."

Jack gave her an awkward hug before turning and kneeling down beside Apple. "These bites look nasty," he said, gently patting her neck.

Mia touched his shoulder. He glanced up and saw that she was beckoning him to move away from Apple. He stood up and followed her to the tree line.

"The bites are deep, Jack, and Apple is losing a lot of blood. I fear that there is nothing can be done to save her now."

"You can't heal her with magic?" he asked, although he already knew the answer.

Mia shook her head. "I would need the help of the elements of Spirit and Earth, which two of my sisters have—but even if they were here, we could not use the power. Healing is forbidden practice."

"Why is heal—" Seeing Mia's anger, he broke off his question. He understood that she wasn't going to explain anything about magus healing. He sighed deeply. "Does she understand that she is dying?" he asked instead.

Mia nodded again. "It will be painful for her, Jack, to bleed to death."

Jack's face paled. "Ask her if she wants me to ..." He gestured to his sword, unable to finish the words.

Mia understood his offer and moved to speak with the horse. She knelt for a moment beside Apple, nodded, and signalled Jack to come over. "She understands, Jack, and she asks you to help her on her way," she told him, her voice breaking slightly.

Jack closed his eyes, preparing himself. He wished his blade was clean, but he didn't have time. He didn't want her suffering any longer.

"What is happening?" asked Lily in confusion.

Mia took her by the hand. "Apple is dying, Lily. Jack is going to stop her pain. Don't look," she said, turning her away.

Jack knelt down by Apple. "I'll be quick," he promised her before standing. Raising his sword, he quickly drove it through her heart, waiting for a minute to ensure she was dead before removing his blade.

Lily was weeping in Mia's arms. Jack could hardly stand to see her so distressed.

"Is Leena hurt?" he asked Mia, his voice hollow.

Mia shook her head. "She has a few cuts and bruises but nothing more."

Jack glanced at Bailey. "Can you carry two from now on, until we reach Emiscial?" Bailey snorted once, and Jack knew that was his acceptance.

Jack walked down towards the river. "We had best get cleaned up," he said to the group. "We can't go into a town like this." He abandoned his ruined jacket and removed his shirt. He splashed water over his wounds, exhaling sharply as they stung. He ordered Bailey into the river to wash away the blood covering him.

"What of the bodies?" said Lily, joining him by the water. "Should we bury them to hide what has happened here?"

"I shall cover them all with an illusion," said Mia, sitting down on the other side of Jack. "We must get back on the road quickly. It will be evening by the time we reach the village now."

Jack pulled his dirty shirt back on. He checked that Lily had cleaned her wounds properly before preparing the party to continue the journey.

Mia had predicted it right; it was late by the time they rode into the village of Lowfar. The city was twenty miles away, but even at this distance Jack felt uneasy.

"Mia, perhaps you should use your magic again and change our illusions," he said as they approached the first street.

"Why?" Mia asked him, looking suspicious.

"Because it would be safer, don't you agree? I mean, Aidan will learn that Argon is dead, and surely he will send more men to stop us reaching Emiscial. If we were under another illusion spell, they wouldn't know it was us. It could mean a safe night's sleep, assuming Aidan doesn't come himself."

Mia regarded him for a moment. Jack merely shrugged his shoulders.

"Very well," she agreed. "I suppose it would make more sense."

Jack sighed inwardly in relief. He knew Jarrad was dead, but that didn't mean he wasn't still being hunted.

Mia had to lead the group back up the road, away from the village, to give her room to work the spell without anyone noticing. Jack looked at Lily's new illusion. She looked young and very plain, in a simple, clean-cut brown woollen dress, just like a Sanalow slave girl. He and Mia wore rich fabrics of velvet in many different colours, very popular with Sanalow nobles. Bailey had become bay, and Leena was now chestnut in colour.

"How will we explain Lily riding behind me?" asked Jack.

"We won't," said Mia simply. "Lily, you must walk now. Lead Leena for me, and carry our packs. That is what slaves of nobles in this country do."

Lily dismounted. "Why am I made the slave, anyhow? Surely it would have made more sense if I were the noblewoman. Jack would be closer to me, for one thing."

"That is one reason I do not allow it!" said Mia harshly. "You two shall be keeping your distance from each other. We shall rent two rooms at the next inn—and you shall sleep in mine," she added to Lily.

The party arrived at an inn and found rooms easily. Noblemen never struggled to get accommodation wherever they went. They ate in a private dining room, and after supper Mia took Lily away to their room to sleep.

Jack decided to check on the horses before going to bed. The innkeeper led him out to the stables. The horses were warm and well fed. Jack spent a while talking with Bailey, until finally his eyes began to hurt from tiredness. He thought that it must have turned the early hours by now, so he made his way back inside to get some sleep.

There were still men drinking at the bar, despite the late hour. Jack noticed that they were soldiers, each wearing the uniform of Sanalow. He tensed slightly and hoped the illusion was holding over him properly. The soldiers turned to regard him as he came deeper into the common room; then they returned to their own talk. Jack was about to move towards the stairs when something one of the men said caught his ear.

"The war into the land of Grimfar to storm the underground city is going to prove to be a mighty challenge," one of the men was saying.

"The steward wishes to take their land by force. He is determined to make sure the vermin of Grimfar can never again foul our soil," said a second man

"Emiscial will object, of course. The white witches are allies with Grimfar," said a third soldier.

"I don't much fancy taking on the witches," the second soldier said with a shudder. "Them and the Grimfar monsters will be more than a match for our forces."

"What are you going to do, tell Morridread you're not going to fight?" said the first soldier with a roar of laughter.

Jack's stomach's turned to ice. He wasn't hearing them right. Jarrad Morridread was dead! He had no other family—that was why Jack had been raised to under-steward.

Needing clarity, he approached the bar. "I heard a rumour that Morridread was killed," Jack said, his voice louder than normal due to anticipation.

The soldiers turned to regard him; they took in his expensive outfit. The first soldier spoke to him. "There was a rumour saying Morridread was killed in a fall, but the people who began it were misled. He did have a fall and broke his leg; people mistook the word *leg* for *neck*, My Lord," he added quickly.

"You're a Sanalow noble, aren't you? Surely you know what happens in Sanalow better than most," said the third soldier rudely.

"You dare to question a lord," said the second soldier quietly. "Be careful he doesn't have your neck for this."

The third soldier looked frightened. "Forgive me, My Lord. I forgot myself; too much ale."

Jack waved the man away. "I have been away on business. So the rumour is false then—Morridread is alive and well."

"Yes, he is, except for the slight limp he has now," said the first soldier.

"What are your views on the Grimfar monsters, My Lord?" asked the third soldier. "Do you believe the army of Sanalow can have victory against them?"

Jack wished he could voice his true feelings. "I am sure the steward is capable of making the right decision for Sanalow," he said instead. "You soldiers would do better to honour him in private, or word could reach his ear that you have been openly disagreeing with his commands. I can imagine what he would do to you if he were to find out."

All three of the soldiers looked frightened now. "We meant no offence, My Lord. Morridread is a great steward, and we have every faith in him," said the second soldier.

"I bid you goodnight, then," said Jack before moving away and up the stairs to his room. Once inside, he closed the door and sat down behind it. His head was throbbing and his throat was dry. Jarrad being alive meant that he could avenge his family after all!

Jack had bathed and dressed by the time Mia and Lily knocked on his door. They ate a hurried breakfast, paid the innkeeper, and left to fetch the supplies. Jack knew his eyes were purple and baggy from no sleep. He saw Mia observing him, but she didn't make any comment, and he offered no explanation.

They went into the market to buy the supplies and a new horse for Lily. As they were preparing to leave, Jack spotted the group of soldiers from the inn. They were mounted on their warhorses. One of then spotted Jack and raised his arm in greeting. "Safe journey, My Lord. We are moving on to find new men to honour the steward."

Feeling Mia glaring at him, Jack raised a hand to acknowledge them but didn't speak as they left the village.

"Is that why you're so tired this morning, Jack? You stayed up all night drinking with soldiers!" said Mia in a clipped voice.

Jack growled. "No," he said.

"Jack wouldn't drink with Sanalow soldiers anyway," said Lily from the ground. "They might still be looking for him, even now." She realised then what she had said and looked up in apology. Jack cast her a stern look.

Mia looked very interested in that fact. "We shall talk of this later, Jack."

"It is my life, Mia, and I don't wish to discuss it," said Jack shortly; he was relieved when Mia didn't argue further.

Once they were a safe distance away from Lowfar, Lily mounted her new horse, Belldean. As they had left Apple's tack behind, Jack had bought a new saddle and bridle for the chestnut mare. He saw that Mia was displeased that the bridal had a bit, but as she couldn't remove it until they reached Emiscial, she had to content herself by glaring at it every now and again.

The party began to ride hard. Soon the river was far behind, and the Black Mountains stood tall above them. Mia led them into the mountains and along the winding pathways, which began to narrow the higher they rose. Jack dropped back to make sure Lily rode in front of him. Glancing at Mia to make sure she wasn't watching, he quickly leant out and touched Lily on the arm as she passed him. She looked into his eyes.

"I love you," he whispered, knowing he needed her to hear him say it just once. She giggled quietly; he thought she looked happy. Mia turned round the check on them, and Jack let his hand fall. Lily moved past him, and he fell into step behind her.

17

THE THEANIC ORDER

"The way into Emiscial begins a short distance into this part of the mountain range," Mia told the party as they rode the horses into a deep valley. "The path narrows even more from now on; only one horse will fit through at a time," she instructed Jack.

Lily looked at Mia. "How does Emiscial manage to trade with the other lands?" she asked. Jack understood her confusion; the journey into the mountains was hard riding, and carts couldn't manage on the paths. He waited curiously for the explanation.

"We don't have traders come or go from Emiscial, Lily. We grow all we need for ourselves. People who come to us come to retire and help look after the land and the livestock. Only a handful of people ever get to leave the city once they have entered."

Jack jumped in quickly. "We will be allowed to leave again, won't we?" he asked, wishing the rumours he'd heard had been false.

"Of course. You are coming to us for aid, and we have invited you as our guests, knowing that you must one day leave us again. Don't worry, Jack. Nobody here will force you to take a course of action you do not choose freely," said Mia.

Jack thought that was slightly hypocritical, considering the magus were already taking his true love away to marry another, but that aside, she sounded truthful. Lily turned to look at him, smiling encouragingly.

Mia led them deeper into the mountain valley, where the walls became tall, smooth, and unnatural-looking. Jack suspected magic had been used to cut the rocks. The path was dark, and the wind made a chilling moan.

Jack glanced ahead and saw over Mia's shoulder that they were heading towards a tunnel. Mia stopped in front of the entrance and turned to speak to Jack and Lily. "This tunnel is the way into my city. On the other side is where Emiscial begins."

The tunnel was pitch-black and made Jack feel claustrophobic just looking at it. Mia saw his unease. "The tunnel path is flat and runs straight, but it is fairly long," she explained. "Once we are inside, we shall be able to see."

Mia let Leena enter the tunnel. The darkness swallowed them completely. Lily looked round at Jack. "I don't like this," she said quietly.

Masking his own concern, Jack smiled at her. "Go through, Lily. There is nothing to fear," he said gently.

"You'll come straight behind me?"

"Of course I will. Go on, now."

Lily let Belldean enter the tunnel, and Jack spurred Bailey forward before they disappeared completely. They came through with Bailey nearly on top of Belldean. A strange whistling noise filled the tunnel, and Jack saw something go past him that shimmered like a mist.

"What was that?" he shouted in the darkness.

"Magic," said Mia from up ahead. "We have been sensed by the Order, and they know who we are now. We may proceed into Emiscial."

The tunnel suddenly lit up with a golden glow. Jack looked around in surprise; the glow seemed to be coming from within the wall itself.

"Crystals of light litter these rocks," said Mia glancing back at him. "The fire magus can use them to light even the darkest places. We must press on now; the Theanic Order are waiting for us."

Jack turned to look behind him and gave a start—the tunnel entrance was a solid wall. As he turned slowly around, he hoped he had not just made the biggest mistake of his life. Lily had ridden off after Mia; he quickly caught up to her. The tunnel ran on, and on; it was a tedious journey. Jack was fighting a losing battle against tiredness. Finally a small patch of light appeared up ahead. It grew bigger and bigger the closer they got to it, Jack could see the tunnel exit clearly now. There were trees beyond, and rich green grass covered the ground.

Mia led them out of the tunnel and into the light. Jack covered his eyes against the brightness, letting them slowly adjust.

On his left, the mountain ranges continued to spike ever upward, but on his right Jack could see the land of Emiscial stretching out below him. They had entered at the top of a large valley. Jack could see woodland flowing down and many horses roaming freely. The air was hot and humid; Jack looked up into the sky and saw a great, golden shield above him. He pointed at it. "What is that?" he asked.

"The magic shield," answered Mia. "Orthrillium cast it to keep the magus and King Rain safe from Evelyn Maude when he learnt she planned to kill him for his power. No black magic can penetrate the shield, and the land beneath stays in one season, meaning we don't suffer at the hands of the elements.

"The protection of the shield ends just to the left of us, where the higher mountain paths begin. The Black Mountains are twins of the Great Mountains; they are both treacherous enough to prevent anyone from crossing them."

Jack shook his head, feeling confused. "How did Evelyn Maude manage to kill Orthrillium if he had a magic land to keep him protected?"

Mia looked angry. "He died because he would not listen to me," she spat, her eyes fierce. "Evelyn tricked him, convincing him she had what he desired above all things, the way to heal the Earth Stone he had shattered. Desperate for the knowledge, he ignored my counsel and believed her lie. She killed him on sight."

Jack huffed. "So he betrayed the Fairy and met his fate being betrayed by the Black Witch," he said.

Mia nodded. "Yes, it's ironic, I suppose. Just one of his many mistakes," she said sadly.

Lily was looking round with wide eyes. "It is so beautiful here," she said quietly, "but I don't see any buildings. Where is your temple?"

Mia pointed towards the forest. "In the middle of the woodland is where we live, Lily. Here we have small homes made from plants; we call them domes. We don't have stone cities like Judelen and Sanalow; we live as one with nature."

Lily looked puzzled, but Mia merely smiled. "You shall understand when you enter the forest. We must go down now and meet with the Theanic Order, my sisters of magic and my very good friends."

Mia turned Leena to follow a path into the woodland. It ran downhill, leading them deeper into the trees. The land began to level out, and Mia pointed out the dome plants. Jack had to admit they were pretty amazing. They looked like giant pumpkins that had been hollowed out and carved with doors and windows.

"Do you have to find them growing and choose which one you want to live in?" he asked Mia.

"No, the magus assign places from them to grow in and then plant the seeds, to ensure there is no overcrowding."

"How long do they take to grow?" he asked.

"A day."

Jack nearly fell off Bailey.

Lily laughed with joy. "Just one day to grow a plant that size!" she exclaimed.

"Yes," said Mia, "with the help of a little magic, of course. But then it is up to the person wishing to inhabit the dome plant to hollow it out, take the seed, and carve the windows and door. That way the person can make it exactly as he or she wants it. You can have one room or up to four in one dome, depending on your needs or the size of your family. There are a few empty ones near to the magus's clearing for visitors. You two shall each be assigned one of these for your stay here."

Lily looked around with a grin on her face. "This land is so exciting, I don't know if I'll want to leave," she said.

Mia seemed pleased. "It will be your home now until after the Child of Light has been born and the dark forces have been destroyed," she said.

Jack narrowed his eyes. "If we agree to you plan," he added quietly. Mia ignored his comment and kept riding.

They rode until they reached a large clearing in the middle of the woods; the area was full of domes and people busily hurrying about their business. Jack assumed this was the heart of the city. On the far side of the clearing he could see an enormous dome plant, at least ten times the size of a normal one. He knew it had to be the temple of the Order.

Mia dismounted from Leena, while Jack climbed down from Bailey and helped Lily down from Belldean. The people moving around the clearing were watching them in interest. Mia moved through the crowds, inclining her head every now and then, and people parted to allow the party to pass through.

Mia was heading straight for the temple. Jack watched six women file out to greet them. Each was dressed in a different colour; they looked like rainbow pillars—beautiful, powerful, and strong. He saw immediately that although they were all very different looking, they shared the same yellow eyes and strange hairstyle Mia used. The magus that really caught his eye wore a dress of many colours; Jack counted eight and then he realised that each one of them was being worn by one of the other magus—with the exception of gold and black.

Mia approached the woman wearing the multicoloured dress. "Reanna, I bring before you Lily, the princess of Judelen, and her loyal bodyguard, Jack Orden," she said formally.

Mia moved aside to allow Lily and Jack to be seen. Reanna stepped forward, and Jack studied her. She had handsome features and rosy skin. She was tall and slender, her hair a similar blonde to Lily's. Like Mia, she wore the mask of immortality, making it impossible to place a human age upon her. She, in turn, regarded Jack briefly before fixing her gaze onto Lily. Her rosebud mouth curved into a smile. "Welcome to Emiscial," she said. "My name is Reanna, and I am the head of the Theanic Order."

Lily made a small curtsy. "It is a pleasure to meet you, Magus Reanna. I offer my thanks for the aid you sent me to leave Judelen safely, and the aid that you now give me here in your city." Lily turned to Jack. "May I present my bodyguard, Jack Orden."

Jack bowed low. He could feel all seven of the magus staring at him. He straightened and waited uncomfortably for them to finish conducting their evaluation of his appearance. Then he felt his body prickle with goose bumps; he recognised the cold sensation he had felt during Mia's illusion spells. He stiffened, realising they were probing him with their magic. He locked his jaw, trying to fight down the anger he felt at their rudeness. It took all his effort not to shout at them. *How dare they do something so evasive without permission!*

After a couple of minutes the cold sensation stopped, and Reanna spoke to Jack. "Thank you, Jack, for helping the princess and Magus Mia reach us safely. My sisters and I are aware you have a lot of questions for us, but first you should rest, eat, and freshen up. We will meet in the temple to discuss everything in an hour. You shall be shown to your domes now."

Jack nodded curtly; he didn't trust himself to speak. He watched the two young girls, dressed in pale-green silk dresses, who were now approaching.

"Please show the princess and her bodyguard to their domes," commanded Reanna.

The two girls bowed and then signalled Jack and Lily to follow them.

"Are you coming, Mia?" asked Lily nervously.

"I must remain and speak with my sisters, Lily. The girls will see that you are safe," answered Mia. Mia didn't wait to see them off before walking into the temple, followed by the other magus.

They crossed the clearing once again. Jack looked wildly around. Bailey, Belldean, and Leena had been taken away. "Where have the horses being taken to?" he asked.

"The valley," said one of the girls quietly. "Don't be concerned. They will be quite safe."

Lily smiled at him and took his arm. "Everything is going to be fine, Jack. I can feel it." Jack patted Lily's hand gently. He was not as confident, but he didn't want to worry her.

The two girls stopped them by an empty dome just on the outskirts of the clearing. "This dome is for you, Your Majesty,' said the second girl.

"Thank you," replied Lily with a smile.

The two girls moved over to another dome, just within the trees, outside the clearing. "Your bodyguard may use this dome. There has been food and fresh clothing placed inside already. Someone shall collect you in an hour to bring you back to the temple. Until then you must not leave this area."

Lily thanked the girls again and watched them hurry back towards the temple. She turned to Jack. "I'll come to your dome once I've changed, and we can eat together."

Jack nodded and waited until she was inside her dome before he went to his. He was thrilled about the fresh clothing; he still had on his tattered shirt from after the battle with Argon. Unlike the others, he hadn't had a change in his pack. He stripped off and used the water provided to wash. He checked his fight wounds; his arm seemed to have avoided infection. He examined the new clothing, all made of silk. He guessed it kept everyone in Emiscial cool. He pulled on the dark-brown trousers; they felt like air compared to his leathers. Jack stood grinning and moving his legs, letting the material swish from side to side. When Lily knocked on his door and then stepped inside, he looked up, startled, quickly grabbed the white silk shirt he had been given, and slipped it on.

He smiled at Lily. "You look beautiful," he said, barely able to stop staring at her, in her pale-pink silk gown and her hair loose, shining in the sun. How he longed to run his fingers through her hair, down onto her soft skin, to finally kiss her and embrace her. He smiled fondly at her, wondering if she knew how proud she had made him when she'd accepted his marriage proposal. He had never felt so happy. His thoughts turned dark then, and his smile slipped away. The magus were not going to let them be together. But he couldn't switch off how he felt, even to save the world. Maybe it was selfish, but he couldn't understand how separating two people in love could result in anything good.

Lily eyed Jack in worry. "What's wrong? You're transmitting so many conflicting emotions through the bond, I cannot make sense of them."

Jack rubbed his face. "Everything," he said quietly. He leant forward to smooth her worry lines with his finger. "I'm sorry. Just ignore me—I'm tired. Let's eat!" He moved away and collected the dishes of fruit and berries that had been left on the side. They ate in silence.

When a knock sounded on the door, Jack jumped up to answer it. He found Mia standing outside. "You two must come to the temple now to speak with the Theanic Order."

Jack stayed silent as he trudged back across the clearing. Reanna was waiting to greet them all. "Shall we proceed inside to see if we cannot put your troubled minds at ease?" she said.

Jack nodded once and signalled with his hand for Reanna to lead the way. He moved a step backward to make sure Lily could enter before him. He could feel her concern through the bond and was annoyed knowing it was his doing.

Reanna moved inside and down a short corridor. She reached a wooden door, pushed it open, and led the way into a large room with a round table and nine chairs. She moved to sit at one of the chairs. The other magus were already sitting around the table. They had left three chairs empty next to each other, for Jack, Lily, and Mia. Jack took his seat next to Lily and beside a magus dressed in a blue silk dress. He glanced round the chamber, studying it carefully. There were many doors leading from the room, but they were all shut. He passed his eyes over each of the magus in turn. The one he was seated next to had blonde hair so light it was nearly white. She was petite and reminded Jack of a child's porcelain doll. The magus next to her was in red. Her features were sharp and her hair as black as coal. She looked as if she could handle herself in a fight without difficulty. Jack blinked as he looked at the next magus; she was identical to the red magus, except she wore a yellow dress. *Twins*, he thought with interest. He wondered how that worked in a magic order. He skipped over Reanna and on to the magus in white. She was average in height, and pale, with bright orange hair that stood out sharply against her white dress. It clashed dreadfully with her yellow eyes. She caught Jack studying her and gave him a wicked grin. Feeling embarrassed, Jack looked quickly towards the next woman, who wore brown and looked kind, gentle, and somehow older than the others. She was plumper than any of her sisters and not immaculate in her appearance at all. Her silk was torn, and her light-brown hair was wildly escaping the waist wrap she wore. She sat with her hands on the table in front of her, dirt under her nails, and she was giving the white magus such a stare it reminded Jack of Mistress Stratton. He smiled a sad smile for her. She had died in defence of Lily, and he longed for the day when he could honour her memory. He immediately decided this magus would be his favourite. Mia sat next to her and then Lily. His evaluations done, he turned back to regard Reanna. He realised with surprise that she had been watching him.

She smiled and stood up. "All of us here are going to need time to get to know each other better, and I think introductions would be a good starting place. My sisters, perhaps you would be so kind as to introduce yourselves to our guests and give a brief description of your power within the Theanic Order." Reanna sat back down and signalled for the magus next to Jack to stand up.

Looking nervous, the blue magus stood up. She looked at Lily, avoiding Jack's eye, and wrung her hands. "My name is Emmra, and my powers lie with using the element of water." She trembled and sat down quickly; she turned to the red magus, who frowned at her before standing up gracefully.

"I am Troyan, the fire magus," she said in a confident voice. She sat back down as gracefully as she had stood. Jack frowned, thinking the "brief explanation" was perhaps meant to be a little longer.

Her twin stood up with a beaming smile. "I am Jamella, the spirit magus. Troyan is my sister both magically and earthly." She smiled warmly at her sister before continuing. "My gift is very interesting. Spirit is the binding force; there is no element that it doesn't work alongside. It has the natural ability to control—"

Jack sniffed loudly. "That doesn't sound like a good thing," he said.

Jamella looked at him in interest. "But it is good, because through the control of the elements comes order. The dark forces dislike spirit the most, because it has a duty to destroy chaos. They can use it to bind their twisted magic, but it can be unpredictable; it doesn't always produce the expected results."

Jack listened in interest. "Can you give us an example?" he asked.

Jamella nodded. "I can give you two. Firstly, Evelyn cast a spell on the Guardian to trap him into a human form, but her spell backfired, and her son, the Dark Knight, also became trapped in the form—"

At that Lily gasped. "The Guardian—King Rain—isn't human?" she said shakily.

Jamella shook her head. "No, child, he was made by Orthrillium with his own hands. He has all the elements within his structure; he is made out of mud, baked with fire, cooled in the air, and given a skin sealed with darkness. Spirit gave him life and the ability to change forms, just like the Dark Knight. He can whisper like Mia, and he was created to protect all the light magic, which is hidden safely within him. He has been trapped in human form since shortly after his creation, so he looks and acts like a human; it was one of the earlier spells Evelyn cast."

Lily looked disconcerted.

Jamella continued, "The better example of the unpredictability of spirit is when she tried to destroy the Guardian nearly one thousand years ago. It was just after her destruction of Grimfar. She was successful in firing her spell, but as Mia has made you aware, we learnt about ten years ago that the spirit weaves failed her, and they both ended up in mirror prisons instead."

"Yes, she told us the magus lied to everyone and said they were destroyed," said Jack coldly.

Jamella cast a look at Reanna. "We didn't want to cause a panic in the kingdom until we properly knew what we were dealing with," she finished quietly.

Jack was struggling to listen. Lily had taken hold of his knee and was squeezing it hard. He pulled her off with his hand but kept hold of her hand under the table.

Jamella continued, oblivious. "You know we can unlock the prison, but if we do, Evelyn Maude will be freed too. That is why the vessel must be secured quickly, as we have already—"

Reanna waved her hand in the air. "Sister, let us leave that story for later."

Jamella smiled in apology and sat down, allowing the white magus to stand. "I am Kerri, and my gift is the element of air." She put her hands on the table in front of her and leant forward to speak to Lily, her grin returned to her face. "My sister thinks her gift is special, but with air I could make you fly!"

Jamella laughed good-naturedly. "Indeed you could, but not for long, without my help!"

Kerri tilted her head. "Well, true, but for long enough to show the vessel what it feels like to soar like a bird."

"Hopefully without dropping her on her head!" the brown magus cut in. She stood up to join her white sister. "Then it would be my job to make sure you had something soft to land on. Your Majesty, my name is Kem, and I am in charge of the element of earth."

She inclined her head to Lily and pulled on Kerri's arm to make her sit back down. She gave her a stern look and whispered something that made the white magus utter an apology under her breath.

Reanna stood up again, and they broke off to listen to her. "We assumed Mia had already discussed her gift with you,'" she checked.

Jack nodded, and Lily stared blankly ahead; he squeezed her hand in comfort.

Reanna smiled. "Well, I sincerely hope my sisters have managed to convey to you some knowledge of their powers." She spread her skirt out for them to see all her colours. "You will notice that I wear each of my sisters' colours, and I also wear gold and black. The gold is to symbolise the light and the black the darkness. I wear all the colours because I have a trace of every element within me, except the light. I am gifted with detailed knowledge of every power, and I am able to sense all of them but not physically able to wield any of them. The element of darkness, as you know, is gifted to Evelyn Maude. Were she here, she would sit in black silk. The element of light, however, cannot be wielded by any human being since Orthrillium, and as you are aware, the light currently sits within King Rain.

"He was created from pure magic, so he cannot be twisted by Evelyn, just as the Dark Knight was created from black magic and cannot be turned to the Light. The Guardian was instructed by Orthrillium not to let anyone have the power of the Light, unless it could be used to undo the black magic. So he has been protecting the power, while the Order search for a way to defeat Evelyn Maude and her son." She looked at Lily and then at Jack. "We believe that we have found the solution, and the answer is you, Lily," she said proudly.

Lily tensed as all eyes in the room turned to her. "Explain to me how the Child of Light will destroy the Black Witch," she said. She sounded calm, but Jack could feel her shaking.

Reanna looked at Troyan. "Perhaps you could explain, as this begins with your magic."

Troyan nodded and turned to regard Lily. "My gift of fire is more than just a physical element; there is an emotional element within it. Evelyn Maude uses the darkest, strongest emotions to twist her magic—fear, hatred, jealousy, to name a few—and when we cast the spell to make the world mortal and defeat her army, we unintentionally made these emotions stronger.

"Then we realised a very important fact. When the negative emotions grew, so did one very powerful positive one—love. It remained so strong that even death could not conquer it. The magus began to study the emotion in greater depth and came to believe that love is at its strongest when a child is born. The unconditional love a mother gives to her child is almost as strong as the Light. That revelation led the magus to formulate their plan to create the Child of Light."

"So, what happened to your vessel?" asked Jack.

"Evelyn destroyed it," answered Reanna before Troyan could speak.

"How?" pressed Jack.

"She sent her son to defile the vessel. A child was created and its creation hidden by lies, weakening the love needed for the spell. The Dark Knight killed them both, to make certain we couldn't try again," Reanna said in a hard voice. "That is why we are insisting Lily needs to marry King Rain; human love is too weak on its own. Evelyn Maude and her son are formidable enemies. We cannot take any risks."

"How could they use me to create a Child of Darkness?" asked Lily impatiently. "I am good; I am not evil." Jack felt her squeeze his fingers. "I can love, I am just, so how can I become a vessel for something so dark?"

"We have been discussing this amongst ourselves since you arrived," said Troyan. "We couldn't understand how our plan could benefit the dark forces, but then it made sense. If Evelyn really wants to win against the Light, she must defeat love completely."

"And how can she do that!" spat Jack.

"By seducing the vessel, letting her fall in love with her son, marrying them, and making the child in love—only to raise it in darkness, therefore destroying love and becoming stronger then the Light."

Mia looked at Lily, with gentle eyes. "We believe that is why Aidan did not simply violate you. He was seducing you and exposing you to the darkness little by little, ready to claim you as his wife, make his child, and raise it in his mother's image."

Lily went white.

Jack stamped his foot. "This doesn't make sense! Why can't Lily and I make the Child of Light? If we stay here under the protection of the shield, we should be perfectly safe," he said, his voice rising in temper.

"Because we need the strongest, purest child," shouted Reanna. "We will not risk the only chance we have left on anything other than certainty. You two barely know each other; it's a fools crush!" she spat nastily.

Lily suddenly moaned and slumped forward unconscious onto the table. Jack jumped to his feet and moved behind her. Reanna and Mia also stood up. Mia felt Lily's head. "She's fainted," she informed everyone.

Jack said with a growl, "It is any wonder after what you have just unloaded onto her? Get off her, Mia. I will take her and put her to bed, so she can rest."

Without waiting for approval, he scooped Lily up and carried her from the temple.

18

CONSEQUENCES

The door banged shut behind Jack as he left.

Reanna turned slowly to regard Mia. "You are correct about the boy."

Mia sat back down. "His emotional state is fragile, to say the least," she said.

"He has much love for the vessel," said Troyan, regarding her sisters, "but he is filled with rage and a desire for revenge, a dangerous combination."

"He is very loyal," said Kem.

"He is not easily controlled," contributed Jamella. "He will do what he wants when he wants to do it."

"But not at the integrity of his loyalty," added Kem.

Reanna bit her finger and stood silent in thought. "Troyan, who does he want to take revenge on, the Dark Knight?" she asked eventually.

"He is undoubtedly a target of Jack's vengeance, but I don't think that he is the only source."

Reanna turned to the blue magus. "Emmra, what does your gift of water show you of the boy's strength?"

"He is strong, Reanna. He is not easily manipulated, and yet he has a lot of fear inside him—that makes him vulnerable. He doubts himself at times when he needs to be strong; it could be an obstacle to him in the future."

"I am thinking I should send him away," said Reanna seriously. "There is so much at stake now that we have the chance of making the Child of Light once more. I think the boy will not allow us to move forward. He

172

will whisper to the princess, and she will follow his council over ours, because they are so close. I don't believe I can risk leaving them together much longer. What if they act impulsively and destroy the chance to create the child?"

"Destroy the bond between them," Mia spoke out suddenly. "The bond must be removed from the bodyguard who is already taken by the black power. I can remove Jack's bond at the same time."

"The loss would cause Lily and Jack a lot of pain," said Kerri.

"They have been given a medicine to dull the feelings felt through the bond. It is true that it is probably wearing off now, but if I did the removal tonight, while they sleep, neither will feel as much pain," reassured Mia.

"I believe we should do this," said Reanna firmly. "Does anyone strongly disagree?" None of the magus spoke out.

Reanna looked around the temple at each of them. "It is settled then. Tonight we will remove the bond, and tomorrow we shall deal with their anger."

Jack was sleeping soundly on the floor of Lily's dome. He had remained with her, fearful to leave her in an unconscious state.

The breaking of a bond woke him sharply. Shocked, he sat up, felt for the connection to Drake, and realised it was gone. He knew the magus must have removed it. It didn't feel at all painful, which surprised him. Perhaps it was because he knew of Drake's duplicity, or perhaps because he was no longer really Drake.

Jack was not prepared for the second snap; it cracked like a whip and shook him to his core. Instantly he felt the loss of his connection to Lily. Jack let out a gasp. She was gone—the magus had removed their bond as well! Jack felt numb, and then he felt the burning in his head. It was worse than any pain he had known. He began to shake Lily, until he remembered she would not wake. Trembling and weeping, he climbed onto the bed with her and held her tightly to him. "They're taking you away from me in every way they can," he whispered, his tears soaking the pillow.

Mia came to check on Lily after the bond was cut, and was horrified to find Jack in her bed, spooned up beside her, fast asleep. Mia did not dare tell Reanna, for she feared she would eject Jack immediately from Emiscial.

She left him as he was, and vowed to return early in the morning before anyone else was up.

Jack opened his eyes groggily. He felt motion and didn't understand. Then his eyes focused, and he saw Mia bent over him, shaking him awake. He sat up, yawning loudly, and with his inhalation of air came the return of the pain in his head from the snapped bond.

He stared at Mia, cold fury burning in his eyes. "How dare you remove our bond!" he hissed.

Mia put her hands on her hips, looking equally livid. "How dare you put yourself into the princess's bed!" she spat back at him.

Jack leapt to his feet in anger, his headache forgotten. "She has been unconscious all night. I stayed to protect her, as you didn't bother to warn either of us you were going to cut the connections!"

Mia stepped towards him. "It was necessary, Jack! Now get out of this dome, before Reanna catches you!"

Jack's hand twitched dangerously, he turned and stormed out. He ran behind Lily's dome, breathing hard. He heard Mia moving around inside and the wringing out of a cloth. He thought he heard Lily stirring, and then he heard her groaning. He stayed out of sight and listened.

"Where am I?" moaned Lily.

"You're safe in Emiscial."

"Where is Jack?"

"In his dome."

Then Jack heard her gasp out loud. "What have you done!" she demanded coldly.

"What we had to," answered Mia calmly.

"I can understand removing Drake, but why have you taken Jack's bond?"

"You are no longer in need of bonded guards. You are safe here, and you will be protected until the Child of Light can come and save the world."

"You would force my hand as hard as Aidan would have! I am not yours to command. If you think I am, then believe me, I shall be out of Emiscial by nightfall!" screamed Lily.

Jack heard Mia laugh. "Even you know that to leave the protection of the magus would be a stupid thing to do. You feel angry with us now, but you will come to see the wisdom in our decision to remove the bond. You know you have a duty to do, and it involves you marrying King Rain. What you need to ask yourself is this: could you do it with Jack in your head, thinking his thoughts of loving you?"

Jack froze, waiting for Lily's reply. When she didn't answer, he stepped round the side of the dome and into the doorway. "Is that why you did it?" he asked. "To stop our love from clouding over doing what is needed?"

Mia didn't appear concerned that he had overheard the conversation. She merely shrugged. "It was the main reason, Jack. I shall not deny that," she admitted.

"What other reasons were there?" he asked firmly.

Mia's eyes flashed, and she pursed her lips. "You have been keeping secrets, Jack, from Lily and from the Order."

Jack lost the final thread holding his temper. "What secrets!" he shouted at Mia.

Mia squared her shoulders. "Whom do you want to take revenge on, Jack? Do not say Aidan. We know it isn't him," she said.

Jack felt the colour drain out of his face. "Are you witches mind readers now?" he said acidly.

Mia shook her head. "No, Jack, but we have the power to feel your emotions. Troyan could feel your need for revenge. It is so powerful it is making the Order question whether you should be sent away."

Lily looked at Jack in shock. "Is this true?"

Jack considered his options and decided the truth was the only way forward. "Jarrad Morridread is still alive, Lily," he said. He swallowed, waiting.

"The steward of Sanalow?" said Mia in surprise. "Why would you think him dead?"

Jack knew he had no choice but to explain. He came into the dome and sat on one of the chairs. "I was under-steward of Sanalow, and when I left the army, I heard he had fallen and broken his neck. I found out the night we stayed in Lowfar that it was actually his leg."

Lily covered her mouth.

Mia sniffed loudly. "Jarrad Morridread is a monster, and you were his under-steward. There is something more going on here! What happened between you?"

Jack flew back to his feet, feeling threatened. "He ordered me to murder the woman and children of Grimfar, and I refused to do it, so I became a traitor," he yelled.

Mia folded her arms. "There is still more to this story. You will tell me now, Jack; otherwise I cannot help you."

"I didn't ask for your help!"

Mia stepped towards him. "Whether you did or not, you need it. If you explain this revenge anger you feel and show you can control it, Reanna might let you stay."

"He killed my family!" yelled Jack. "He killed them all just to get back at me! I couldn't save them, so I vowed to avenge their deaths. There, are you satisfied now?"

Mia uncrossed her arms, looking sad. She placed a hand on Jack's shoulder, but he shoved her off. She sighed. "Do you still intend to take this revenge?" she asked, putting her hand down. "If you do, Jack, I believe my sister will remove you."

Lily looked horrified; she had not taken her hands from her mouth.

Jack looked at Mia and then at Lily. Lily gave a small shake of her head. "Please, Jack, don't."

Jack took a deep breath. "Tell the Order that Lily is still my number-one priority. Tell them I am not planning on taking revenge upon Jarrad until after King Rain arrives and the Child of Light is secure. Then I shall leave Emiscial, and with leaving, I shall leave Lily's service. Never again will I return to Judelen, Emiscial, or Grimfar. I shall do what I need to do and disappear forever."

"No, Jack! What are you saying?" screamed Lily; she had tears running down her cheeks.

He rubbed them away gently. "Lily, if I stay I'll only be standing in your way." He stepped away towards the door. "I can't lie anymore. I cannot watch you marry someone else. I shall leave Emiscial as soon as King Rain arrives. You'll be safe then, Lily, and you'll be able to do what is needed."

He couldn't look at her anymore; he shut his eyes tightly, turned, and ran out. Lily screamed his name, but he quickened his pace, walking past his dome and through the woods, until her voice was lost to his ears. He stopped deep in the woodland and sat down behind one of the trees. Only then did he allow himself to cry. He knew that what he planned to do was the only way forward, but it didn't stop his heart from breaking.

19

LOVE AND BETRAYAL

Jack and Lily had been in Emiscial for twelve days. After the rough start, Lily had now grown close with the magus and was on first-name terms with each of them. She had barely seen Jack since the morning he had announced he was going to leave. He had sent a message to the Order to let them know he was working near the horses' valley and that they were to send word if Lily needed him for anything. Whenever Lily returned to her dome at night, Jack was already at his own, waiting to check that she was well and take any instructions she needed to give him. Their conversations were always short and oddly formal, and Lily found it hard to hide her hurt at this change in him. She made herself believe it was for the best and he had done her a favour. It was silly of her to ever have loved him in the first place. She was a queen, and she would marry a king, not an ex-soldier from a foreign army!

The magus were each taking it in turn to teach her more about King Rain and about the history of magic. Last night Reanna had told her that King Rain had nearly reached Emiscial. He was travelling with the king of Grimfar, whose family had always had the responsibility to keep him safe, ever since they'd discovered the prison in Mount Dragonia during their tunnelling. Lily had meant to tell Jack about his friend's imminent arrival the previous night, but she'd been so angry with him she had gone to bed without a word. Now it was only two days until King Rain would arrive, and her heart thumped wildly at the thought. She understood the duty she must perform, but she couldn't shake a deep-seated feeling that something was very wrong.

"Fear is a powerful emotion," said a firm voice behind her. Lily jumped and spun round to find Jamella standing quietly behind her. She stood up from her seat next to the temple. "You made me jump!" she said.

Jamella spread her hands in apology. "I did not mean to," she said. "I have come to take you through your lesson for today."

Lily nodded. She had been waiting by the temple for one of the magus to do just that.

"Shall we sit?" Lily allowed the magus to sit first before sitting beside her.

Jamella regarded Lily seriously. "My sister, Emmra, has felt your fear growing inside you every day. I have been requested to ask you what is so terrifying to you," she said.

Lily knew there was no point in lying. The magus could sense when she was being untruthful. "I have been worrying about King Rain."

"What about him?"

"I am deeply concerned about being married to something not human. I know he is pure and good, but it feels unnatural."

Jamella smiled. "You have nothing to fear. King Rain might not have been born in this world, but he looks, feels, and acts human. Remember, Aidan isn't human either, but you did not know it. It will be the same with Rain."

"Yes, but they are both forced to be like humans. What happens when the world is healed, and the spell is broken?" asked Lily

"He isn't going to disappear in a puff of smoke. Lily, please don't worry. I promise you he is perfect."

"I don't know why I am so afraid of him," said Lily, shaking her head. "I am not afraid of the magus, and you are the same as he is."

"We are not the same," said Jamella sternly. "We were born to this world. We have faults, just the same as any other human, but ours are less obvious after four thousand years."

"Will we be restored to immortality after the war?" asked Lily.

Jamella nodded. "Yes, when the Child of Light cleanses the world, I believe immortality will return." Jamella smiled at Lily. "It is time for your test."

Lily's swallowed hard, but Jamella's eyes sparkled. "Come now, you must stop worrying; you will remember more than you think. Tell me first, what are the eight elements that made the world?"

Lily bit her lip. "Earth, fire, water, light, and air. Those are the natural elements. The two hidden elements are spirit and whispering."

"And the eighth?" asked Jamella.

"Darkness," remembered Lily. "But no 'gifted' ones who are discovered with that power are allowed to develop it, because it can be tainted."

"What are the 'gifted', and how did they come to be?"

"Humans who were found to be worthy of possessing a magical ability by the magus. They were your army, but Evelyn Maude copied your idea by casting the darkness out into the world and making her own army. She grew stronger than the magus and destroyed your army; the magus in turn destroyed her army by making humans mortal and too weak to wield magic any longer. The few gifted who were in Emiscial during the downfall of Grimfar can no longer advance their powers, until the mortality spell is removed," recapped Lily.

"Very good," Jamella congratulated Lily. "If you have no other questions, you may go and enjoy some free time."

Lily raised her hand. "I have one question."

"Go on," said Jamella kindly.

"When Evelyn Maude is free from her prison, what do you think she will do first?"

Jamella looked thoughtful. "She will need to reunite with her son, and I imagine she will continue to prepare her new army. Try not to worry. She cannot reach you here, and the Child of Light will be made before she knows what has hit her."

Lily hoped she was right. She smiled and excused herself. She decided to use her free time to walk in the woods and found herself wandering all the way to the valley of the horses. She hid in the tree line and watched a group of people up ahead. Jack stood among them, laughing and talking with a very attractive girl who was handing round drinks. As she watched Jack, Lily felt as if her heart had been broken all over again. Jack looked content; he had forgotten her. Lily turned away from the happy scene and ran back into the woods.

She came back to the clearing and crossed to the temple. She was not supposed to enter without permission, but she really needed to find Mia.

She went inside and up to the door of the chamber they had used when they had first met. She heard voices talking quietly on the other side. Something they said caught her ear, and she leant closer to the door to eavesdrop further. Her eyes grew wider with every word she heard.

Jack stood before the white magus with his arms crossed; he was worried about Lily. When he had arrived back at his dome the previous evening and waited for her to come to hers, she had refused to speak with him again, just as she had the night before. She had gone straight into her dome, shut the door, and refused to answer his shouts. He could tell she had been crying.

Jack had sent a message to the magus to ask that one of them come to speak with him about Lily. Kerri had responded only that morning. *Better late than never*, Jack thought.

She stood before him, with her bright grin plastered on her face, as usual. "She is fine, Jack," Kerri told him in a bubbly voice.

"Are you certain? She hasn't spoken to me for two nights now, and last night she had been crying. You haven't told her anything that would upset her, have you?"

Kerri rolled her eyes. "The vessel had a long day yesterday, Jack, and had a lot of new information to take in. I shouldn't worry if she didn't feel like talking. I expect she will feel better this morning after a good night's sleep."

Jack's shoulders slumped. He'd left early that morning to get to the valley to help with the crops. Perhaps he should have waited to see Lily first.

"So, have you seen her this morning?" he asked Kerri.

Kerri shook her head. "Jack, it is barely sunrise. We don't drag the vessel from her bed, you know! I am heading back to the clearing. I am certain she will be in the temple eating breakfast when I get there."

Jack sighed. "How long is it now before King Rain arrives?"

"He will arrive tomorrow," Kerri told him. "Now, stop worrying about Lily. We will tell you if she needs anything."

Jack thanked her and let her leave. He got back to working on the ploughing. It was probably the arrival of King Rain tomorrow that had unnerved her, although he still suspected the magus had had some part to play.

For three hours he worked solidly, keeping his mind off Lily as much as possible. Bailey came to the top of the valley to see him; Jack stopped planting and stood patting him idly. The family he was working with had moved further into the valley to plant more seeds. He had offered to stay behind to finish off the row they had begun two days ago. It should have been finished yesterday, but the family had interrupted their work to celebrate their only daughter's engagement to a man who worked in the woodland. Jack had been invited to join them, and for the first time in a long time he had laughed and felt good. He had congratulated the girl on her engagement and envied her because he could never marry the woman he truly loved.

Bailey gave Jack a nudge to make him carry on stroking his neck. Jack began the action again with a smile for his friend. "I really must get back to planting the last of these seeds," he said seriously. "It is strange to be here, with only one season. It must be late summer in the real world."

A party of people was walking out from the woodland into the valley. Jack looked over in interest, and his eyes grew wide when he realised it was the Theanic Order, all seven of them. They approached him quickly, talking in urgent whispers amongst themselves.

Jack waited for them to reach him before offering a bow. "Well, I've had the pleasure of Kerri already this morning. What brings the rest of the Theanic Order to the valley?" he asked in interest. He smiled warmly, but when he saw the stony faces of the magus his smile slipped away.

Reanna stepped forward, saying, "Jack, we need your help."

Jack realised that this was something very serious, and his heart skipped a beat. "Lily?" he asked.

Reanna nodded. "She has gone missing, Jack. She did not turn up for breakfast a few hours ago, and we have sent messages to every part of Emiscial within the shield. No one has seen her! You were our last person to check, but we see she is not here, either."

Jack wondered why he was the last person to be checked. "I have not seen her since last night," he told them. His mouth felt dry. "I told Kerri earlier I was worried about her."

Reanna looked scared. "I told Kerri not to tell you what Lily learnt yesterday, but I believe you were right in thinking it is what we said that has driven her to run away."

"What did you tell her?" shouted Jack angrily. "Where has she gone?"

"There is only one place she could have gone, Jack," said Mia quickly. "There is a path into the high mountains not far from the tunnel entrance. I believe she meant to try and leave Emiscial, but the tunnel was sealed, so she has gone into the mountains to try and climb her way out."

Jack raked a hand through his hair. "She has a three-hour head start?" he checked.

"Yes, she could not have left in the night, for we have night watchers who would have seen her go," said Reanna.

"Then I shall catch up to her quickly, for I can climb better than she can," said Jack, taking hold of Bailey's mane. "Take me to the mountain path, my friend," he said, climbing up onto his horse.

"Wait, Jack, there is something else you must know," shouted Kerri. "There is a snowstorm brewing at the mountain peak; it will hit in a few hours' time, and it could last for many days. You must find Lily quickly and get her safely back inside the shield before it comes; otherwise, you will freeze to death."

Jack nodded. "I understand, and I will find her," he assured them. He spurred Bailey into a gallop and headed for the mountain path, leaving the anxious Theanic Order behind him.

20

THE HIDDEN REALM

Bailey pulled to a stop outside the shield, at the start of the mountain path, and Jack climbed down. "If only this wasn't so narrow, boy, I would take you with me. Go back into the shield and wait for me to return. If I do return," he added under his breath.

Bailey gave him a push. Jack patted him goodbye and began to scramble up the steep and narrow rock path. He climbed and climbed as fast as he could, until his legs ached and his hands bled from rock cuts. His body shivered from the cold air, for he was still wearing his silk shirt and trousers. He hoped that Lily had wrapped up warmly.

After hours of hard climbing, Jack came to a flat part in the mountains. There was a small cave buried into the mountainside. Jack looked around hopelessly. "Lily!" he tried calling. He looked up the next part of the path. It was even steeper, but he could just make out the peak above, so he began to climb upward again. The air was growing colder, and small flecks of snow were beginning to fall from the sky. He knew he was running out of time before the storm would hit.

It took another hour to reach the top. Jack pulled himself up the final part and looked around for some sign of Lily, but there was none.

"Lily!" he called again. "Lily, where are you?"

"Jack!" cried Lily's voice. He looked round to see Lily staggering towards him.

Jack rushed towards her. "What are you playing at!" he screamed, "You've had me worried sick. Why did you run away?" He looked at her ripped blue-silk dress and then at her lips, which matched the gown's colour. He wrapped his arms around her to warm her up. "We have to get back down, Lily; there is a storm coming, and we'll freeze up here."

"No," said Lily, pulling away. "I'm not going back, Jack. I can't face it."

Jack grabbed her wrist. "You've got to, Lily, you know that. You have to do what is needed to save the world!" he insisted.

Lily's face grew angry, and she pulled from his grip. "That's easy for you to say—it's not you that has to do anything! You're all secure and happy in your new life. You don't care about me at all!"

Jack stared at her in disbelief. "Lily, of course I care about you," he said, feeling stung. "I've come to save you."

"Only to return me to *them*, and see me save the world. You didn't come to save me for any other reason," she spat.

Jack spat right back. "I came to save you because I love you, and I won't stand by and watch you die!"

Lily turned away. "You don't love me; you've forgotten me. You have stayed away from me for days, and I saw you yesterday, with that other girl."

Jack took a moment to absorb the information. "That other girl is the daughter of the family I am working with. She got engaged yesterday—but not to me!" he added quickly. "I was congratulating her with her family. They have been very kind to me."

"Why are you working at all!" said Lily, quickly changing tack. "You're supposed to be my bodyguard, but you've been out in the valley instead."

"Yes, because I can't bear to be around you, with the love I feel for you, any longer," he blurted out. He rubbed his face with freezing fingers. "It will kill me to see you marry King Rain, and you won't do it if I am around to distract you. I went away so you would feel free to do what you have to, and yes, a part of me hoped my leaving would hurt you, so you would forget me," he said honestly.

Lily shook violently from the cold. "I tried to forget you, Jack, but I couldn't do it. I came up here to escape from it all."

Jack walked over to her and rubbed her arms against the chill. "You know you have to face this, Lily. It is too big to run away from," he said.

Lily began to cry. "I fear, above everything else, that you will hate me if I marry Rain, knowing that I love you."

Jack shook his head. "I will never hate you, Lily. I wish things could be different between us, but you have to marry Rain, and I understand that."

"Will you still love me?"

"I'll always love you, Lily," said Jack, fighting back tears of his own.

"Will you stay?"

"No," he said shortly. "I can't stay, Lily. I must do what I have to do, to avenge my family."

"You could do that and then come back," pleaded Lily.

"No, Lily, I couldn't stand it. I would rather be away from you forever than be with you and not able to have you. It would rip you apart as badly as it would me."

Lily wiped her tears from her frozen cheek. "I know," she said hopelessly. She reached out and took Jack's hand. He pulled her to him, and she wrapped her arms around him; he wished they could stay that way forever.

He moved away and held her face to wipe away the stray tears. "We have to get off this mountain before this storm really hits," he said, pulling her back towards the path that would lead them down.

They managed to reach the small flat place in the mountain when the snow fell thickly from the sky. "We'll not make it back," shouted Jack over the rush of the wind. "There is a cave over there. We'll have to hide out in it until the storm dies down."

He pulled Lily to the cave and pushed her inside ahead of him, so she was out of the wind. It wasn't very deep, and Jack knew that if the storm lasted days they would freeze to death. He prayed it would pass in a few hours.

He moved Lily as far back as the cave went and then sat down with his arms around her to keep her warm. Lily shook from the cold, and her skin felt like ice. Jack felt little better, but he was stronger than she was. He knew that if he was suffering, then she must be suffering worse.

"How long will the storm last?" asked Lily through chattering teeth.

"It could last hours or days. Pray for hours, Lily," said Jack, hugging her tighter.

"I'm sorry I wasted so much time on the top with talk. I've risked your life as well as mine."

"That doesn't matter now. We just have to hope the weather changes," replied Jack, fighting back a shiver.

"I wish I had never dragged you up here, Jack," said Lily, her voice full of regret. "I wish I could find you somewhere safe to be out of the cold."

"You didn't drag me anywhere. I came because I wanted to come," said Jack quietly. He was studying the snowstorm; it didn't look as if it would ease anytime soon. He kissed the top of Lily's head. "If we die here on this mountain, I will die happy, because I know you love me," he said.

Lily stood up suddenly.

"What are you doing?" he hissed.

Lily was examining the cave wall behind them. "I felt my hand go through the wall, Jack!" she said in shock.

"What!" cried Jack. He jumped up and scanned the wall.

Lily looked at him and lifted her hand. She placed it on the cave wall—and her hand disappeared through it. "See!" she said as she drew her hand out.

"It's a doorway of some sort," said Jack. He glanced at Lily, but before he could stop her, she had walked through the wall.

"Lily, Lily!" he screamed. "Can you hear me? Come back through!"

Lily's hand came back through the wall, making him jump. "Take my hand," her disembodied voice told him. Jack took it, and she pulled him through the wall. He stepped out into a large underground cave. The ground was covered with green moss, and there was a huge waterfall flowing from the cave roof. It ran into a brook that flowed away beyond his line of vision. The air was warm and humid, very much as it was in Emiscial.

"What is this place?" he asked wearily.

"It's magical," said Lily, blowing on her chilled hands. "Let's explore." She pulled Jack along by his hand.

"Slow down. We don't know anything about this place," he said, looking round uncertainly.

Lily paused and considered Jack. "What do we need to know? It is dry, and warm, and lovely. We can see the way out of the cave," she added, looking back at the place they had entered. "Look, Jack, there are fruit trees here. Let's get something to eat. I'm starving."

Fruit trees growing in a cave was slightly odd, thought Jack. They truly must be in a magical cave. He followed Lily without protest, for he had to admit he, too, was hungry.

Lily reached one of the fruit trees, which grew large, soft, yellow, peaches. She picked two and gave one to Jack. He bit into it and moaned with pleasure. It was sweet and tasty. He ate it and helped himself to another three.

Lily had settled herself down on a thick patch of moss; she patted the ground, and Jack sat beside her. "Do you think anyone lives here?" he asked.

"We've been here a while, and I haven't seen anyone," said Lily, looking around. "I was thinking, though. It was funny how I said that I wanted to find somewhere to keep you safe, and then the next thing I knew I was able to enter this place. Maybe it is a special place for people to come to in times of need."

"That's possible," said Jack smiling. "I think it is made of white magic. It feels similar to Emiscial, but if it is, why didn't the magus tell me it was here when I came to rescue you?"

Lily sat up suddenly and fixed her eyes on Jack. "Let's stay here," she said in excitement.

Jack barked a laugh. "We can't stay here," he said. "We don't really know where we are, and it might not be safe."

"Well, nothing bad has happened yet," said Lily. "Why should anything bad happen now? Please, Jack, will you think about it? It would mean you and I could stay together."

"What about King Rain and the world needing the Child of Light?" he said seriously.

Lily scowled darkly. "I don't care anymore."

Jacked looked at her face, feeling shocked, "What have the magus told you that's upset you so much?"

Lily's whole posture slumped. "Jack, I found out who the other vessel was. It was my mother," she said sadly. "She and my father agreed to make the Child of Light, but the magus lied to us about a part of their story. They said Aidan killed her, but he didn't—they did."

"What?" shouted Jack in horror.

A sob racked Lily's body. Jack put his arm around her, rubbing her back. "That isn't the worst of it," sniffed Lily. "The boy my mother carried was Aidan's. The magus said she lied about the violation and weakened my father's love for her, but she didn't. He knew the baby wasn't his and planned to raise him as his son anyway. That hindered the magus's plans for the Child of Light, so they tried to abort the child without my parents' knowledge, to cleanse them both, so they could try again to make a child of love." She drew in a sharp breath, tears splashing on the ground. Jack kept rubbing her back, making soothing noises and trying to help her calm down. She drew her knees up and hid her head, weeping uncontrollably. He stayed silent, letting her regain herself. It took her several minutes, but then her sobs began to ease.

She sat up, rubbing her bloodshot eyes relentlessly, and wiped her face on her arm. "The magus sent to do it gave the wrong dosage of poison and killed my mother by mistake," she finished, squeezing her eyes shut in pain. "They won't tell me who did it. I know it was Mia who brought the serfdom that was meant to provide my mother with loyal guards to protect her and the child."

Jack shook his head. "Lily," he whispered before pulling her into a tight hug. He let her bury her head into his shoulder and cry as he held her. He felt horrified by her discovery—and murderous towards the magus! He kept silent until he felt her calming down again; he knew what he wanted to do.

Jack broke away and held her face. "I am yours, Lily, in every way. Command me, and I will obey you," he promised her.

Lily looked overwhelmed with relief and happiness; she flung her arms around him again.

Jack hugged her back and ran his fingers through her hair. It felt exactly as he had imagined it would.

Lily moved out of the hug and ran her hand over Jack's face. "What I want to ask you to do is going to change the fate of the world," she warned.

Jack felt his heart quicken. "Are you saying you want to marry me," he asked. He could barely breathe.

Lily took a deep breath. "The magus have made so many mistakes that I don't trust their judgement. From now on, I'm choosing to trust my own," she said quietly. "Marry me, Jack. I love you! How can that be wrong?" she asked.

Jack cried out in joy and hugged her so hard. "I truly, deeply love you," he whispered into her hair. "You're right; it can't be wrong."

He let her go and studied her face, feeling his love blossom inside him. He closed his eyes, took a deep breath, and leant forward to kiss her. Finally he felt her lips on his, soft, and warm, and they both smiled simultaneously. Jack put his hand behind her neck and gently gripped her hair. As he made the kiss more passionate, he felt Lily take hold of his arm. Without breaking the kiss, he guided her backwards so she was lying down in the moss, and moved himself slightly on top of her. He let his hand run down her body, exploring her through the silk, and she gasped.

Jack drew away, panting hard. "Do you want me to stop?" he asked seriously.

Lily's breathing was fast and her eyes bright; she shook her head. "No, don't stop," she said. She suddenly giggled a sweet, nervous sound. She moaned and squeezed her eyes shut. "I don't know what to do," she said in a whisper.

Jack laughed gently. "Neither do I," he said. "We can learn together."

Lily opened her eyes; she licked her lips and nodded.

Jack kissed her lips again before moving to her jawbone and all the way down her neck. He listened to her noises and studied her responses. Everything he did came naturally to him, and everything she did in return felt amazing. He felt shy as he undressed and tried not to make her feel that way when he removed her dress. She looked scared when he moved on top of her, so he slowed down and made sure he began the lovemaking gently. Only when she was ready did he increase the depth and speed. She held him tightly, and he felt honoured by her faith in him. They were finally together in every way, and he felt complete.

When it was over, Jack wrapped Lily in his arms. She fell asleep quickly, and he watched her until his eyes grew heavy and he, too, nodded off.

When Jack stirred, he could hear water flowing. He was warm and comfortable. He remembered where he was and smiled at the memory of the night before. He kept his eyes closed, reliving it second by second in his head. When he felt Lily's hand stroke across his stomach, he reached for it and squeezed. "Have you been awake long?" he asked, opening his eyes. She was sitting next to him, grinning at him. He sat up and kissed her cheek.

"I was enjoying watching you sleep for a change," she said playfully.

Jack ran his hand over her bare back. "Some bodyguard I turned out to be," he said teasingly.

Lily smiled a mischievous smile. "Do you have any regrets?" she asked.

Jack kissed her shoulder. "I'm meant to be with you, Lily. I will never regret choosing to embrace my destiny," he said, stroking her back again. "Do you have any regrets?" he asked, hoping she would say no.

"Only one," said Lily. Jack froze. She saw his reaction and smiled. She lay down and pulled him beside her again. "That we are not married," she finished, touching his chest.

Jack grinned. "Let's fix that. I, Jack Orden, take you, Lillian, Princess of Judelen, to be my wife."

Lily smiled happily. "And I, Lillian, Princess of Judelen, take you, Jack Orden, to be my husband."

"Done," said Jack, rolling towards her so he could kiss her again.

A breeze blew through the cave, and a faint chiming noise floated on the air. Jack broke off the kiss and looked around. He sat up quickly.

"What was that?" asked Lily.

Jack had no idea. "Get dressed quickly," he said, reaching for his clothes.

Lily grabbed her dress and slipped it on. Jack finished dressing, jumped up, and helped her to her feet.

"Do you think it was something bad?" asked Lily in a frightened voice.

"I don't know," said Jack, looking around.

Lily let out a gasp.

"What is it?" said Jack, spinning round.

"Don't you see it?" asked Lily, pointing to the waterfall. Jack looked, but there was nothing there.

He shook his head. "What did you see?" he said.

"It's the Unicorn, I'm sure of it," said Lily, stepping away from him.

He grabbed her hand. "Don't wander off," he told her, but his voice died in his throat when he saw it too. How was it possible for the Unicorn from the Trio to be standing in this cave?

Jack's awe turned quickly to anger, and he stepped forward. "Why are you hiding in here? Why aren't you helping to fix your world," he yelled.

Lily squeezed Jack's hand. "Stay calm, Jack," she begged him. He heard the fear in her voice.

He looked down at Lily. "I don't care what he is. We deserve an explanation as to why humans have been abandoned by our creators to suffer pain and death. Why did you leave us?" he demanded, staring back at the Unicorn.

The Unicorn seemed to be staring just as hard back at him; stubbornly Jack waited out the silence.

"You are angry," the Unicorn finally whispered. Jack was taken aback by the sensation of the telepathy.

Jack nodded curtly. "I am angry. The world is falling apart; people are dying. Why haven't you done anything about it?" he asked, feeling bitter.

"We lost control of our creations when Orthrillium broke the Earth Stone," the Unicorn whispered. "The Fairy died, and we did not know that could happen. We trapped humans into a tiny pocket of our world, fearing their destructive powers—"

"What do you mean, 'trapped'?" interrupted Jack.

"It was the last act we did before leaving you to your fate. We did it immediately after Orthrillium broke the Earth Stone and refused to surrender it, instead choosing to split the magic with his Theanic Order. We made the mountain ranges, and the deserts beyond, and the sea beyond them, to make certain humans could not spread their infection into the rest of the world. Then the Dragon and I fled to different hidden realms, knowing the world was beyond our power to fix. Then came the greatest betrayal in Evelyn Maude's murder of Orthrillium, her ability to create black magic, and the War of Power, causing chaos and destruction."

"But surely you have powers beyond hers?" shouted Jack. "You made her—you must be able to destroy her!"

"We don't have the power to destroy our creations. The Trio made the world; only the Trio can unmake it. Orthrillium's betrayal was unexpected and the results catastrophic. If this world is to be repaired, humans must do it."

Jack stepped forward. "Tell us how to do it. Is it through the Child of Light?"

The Unicorn pawed the ground. "I have been listening to the magus. They have made many errors, but this plan has the chance of success."

Jack looked down in guilt. "Have we now destroyed the power?" he asked seriously.

The Unicorn lifted its head. "No, you haven't. You have made it come into being. You have made the child in love, and now there is a chance the world can be healed."

Lily gasped and grabbed Jack's arm; he looked down at her. She had tears in her eyes; her other hand was unconsciously touching her stomach. He put his hand over hers, on the spot where their baby was now growing. He was going to be a father!

Jack looked back at the Unicorn. "Can you infuse the child with light?" he asked hopefully.

"That is beyond my power. You need the light the Guardian protects, to be given when the child is born."

Jack looked back down at Lily. "We'll just stay in Emiscial until then."

Lily looked worriedly at Jack. "I don't think the magus realised the infusion can't happen until after the birth," she said.

Jack began to pace. "Nine months is a long time to wait. Evelyn and Aidan will stop at nothing to destroy us, but what can we do? Can you help us?" he asked the Unicorn.

"I let you into the hidden realm because I felt your love. It is the only thing left that could be powerful enough to mend this world. My belief in that is the reason I will continue to aid you. Let the vessel come here to me."

Jack let go of Lily and guided her in front of him. She walked slowly towards the Unicorn, looking uneasy. Jack felt apprehensive, but he nodded encouragingly at her when she glanced back at him. She stopped directly before the Unicorn and waited.

"Hold out your hand," he commanded.

Lily raised her left hand and turned it palm upward in front of the Unicorn. Jack could see she was trembling slightly. He shifted his stance in case he needed to move quickly.

The Unicorn lowered the tip of its horn onto Lily's outstretched palm, and her fingers twitched slightly. The horn emitted a golden light. It lasted only a second, and then it disappeared. Jack squinted to see what it had done to Lily: he could just make out something gold sitting on the palm of her hand. The Unicorn drew away, and Lily closed her hand over the object. With a small bow, she retreated back to stand with Jack. He studied her hand in interest.

Lily opened her palm and showed Jack the ring she now held. It was solid gold, cut into two figure-eight pieces that crossed each other. Nestled in the middle was a small piece of multicoloured smooth stone that shone in the light. They both turned back to the Unicorn, awaiting an explanation.

"I have given you a ring that will protect you and the child from death in any form. It will also alter your natural pregnancy cycle. The child will be born within two weeks. You must wear the ring for the powers to work. Be cautious that the dark forces do not learn of it and take it from you.

"The stone in the centre is the last remaining piece of the Earth Stone. The child will need that if the plan works. Let your husband put it on your finger; it will seal your union."

Jack carefully picked up the golden band. Lily extended her fingers for him to slip it on; it fit perfectly. Jack raised her hand and kissed her finger, feeling the ring beneath his lips. Lily looked overjoyed.

Jack looked back at the Unicorn. "I don't know how to thank you," he said sincerely.

"It is I who should be thanking you. You have given me hope. If you need help again, I will aid you. But keep me hidden for as long as possible—otherwise, Evelyn Maude will be able to find and destroy me. If she takes my power, you will lose the advantage the Child of Light has given you. You must return to Emiscial. You have work to do."

Jack took Lily's hand. "Let's go," he said hurriedly. "We have a lot of explaining to do."

A flash of golden light blinded his vision. He blinked sharply and found he was no longer in the hidden realm. He and Lily had been transported back to the bottom of the mountain path, just outside the protective shield. He glanced back up the mountain, silently thanking the Unicorn.

Lily was doing the same. Her eyes caught Jack's, and she laughed. He kissed her gently.

"They're here," a voice shouted. Jack turned around to see Troyan, Kerri, and Jamella standing just inside the shield. He sighed in relief, and leading Lily by the hand, he ran towards them.

Jamella suddenly stepped backwards. She raised her hand, palm up, towards them.

Jack moved to pass through the shield, but his entry was blocked. "Let us in!" he shouted in an urgent voice. "There is so much we need to tell you."

Jack looked at their faces and saw they were furious. He glanced at Lily and lowered his eyes to her stomach. He realised they could sense the baby—but they didn't understand!

He looked up in horror. "Where is King Rain? I must speak with him!" he called, looking at each woman in turn.

"He is in the temple, with Reanna and the other magus," answered Troyan, her voice cold and emotionless. "The king of Grimfar has escorted him here safely."

"Niar's here," said Jack, and he felt a wave of hope. "I know what you are thinking, but we haven't done anything wrong. We have made the Child of Light!"

Troyan sneered at him. "You have destroyed any chance of that!" she spat. "Were we not clear enough to you? Why would you do this?"

Jack banged on the shield. "You don't understand! You must let us in. We can explain!"

The three sisters exchanged looks, and Kerri shook her head. Jack cursed loudly and banged on the shield again. Lily suddenly screamed, and every eye turned to her. Something was approaching from the mountain path. It was a funnel of air, twisting round and round at high speed and heading straight for them.

Jack grabbed Lily and moved her next to him. He turned his back to the twister to address the magus. "What is that? Is it you?"

Jamella studied the twister. "It is air being manipulated by some sort of spirit creature. It is black magic."

"Then let us through before it takes us!" screamed Lily.

"You have defiled the vessel, and you will not defile our realm," shouted Troyan in a temper. "If that thing has come for you, then good riddance to you both. You are wicked children!"

Jack didn't have time to plead with her again; the twisted air was upon them. He felt it take his arm in an iron grip, and he fought to pull free. It had hold of Lily, too; she was frantically trying to break its grip. Suddenly they were lifted into the air.

Lily screamed in panic. "Help us, please!" she begged the magus, but they didn't move.

The twister took them higher. Jack heard someone shouting. It sounded like a man's voice, and he looked down to see Niar sprinting towards the shield. He pushed through the magus and leapt into the air, grabbing Jack by the ankle. Their combined weight forced the spirit creature to release Jack. He and Niar fell to the ground, landing hard. Jack was on his feet in a second. He looked up, but it was too late. The twister had risen beyond his reach; it was carrying Lily away towards the mountains. Jack could hear her screaming until the sound faded in the distance.

He felt a hand on his shoulder and looked up into the face of his friend. Niar looked back at Jack in sympathy. He steered him under the shield, which Jamella had unblocked. Niar released Jack to straighten his grey silk tunic and brush dust off his black hair.

Jack felt numb. He collapsed onto the ground as energy left him and loss filled its place.

Niar held his shoulder again, and squeezed it in comfort. "My friend, I am so sorry that this tragedy has befallen you." He turned angrily to the three magus. "Why have you done this? Explain yourselves!"

Troyan raised an eyebrow at him. "We do not answer to you, King Niar. You are a visitor here."

"You will answer his question," said a voice so deep it vibrated in Jack's head. He looked up and saw a man coming towards him. He was nearly seven feet tall, with plaited white hair down to his ankles. His face was smooth and long, his irises pure white.

Jack swallowed a lump in his throat, and drew himself onto his knees, keeping his eyes downcast. "King Rain," he said.

King Rain reached down and extended his long pale fingers towards Jack. Jack took his hand, and the Guardian pulled him to his feet. He stood regarding him for a moment.

The king turned back to Troyan. "Explain why you have done this terrible thing," he said. Jack was shocked that there was no emotion in his voice or change in his tone. Jack knew he wasn't human, but Aidan displayed emotions. He wondered why Rain did not.

Troyan drew herself to stand taller. "Jack Orden and the vessel have, against our orders, taken each other, and she is now pregnant. They have destroyed the chance to make the Child of Light, so my sisters and I banished them from Emiscial."

Reanna suddenly appeared besides King Rain. She was panting as if she had been running, and she looked livid. "Do you have any idea what you have done! You have just sent Lily into the hands of Evelyn."

"What does it matter!" shouted Troyan. "She will have no use for her. They deserve to be punished, Reanna."

"It is you three who shall be punished!" screamed Reanna.

"Punish *him*!" shouted Troyan, pointing at Jack. "He has destroyed everything."

Reanna's face lost its anger. She glanced at Jack and back to her sister. "No, Troyan, we were wrong. Jack has been right all along. He was meant to make the Child of Light."

Troyan's eyes widened in shock. "But we were certain she needed to marry King Rain, and the child needed to be his," she said.

"The vessel was not meant to be with me," said King Rain. "I am here to infuse the power into the child she created with the man she loved, just as I would have done for Elizabeth and Symon. The Order was foolish to think I would take an earthly wife. That unnatural act could never create the Child of Light. My job has always been to be the child's teacher and protector."

Jamella cried out and dropped to her knees. Kerri and Troyan did the same, and all three stared at the ground.

King Rain turned to Reanna. "We must help Jack to get his wife back."

Jack found his voice again. "You all need to listen to me; there is very little time. My child will be born within the next two weeks. It doesn't matter how I know that," he added, as Reanna looked ready to question him. "We need to stop Evelyn Maude and Aidan from being able to form any plans."

Reanna nodded. "Of course, Jack, the Theanic Order is at your command." She glanced at her sisters on the ground. "King Rain, what should I do with them?"

Jack glared at the three women coldly; he knew what he would do given the choice.

"Do nothing. They must live with their mistake, and it is for them to try and repair it," answered King Rain.

Reanna nodded, and she looked at Niar. "I need your help, King Niar, Jack is going to need an army to help him get back to Judelen safely to rescue Lily."

Niar stepped forward. "Without hesitation I will help my friend, but he is going to need a bigger army than I can raise." Niar turned to Jack. "You must go home, Jack, and take your rightful place as the steward of Sanalow."

Everyone went silent, turning to stare at him. Jack considered Niar's words and nodded. "I think you're right, and I must leave immediately. That thing will carry Lily quicker than I can march an army." He turned to King Rain. "I'll get her back here as fast as possible."

Jack needed Mia. He looked round for her and spotted her standing quietly under one of the trees. He strode towards her, saying, "I need your help." He pulled her slightly into the forest, where the others couldn't overhear them speaking. Mia waited in silence for him to explain.

He raked a hand through his hair. "Mia, I am so angry right now with the magus that I want to kill all of you!" Mia blanched at his words, but he ignored this and carried on speaking. "That being said, I trust you enough to believe you would never intentionally harm Lily. I need you to do a job, but you cannot tell Reanna, Rain, Niar, or your sisters." She nodded her agreement, and Jack continued, "I need you to follow the path Lily took into the mountains. After a few hours, you will come to a flat area with a cave. Go inside the cave, and say out loud that I have sent you to ask for help."

Mia opened her mouth to speak, but Jack cut her off. "You need to trust me, and I need you to go now. What I need is something powerful enough to destroy Aidan's army and delay anything he or his mother may be planning. Topple Judelen if need be. Don't worry about Lily; she'll be safe."

Mia looked utterly confused, but she nodded again. She grabbed Jack and pulled him into a hug. He tensed, but he understood the gesture and hugged her back. She broke away from him and ran straight out of the shield and onto the mountain path. He watched her go, feeling grateful that she trusted him.

"Where is Mia going?" shouted Reanna, running to Jack.

"She has a job to do, Reanna, and so do you. I need horses." He turned to Niar. "I need you to come with me to Sanalow." Niar nodded readily.

Jamella leapt to her feet. "Jack, I am so sorry! I cannot believe what I have done. Please take me with you. I believe I can help you with those spirit creatures. Let me try and repair what I have broken."

Jack looked upon the yellow magus, feeling hatred. He wanted to punch her, but he knew he would never strike a woman. He forced himself to calm down and see reason in her offer. "You should come, and I want to take Kem as well," he said to Reanna. She nodded her agreement.

"Someone needs to go to Grimfar to rally Niar's people," said Jack.

Troyan stood up and bowed. "I'll go, Jack."

Jack nodded. "Have them ready to meet me where the colony was, as soon as I have claimed Sanalow."

As soon as the horses were ready, Jack, Niar, and the magus mounted. Jack signalled for Kem to lead Belldean.

Reanna approached him and touched his leg. "I cannot express to you how truly sorry we are that this has happened," she said.

Jack sniffed. "Let's just hope I can find Lily and get her back here to King Rain so that we can repair this mess," he said angrily.

Reanna nodded and stepped away from him as he heeled Bailey into the tunnel.

21

BACK IN JUDELEN

Lily waited anxiously in the darkness. She was in a cell beneath the palace, her arms strapped in chains that hung down from the ceiling; they ached from the pressure. She shivered uncontrollably, for she was still wearing only her ripped blue dress made of pure silk.

The journey back to Judelen had been much shorter then she had hoped. The creature in the air funnel had delivered her to Drake, and he had brought her here.

Lily wondered whether the Black Witch was here by now. She was trying not to think about seeing Aidan again or the creature that was using her father's body. Instead she tried to think up a way of escaping, but she knew she had no chance alone. She must put her trust in Jack to save her.

She thought of the magus and sighed, hoping they would help him. She took a deep breath and looked around the gloomy room. There was nothing she could do about the magus, or Jack, and she needed to focus on keeping herself and the baby safe from Aidan. She glanced at her ring. She must not let that monster know she had it, or he wouldn't hesitate to kill her.

The cell door burst open. The sudden appearance of torchlight made Lily turn her head away.

"The Overlord wants you," said Drake from the doorway.

"You don't have to do this, Drake," pleaded Lily. "Remember who you were before the dark forces took you over. You were my protector. I need your help!"

Drake rolled his eyes at her plea. "I was never your protector. I was given this body when I was in the service of your mother," he said as he undid the chains holding her. "The serfdom never worked properly on Argon and me. It was us who helped Aidan defile her. And we manipulated your father into trusting Aidan's letters, fuelling his belief in the invisible land beyond the mountains."

Lily's arms dropped, and she rubbed her wrists. "So, it was all made up? Shangol and its people don't exist?"

Drake shook his head. "The Overlord built Shangol City within the Great Mountains to protect his mother's prison. It's filled with black creations, but no human lives there. I think he quite enjoyed filling your head with lies about his imaginary people; he has a gift for manipulation."

"Where is my father?" asked Lily.

Drake smiled coldly. "You know as well as I do that your father is dead. Salzar, however, is busy with king's business. Come, the Overlord doesn't like to be kept waiting."

Drake dragged Lily from the cell and took her up a narrow staircase into the main palace. He led her quickly through the corridor towards the greeting chamber, passing many servants and guards along the way.

"Have you taken them all?" asked Lily, looking at their unconcerned faces as they watched their queen being dragged through the palace.

"We stopped hiding our presence after your escape. The palace has been cleansed of any pure souls that were left. They are all hanging up in the main square alongside Will and Ryan, and we even put Mistress Stratton up there too!"

Enraged, Lily swung for Drake, but he held her back easily. They reached the greeting chamber, and Drake opened the doors without knocking. He pushed Lily inside ahead of him and closed the doors behind her.

The room looked different than when she had last been in it; the walls were now black and silver.

Lily turned her attention to the far end, where the thrones were placed. Aidan sat in the throne he had always used. He watched her with a calm face, but she could see the amusement in his eyes.

Slowly he got up and crossed the chamber towards her. He spread his hands out in front of him. "Welcome home, Lillian. You have no idea how pleased I am to see you!"

Lily kept her eyes locked on Aidan's. "I think your pleasure is to be short-lived. You've lost, Aidan. You cannot use me anymore to make your Child of Darkness."

Aidan laughed. "I know all about you, and the boy, and your marriage," he said unconcernedly.

"I'm pregnant, Aidan, with my husband's child, the Child of Light," said Lily with her head held high. "The child was made in true love. You can't taint that!"

Aidan tilted his head. "Oh, but I can, Lillian. I can and I will."

Lily shook her head. "I will never be your queen," she sneered. "Your plan to make me fall in love with you has failed. My husband is going to return to Judelen; he is going to rescue me and kill you!"

Aidan laughed in delight. "I certainly hope he will try, but he may find himself outnumbered, as every person left in your city is now a part of my new army. I also have other creatures at my disposal—wind riders, Shangol beasts, and don't forget my mother! She is free of her prison and on her way from Shangol to meet us on our journey. By tomorrow you will be at her mercy in the Great Mountains, where I doubt even Jack will be able to find the way through."

Lily raised her hand and slapped Aidan hard across the face. His head whipped to the side. Giving a low growl, he advanced upon her slowly. Lily stiffened and stepped back against the door. He didn't stop until he was so close that their noses touched. He studied her face, and then suddenly he grabbed the back of her head to hold her still and kissed her passionately. She pulled sideways, trying to break his grip, but she couldn't move him.

He broke off the kiss and took a step back, wiping his mouth. "I see marriage agrees with you," he said mockingly. Lily said nothing; she merely regarding him with a stony expression.

Aidan's eyes narrowed slightly. He took Lily's arm and steered her into the chamber towards the thrones. She struggled to get free, but he tightened his grip. He reached his throne, pushed her onto her knees before it, and went and sat in his seat.

Lily made a vexed sound as she straightened up but stayed on her knees regarding Aidan, trying not to give him any satisfaction.

"I see your little road trip to Emiscial has done nothing to improve your manners," observed Aidan. "No matter. Soon you will be delivered into the hands of my mother. She will have great satisfaction moulding you with her powers until you are a perfect little slave. For her pleasure and mine," he added with a nasty smile.

Lily's stony façade slipped slightly. "Why bother with this game? I know I cannot give you the Child of Darkness."

Aidan leant forward. "I'm not lying, Lillian. Your child *will* be the Child of Darkness."

"That's impossible," spat Lily. "It is made from love, pure—"

"Yes, yes," shouted Aidan, sitting up straight. "That is what makes it perfect." He gripped the arms of his throne tightly. "My mother is a very clever woman. She has discovered a way to defeat love—"

"I know," said Lily coldly. "That is why you came to Judelen, to seduce me and trick me into having your child, in your tainted version of love."

Aidan looked impressed. "The magus have been doing their homework," he said, "but so have we. And we now believe we can twist this pure child—and the best part is, you are the one who will help us do it!"

"I will not," said Lily firmly. "I will never help you."

Aidan nodded slowly. "I agree. You will not help me, but you will help your child. I am going to take you back to Shangol, and there you will stay to raise your child with me. You will love it unconditionally, and even when my mother has finished filling it with her black magic, and it begins its evil deeds, you will still love it."

Lily put her hands on her stomach, and a tear fell from her eye.

Aidan scoffed. "Because you will love it no matter what it becomes, my mother will be able to use it freely to destroy the light. You will be our saviour, Lillian."

Lily couldn't speak. She remained on her knees, her hands covering her belly in a protective manner. She knew what Aidan said was true. She already loved this child, and she had already vowed to protect it forever. She closed her eyes in a silent prayer; she needed Jack more than ever to save them. If he didn't succeed, they would be lost.

22

JACK'S REVENGE

The journey from Emiscial to Sanalow had taken half a day. Jack sat upon Bailey, studying the city's outer walls. Niar, Jamella, and Kem sat beside him. All the members of the party wore riding cloaks to conceal their identities.

"The plan will work, Jack," said Niar reassuringly. "The magus need to go in first and conceal themselves by the circle, if that is where you choose the fight to be."

Jack nodded, keeping his eyes on the gates. They didn't appear to be manned. "It is a big area, where fewer people can get hurt. We should be able to reach it safely without the guards detecting me." He turned to Kem and Jamella. "You two go now. Niar and I shall wait for one hour before we follow you into the city."

The magus nodded and rode their horses towards the city gates. Jack watched them until they were out of sight; he ran his battle plan over and over through his head.

"Are you prepared to face Morridread?" asked Niar.

"I have been ready to fight him since he murdered my family," said Jack coldly.

Niar frowned. "Remember not to let emotions get in the way of your fight! He will try to trip you up that way."

Jack looked kindly upon his friend. "I shall call upon the deep calm, I promise. Jarrad shall not trip me up or defeat me."

Niar smiled in approval.

When the time came to ride into the city, Jack's senses were fully prepared. He kept his head down; hoping no one would recognise him or Niar before he was ready. He reached the circle and immediately checked for Kem and Jamella; he relaxed slightly when he spotted them concealed on opposite sides. They both nodded to him.

Jack lowered his hood and looked around the circle. He spotted a young boy playing on the outskirts. Jack pointed at him. "You, boy! Go quickly and pass a message to the city guards. Tell them to inform Jarrad Morridread that Jack Orden waits for him here in the circle. Tell them I challenge Morridread for the rule of Sanalow, and he must fight me here and now, or I shall take it with my army."

The boy looked terrified and excited all in one. He ran off as fast as he could. Jack saw him encounter guards on the far side of the courtyard. At the boy's words, the guards studied Jack, looked beyond him at Niar, and ran into the steward's hall. Jack waited in silence, concentrating on the deep calm. The few people walking in the circle had heard the order Jack had given to the boy. They stood watching Jack in interest, but he ignored them, keeping his eyes fixed on the door, waiting for Jarrad.

Jack hadn't been waiting long before a large group of guards piled out of the hall, followed by Morridread himself. He looked just as he had when Jack had last seen him, still thin-faced with a crooked nose and wide chin. His black hair, to his shoulders, was stock straight, unlike Jack's short brown curls.

Niar tapped Jack's shoulder and signalled for him to hand over Bailey's reins. Jack dismounted and gave them over. He took a few steps forward, keeping his hand resting on his sword hilt.

Jarrad watched him, his face expressionless. "Surround them!" he ordered the guards. They quickly obeyed, forming a circle around the edge of the courtyard, keeping Jack and Niar inside. They parted to allow Jarrad to come into the circle before sealing the gap.

Jarrad limped into the circle. He stopped to face Jack but stayed far enough back to be out of sword range. "I wondered how long it would take for you to return, Jack. I always knew one day you would," he said.

Jack smiled, although he felt no humour. "It seems you were correct, Jarrad, for here I am."

Jarrad held his arms out; he looked pompous. "Have you come to fight me, Jack?"

"Yes," said Jack, his eyes locked on Jarrad's.

"I'm afraid not!" said Jarrad, folding his arms.

The whistle of an arrow being let loose from a bow rang in Jack's ears. He glanced up and saw it flying towards him from a nearby roof. He watched it approach, his heart quickening. A few feet above his head, the arrow hit an invisible shield and broke in half. Its remains fell to the ground. Jarrad looked from it to Jack in astonishment.

Jack tried not to give away his relief that his plan had worked. He made sure his voice was calm when he spoke. "I figured you'd attempt something like that, Jarrad. That is why I have brought magus with me, to make sure our fight stays between you and me," he said.

Jarrad looked round in alarm. "Witches, here—that's not possible! You're lying!" he said.

"Explain the shield then!" said Jack loudly. "Try firing more arrows if you like, or send your men into the circle to cut me to shreds!"

Jarrad turned to the guards. "Kill him now!" he screamed.

The guards moved forward, but the invisible shield stopped them from taking more than two steps. "We can't enter the courtyard, My Lord," one of them shouted.

Jack offered up another silent thank-you to Jamella. "Let's stop wasting time, Jarrad. You cannot leave this courtyard until you kill me or I kill you," he said.

Jarrad looked sceptically at Jack. "How can I know that your witches won't interfere with the fight?"

"I give you my word that they are forbidden to interfere," answered Jack. "Even should you kill me, they are ordered to take no revenge upon you. They and Niar shall simply leave."

Jarrad pointed sharply at Jack. "If I kill you, then know this: that Grimfar monster will die shortly after," he said. "He was sentenced to death alongside you, and I shall carry out that sentence!"

Jack heard Niar walk forward. He turned to regard him.

"Very well," shouted Niar. "If you defeat Jack, then I swear to you I shall hand myself over to you for execution."

Jack glared at him. "You'll do no such thing!" he hissed.

"You are too late, Jack. I accept his word," said Jarrad, sounding delighted.

Jack turned away from Niar, his mouth dry. "So, are you agreeing to my challenge?" he asked Jarrad.

Jarrad nodded. "I accept your challenge, Jack Orden. If you defeat me, then the rule of Sanalow will pass to you on the moment of my death. If I defeat you, I shall maintain my title, and I shall kill both you and the Grimfar monster, King Niar!"

Jack drew his sword. "Then let this fight begin," he said.

Jarrad brought his sword up and gripped it hard beneath his fingers. He wasted no time in making a strike; he came in high, but Jack pushed his blow aside with ease, quickly striking one of his own. Jarrad skipped backwards to avoid his blade.

Jarrad gave Jack a twisted grin. "I thought time on the run would have made you lazy," he said.

Jack laughed at Jarrad's pathetic attempt to wind him up. He couldn't resist replying. "I was only a wayfarer for one year. I have been a fully trained bodyguard since winter ended," he said, making another quick strike.

Jarrad pushed his blow aside and struck three times in a row. Jack danced away from him, fending off his blows.

Jarrad let him retreat, looking amused. "Who was stupid enough to hire a deserter?" he asked.

Jack knew he would feel a boyish pleasure with his answer. "The princess of Judelen," he informed him.

Jarrad froze, and Jack threw in an attack, but Jarrad quickly recovered and pushed his blade away.

"Nice lie, Orden," he hissed. "As if she would ever hire someone like you!"

Jack felt annoyance ebb into the deep calm. Jarrad attacked him again and Jack attacked back, their blades ringing loudly with each blow.

Jarrad was too focused; Jack needed to break his concentration. He had an idea. "She did hire me," he said quickly, "and not only that—she is now my wife."

It worked. Jarrad stopped attacking, lowering his sword slightly. The hesitation was enough for Jack to knock his sword from his hands. Jarrad came to and dived across the ground to retrieve it, he brought it up before Jack could strike a deadly blow, and with a quick movement he cut Jack's leg. Jack hissed sharply as blood began to leak from his wound. The Emiscial silk offered poor protection compared to his usual leather trousers. He jumped backwards to steady himself.

Jarrad was back on his feet, looking triumphant. "Did you hear that, my guards?" he shouted to the watching crowd. "Meet Prince Jack Orden, married to the princess of Judelen, he is!" The guards laughed out loud. Jack pushed his rising anger away, searching once more for the deep calm.

Jarrad was regarding him coolly. "Things have certainly changed for you, Jack! I'm afraid my time here has been quite uneventful since the night of your escape," he commented calmly.

Jack snarled under his breath, "I heard you broke your leg. I was rather annoyed to learn it was not your neck!"

Jarrad raised his eyebrows. "I don't believe that, Jack. You are not the type of man to be happy when his chance for revenge gets ripped away from him. We all knew that you would return to Sanalow to avenge your family. It was such a shame there was never any hope of you saving them!"

His temper took hold, and Jack launched at Jarrad with a scream of pain. Jarrad pushed his blade aside and thumped him hard in the stomach, causing him to drop to the ground.

"Didn't I teach you anything!" yelled Niar from the sidelines. Jack looked back at him and struggled to his feet. He felt stupid; letting his emotions rule him would kill him. He had to stop.

Jarrad had waited for him to get up without attempting to attack further. He smiled as he looked at Jack, all covered in blood and dust.

"As I said, it was a shame that you couldn't save them. We all heard you crying like a baby. Did the monster stop you from coming back to defend their bodies?"

Jack started shaking with anger, and he tried desperately to calm himself.

Jarrad had his sword hilt resting under his chin, his face totally relaxed. "I knew you would one day return, Jack, so I thought it would be nice to give you the chance to do what you failed to do."

Jack looked at Jarrad in confusion. "I don't understand," he said.

Jarrad lowered his sword hilt; he had a nasty glint in his green eyes. "The chance to defend their bodies," he said slowly. "I kept them in cages for you—look."

Jack knew he shouldn't do it, but he couldn't resist. Turning to look where Jarrad was pointing, he saw three cages. Each held a skeleton, and one of them was very small.

It took all his strength, not to move towards them. He turned back to Jarrad, knowing he must not react. "What use are bones to me? I feel nothing for remains, Jarrad," he said, forcing his voice to stay even.

Jarrad looked angry that Jack was not upset. He raised his sword again. "Then let us finish this fight, Jack, and see who shall be joining the dead!" he spat.

Jack regained the deep calm and pushed away Jarrad's first blow. He struck back with a strong blow. He calculated the next one and aimed lower; it was deflected. He moved onto another pattern, then another, then another. For several minutes the two men fought without stopping. Jack was hot. His body was covered in sweat, his hands sticky over the sword hilt.

Jack got lucky and managed to hit Jarrad across the stomach with his sword, leaving a tear in his flesh, but he was not quick enough to avoid getting slashed on his shoulder and then his face.

Jarrad smiled at the wound across Jack's cheek. "You almost match the monster now," he said mockingly.

Jack didn't rise to the provocation but continued to fight. He was tiring, but Jarrad didn't look to be. Jack moved backwards to give himself chance to calculate. He trod on something hard under his boot, his foot slipped, and he crashed backwards onto the ground. He looked down and saw a pebble had caused his slip. Jarrad kicked Jack's sword away with his foot and brought his blade up to Jack's throat. Jack lay still, feeling death creeping toward him.

"I see it is you that shall be joining the dead!" snarled Jarrad.

He raised his blade, and Jack knew this would be the fatal blow. In desperation he reached up and grabbed the blade with his hands. It sliced easily through his skin, sending blood pouring down the blade and onto his face. Jack felt the pain searing through him. His body went cold and his vision started to blur—he had to act fast. With all his might he pushed the blade upward. The hilt connected with Jarrad's nose; it crunched as it broke and blood began to run from it. Jarrad dropped his sword. Jack rolled away and scrambled onto all fours searching for his. When he picked it up, his hands could barely close round it. He had lost sight of Jarrad, so he pushed himself back onto his feet and spun round, feeling dizzy.

Jarrad was distracted; he stood moaning and cradling his face.

"Finish him, Jack!" shouted Niar.

Jack gritted his teeth and approached Jarrad. He tried to swing his sword, but it slipped from his grasp, and he screamed in frustration.

Realising Jack was there, Jarrad lowered his hands from his broken nose, and with a snarl, he ran for his own sword. Jack staggered into him to stop him from reaching it; the impact put them both on the ground. He punched Jarrad, and Jarrad punched him back.

Jarrad's hands took hold of Jack's throat. "I don't need my sword to kill you!" he hissed.

Jack tried to loosen Jarrad's grip on his throat, but his hands slipped on his blood. He couldn't inhale; his throat made a rasping sound from the effort. He swung, hitting Jarrad on the arms, but Jarrad didn't stop choking him. The world was turning black, and Jack knew he was close to unconsciousness. He made his hand form a fist for one final attack. He punched upward, connecting his fist with Jarrad's nose.

With a scream, Jarrad let Jack go and once again cradled his face. The air rushed back into Jack's lungs, and he swallowed painfully. Forcing himself to sit up, he crawled towards his sword once more. He staggered to his feet and used it as a walking stick to steady himself. Jarrad still lay on the ground. Jack dragged his sword back to where he lay, his hands protested sharply.

Jarrad twitched as Jack came to rest standing over him. He looked around, bewildered, before locking his eyes on Jack's. Jack kicked Jarrad hard in the side of the head; the blow stunned him, and he stared blankly ahead. Jack quickly knelt down and brought the sword blade over Jarrad's neck.

"Go join the dead, Jarrad," he said, using his weight to push the blade downwards and slice his throat open. Jarrad choked on his own blood, began to spasm, his eyes clouded over, and he lay still in death.

Jack fell beside Jarrad's corpse, exhausted. He heard feet running towards him. Niar appeared at his side and knelt down beside him. "It is over, Jack. You have won!" he said.

"Cut them down," said Jack, his voice hoarse.

Niar looked confused; then his eyes widened, and he turned to regard the cages.

Jack looked at his friend, a tear running from his eye. "Get my family out of those cages, I beg you, Niar. Do it now!" he said weakly.

Niar looked at Jack in pity, but he shook his head. "On your feet, Jack. I shall do as you ask, but you must now address these guards, as their ruler," he said firmly.

Niar got up and seized Jack under his armpits. He pulled him easily to his feet and made sure he was able to support himself before letting him go.

Jack looking at the guards around the circle. "Let it be known that I, Jack Orden, have taken over the rule of Sanalow," he said, his voice hollow. "Let the city know that Jarrad Morridread lies dead, and that so shall all who choose to resist me." He bent over to catch his breath.

The guards around the circle all saluted Jack and cried, "Jack Orden, King of Sanalow!"

Jack straightened up and frowned at the title.

Niar touched his shoulder. "Your marriage to Lily makes you the king in this city," he explained.

Jack acknowledged the guards with a nod of his head; he turned silently to Niar. Niar nodded in understanding and ran towards the cages. He called two guards from the edge of the circle to help him.

Jack's legs gave way, and he fell back to the ground.

"Jack!" shouted a voice from beyond the guards. He saw a flash of a yellow dress and knew Jamella was pushing her way through the guards.

A moment later she was on the ground next to him. She picked up one of his hands. "You are badly wounded," she said seriously. "You may not be able to use your hands again." She looked mortified at the thought of Jack's disability.

"Thank you for your shield," said Jack weakly.

Kem appeared beside Jamella, holding a handkerchief. She knelt down on the other side of Jack. "Don't talk now," she said, wrapping Jack's hands.

"I have ordered guards to bring water and bandages, so we can clean these and stop you losing more blood."

Jack nodded slowly. It was an effort to keep his eyes open; he just wanted to go to sleep.

"What further orders, Your Majesty?" said another voice. Jack didn't recognise the speaker.

"He needs rest and to be inside, guard," said Jamella. "Go and arrange a room for your king, quickly."

Niar returned then. "Jack, the cages are down," he said. "What would you like me to do with the bones? We've laid them out, so you can see them if you like."

Jack didn't respond; the pain had left him, he just wanted to lie peacefully for a while. People were talking near to him but their voices were growing distant.

"He has lost too much blood!" said Kem seriously. "King Niar, what can we do?"

"Heal him," said Niar simply. "Earth and Spirit are all that is needed to sustain his life."

Kem and Jamella both gasped. "It is forbidden," said Kem quietly.

"He cannot die! The fate of the world lies on his shoulders—so forbidden or not, it is necessary!" shouted Niar. "I will explain to Magus Reanna on your behalf. Now do it!"

Jack felt their hands touch his shoulders. His body went cold; the pain returned sharply and then ebbed away again. Jack's tiredness disappeared. He sat up and regarded the magus. They had their eyes closed and kept hold of his shoulders. He held his hands out in front of him—and watched the deep cuts sealing up. He gasped in surprise.

Kem and Jamella opened their eyes and slumped backward, letting go of Jack's shoulders.

"How do you feel, Jack?" asked Niar.

Jack was still staring at his repaired hands. He stroked his mended facial wound and checked his leg. "How did you do this?" he demanded.

He heard Kem sigh. "We used our powers to heal you."

Jack looked at them seriously. "Mia told me it is forbidden to use healing," he said.

Kem stood up and held a hand out to Jack. He took it and got to his feet. She looked at him sternly. "It is forbidden magic, and we know what you must be thinking. You can see that with its power you would never have to face injury or death again. But you must understand that it is for that reason we don't use it. A power this strong in the control of a mortal could cause great damage to the natural order."

Jamella nodded and studied Jack. "Jack, we have to trust that you will forget this ever happened and never ask us or force us to use it again, because it will turn your soul black. Trust me in what I am saying. You must not seek to conquer death until the mortality spell is removed in the correct way, by the Child of Light."

Jack looked at Jamella, feeling hurt. "I didn't ask you to do this."

"No, I did," said Niar quietly. "I'm sorry, Jack. Maybe I shouldn't have, but you need to live! I'll accept the consequences for my actions later."

Jack looked up sharply. "What consequences?"

Niar didn't answer the question. He began to steer Jack towards the hall. "You must go indoors now and rest. The magic saved your life, but you lost a lot of blood, and your body will need time to recover."

"I must see my family first," said Jack firmly. "I must say goodbye."

Niar didn't argue; he led Jack to where the bones were laid out on the ground. Jack stood staring at them until finally Kem insisted he go inside. He reluctantly obeyed. "I'll arrange for them to be buried tomorrow," said Niar quietly. Jack nodded his agreement.

He entered the steward's hall. It was far less glamorous then Judelen Palace; all the walls were bare and made of cold, grey stone. The floors were not covered, and it had a neglected air to it.

"What do you want to do about Jarrad's body?" asked Jamella.

Jack looked sideways at her. "He shall be burnt and his ashes thrown in the wind," he said coldly. "He was not worthy to rest in the graveyard of the former rulers of Sanalow."

The sound of running footsteps drew Jack's eyes; two men came hurrying down the corridor. One was tall, with black, curly hair and olive skin. The other was stockier, with short, straight brown hair. Both wore brown leather trousers, tucked into knee high boots, and the traditional red jacket of Sanalow soldiers. Upon seeing Jack, they both broke into grins, and when Jack realised who they were, he grinned back. "Sam! Leon! How happy I am to see you two are well!"

Sam and Leon stopped in their tracks to bow to Jack. "Your Majesty," they said in unison.

Jack felt happiness expand inside him. "Stop that now!" he said playfully, pointing at both men sharply. "I am, Jack, nothing more, to my friends." Both men came closer, and Jack embraced them in a brotherly hug.

Leon broke away and patted Jack on the back. "We couldn't believe it when we heard the guards say you had returned. We would've come to the fight, but our late commander ordered us to remain inside."

"Good," said Jack seriously. "You would have distracted me!"

Leon grinned.

"There is so much to talk about!" said Sam, his round face beaming.

"You must wait until tomorrow. The king needs to rest now," said Kem in her most authoritative voice.

The two men nodded and fell into step with Jack, to escort him to his room. They saw him safely inside and left with the magus, to let him rest.

Jack didn't bother to examine his room. He walked straight to the bed and threw himself on it, not bothering to clean up, undress, or even remove his boots. Sleep claimed him quickly.

The following morning, Jack was bathed and dressed in fresh brown leather trousers and boots and a white cotton shirt and navy-blue velvet jacket. It was a relief to be out of the Emiscial clothing. He felt refreshed, and he wasted no time in summoning his friends and the city council to begin preparing for the trip to Judelen. Before he could leave Sanalow, he needed to raise somebody to be his under-steward, so he chose Leon.

"I don't know what to say, Jack!" said Leon. He ran his fingers through his black curls, his green eyes wide in surprise.

Jack held back a sigh. "Say yes, Leon. You know as well as I do that you are the best man for the job. I would only trust you or Sam in my absence. I know Sam holds the position now, but he is better skilled to ride with me and fight," he said. "I know this has come as a surprise, but I must have your answer. I need to be on the road to Judelen today, if possible, or tomorrow at the very latest."

Leon studied Jack. "You've given me a lot to think about, Jack. Not just the position you offer me, but all the problems we must prepare for. The people are panicking. The city is divided, with those loyal to Jarrad and those loyal to you. There is fighting in the streets. On top of that, there is Niar to consider. Most people in the city either fear Grimfar or hate its people. I am worried that if you leave so soon after taking command the city will break down altogether."

Jack did sigh this time. "I must leave! My wife needs me, and I need you, my friend. Please take the position and help me fight this war."

Jack watched his friend fidgeting restlessly while he waited for the answer. Finally Leon nodded. "All right, Jack. I shall accept."

Jack punched the air. "I knew you would help me," he said, slapping his friend on the back.

Leon looked pensive. "I will do my best, although I am unsure how much good I will be," he said.

"Niar is thinking up a plan to help keep Sanalow in order," said Jack reassuringly. "Gather the council. The quicker we put things into place the better."

23

MIA'S PLAN

Lily sat on the floor in the cell with her head resting on her knees. She was cold and tired; her new black woollen dress itched uncomfortably. Aidan had kept her in the greeting chamber for hours, delighting in his vindictive punishments. She wanted to sleep but tried hard to fight it. Aidan was busy making plans to leave the city. Lily hoped Jack had set off quickly from Emiscial, for he had more ground to cover to reach Judelen than Aidan did to reach the mountains and his mother.

The cell door opened, and Lily looked up to see Aidan in the doorway. She stiffened and watched him fearfully; she felt cold sweat run down her back. She steadied her breathing and adopted her stony façade once more.

"I do wish I didn't need to lock you away in here. If you would just submit to me, then we could make your accommodation so much more comfortable."

"Never!" screamed Lily with more bravery than she felt.

Aidan recoiled slightly but recovered his composure quickly. "As you wish," he said. "I do hope you are not sitting here dreaming about being rescued by your husband."

"Jack will come," said Lily simply.

Aidan laughed. "He has forgotten you, Lillian."

"Jack would never do that," she shot back.

Aidan tilted his head to one side; a nasty grin set on his face. "But will he ever forgive you?" he asked.

Lily felt her cheeks flush as she remembered the violation Aidan had inflicted on her in the greeting chamber. A single tear rolled down her cheek; she wiped it away in annoyance. "I have done nothing to be ashamed of. Jack will not hate me for your cruelty."

Aidan took a deep breath. "King Jack Orden will not be able to look at you without feeling disgust!"

Lily turned to Aidan. "Jack is not a king," she said scathingly.

"Yesterday he challenged and defeated Jarrad Morridread, steward of Sanalow, and took over as ruler," said Aidan, watching her reaction.

"Jack's in Sanalow," said Lily quietly to herself. She had thought he would be on the road to Judelen. She knew he'd wanted to take revenge on Jarrad for killing his family, but surely her life and his child's life were more important.

Aidan's eyes glinted. "As I said, he has forgotten you."

Lily looked up sharply, comprehension dawning on her. "No he hasn't. He is raising an army to defeat you!" she said feeling triumphant.

Aidan looked livid. "Well isn't he a clever boy! No matter; he will be too late," he said angrily. "We will be leaving shortly, and my army is ready for battle. He will meet it before he even sets foot in Judelen."

Aidan left, slamming the door closed behind him and putting Lily back into darkness.

"Hurry, Jack," whispered Lily, a taint of worry washing over her.

It was getting late into the afternoon, and Jack was in the steward's hall with Niar and Leon. They had quickly sworn him in as under-steward and high advisor of Sanalow before the council.

"I am confident my plan will help keep order while we are away," Niar told Jack. "We need to execute it quickly, so we can leave."

"I agree," said Jack. "We will leave Judelen at first light."

A knock sounded at the door.

"Come," called Jack.

Kem stepped into the room; she looked worn out from her journey.

Jack looked at her in interest. "What news from Emiscial?" he asked.

"Reanna says that Mia has been down to visit her and give instructions to the other magus; she warned that the plan will begin shortly. She intends to cause an earthquake to topple Judelen, and she said something about breaking open the dam."

Jack's heart lurched. "I hope Lily will forgive me for the damage I am about to inflict on her city," he said with a frown.

Kem shrugged. "You assured me she will not be harmed during this attack, which is the main priority. As for the city, it can be rebuilt."

Jack hoped so, for if not, his wife would be furious, life saved or not. "Did Reanna have anything to add?"

"She just wished you luck."

Jack bit his lip. "I need all the luck I can get."

Kem moved closer to Jack to whisper in his ear, "Time is against you, Jack, so King Rain is secretly going to leave Emiscial, after you have left Sanalow, to meet you on the road. But you cannot tell anyone, not even your friends."

Jack sighed deeply. If Rain left the shield, he could be destroyed; the odds were stacked against him. "I intend to reach Lily in less than a week. Once I have secured her, I shall leave the army in Judelen and ride ahead with her, to get her to Rain before she gives birth."

Jack turned to Leon. "I need to go now and address the city with my counsellors and Niar. Kem, are you happy with Niar's plan?"

Kem nodded. "Jamella and I agree it should be enough to scare the city into keeping order."

Jack was displeased that he needed to use fear as a tactic, but he could not risk a rebellion starting in Sanalow while he was away.

He travelled up through the hall until he reached the balcony, which was used to make public announcements. The steward's hall was the tallest building, so he was high enough up to see most of the city spread out below him. His people lined the streets, waiting to hear his announcement.

Jack stepped forward onto the balcony and fixed his eyes on the crowd. "I stand before you this day to tell you that Sanalow is changing under my rule." His abrupt statement shocked the entire crowd to silence.

Jack continued, knowing he had everyone's attention. "Under the rule of Jarrad Morridread, Sanalow has become a city full of hate and wrongdoing. I know there are many people standing below me who would disagree. You would tell me Morridread was the greatest ruler Sanalow ever had. I stand before you now to tell you that you are mistaken. Morridread was nothing more than a murderer. The greatest ruler Sanalow ever had was Orbressen Fanlar. He searched for peace, never war; he fought for right, never wrong. I shall follow his guidance and rule you as he once did.

"My first duty as your king is to restore what Morridread tried to destroy. Sanalow and Grimfar will be at peace once more."

The crowd below gasped in shock as Niar stepped forward to join Jack in the centre of the platform.

"This is King Niar of Grimfar. We have signed a contract between us that unites our lands. Our armies shall fight side by side, and our people shall all live together in peace."

Jack's voice grew firmer. "I do not expect all of you to agree with my actions, but know that while the power of rule is mine, this is the way things shall be. I must now inform you that personal business is taking me away from Sanalow today, and I may be gone for a while. Leon Myere has been appointed as the under-steward of Sanalow. To secure Grimfar's rights, there will be a joining of councils, and as independent advisers I am leaving two magus from Emiscial."

The crowd gasped in awe.

Jack smiled to himself at their reaction. "The magus are very powerful, as you are aware. I have told them that lawlessness may be dealt with by use of their magic powers.

"Shortly, you will all feel the earth shake, but do not be afraid. This is not an attack upon you. The kingdom is under attack from the dark forces once more, and I will lead our army to defeat them. I expect you, as my people, to follow my commands and the commands of those I appoint to rule with me. Now I order you all to retreat to your homes and get ready for the earthquake. Do not leave your homes again until the magus inform you that it is safe."

Jack and Niar bowed to the people before turning away and moving inside.

"I hope Mia is able to begin the plan soon," Jack confided to Niar. As if she had heard his wish, the ground began to rumble. It wasn't a big movement, and it ceased after a minute.

"That must have been a warning from Mia that she is about to begin," said Niar.

Jack knew he had no time to waste. He turned to Leon. "Send the council into the city to make sure everyone is going home and staying there. The next earthquake will be much bigger. When it is all over, open the treasuries and use the gold to ensure everyone has enough food, water, and clothing. Any damage done to homes must be compensated."

"To make sure the whole city doesn't go hungry will take all the gold you have, Your Majesty," a council member said in shock.

Jack turned around sharply. "I see no need to have a treasury full of gold for me to admire! I shall see that my people are well looked after. My wife is queen of Judelen; Judelen is much larger then Sanalow, and yet her people are not starving. I shall ensure Sanalow is the same! And Grimfar's people have no gold. They are forced to live below ground to escape death from their polluted air. They have to cope with life-changing deformities, and yet not one person is neglected. Sanalow will be the same!" The council member bowed low and backed away.

Niar smiled warmly at Jack. "You shall be a fine ruler, Jack. I am in your debt once again, for allowing us to leave our underground city."

Jack took Niar by the shoulder. "I should have done more to help you when Jarrad made his original plans. I let your people down, Niar. What I do now will never fully make up for that."

"You are mistaken, Jack. You really must start believing that you are a good man," said Niar kindly.

The ground began to shake again. This time, as predicted, it was harder and showed no sign of relenting.

"This is it," Jack warned the others. He prayed it would work to stop Aidan and his mother from hatching their plans.

24

BROKEN

Lily struggled in Drake's firm grip as he dragged her up the stairs from the cells.

"Stop it," hissed Drake, shaking her firmly.

"You think I'll just let you take me," spat Lily. "I shall fight you with everything I have!"

Drake's fist connected with her face, causing stars to appear in her vision. Lily fell to the floor; she tasted blood from her split lips. Drake dragged her up by her hair and flung her ahead of him down the corridor. Lily was too shocked to fight him again. Drake was taking her back to the greeting chamber. He opened the doors and walked her inside.

"What happened to her face?" asked Aidan as soon as Lily entered the room.

"She attempted to escape," said Drake calmly. "I had to hit her to control her."

Aidan regarded him with cold black eyes. "If you touch her again, I shall inflict you with twice as many wounds as you give her!"

Drake bowed low and kept his eyes downcast.

Aidan turned to Lily. "It is time for us to leave Judelen. A carriage waits outside to take us from the city." Aidan turned to the man sitting next to him. "Salzar, you shall remain here, to ensure the army is fully equipped to fight the boy, if he arrives."

Lily knew her father was dead, and yet he sat before her on his throne—at least his body did. It felt confusing, and it made her heart ache. She dropped her gaze from him.

"Let's go," said Aidan, stepping towards the door. He took hold of Lily's arm and steered her out of the room. He kept hold of her as they walked off down the corridor, but his grip was not tight. Lily had an idea. She began to study the doorways off the corridor, searching for the one she needed to make her escape. Suddenly the ground shook. It was a small tremor, and it passed quickly. Aidan and Drake exchanged looks. Aidan waited for a few seconds, and upon deciding all was well, he continued to walk down the corridor. The tremor came again, and this time it was so violent it caused everyone to stumble against the wall. The ground continued to shake, and Drake fell to the floor.

"What is this?" shouted Aidan in total confusion.

Lily felt Aidan's hand release her arm, and she took her chance to escape. She kicked him hard in the knee. The impact, combined with the earthquake, unbalanced him, and he fell to the floor beside Drake. Lily ran as fast as she could, holding onto the walls for support until she reached a storeroom. She pulled open the door, stepped inside, and hit the darkest stone in the far wall. A hidden doorway appeared, leading upward, and she began to climb the stairs. She could hear Aidan screaming for Drake to grab her. Lily kept running up the stairs without looking back. She came to a solid wall and hit the darkest stone to make it move. She burst out into a corridor on one of the upper levels, near the bodyguards' chambers. She surprised a servant, who was clinging to the wall in panic. She quickly lashed out at the woman to stop her from revealing her position. Footsteps were growing louder on the hidden stairs behind her. Lily continued to run. She knew she couldn't use the stairway she and Jack had used to escape, so she quickly dived into another storeroom before her pursuers came out into the corridor. She found the darkest stone and touched it. The wall slid away, and another stairway appeared, again going upward. She climbed as fast as she could and burst out onto another level. Lily looked around, trying to get her bearings. She began to run along the corridor, past her chambers, looking for another storeroom. She found one and repeated her pattern; another stairway appeared, and again she ran upward, panting from the effort.

The corridor she entered bent round in an endless circle. It held no other doorways except an open archway, which led directly onto the roof of the palace. The ground continued to shake, and she felt the palace buckle under its effect. With a sharp crack, the walls around her began to split. The glass windows shattered, and the whole building groaned in protest. A part of the floor gave way, and rubble fell down into the level below. The ceiling above her started to cave in.

This must be the magus, Lily thought to herself. Jack was attacking Aidan and his army.

Lily ran through the archway onto the roof. Below her the city lay in ruins. Suddenly there was a bang so loud she had to cover her ears. The dam behind the city had split down the middle, and with a mighty explosion, the water burst from it and poured down upon Judelen, sweeping away everything in its path. The palace shifted beneath its current, and Lily was thrown to the floor. A hand grabbed her from behind. Lily looked up to see Aidan.

"Nowhere left to run!" he said, bending over her. He surveyed the broken dam and the destroyed city and cursed out loud. "This magic is too powerful to belong to the magus alone," he said to himself. He closed his eyes and smiled. He looked at Lily and pulled her up to her feet; she held him for support.

"It appears Jack has found a new powerful alley," Aidan told her. "But one broken creator is no match for the powers of my mother."

A great ball of pulsating black magic shot into the air high above the Great Mountains. It began to move towards Judelen. It passed over the city and into the west towards Emiscial, gathering speed as it went. After a few minutes, there was a distant explosion, and the ground stopped shaking.

Lily realised the magic had been aimed for the Unicorn, and she knew he was dead. Fear swept over her.

Aidan looked at her in triumph. "Now my mother has two-thirds of the power of creation at her disposal. She is so powerful you cannot hope to beat her." He laughed and moved to drag Lily back inside the ruined palace.

The foundations of the palace finally gave way to the raging water, and the whole building began to fall apart, a chunk at a time. Lily broke loose of Aidan's grip and ran to the edge of the roof. "Get away from me!" she cried as Aidan advanced towards her. He raised his hands in submission.

"Move away from the edge, Lily," he said in urgency. "If you fall, you'll die!"

Lily smiled and touched her ring. "Not today," she said, and she turned and threw herself off the building.

Aidan rushed to the edge and saw her land in the waters below. Realising something must be protecting her he cursed out loud and jumped off after her.

The remaining palace disappeared under the currents. The city was now buried under a vast lake. Water poured though the city gates, spilling over the moat and flooding the land beyond. It continued raging down into the valley below, towards the river and the Judelen Pass.

Jack and Niar, meanwhile, had left Sanalow City and were in the colony, preparing the army. Mia and the Unicorn were managing to keep the earthquake's effects upon Sanalow to a minimum, leaving the city reasonably unharmed. Jack was pleased that the shaking was not delaying him from making his preparations. Hopefully the men would manage to rest that night and be fresh to march in the morning.

"How much damage do you think Mia is doing?" Jack asked Niar, walking beside him.

"I don't think there will be much left of Judelen," said Niar.

Jack looked down, feeling guilty.

Niar smiled reassuringly. "I promise you your wife will understand, Jack. She will know anything you do is only done in your fight to protect her."

That wasn't what was bothering Jack. "I just wish I could have warned her. She must be terrified," he said.

Niar considered him for a moment. "Are you certain she will be safe from an attack of this magnitude?"

Jack looked at him sharply. "Of course I am!"

Niar gave his friend an apologetic look. "Sorry, Jack, that was a stupid question. I know you are worried, but we must think about the long march ahead of us. We do not know for certain what advantage Mia's attack will bring us."

Jack studied the soldiers rushing all around him. He had at least two thousand at his command, which he hoped would be a match in numbers and strength for the Judelen soldiers. He knew he had no defence against magic, but hopefully Aidan and Evelyn were too busy dealing with the attack on Judelen to seek him out personally. Jack spotted Sam. "Make sure all the commanders are with their groups and that everyone is staying safe." Sam nodded and rushed off.

A darkening of the sky made Jack look up. He gasped to see a huge sphere of black magic flying at high speed towards his location. Panicking, he thought it was aimed for the army, but it flew over Sanalow and into the Black Mountains. There was a deafening explosion, and the earthquake ceased.

"I think we just lost our advantage," said Niar in concern.

Jack looked with horrified eyes at his friend. "Mia," he whispered.

Niar swallowed hard and shook his head. Jack knew what he meant. Mia must be dead, but if she was, then he had doomed the Unicorn along with her.

Reanna lay on the ground near the tunnel entrance. She stared at the mountain where Mia had gone to carry out the attack. Fear engulfed her. The entire peak of the mountain was missing, destroyed completely. There was only a deep crater, smouldering from the heat of the magic's impact, left in its place. If Emiscial had not been shielded, it would have been obliterated in the blast. Reanna knew there was no hope that Mia could have survived the blast. She felt consumed by loss. She looked wildly around for her sisters. The land was eerily quiet.

At the sound of footsteps, she whipped her head round. She saw Emmra and Kerri rushing out of the trees towards her.

"Reanna, we're so glad you are safe!" said Emmra. She extended a hand and helped Reanna to her feet.

Reanna brushed down her silk. "Have you seen the others? Are they well?"

"Troyan was with the gifted. I think King Rain was helping her, so they should be all right after …" Emmra's voice trailed off. She looked out of the shield at the destroyed mountain and covered her mouth. "Poor Mia," she whispered, lowering her eyes.

Reanna stood beside her, and for a moment they surveyed the ruins in silence. "Do you think she did enough to stop the Dark Knight?" asked Kerri quietly.

Emmra turned to look at her. "I felt the water flows when the dam broke; they were strong enough to level the city." She frowned and turned to Reanna. "Mia didn't have the type of power to carry out this attack. How did she do it?"

"She had help," said a male voice behind her. The three magus turned to see King Rain approaching, and Troyan followed behind him. She looked out at the mountains and shook her head sadly.

King Rain joined the line and studied the scene.

Reanna watched him. "Who helped her?" she asked.

King Rain glanced down at her. "The Unicorn, I believe. The power used would indicate him," he replied.

Everyone gasped, and Kerri and Troyan exchanged shocked looks.

Reanna put a hand on her heart. "The Unicorn! But he and the Dragon fled after they trapped us on this island. Orthrillium said they would leave us to our own fate."

"They did," said Rain. "However, it would appear that Jack and Lily have restored hope to them. The Child of Light is the way to fix the world. We must be very careful now how we proceed, Reanna. Evelyn Maude has destroyed the Unicorn. If she has his powers, then Jack will not stand any chance of rescuing Lily from her."

Reanna looked hopefully at Rain. "I don't think she does have all of his power. What was it Jack said about Lily—that she would be safe from the attack? It is obvious that they met the Unicorn in the mountains. He must have protected Lily and the child."

"He did."

Reanna heard the new speaker and spun round. Her face split into a wide smile. Mia was coming towards the party from the direction of the valley. She looked a little worse for wear; her dress was torn, and she had a graze on her cheek.

"You're alive!" shouted Reanna, running to embrace her.

Mia hugged her back and stepped away, tucking her loose hair back into her waist tie. "I am," she said wearily. "The Unicorn expelled me from the cave before the magic could hit. I ended up just outside the shield, near the valley. I made it inside before the explosion. He died helping Jack and saving me."

"Do you know if he released his power before his death?" asked Rain.

Mia looked thoughtful. "I know Lily has a ring that is keeping her alive, and shortly before the black magic came, the Unicorn looked like he was shrouded in mist. Tendrils were floating away into the air. It was beautiful," she said.

"I think he sent it away. He must have known his death was approaching. Perhaps the Dragon has it. Wherever it is, it is not in the reach of Evelyn Maude, and that is a very good thing."

"She will go after Jack!" said Mia sharply. "When she realises she hasn't got that power, she will strike him dead!"

"She will wage war upon him, but what will she do with Lily, I wonder," said King Rain.

Reanna looked round seriously. "I've had a sickening thought. I think we have made yet another mistake of catastrophic proportions."

"What else could we possibly have got wrong?" asked Mia angrily.

Reanna regarded her. "We've given her the Child of Darkness. She will use Lily's love for that baby to destroy everything. When it is born, she will fill it with black magic, and it will do awful things, but Lily will never stop loving her child. Even her hope of fixing it will give Evelyn Maude the power to conquer love."

Mia squeezed her eyes shut. "We are so stupid! We have to warn Jack. He must quicken his pace to Judelen." Suddenly Mia disappeared.

Reanna looked round in shock. "Where did she go?' she cried to the others.

Just as suddenly Mia reappeared, looking surprised and frightened.

"What happened, sister?" asked Reanna, looking her up and down.

"I was thinking about Judelen, and the next thing I knew, I was there! I don't know how I did it."

"With the power from the Unicorn," said Rain thoughtfully. "He has given you the power of teleportation!"

Mia looked thoughtful. "If I understand it right, I can disappear and reappear at will. I could go to Judelen and rescue Lily."

"No," shouted Reanna. "You must be very careful and not rush into Judelen blind. If you appear before the Dark Knight, he will feel this power, and he will destroy you to claim it for his mother. You must not be detected. You would do better to go to Jack and transport the army to Judelen. He can rescue Lily, and you can bring them all back within a matter of hours."

Mia nodded. "Then I shall do just that," she said. A sharp pain shot across her head. She leant forward, and grasped her knees. "I feel unwell," she said quietly.

King Rain guided her to sit down on the floor. "You need to rest, Magus Mia. You have to adjust to your new powers."

"There's no time—" Mia didn't finish; she passed out on the ground before them.

Reanna rushed forward, but Rain held out his hand. "She'll be all right, Magus Reanna. But she must rest, and so must Jack. Leave them be tonight. Tomorrow morning they can travel to Judelen, refreshed and ready to fight."

25

---❦---

THE COUNTER-ATTACK

Lily's head broke through the water; she took a deep breath of air and coughed uncontrollably for several seconds. She glanced around her, keeping her arms moving to stay afloat.

The city was gone, buried beneath a lake that was being held in by the outer walls. The current from the mountain river was strong. It carried several dead bodies and broken parts of the city past her, towards the city gates.

Lily couldn't see Aidan anywhere. She had heard him land in the water not long after she had. She had dived under to hide from him, until finally the need for air had brought her back up.

A body floated into her back, and with a shudder, Lily pushed it away. So many innocent people had died in the attack, and she felt sick thinking about it.

Shouts echoed in the distance. Lily saw there were survivors outlined on the city walls. She had come up behind a large cart, which blocked her from their view. The current was flowing in the opposite direction than she needed to go in. Lily took another deep breath and dived back under the water, fighting against it and trying to get clear of any survivors. Evening was falling. If she could escape the lake and get into the forest, she could use the growing darkness to cover her. She could sneak over the Pass and back towards Sanalow.

She resurfaced at a section of the outer walls and quickly looked round to see if anyone was nearby. The survivors were all closer to the main entrance. Relieved, she pulled herself up onto the wall and looked down. She was very high up; it would be a difficult descent. She checked her finger for the ring and found it safe. She shut her eyes and steadied herself; she had no option but to try and climb down.

When a hand grabbed her on her back, she screamed. She had to hold onto the wall to prevent herself from falling back into the lake. She looked behind her to see Aidan. "Get off me!" she cried.

He looked up at her in anger. "What a clever girl you turned out to be, very deceptive. I never knew you had it in you!"

Struggling to get free, Lily turned around and seized a handful of Aidan's hair, pulling it as hard as she could. His head whipped backwards, and reflectively he raised his hands to his head to stop her, letting go of her arm. Suddenly he drew his hand back and slapped her hard across the face. The force of the blow caused her to lose her balance, and screaming, she fell off the wall.

The air rushed past Lily as she fell, spinning around and around. When she hit the water of the moat, the impact stung sharply. She resurfaced gasping. She swam as fast as she could, until she could drag herself out of the water and flee across the flooded land and into the forest. Tripping over an exposed root, she tumbled down the steep slope of the valley, digging her nails into the soil to stop her descent. She drew herself up onto her knees and examined her body. Everything appeared to be fine, with no broken bones. She sighed in relief, rubbing her stomach. The magic in the ring had kept her alive once more.

Lily knew that Aidan would follow her, so she dragged herself up and began to run quickly through the silver trees and thick ferns beneath. She was trying to put as much distance as she could between them. Her wet clothes clung to her body, and she shook from the cold.

She ran without stopping until it began to grow dark. The forest filled with shadows that danced in the moonlight. When Lily could no longer see in front of her face, she stopped running and collapsed behind a tree to rest. She stopped for one hour, letting her eyes adjust to the dark, until finally she could pull herself back to her feet. She moved slowly, feeling her way along with her hands. Nothing stirred in the forest, and the silence was terrifying. No wind blew the trees, and Lily fought back tears as the shadows continued to dance around her. Her body felt painfully cold.

The sound of running water caught her ear. She hoped she was nearing the Pass. A snapping twig made her jump, and Lily clapped her hands over her mouth. She could see the black outline of someone moving towards her in the darkness. She stepped back quietly, not letting her eyes leave the outline of the person. Back and back she went, one step at a time, her hands still over her mouth, until she bumped hard into a tree. The outline of the person grew bigger, and hands grabbed her arms. She fought in vain to free herself.

"Give it up, Lillian! You will not get away from me again," snarled Aidan in the blackness.

Lily tried to twist from his grip, but she was exhausted. Her head felt light, and she fell to the ground. Aidan made a disgruntled noise. Suddenly the air around them lit up with a pale-blue glow. Floating above Aidan's hand was a ball of blue light. He left it hovering in the air and sat down next to Lily. He snatched her left hand into the air and stared at her ring in disgust. "That's a clever piece of magic the Unicorn gifted you."

Lily screwed her fingers into a fist to protect the ring.

Aidan smiled bitterly. "I am not going to take it off you. I need you and your child alive, so until you reach my mother you may keep your magic ring."

Lily sighed in relief. Her body ached with cold and tiredness. She felt her eyes closing, and she had no strength to open them again.

Aidan looked down at her in annoyance. "I see there is no way I can move you tonight without aid. As your husband has effectively managed to destroy most of my hosts, I will just have to wait until tomorrow." He settled his back against a tree and crossed his arms. "Don't worry, though. I still have a mighty spirit army, and it is already on its way to Jack. With a little luck, he will be dead before tomorrow ends. If not, he has no chance of catching up to us once my wind riders tear his army to shreds."

Lily groaned, unable to answer. She heard the words, but they felt numb inside her brain. They couldn't win; everything was against them. She gave up, shutting out the world and everything in it.

The first night for Jack and his army had been uneventful. They had rallied early and were marching at a good pace. Jack was pleased that they would have covered a lot of ground before dark fell again. He only wished he knew what effects the attack had had upon Judelen, and what Aidan's plans were.

Niar rode next to him with his face set in thought. Jack had chosen to confide in him about the Unicorn, and he seemed deeply concerned. Jack knew Niar would be taking all the information and using it to formulate new plans. He didn't like to disturb him and so rode along in silence, letting his own thoughts run free.

Suddenly Bailey neighed in fright, rearing up and nearly causing Jack to fall from his saddle. Jack steadied his horse and glanced down to see what had spooked him. He saw Mia standing on the road and laughed out loud. His men were drawing swords, but Jack signalled them to stand down.

"Where did you come from?" he shouted, delighted that she was alive. He kicked his feet from his stirrups and vaulted off Bailey. Running to her, he hugged her tightly; then he let go and kissed her on the cheek. "I thought you had been killed," he said, holding on to her arm. "I'm so glad you're all right!"

Mia stood holding her cheek. She looked stunned by his display of affection, but a smile spread over her face. "The Unicorn gave me powers to teleport. I would've come to you last night, but I was weak after the infusion. I am stronger now, and I'm here to take you all to Judelen."

Jack's delight at seeing Mia faded slightly. "He died helping me—he trusted me that much."

Mia took hold of Jack's hand. "Yes, Jack, he did, and rightly so. You are the saviour."

Jack shook his head. "Lily is," he said quietly. "She is the one who convinced me to follow my destiny."

Niar rode forward on his horse. "Forgive the intrusion Magus Mia. It is wonderful that you are safe and to hear that you have powers to help us. Did your plan against Judelen work? Is the city destroyed?"

"Yes, the combined force of the earthquake and the destruction of the dam was enough to destroy Judelen completely," she answered.

"Can you use your powers to go to Judelen and snatch Lily from Aidan?" asked Jack eagerly.

"If I could do that, Jack, I would have already," she said, sounding exasperated. "I have to be very careful. If the Dark Knight or Evelyn Maude get their hands on my power, then we are in a lot of trouble."

Jack raised his hand submissively. "I understand, Mia. I don't want to place you into any more danger then I already have. Take the army and me as close as you can to the Great Mountains."

Mia nodded, and Jack signalled for Belldean to be brought forward. "Mount up, Mia, and tell me what we have to do to transport us all." He gave her a leg up before running back to Bailey and remounting.

"I will require everyone to be touching some part of someone else, be it horse or person, to make the transfer," she instructed.

Sam and Niar heard her instructions and broke ranks to go and inform the rest of the commanders to spread the word.

"We'll just need a few minutes to make sure everyone is joined," said Jack.

Mia rode Belldean up to Bailey; she was studying the columns. Niar and Sam reappeared and signalled to Jack that everyone was ready.

"Time to go," said Mia; she looked a little apprehensive. Jack took hold of her arm and squeezed encouragingly. Niar began to bring his horse closer to Bailey.

"Jack!" shouted Sam, pointing along the road ahead of him. "We're under attack!"

Jack looked up and saw hundreds of wind riders coming down the road, swirling towards them. Sam was trotting his horse back towards the front of the columns.

"Sam, grab someone!" screamed Jack, but before Sam could extend his arm, Belldean reared and pulled Mia from Jack's grip. She shied to the side, with Mia frantically trying to steady her.

Jack had no choice but to move away himself. *Sound the alert to the columns! We're under attack!* he screamed.

The officers broke out of the column and galloped down the ranks, screaming that they were under attack.

"How do we fight these creatures?" Jack shot at Niar.

"You must just break free if they take hold of you!" answered Niar.

"Spread out!" ordered Jack. "Don't let them take large groups of you."

Soldiers began to push each other, but there was no time. The wind riders were upon them and began a ruthless attack upon Jack's army. They swept up and began to snatch people and catapult them through the air. The sound of men and horses screaming filled Jack's ears.

Jack heeled Bailey to where Mia was still struggling with Belldean. He grabbed her reins. "Stay close to me," he told her.

A wind rider darted sideways and came for Jack. He stiffened as it grabbed him and lifted him clean from the saddle. The wind rider didn't throw him to the ground but attempted to carry him off. Jack fought against the flows so hard that he managed to fall from the twister, but he landed painfully on his knees.

Niar appeared by his side. "Are you hurt?" he shouted down.

Jack shook his head and pushed himself back onto his feet. Bailey came up beside him, and he mounted quickly.

He surveyed his army; it was in trouble. Panicked men, without a clue of how to fight without swords, were dying everywhere. Jack saw that the Grimfar warriors were managing to avoid the wind riders, due to their strength.

A group of men close to Jack were pulled into the air and thrown through the sky at terrifying speed, until they were smashed in a heap upon another group of soldiers.

"We don't stand a chance!" shouted Jack towards Mia.

Sam rode up to beside him. "Jack, the army is being defeated!"

Jack looked at his men, feeling broken. "Mia, transport as many as can go to Judelen—now!' he shouted.

Mia grabbed one of his arms, and Sam grabbed the other.

"Niar, take hold!" ordered Jack.

A wind rider seized Niar before he could obey. It picked him up, and another joined it; together they were strong enough to stop Niar's attempts at freedom. They carried him straight up into the air.

"No!" screamed Jack, watching in horror. The riders didn't hurl Niar back down; they carried him away towards Judelen.

Mia's grip on his arm tightened. "Sam!" she shouted. He gripped Jack tighter, and Mia closed her eyes. They disappeared, and when they reappeared, they were in a small clearing within Judelen forest.

The silence after the noise of the attack startled Jack. He glanced around at the others, checking they were OK.

Sam looked round with wide eyes. "I don't think I'll ever recover from all this magic!" he said in a shocked tone.

Mia turned to Jack. "I must leave you and quickly go to Sanalow and Emiscial. I can take Jamella and Kerri back to the road to destroy the wind riders, and hopefully save some of your army." She didn't wait for approval before disappearing.

Jack stared at the empty air where she had stood; he wasn't sure where he was, so he began to look round for a landmark.

Sam adjusted his seat. "How many men do you think we lost?" he asked sadly.

"Too many," replied Jack, still studying the forest. "But we can't grieve for them now, Sam. We need to find a road to the city."

Sam began to study their surroundings. "I think the city is in that direction," he said, pointing slightly to the north.

Jack agreed with his assessment. "Let's try to find a path," he said.

"Will Magus Mia be able to find us again if we move around?" asked Sam.

Jack considered his question. "I think all she has to do is think of us, and the magic will bring her straight to our location," he said.

Jack stopped Bailey and listened hard. "Did you hear a noise, Sam?" he whispered.

Sam stopped his own horse and listened intently. He nodded silently and pointed into the forest slightly to the left of them. Silently, both men drew their swords.

It sounded as if someone was walking through the trees, snapping twigs beneath their feet. Jack scanned the trees, but they were thick in most places and he could see nothing between them. "Whoever it is, they're heading in this direction," he whispered to Sam. They sat waiting in silence.

A lone figure walked out from the darkness of the trees. Jack took in his dark hair and ponytail. "Drake, I won't say it is a pleasure to see you again!" he said.

Drake stopped dead in his tracks; he looked shocked to see Jack and Sam. "How do you come to be here so quickly?"

"Now, that would be telling!" said Jack mockingly. He noticed Drake had no weapon. "How did you come to be alone in these woods? Have you run from the service of the Black Witch? Are you a deserter?"

Drake laughed. "Really, Jack, that is pathetic, even for you. Why would I leave the service of the most powerful woman to walk the earth? If you think the destruction of Judelen will stop her taking the vessel, you are wrong. Even as we speak, Aidan is taking Lily towards the mountains and his mother. Soon the Child of Darkness will be made."

Jack smiled. "There won't be a Child of Darkness. Lily's pregnant," he said smugly.

Drake looked amused. "So I believe. Don't you understand, boy? It's *your* child that is going to be infused with twisted darkness, and then it will destroy the world. You must be so proud!"

Jack knew he was lying, trying to provoke his temper. He stayed calm. "I think it's time for you to die, Drake."

Drake looked utterly at ease. "You'd have to catch me first, boy!" He turned on his heels and ran back into the trees.

Jack kicked Bailey into a canter, but as he reached the tree line, he had to pull him up, for the gaps between the trees were not large enough to fit through on horseback.

"I'll hunt him on foot!" shouted Jack to Sam whilst swinging off Bailey.

"Give him up, Jack. He will be long gone, and we must find the city," counselled Sam.

Jack growled as he stood scanning the trees, but he could not hear or see Drake anywhere. He accepted defeat and climbed back onto Bailey.

"Look, Jack! There is path up ahead," said Sam. "If we can find the city, we can cross over into the mountains."

Eager not to waste any more time, Jack led the gallop along the forest path. They rode all day, and eventually they arrived at the ruined city. Jack gasped and his eyes grew wide as he saw the waterfall pouring from the main gates and into the moat, which had overflowed and drowned the surrounding land.

They found a safe place to wade across, and once over, they studied the mountains. "There," said Sam, pointing out a pathway into the lower peaks.

"If these mountains are anything like their twin, they are a maze, and we are going to struggle to get the horses past the lower parts," said Jack quietly.

Sam shrugged. "We knew this wouldn't be easy. We just need to go as far as we can as quickly as we can."

A noise in the air made Jack look up, and he saw two wind riders coming over the forest behind them. "Quickly! Move the horses under that birch tree," he ordered. Sam didn't hesitate, and both men quickly hid out of sight.

"Look, Jack," whispered Sam. "It's the two that took Niar! I can see him hanging down between them."

Jack felt his luck changing. "We mustn't lose sight of them, Sam! If we're fortunate, they will lead us through the mountains to Aidan."

He kicked Bailey and began to pursue Niar and the riders, Sam following closely behind him.

The two men were able to follow the wind riders without difficulty until late afternoon. Then they hit a narrow path the horses couldn't travel through, and they lost sight of them.

Jack cursed again and again, but he knew there was no point in regretting. He just had to keep climbing and hoping to find them again."

26

REUNITED

Aidan dragged Lily along the mountain path. It was narrow, with a deep canyon dropping below them on one side and a steep cliff climbing upward on the other. She could barely keep up with his pace, and for what felt like the hundredth time, she tripped and fell to the ground. When she landed dangerously close to the canyon edge, Aidan stamped on her back to stop her moving. She grunted and lay on the stones, panting hard, sweat dripping off her skin.

Aidan sighed deeply and dragged her back to her feet. He moved her to stand with her back against the cliff face. "Stop these stalling tactics! We are so close now to my mother that you have no chance of saving yourself," he said viciously.

Lily wiped the sweat from her forehead; her face was red. "I'm not trying to use tactics, you monster! I am human and pregnant—I cannot manage to keep up your pace. You have been pushing me since the forest this morning. I am going to collapse."

Aidan stepped forward, looking concerned. He felt her forehead, but then he smiled cruelly. "You'll be fine, Lillian. You have a magic ring, after all." He turned her sharply and shoved her up the next part of the mountain path. The path became slightly wider, and Aidan steered Lily around a bend, keeping her by the cliffs.

He heard the whirling air of the wind riders and looked into the sky. "It appears we have company," he told Lily, pushing her onto her knees. "I wonder if they have brought me the boy—that would make my day!" he said with a laugh as he watched two riders lowering down towards him.

They dropped Niar from their hold and flew away, back towards Judelen. Niar fell hard and staggered sideways but quickly found his balance. He glanced down into the canyon and took a step away from the edge.

Aidan looked at him in disappointment. He assessed Niar's facial deformity and his build. "Well, you're not the boy, but I guess my creatures thought the king of Grimfar was a worthy prisoner."

Lily looked past Aidan and up at Niar. His eyes met hers. He smiled warmly at her. "I'm glad you are safe, Your Majesty," he said.

Aidan stepped forward. "Don't speak to her," he warned. "She is my prisoner."

Niar's eyes snapped to Aidan; he reached for his sword.

Aidan held his palm upward, and a ball of black magic appeared in his hand. "Draw your sword and throw it into the canyon," he ordered.

Niar clenched his fists. He glanced at Lily. Then he drew his sword and tossed it away.

Aidan did not let the magic fade away. "Get on your knees, and put your hands on your head," he commanded.

Niar obeyed, locking his fingers behind his head. Lily shook her head sadly at him; a single tear fell from her eyes.

"I want information, King Niar," continued Aidan. "Where is the boy and his army?"

Niar's grey eyes flashed, he didn't answer.

Aidan tilted his head. "You will answer my questions or I will kill you," he promised.

Niar sniffed at the threat. "Go ahead, Dark Knight, for I will never betray my friends."

"Very well," said Aidan simply. The ball of magic flew from his palm into Niar. Niar convulsed sharply, his jaw clenching tightly. Lily screamed, but Aidan ignored her. Niar's eyes began to bulge, and blood trickled from his ears and nose. Lily sobbed as she watched Aidan's painful torture. She looked round wildly and found a sharp piece of slate. Aidan had his back to her. She picked up the slate and jammed it through his leather boot, and into his ankle, ripped it out, and jammed it in again. She kept repeating her pattern, showing no mercy.

When Aidan felt her attack, he turned round and grabbed her arm. The spell over Niar was broken, and he fell panting onto the path.

Aidan dragged Lily up and shoved her into the cliff face. "I am going to enjoy breaking this spirit of yours," he told her cruelly. "Attack me again and I'll make you pay dearly for it!"

Lily looked past Aidan and into the face of Niar, who had risen, undetected, to his feet. He wiped his bloody nose with the back of his hand and, without warning, put his arms tightly around Aidan, pulling him backwards.

Aidan elbowed Niar to break his hold, but the king of Grimfar didn't flinch. He stepped backwards again, getting closer to the deadly drop.

He kept his eyes on Lily as his feet found the canyon edge. "Run," he told her, before he stepped off, dragging Aidan down with him.

Lily's hand extended towards the drop, and she cried out in pain. She listened to Aidan's screams growing fainter, until she finally heard a distant cracking noise.

She covered her face in horror and willed herself to calm down. Full of adrenaline, she jumped to her feet. Her stomach clenched, and she doubled over; she felt it expand slightly. She touched it in fright, but knowing she had no time to lose, she tried to focus her mind on the journey back out of the mountains.

27

BIRTH AND DEATH

Jack and Sam were running up a steep path. Jack kept his body as close as he could to the mountain. The path was narrow, and there was a nasty, deep canyon on his left, waiting to kill him if he fell into it. He heard Sam panting behind him.

He paused to catch his breath and studied the path ahead. It climbed sharply, curling round and out of his line of vision. He hoped that once he reached the bend he'd be able to see more.

He glanced back at Sam. "Are you good?"

Sam took several deep gulps of air and nodded. Jack licked his lips and continued the climb.

A scream filled the air; it vibrated off the mountains. Jack stopped running to listen. He would swear it sounded like Lily, and his stomach dropped sharply.

Sam put his hand on Jack's shoulder. "I heard it too, Jack. If that was your wife, it means she is close."

"But why is she screaming?" said Jack in fear.

Sam slapped his back. "Let's go and find out," he said firmly.

Jack began to sprint again, ignoring the protesting of his muscles. Another scream filled the air. This one sounded male, and it lasted longer than the first.

Jack put it out of his mind, climbing onwards until he reached the path's curve. He heard the sound of rocks sliding and footsteps coming towards him. He flattened himself against the cliff face and drew his sword, waiting to surprise whoever appeared around the corner.

A woman flew into sight, slipping around the corner and only just regaining her balance. She was dressed in black wool. Her blonde hair was loose and blowing wildly in the mountain wind. She looked up and stopped dead at the sight of Jack.

"Lily!" he cried out, stepping towards her. He dropped his sword and reached out to grab her arm, pulling her towards him.

She threw her arms around him and wept on his shoulder in relief. He kissed her hair, her cheek, and eventually her lips. She kissed him back as if she wanted to devour him; Jack didn't want the kiss to end.

Sam jabbed him on the shoulder. "Jack, we need to go," he said urgently. He picked up Jack's sword and thrust it at him.

Reluctantly Jack stopped kissing Lily and drew away. He took his sword and put it back in its scabbard. He looked Lily up and down. "Are you OK? Is the baby OK?" he asked.

Lily smiled through her tears, her lip trembling. "We're fine, Jack. Thank goodness you found us!"

"Where is Aidan?" he asked scanning the path behind her.

Lily bit her lip. "Your friend King Niar was here. He threw himself into the canyon—and took Aidan with him."

Jack stiffened in shock. Niar was gone! He felt tears falling down his cheek. Lily leant forward and kissed them away. "He saved my life, Jack. He is a hero."

Sam shuffled his feet, and Lily regarded him uncertainly. Jack shook himself, wiped his face, and took her hand. "This is Sam, from Sanalow," he explained. Lily gave Sam a small nod.

Sam bowed low. "Your Majesty," he said. "I wish we could be meeting under more pleasant circumstances."

Lily managed a small smile. "Me too, Sam."

Keeping hold of her hand, Jack signalled for Sam to lead the way back down the mountain path. "We need to get back to the horses and ask Bailey to whisper to Mia to come and teleport us away."

"How can Mia do that?" asked Lily.

Jack squeezed her hand. "Long story short, I sent Mia to the Unicorn to delay Aidan's plans, by toppling Judelen. The Black Witch destroyed him, but not before he gave Mia some of his powers."

Lily's mouth fell open. Jack kissed her head. "I'm sorry about Judelen," he said gently.

Lily shook her head. "It was a good plan, Jack. You destroyed Aidan's human army."

Jack looked at her nervously. "I thought you'd be so angry with me."

Lily laughed gently. "I'll see how I feel when the shock of all this wears off!"

The sky overhead rumbled loudly and turned red. Seeing the darkening sky, Jack put his arm around Lily.

"It's her, Jack," said Lily, trembling. "It must be her!"

Jack gritted his teeth. He knew she was right. They were about to come face to face with Evelyn Maude.

"Run," he shouted, pushing Sam ahead of him and dragging Lily behind.

Lightning forked in the sky. Lily jumped as it flashed above them.

Jack ran as fast as was safe, keeping of the heels of Sam. The path down was steep but straight. There was a blinding flash of lightning, and the path in front of them split open, leaving a deep, wide crack. Sam flung himself backward to avoid falling into it. Jack ran into him, and Lily ran into Jack. All three of them ended up in a heap on the mountain path.

Sam clambered off Jack and helped Jack get up off Lily. Jack pulled his wife to her feet. "I'm OK," she asserted before he could ask.

He turned back to Sam. "Do you think we can jump that?" he asked, glancing at the crack.

Sam wiped his brow and stepped closer. "I might be able to, Jack, but I don't think the queen will make it."

Jack joined him by the crack. He groaned, knowing Sam was right. "You need to jump, Sam, and run for the horses. Get me some rope from the saddle packs to help get us across."

The sky continued to grow darker behind them.

"Hurry, my friend. We've not got very long at all," said Jack.

Sam moved past Jack to give himself a run up. Jack took hold of Lily and flattened her against the cliff face. He took a deep breath and watched Sam as he prepared to jump.

Sam checked his footing and sprinted as hard as he could towards the crack. He sprang into the air and flew across. His body cleared it, but his foot caught the edge, and he landed roughly.

Jack's heart was in his throat as he stepped forward. "Sam!" he shouted.

Sam rolled onto his back and drew his foot off the edge. He sat up, checked his ankle, and then sighed in relief. "It's good—I'm good," he said. He jumped back to his feet and carried on running downwards. Jack watched him until he was out of sight.

Lily rushed to him and hugged him tightly. Jack kissed her head and ran his hand down her back, where his skin caught on the coarse wool. He felt the material between his fingers. "What other cruelty did that monster subject you to?" he asked seriously.

Lily swallowed hard. "None of it matters anymore. He's gone, and we need to escape his mother."

Horrid scenarios filled Jack's mind, but he didn't ask any more. He rubbed her arms. "OK," he said gently.

Lily looked up sharply. "You should jump the crack, Jack, and then let me try too. If I fall, I'm not going to die, because of the ring."

"That may be true, Lily, but if you fall into the canyon, how will I retrieve you from it?"

Lily looked downcast. Jack stroked her hair. "We just have to hope Sam can beat Evelyn back here," he said.

The ground shook slightly. Jack pulled Lily back against the cliff, and then he heard it, the tinkling of rocks moving beneath feet. He looked up the path to the place where he had been reunited with Lily. A silhouette had appeared in the distance. Jack looked up the cliff face, but there was no way they could climb it. He stepped towards the edge to study the canyon, but its walls were smooth. They had no way of escaping.

The witch was getting closer. Jack looked for some sign of Sam, but there was none.

Lily appeared by his side. She grabbed his face and kissed him. He pulled away. "What are you doing?" he asked.

Lily took hold of his face again. "If this is the end, then I intend to go out with love and passion burning inside of me!"

Despite the dire circumstances, Jack couldn't help but laugh. He kissed her again, knowing it was better than any words he could say.

Then the witch was upon them, and they broke apart, staring at her defiantly. Jack drew his sword again and moved Lily behind him.

Evelyn Maude stopped a short distance back from Jack and Lily. She smiled, showing teeth bared beneath her blood-red lips. Her beauty shocked Jack. He'd expected her to be ugly outside and in, but she had radiant, milky skin and an hourglass figure that she showed off in a tight black velvet gown. Her silver hair was piled in a messy bun on top of her head, with loose tendrils lying curled upon her cheekbones. Jack shuddered; her eyes appeared to be missing from the sockets, but then a flash of lightning illuminated her pure-black eyeballs. He watched her, feeling mesmerised and terrified at the same time.

"Ahhhh," she sang in a high-pitched voice. "We meet at last, my vessel." She tilted her head towards Jack. "And you must be her husband. I am guessing from the passionate display you gave."

She laughed a light trill and pursed her lips. "I'm glad my plan to keep you on the mountain path worked," she said, eyeing the crack. She raised her finger and waggled it at Lily. "Tut tut, dear one, for injuring my son. That will not do, will it?"

"It's only a shame I couldn't kill him," said Lily, with real venom in her voice.

The smile faded from Evelyn's face, and she raised her chin. "Be careful, dear one. I have been known to have a short temper. Comments like that are going to hurt your husband more than they hurt you, while you wear your magic ring." She laughed at Lily's surprised expression. "My son has been whispering to me. I know the Unicorn gave it to you, and I know he has cast a little spell to speed up your pregnancy. He is a clever beast. I will take his power from you shortly, and soon enough I'll find out where he hid the rest of it."

Lily gripped the back of Jack's shirt; he put his hand behind him for her to hold onto. The witch watched the display and grimaced. "Desist with your displays of affection! They greatly turn my stomach."

Jack didn't let go of Lily. He stared coldly at Evelyn. "Good. I'll happily use my love as a weapon against you," he said.

Evelyn's smile returned. "I like your fire, boy. I might keep you as a pet, but first things first. I need to return my vessel to Shangol."

"Over my dead body!" growled Jack, raising his sword.

Evelyn flicked her hand, and Jack's sword was ripped from his grip. It flew over the edge and into the canyon. She pointed a finger at him. "And you will be next, boy, if you don't do exactly what I say. Now, lead your wife back up this cliff path ahead of me."

Jack didn't move. "No," he said calmly.

Evelyn threw her head back and screamed in annoyance. "Fine!" she spat. "Have it your way. Die if you want to." A ball of black magic appeared in her hands. Jack squared his shoulders and stared death coldly in the face. Suddenly Lily spun him round, so he was facing the crack.

He stared over his shoulder at her. "What are you doing?" he hissed.

"Saving your life," she said fiercely, firmly gripping the backs of Jack's wrists.

The magic Evelyn had planned to use on Jack was already in motion. It hit Lily in the chest, and the impact threw her backwards at high speed. Jack screamed as he was pushed along with her. They sailed through the air and over the crack. The ground approached fast, and Jack straightened his legs out in front of him. He landed on his bottom and slid away down the steep path. Lily screamed as she bounced over his head. He reached up and grabbed her dress, pulling her down in front of him. Then he gripped her firmly with one hand while trying to slow their descent with his other. The rocks tore through his clothes, leaving cuts and burns along his legs. After what felt like forever, they began to slow down. Jack exhaled as they came to a stop. He immediately looked behind him; he thought he could see the distant silhouette of Evelyn high above them.

He tapped Lily on the shoulder. "We need to run!" he said.

Lily scrambled up, her dress in tatters and matching cuts and burns littering her legs. She wasted no time with words but began running. Jack followed.

The path began to widen out, letting them increase their speed. Jack started to see distant trees over the lower peaks in front of them.

Lily raised her arm and pointed down the path. "It's Sam!" she shouted.

Jack saw Sam below; his friend was running towards them, rope clenched in his fist. Sam heard them approaching. When he realised who it was, he raised his fist into the air and cheered loudly.

Lily reached him, and he grabbed her by the waist to slow her momentum. Jack stumbled and slid, grabbing the cliff face to stop from running Lily over.

"Jack—how did you get over the crack?" asked Sam, looking impressed.

Jack bent over, letting air fill his lungs. "Long story." He was wheezing. "How far until the horses? We need to get out of here *now!*"

Sam began running back down the path. "They're just round the next bend. Jack, I told Bailey to summon Magus Mia; hopefully she will arrive soon," he shouted over his shoulder.

Jack hoped so too. He saw Lily clutching her stomach. He stopped running and grabbed her arm. "Are you all right?" he asked in concern.

"Stitch," said Lily shortly, out of breath. "And the baby has begun to have growth spurts—feel it." She guided Jack's hand to her stomach. He touched it gently and felt the small bump, drawing away in surprise.

"I know the Unicorn sped up the pregnancy, but that feels so strange!"

Lily groaned. "You should see what it feels like for me!"

Jack smiled. He would never dare tell her, *No, thank you,* out loud.

They reached the horses, and Jack got Lily onto Bailey before climbing up behind her. "We need to get back over the flooded land and down to the Pass as fast as possible," he told them.

The sky was growing dark. Jack looked up in confusion; it wasn't Evelyn's red sky. It looked more like dusk, but it was too early.

"Ride hard, Sam!" he shouted, knowing that whatever was happening wasn't good.

The trio galloped down the mountain path towards Judelen, while the sky continued to darken; it had turned pitch black by the time they'd left the Great Mountains behind them. It stayed pitch black for several minutes before beginning to lighten once more.

"It's as if time has been altered!" shouted Sam.

Lily stiffened in Jack's arms. "What if it is! Evelyn could be forcing the time difference to bring forward my labour."

Jack had an epiphany. "She thinks it will slow us down and give her time to snatch you back, but she doesn't know about Mia's powers, and she thinks Rain is in Emiscial. But he isn't! He left in secret to meet us on the road. Before she knows what's hit her, the Child of Light will be made, and that will be the end of her!"

"Unless she catches us and makes the Child of Darkness first—or worse, she kills us to stop any child being born!" shouted Lily.

Sam looked shocked. "So Drake wasn't lying!"

Jack cursed and heeled Bailey to gallop faster.

The light continued to grow and then began to dip back down into dusk within half an hour.

Jack was frantically trying to work calculations in his head. "Seven hours!" he shouted. "If each day passes in half of an hour, fourteen days will elapse in seven hours!"

Lily hissed sharply and doubled over. "It could be even less," she warned. "There is the time between my capture and now to consider." She sat up and moaned loudly. "Jack, the baby is growing quickly. It hurts."

Jack moved his hand onto Lily's stomach; he could feel it swelling beneath his fingers.

"Hang on, Lily. Mia's coming. We'll get you to safety." Jack had a dreadful thought. What if Mia hadn't arrived, because she was hurt? His whole plan rested on her and her powers. What would he do if she didn't appear?

They kept riding hard, wading with the horses back over the flooded land. They eventually found a path that would lead them down to the Judelen Pass.

The next few hours of riding were tough for Lily. She was in agony, her swollen belly pressing painfully into Bailey's neck.

Finally they saw Judelen Pass below them. Jack swung off Bailey to give Lily more space and ran as fast as he could beside him.

"Get up with me!" offered Sam.

Jack climbed up behind him, and they galloped down the path, slowing as they reached the stone steps of the bridge. They began crossing the Pass. The river's water level had risen so high that it came right up beneath the arched columns. Jack was relieved that they had held after the attack.

An ear-splitting shriek from Lily and a sickening thud made Jack jerk his head round. Lily had fallen off Bailey and was lying on her back; her face screwed up in pain.

Jack pushed backwards off Sam's mount and ran to her. "Lily, we need to get you back on Bailey," he said urgently.

Lily's face was flushed, and she was panting shallowly. "It's too late," she cried out. "The baby is coming *now!*"

Blind panic took hold of Jack. Sam appeared at his side. "This night that is falling now is the fifth hour, Jack," he warned.

Jack looked desperately at Bailey. "Where is Mia, boy? I need her here now, and I need King Rain!" Bailey snorted and pawed the stone floor of the bridge nervously.

Lily grabbed Jack's arm. "I can feel another contraction. Jack, help me!"

Jack turned to Sam. "Sit behind Lily, take her hands, and help her breathe," he said.

Sam looked terrified, but he did as Jack commanded. Lily seized his hands, and he winced at her grip.

Jack carefully moved Lily's dress slightly higher. He felt her stomach; it felt like a rock.

"Do you need to push yet?" he asked her.

"No," moaned Lily, "but I think that will happen soon. Feel for the baby's head, Jack," she told him.

With trembling fingers, Jack felt between Lily's legs. There was a large gap between her stretched skin, where he felt something smooth and hard. He looked down. "I can see the head," he told her.

He moved backwards and pulled his jacket off, laying it down between Lily's legs. "When you feel the urge to push, grit your teeth and push as hard as you can."

Lily nodded. Sam removed his belt and gave it to Lily to bite down on. "My mum said it helps," he advised quietly.

Jack wished Sam's mum was here, or his Aunt Shannon! They would be much better at this than him.

Lily suddenly started waving her arms around, her eyes wide.

"Do you feel like you need to push?" asked Jack, and she nodded. "Then do it, and keep going."

With a muffled scream, Lily pushed. Jack kept watch on the baby's head; it was definitely moving. "Well done," he told Lily. "Keep going." Lily continued to push for another minute before she collapsed back, panting.

Jack rubbed her leg. "It's nearly out. You need to do one more big push, Lily."

She narrowed her eyes and said something to him, but she was still biting down on Sam's belt, so her words were muffled. He was secretly glad; he suspected it hadn't been a nice comment.

A few minutes later Lily moaned again as her stomach tightened. Jack got ready. Sam held her hands tightly and made soothing noises at her. Lily screwed her eyes up, and the screaming began again.

The baby's head popped out into Jack's hand, and he held it gently. "Lily, the head's out. Keep going. I love you!"

The baby's shoulders emerged, and Jack wiggled his finger under an armpit and dragged it all the way out. He carefully lowered the baby onto the jacket, making sure its head was supported. It began to cry loudly. He wiped it down and smiled. "Lily, it's a girl! We have a daughter!" He wrapped her up and lifted her into Lily's arms.

Sam discreetly handed Jack a dagger, and he cut through the cord.

The fifth night drew to an end, and dawn began to break. Evelyn's spell ceased when the sun reached its natural position.

"She's got red hair," said Lily, studying her daughter, all her pain forgotten.

Sam moved from behind her and took Jack's place, so he could sit with Lily and the baby. She had stopped crying and gone fast asleep.

Jack touched her small red curls. "She is beautiful," he said softly.

Lily hissed sharply. Sam smiled apologetically as he removed the afterbirth and disposed of it in the river. He took his own jacket off and placed it over Lily's legs, preserving her modesty.

Bailey gave a whinny of alarm—Mia had popped up beside him. She touched his neck to calm him down.

"About time!" shouted Jack, but he was smiling at her.

Mia was filthy and breathing hard. She gave Jack a cold look, but then she spotted the baby and fell to her knees. She grabbed Bailey's leg to steady herself.

"Fetch King Rain as fast as you can," Jack told her. Mia nodded numbly and disappeared. She was still touching Bailey, so he disappeared with her.

"Wouldn't it have been better to send the baby with her?" asked Sam.

Jack realised his mistake. His stomach dropped sharply, and he cursed.

Lily looked up at him calmly. "It's all right, Jack, they'll be here in a minute."

"Jack, I think we need to find some cover. The witch is on her way, and we are too exposed here," said Sam seriously.

Jack nodded and took the baby off Lily. "Take her, Sam. I'll carry Lily into the trees; the savannah is too open." Sam scooped up the princess and moved off the Pass into the forest.

"Aranelle," said Lily with a smile as Jack picked her up. "I want to call her Aranelle."

Jack smiled and kissed her gently. "Then that is what we shall name her," he agreed, walking towards the steps.

He felt wind suddenly rippling the air; he looked up the path towards Judelen and saw Evelyn Maude and Aidan flying towards them, being carried by wind riders.

Everything happened in a blur. Jack glanced at the trees to check that Sam was hidden, and he turned to run with Lily across the Pass. A wind rider flew over his head and dropped Aidan, blocking his escape. Aidan fired a ball of magic at Sam's horse, and it disintegrated into dust. "I learnt my lesson after Argon's misfortune," he said nastily.

Jack turned his back to him, only to face Evelyn, who was standing on the opposite side. The two of them were trapping him and Lily between them.

"Where is the child?" said Evelyn coldly.

Jack shook his head. "Nowhere you'll find her."

Evelyn's eyes widened. "A girl—how delightful! A daughter to go with my son—"

The woods behind her suddenly filled with a golden glow. Evelyn turned round sharply. Jack could see in the middle of the light the outline of King Rain, bending over Aranelle in Sam's arms.

Evelyn produced a ball of black magic and launched it towards the trees; it smashed through trunk after trunk on its way towards Rain.

"No!" screamed Lily in Jack's arms.

Jack thought he saw Sam running, before the ball of blackness consumed the golden glow. There was a high-pitched noise, like a whistle.

It hurt Jack's ears, and he fell onto his knees, feeling disorientated. He looked up and saw the golden light had gone.

Evelyn clapped her hands. "Finally, I have destroyed that infuriating Guardian of the Light!" she cackled. She laughed a victorious laugh, but suddenly it caught in her throat. She inhaled sharply, her eyes began to bulge, and her body violently convulsed.

Aidan ran past Jack. "Mother!" he cried.

Evelyn looked up at him, her face distorted. There was a blinding flash of light, and she vanished.

The two wind riders unravelled and were gone.

"No!" shrieked Aidan. He turned sharply around to face Jack. "You've not won yet, boy! The Child of Light may be here, but my mother destroyed the Guardian, so we are not defeated."

Jack's heart thumped wildly as Aidan produced another ball of magic. "I'm finally going to kill you—the bodyguard who never knew when to quit!"

Jack's little finger tingled. He glanced down, distracted, and saw that Lily had slipped the magic ring onto his finger. He went numb.

"It's got to be you who lives," she whispered. "You're the only person who can fight the magic."

"No!" he moaned, but before he could say anything else, the magic hit them. Lily died instantly in his arms.

When Aidan saw that she had fallen instead of Jack, he laughed coldly. "I think this is even better justice, boy. Now you will have to live without her!"

With a snarl, Jack leapt up and ran straight at him. Aidan disappeared in a puff of black smoke. Jack fell through where he had stood and hit the bridge, grazing the side of his face.

"Jack," he heard Sam scream, and he felt his friend tugging on his arm. "Mia has taken the baby to Emiscial. She's coming back for us shortly. We need to get Lily." His eyes found Lily's corpse, and he fell to his knees beside Jack. Jack felt the sobs break free from his body, and he screamed into the dirt. Sam held his shoulder tightly.

Mia reappeared next to them; she surveyed Jack and Sam and turned to see Lily's body. Her hands covered her mouth, and tears sprang to her eyes.

Sam left Jack and ran to Lily. He took her arms and dragged her over to the others. "Get hold of Jack," he told Mia. She knelt down; keeping her eyes fixed on Lily, and took his hand weakly.

Sam took her other arm. "Go, Magus Mia!" he shouted.

Mia transported them to Emiscial, where they arrived outside the temple. Except for Kem, all of the magus were waiting for them. Bailey stood near to Reanna, who stood holding Aranelle in her arms. She glanced at Sam, at Mia, at Jack, and eventually Lily. She gasped. "What happened to her?"

"I happened to her," answered Jack in a hollow voice. "I sent Mia for Rain, not thinking, and she died because of my idiocy. People keep dying to save me." Fresh tears ran down his cheeks.

Mia held him tightly. "Stop this, Jack. You are not responsible for her death."

He pushed Mia away and stood up. "How many people have died today because of me?" he spat.

Mia stood up slowly. "Many people died, Jack, but not one of them died because of you. They died fighting for a cause they believed in. You might now be the leader of that cause, but you didn't start this war."

Jack's anger left him as quickly as it had come. His shoulders slumped; he felt his grief eating away inside. He looked at Lily's body. Could the magus bring her back to life? He looked up at Jamella but then heeded her warning from Sanalow. He fought his desire to ask her to use healing, pushing it firmly from his mind. He knew he couldn't let his own selfish desire to have Lily back risk Aranelle's future.

Aranelle began to cry, and he rushed over to her. He held her tiny finger, and she stopped crying instantly. Jack stood hypnotised as she gazed up at him. Her left eye was green, and her right was blue. He felt the bonds of unconditional love settle over his heart, but even that couldn't ease his distress over losing Lily.

Reanna held Aranelle out, and Jack gingerly took her in his arms. "She looks like Lily," he said, kissing her soft head of hair. He studied his daughter. "Bring your mother back to us, my sweet child, and put an end to pain and death. Can you do that for me?"

The whole sky shimmered like glitter, and Jack heard a musical sound like tiny bells tinkling. He felt his body go cold. Mia gasped and pointed at him. He looked at his hands. The wounds he had suffered in the mountains had completely healed!

Jack looked at Aranelle in shock. "My child, you're a miracle, but I fear the saviour's path you must walk is going to be perilous. But I promise you, my love; you'll never be alone. I'm here with you—always."

Bailey approached Jack and nudged his shoulder. "Hi, old friend," Jack said gently. "We have a lot of work to do. I hope you're ready for another long journey."

Bailey snorted once; Jack took that as his acceptance.

Epilogue

The Order had all gathered in the temple. Mia sat around the wooden table with her sisters, reading the report Kem had brought back with her from Sanalow.

She looked up. "I can't believe it," she said in a stunned voice.

Kem nodded. "It's unbelievable but true. The child has reversed our mortality spell, and people are rising from the dead. I've seen them with my own eyes!"

Mia smiled. "It's what Jack asked her to do."

Reanna looked serious. "Aranelle needs to be managed carefully. King Rain is gone, and Jack doesn't have the knowledge to teach her about the Light." She looked around at them all seriously. "My sisters, we must help raise this child in Rain's place."

Troyan frowned. "Will Jack let us, though? He is still so angry about all our mistakes. He is talking about taking Aranelle to Sanalow as soon as she is feeding well," she said seriously.

Reanna banged her fist on the table. "He cannot do that! He would be putting her life in danger."

Mia cleared her throat. "Reanna, Jack is not about to endanger Aranelle. He understands that Rain's death meant Aidan lived. He saw for himself that Aidan's no longer trapped in his human form. Evelyn's fate is uncertain, but I don't believe she is dead. I personally suspect she has been imprisoned again.

"Jack wants the very best for Aranelle. He knows she needs to learn about her power in order to use it properly."

"He just misses Lily," said Emmra quietly. "When she returns, he will be healed."

"Healed and much harder to control," said Reanna sharply. "But it is good he doesn't realise the resurrection magic cannot penetrate Emiscial's shield."

The others regarded her in interest. "What do you mean, good?" asked Mia angrily.

"We need Jack to stay in line," said Reanna. "We must push for a strong alliance between him and the Order."

Mia felt cold. "What are you planning now?" she asked sternly.

Reanna licked her lips. "I'm planning a spell that requires all of our powers—a spell to block Lily from returning."

Mia flew to her feet. "Are you insane? You cannot do that to him!"

Kerri stood up. "It makes sense, Mia. The most important thing right now is for Aranelle to learn her powers. If we have a strong alliance, that will be much easier."

"But why do we need to prevent his wife returning! How can that help?" spat Mia.

"Because it will leave him free to marry again," said Reanna.

Everyone's eyes fixed on Mia. She held her throat in horror. "I can't marry Jack! His wife died a few hours ago! Her body rests in a dome in our clearing. How could you even imagine he would suddenly marry me?"

Reanna waved a hand in annoyance. "Not straight away. It will take years of hard work. You need to be a good friend to him, nurture him, and counsel him. In time he will grow to love you. Your union will be vital for Aranelle's future."

Mia shook her head and turned to leave. "This is disgusting. I'll hear no more about it!"

"I demand a vote of the Order to decide the matter," shouted Reanna.

Mia stopped walking. Her heart sank. "Don't do this, Reanna, please."

Reanna ignored her and turned to her other sisters. "All those in favour of my plan to block Lily's return, and for Mia to become Jack's new wife, to forge an alliance and protect Emiscial's future dealings with Aranelle, raise your hands."

Every sister but Mia raised her hand.

"You fools!" whispered Mia. "Haven't we made enough mistakes?"

"This is to protect the Child of Light from her father's fragile emotional state. He is too unpredictable to trust fully," answered Reanna.

She regarded the others. "To block the resurrection spell, I need to be able to wield all of my powers. We need to join together to give me the strength to do that. I propose a blood link."

Mia gasped. "Reanna, you cannot touch that! It is too dangerous! You'll be combining magic, and there is a massive risk it could twist."

"You've been outvoted, Mia. We are doing this," said Reanna coldly. "You cannot go against a vote of the Order. It is binding magic from Orthrillium himself."

Mia closed her eyes. Taking a small knife from her pocket, Reanna slit both her palms open and handed the knife to Kerri, who followed suit. She waiting in silence until all her sisters stood with blood dripping from their wounds.

"You too, Mia," she ordered. Bound and broken, Mia took the knife and cut her hands. She threw the weapon onto the table.

"Join hands," commanded Reanna. One by one the magus took hold of each other's hands, their blood mixing together. Emmra had hold of Mia. Reanna held out her other hand, waiting for her to complete the circle.

Mia stood sobbing, staring at her bleeding palm.

Reanna regarded her in anger. "Now, Mia!" she shouted.

Mia extended her hand with her fist clenched; reluctantly she opened her hand and took Reanna's. She felt the pull of the magical contract fall upon her, like an invisible cloak.

Reanna's eyes shone. "It is done," she said. "I shall cast the spells to block the resurrection of Lily."

Mia dropped her sister's hands and walked towards the door.

"Not a word about this to the boy, Mia," hissed Reanna. "That's an order!"

"I cannot disobey your direct commands," said Mia frostily. She reached the door and pulled it open.

"One more thing, Mia," said Reanna.

Mia turned round sharply. "What?"

Reanna put her hands on her hips. "Don't fall in love with him," she said.

"You cannot command my emotions!" hissed Mia.

Reanna scoffed at her. "It is a warning, not a command. I tell you not to do it for your own protection."

Mia sniffed. "My protection indeed!" She pointed sharply at her sisters. "It is all of you who need protection. You keep meddling, trying to manipulate and control things you shouldn't touch!"

"*We*," said Reanna simply. "*We* have meddled, and *we* do what is necessary!"

Mia laughed bitterly and walking out of the room.

Reanna called out to her. "If you ever break your vow, Mia, I'll make sure he knows it was you who poisoned Elizabeth."

Mia put her hand on her chest. She stopped dead just beyond the room and spun around to face Reanna. "No, you couldn't—you mustn't! He'd kill me!"

Reanna approached the door slowly. "I know!" she whispered, slamming it shut in Mia's face.

Index

The Cities of the Human Kingdom (in alphabetical order):

Emiscial. Built by Orthrillium and protected from black magic by the magic shield.

Grimfar. Built by the magus and humans.

Judelen. Built by the magus.

Sanalow. Built by humans.

Shangol. Built by the Dark Knight.

Uxtellier. Built by humans.

Characters of importance (in order of appearance):

Jack Orden. Wayfarer; bodyguard of Princess Lillian; husband of Princess Lillian; king of Sanalow; leader of the army of the Light; father of the Child of Light.

Bailey. Jack Orden's horse; protector of the Light.

Tomas. Bodyguard of Princess Lillian.

Princess Lillian. Princess of Judelen; the vessel; wife of Jack Orden; mother of the Child of Light.

Drake. Former bodyguard of Queen Elizabeth; servant of the Dark Knight; bodyguard of Princess Lillian.

Argon. Former bodyguard of Queen Elizabeth; servant of the Dark Knight; bodyguard of Princess Lillian.

Ryan. Bodyguard of Princess Lillian.

Will. Bodyguard of Princess Lillian.

Mistress Stratton. Maggie; former mistress to Queen Elizabeth; mistress to Princess Lillian.

King Symon. King of Judelen; father of Princess Lillian; husband of Queen Elizabeth.

Sir Aidan. Ruler of Shangol; the Dark Knight.

Queen Elizabeth. Queen of Judelen; wife of King Symon; mother of Princess Lillian.

Salzar. Spirit creature; servant of the Dark Knight; controller of King Symon of Judelen.

Orbressen Fanlar. Former steward of Sanalow; mentor of Jack Orden.

Niar. King of Grimfar; protector of the Guardian; Joint ruler of Sanalow; protector of King Jack Orden.

Revir. Son of King Niar; prince of Grimfar.

Jarrad Morridread. Steward of Sanalow.

Uncle Jon, Aunt Shannon, and Cousin Tommy. Family of Jack Orden.

King Rain. Guardian of the Light.

Leon Myere. Under-steward of Sanalow; high advisor to King Jack Orden.

Sam. Bodyguard of King Jack Orden.

Aranelle. The Child of Light.

About the Author

———❧———

A bigail Ruth Pearson was born in Bracknell, Berkshire, on January 28, 1981.

Her parents moved to Broseley, Shropshire, before she turned two, and moved again when she was seven, to settle in Cuddington, Cheshire.

She left high school, passing all her GCSEs, and attended Reaseheath College, gaining a National Diploma in animal care.

She went into work, and began her career working with animals. She has a particular fondness for horses and goats.

She began her own family at the age of 19, and today she is a blessed single mother of four children (three daughters and one son).

Since 2005, she has swapped animals for children and has enjoyed working a variety of support roles in a primary school. She is currently taking a career break to take care of her son with special needs. She still loves animals and is known as the "cat whisperer" to her friends—although she thinks "crazy cat lady" is a more accurate description.

She has a love for writing and poetry. She has entered several United Press competitions, winning the chance to publish her poems in several different books. She also has her own poetry book, *Through My Eyes*, which was published by United Press as a prize for her work being selected numerous times for their other publications.

The Wayfarer's Journey is her debut novel, which she wrote over fifteen years ago and archived while she focused on raising her children.

It has always been her dream to see this story become a published book, so she can introduce Jack to the world. Now, thanks to AuthorHouse UK, her dream has come true.

Look out for her next book, *The Child of Light*, which is the follow-on story for *The Wayfarer's Journey*. AuthorHouse UK will publish it within the next few months.

Blurb

Jack is travelling to find a new life, leaving behind him a dark and painful past. He hopes he'll find salvation in the mighty city of Judelen. An accident on the road brings a princess into his life, along with the discovery of a deadly plot brewing within her palace.

To protect her, Jack must help fight a battle between light and darkness that has been raging since the dawn of creation.

Can one man's love fix a world broken by betrayal?

Printed in Great Britain
by Amazon